WINNING

WINNING

Craig Dinsell

This first edition published in 2020 by:

Loudhailer Books
13 Lyminster Avenue
Brighton
BN1 8JL

www.loudhailerbooks.com

A CIP catalogue record for this book is available from the British Library.

ISBN 9781914158001

Search out our hearts and make us true;
help us to give to all their due.
From love of pleasure, lust of gold,
from sins which make the heart grow cold,
wean us and train us with thy rod;
teach us to know our faults, O God.
For sins of heedless word and deed,
for pride ambitions to succeed,
for crafty trade and subtle snare
to catch the simple unaware,
for lives bereft of purpose high,
forgive, forgive, O Lord, we cry.

Hymn
William Boyd Carpenter KCVO
1918

For Poetry makes nothing happen: it survives
In the valley of its making where executives
Would never want to tamper

In Memory of W. B. Yeats
W. H. Auden
1939

Thanks to Julian Dinsell, Barbara
and Jeremy Griffiths, Mark Wellman,
Andy Doyle, William Trego and David Haviland,
editor extraordinaire.

For Sheila, without whom nothing
would be possible.

CONTENTS

CHAPTER ONE

She has not killed yet but she will. Or at least that will be the accusation.

Grace and I did not know one another well when it all started. In retrospect we were both holding the knife by the blade. My name is Fen Morgan and at the time, I was the Chief Investment Officer at XelFunds. It was inevitable that we and everyone around us would be wounded. Now to me, even her name, Grace, sounds like an ironic joke.

I often recall what she told me of her fateful early morning encounter with Miles. From that beginning, he did not stand a chance. I see now what she must have seen. I hear what Miles must have heard.

An angry mist simmers apprehensively around the towering shards that glint along the Hudson. A lone commuter ferry, brimming with blank faces, slices the sullen current across to the World Financial Center from Paulus Hook.

On floor thirty-nine of Tower One, Grace has infiltrated his citadel, loaded for bear, festooned in the war paint and vague smile she devised especially for confrontation with men of his type. Her pugilistic advance halts an arm's length from him, his acrid breath assaults the space between them. At an impasse, the imperceptible tapping of her right foot probes his space, signaling the frustration that gnaws her stomach.

A formidable though indolent adversary, Miles barely acknowledges her arrival with a dismissive purse of his large lower lip. As ever, he is uncertain of her agenda. At other times he has laughed with her and shared a conspiratorial look, but always felt himself to be her prey, not quite worth the effort of entrapment. They are in a war of attrition. She is Mata Hari, he is France. He knows he will capitulate.

Grace has spent months strategizing how to reach him but he has evaded her calculus. She reaches to touch him but his essence is thick, like a layer of clay which cloys her efforts to connect. He is too impenetrable for her to grasp. They exist in different dimensions. His indifference to her descends like a curtain on each occasion they are compelled to meet.

Always the outsider, Grace beats on the doors of the boys' club that is the Equity department but despite her outrage, remains uninitiated. She tells herself it's all about conversations and building relationships and here one of her most important is going south, fast.

The atmosphere is viscid. The pervasive hiss of deadening white noise snakes between them, ringing in the crook of her ear. She takes in the glowering sun's slow ascent as it pours between Titian clouds suspended before his office window. Suppressing her frustration, she suffers the silence while he procrastinates.

Miles is incredulous. "He actually did this?"

Grace notes the fatigue in his eyes as he reads the document she handed him and is mesmerized by the way the florid oval of his face parts to reveal his yellowing teeth. Miles has the look of a man hollowed out as if he suffers each tawdry day as a tide of frustration excoriating his soul.

"That's what they told me. It's all in the report on the investigation." Despite her contempt for Miles she continues to smile. Her voice confident, inviting him to parley.

"So, you think we have to fire him?" The comment is neutral. A momentary truce between them, perhaps. Miles perpetually questions her origins and identity, yet seldom gets beyond the seduction of the mannequin Grace presents before him.

"Maybe, depends on today." Grace takes a slight step back and breaks her eye contact which has been drilling into his skull since he raised his head to glance sideways at her.

"Shit." Miles spits the expletive towards her. It is her shit. She has trodden it into his office. "Are you sure about all this?"

"You can never be totally sure." She will not give him an inch.

"You understand the implications for the business?" *Of course you don't,* he wants to add, *you are a neophyte.* His body language says it all.

"Yep." She has heard this time and time again, the Goths plodding across the plain, discounting anyone's experience but their own.

"He's our best guy in Growth." His tone is plaintive, as if mourning a lost soul.

"I know." Grace is beginning to calm and gain control. Miles is like a child who is having his toys confiscated. It is almost amusing to her.

"In fact, he's the only guy that I actually trust to lead that team."

Grace imagines Miles trudging through the office in sackcloth ringing a bell, moaning, "Woe is me for I am undone!"

"But do you honestly want to keep him after reading that report?" she says.

Miles is distracted. He does not respond to her question. He stands offering his morning obeisance before his Bloomberg screens. His routine communion with the stock market has resumed despite her presence. His bleary eyes pick at market data, as he scratches his thigh and yawns. Skin folds loosely below his jaw. He sips the double espresso he bought on his way into the office.

Grace watches his stomach lapping against the edge of his standing desk. His appearance strikes her as that of a cockerel, a rumpled paper bag, topped by a wattle and comb of scraggy auburn hair.

She observes his eyes drifting over to the Perspex box on the side of his desk that contains his insulin pen, and making a mental note to check his levels at the end of the meeting.

"Where's the guy from Compliance?" Miles asks, his head still down, lips puckered as he absently scans the front page of The Journal lying on his desk. A piece on the BRIC economies diving economic growth has caught his eye.

"He had a conflict." Her thoughts excoriate him—*Conflicted right enough. He is an outright coward. Unless there is some potential advantage to him personally for confronting Investments, the guy from Compliance will run for the hills.*

"What do you suggest, then?" He swivels his Phasianidae-like head towards her.

He has given her an opening. Like a vixen she enters the hen house. "This is about managing risk." Her plan is to employ stealth.

"Risk? How's that then?" Miles is confused. *How can this people issue constitute a risk to assets?*

"Risk to the culture and our reputation as a firm." *Voila. Think about it!* But on reflection Grace doubts he will get it.

"That's pure business school bullshit." And Miles does not.

"Some of us have to live in the real world." He spews the retort at Grace. "We don't have a planned successor. Viser has been so successful on that fund for so long that he's become a one-man institution!" Miles is conditioned by years of ducking and weaving within his silo.

"This is not a theoretical case, Miles. It's a test of our seriousness about what we want as the workplace climate." She is speaking in tongues to him. Using a foreign language.

"What's that?" He does not possess the gift of interpretation.

A light goes off in Grace's head. *I am incomprehensible to him. Miles has been dragged kicking and screaming to all the briefings, completed all the training, sat in the pew suffering the sermonizing, but he has not heard a thing.* She takes a deep breath.

"Look. We all sat in that conference room last week talking about being 'values-driven' in terms of products and people. Why we need to be different." The words gush from her, more passionate than persuasive, as from a rock struck in the wilderness of his comprehension. "We agreed we need an unconventionally strong culture to sustain diversity of ideas, that we need to be better than the competition. And now when the rubber hits the road, when there's a price to pay, when it could hurt us in the short term to make the appropriate decision, our first instinct is to run for the hills." And there it is before them both. So clear, yet entirely opaque.

"Really? Who's making the money to pay for your bonus and that vacation to Asia you just took? You want the product, but you don't actually want to know what's going on behind the curtain in the sausage factory."

"I don't think you get the..."

"You are naive if you think we are anything other than... May I be frank?" Miles says, strutting to the window, his head drawn back for another salvo. He is incapable of dissimulating. She stays put by his desk and raises her eyebrows.

"You're smart. I know that, but you're insufficiently experienced in the business here and honestly, I don't know whose side you are on. Seems to me like you're trying to pick out the black pepper in fly shit." Again, the chicken coop.

"Whoa, where's this coming from? It's not a matter of politics. It's a matter of ethics." *Nicely put, Grace,* she tells herself. *Theoretically correct. But there is no flesh on it.* She knows intuitively that he wants her to be his seductress. But today she will only read him the manual.

"Really, you're going to lecture me on ethics? Tell me. Give me a situation when you genuinely sacrificed anything for ethics. Would you be working for this firm if you did?" Miles has turned from the window to face Grace full-on. The beak of his nose points towards her. The corners of his mouth are coated with saliva.

"Times are changing, Miles," she says, head downcast, brushing the black sleeve of her Tory Burch blouse.

"Don't tell me that you've not done your fair share of jumping for the jelly beans to get up there with the big boys." Miles gives her a lascivious grin from beneath the red of his comb and slowly looks over the taut body she earned kickboxing, and now wears as couture to camouflage her jangling emotions.

This is going a lot further and faster than Grace anticipated. "This is a great conversation but can we put the genie back in the bottle a bit?" She leans back and drops her shoulders. "We've got a lot of shit to clear up. This may not be your fault or mine, but it's thrown up on our watch. And it's become a corporate level issue. Senior management has delegated dealing with this to us. Let's keep on message. Let's call him up here. You give him your decision. I'll take it from there."

"My decision? Since when do I get to make decisions around here anymore?"

He thinks but does not say, *There is assuredly no cheap grace. Ironic she has that name, Grace. This woman is a real hard-ass. But worse, obvious to all, she is an inexperienced hard-ass with connections and more than a touch of arrogance.* Last night, he watched the Boston Red Sox, drinking Sam Adams, alone in his apartment. He had drunk too much again hoping for a break in the Curse of the Bambino. *But who's counting?*

Grace feels the managed white silence suffuse the glass bowl that is Miles's office as it leans on her, compressing her chest. He is again distracted. Atop his shambling frame, which has stalked sideways back to stand at his desk, his brain sprints through the numbers. Unconsciously competent, he quantifies the yield curve, weighs the market risk and projects the Q4 return for the portfolio. He usually loves this moment in his day where he can roam alone and unfettered on the efficient frontier. But this morning she has ruined the moment.

To Grace he must have appeared inert, as if basking in the warm barnyard sun. She told me that he suspected that further in, his emotions were churning and less easy for him to analyze. Her sense was that his feelings towards her previously were, to say the least, ambiguous and until this morning, inconsequential. At this instant it seemed he hated her. He despised her bureaucratic rigor and what she was forcing him to do. He clearly knew instinctively that she traveled alone taking no prisoners. But most surprising to her, she sensed he feared her.

Investment performance against the benchmark had been a challenge for the past two quarters. Miles was swinging for the fences between the rock of how his personal stock-picking performance looked to his department and the hard place of his risk appetite for the portfolios he oversaw. All this crap was piling up.

Miles looks drained and glances at his watch. The phone on his desk rings. "No, not now Jade!" he shouts and slams it down. "What time is all this supposed to happen?"

"Now," Grace answers. She knows that if she doesn't push this morning, Miles will lose his resolve. He will probably go for an early liquid lunch and take the afternoon off. *Pathetic, but he's done it before.* She decides to sit on one of the black mesh designer chairs that are placed before Miles's desk and give him some space. Somehow, the room is further off-balance.

The last week of torrid August in New York. Monsoon rain is forecast for later. The day has a personality disorder. As Miles steps back and forth between desk and window he has the demeanor of being isolated and alone despite Grace being present in his glass-walled office. The space they occupy feels more cell-like than salubrious.

From the expression on his face, Grace speculates that Miles's head is more than usually overcrowded and is in a really bad place. It seems to her that his unease is rising from his stomach to his throat. She can smell the bile from last night's beer as it sours in his mouth.

Miles tugs absently at the sleeve of his open-collared shirt and makes an odd clucking sound as he brushes the back of his incisors with his tongue. "You say that you've got all this on him. But who says it's true? Maybe there are alternative facts?" Like everyone, Miles has unconsciously acquired the lingua franca.

"Honestly Miles, this one is staring you in the face." She is brutal. In his cuckoo world she is Nurse Ratched.

"It may seem like that to you, but I suspect that there is more than a little daylight between the way you see this and the way it may have happened." He pushes back. He does not want the electric shock treatment she is offering.

"Okay then. Let's call the meeting off and see where the chips fall. It's up to you."

"No way. I can see that one coming. I refuse to take action and you pin any consequences on me. Let's do it and get the whole thing over with." His voice is flat. "This one is on you, Grace. It's your reputation as well as mine."

"I'll call him up." Grace feels the tension in her neck as she pulls her phone from her Dior book tote. "Peiter, it's Grace. Can you join Miles and me in his office? Yes Peiter. Now please."

"Where is he this morning?" Miles asks.

"Sounded like his office on thirty-eight. Want to go over the process again?" Grace inquires.

"No, I've got it. I just tell him there's been a decision and you take it from there, correct?" says Miles, contempt lingering in his voice.

"I don't think we're there yet. You need to put the compliance issue and the people issues to him and see what he has to say."

"And if he takes the Fifth?" Miles asks.

"He's not going to do that. He's going to have some sort of story. 'Alternative facts' as you put it. He's a smooth operator," Grace replies.

"Yes, but if he fesses up. What happens then?" Miles insists.

"Well, given the gravity of the compliance issue and people problems we're going to have to give him the choice between resigning and being fired. If it goes that way the better choice will be to suspend him. Finish our investigation. Consult everyone and then determine action. There are a lot of angles here—he will, I am sure, bring in some hotshot lawyer."

"What does Cynthia, our esteemed legal advisor think about this?" Miles drips with cynicism.

"She's totally in the loop. Her view is that the compliance case is soft, but we have a legal case to fire him because of his actions on the people side—contingent on our substantiating cause."

"Maybe that's what she says today, but I've had the unwelcome experience of her having pissed all over me inside the tent before. I've got zero trust in her." Miles is picking again. "Do you really think you are doing the right thing in handling it this way?"

"Do you think we have any alternative given what Ken Harding had to say? And besides, there is more." Grace faces Miles head-on, pushing back at him across the barnyard.

Alarmed Miles asks, "What do you mean, more?"

"There is something else. Trust me, you want to resolve this situation now before we get into a world of hurt." She shows him just enough stick to get him over the line.

Miles turns once again to the window. Grace sees this. *He is always looking at what is in front of him. His eye is always on the near, never the far.*

Absently, Miles says, "So I'm your puppet here. I probe, depending on the outcome he is out or in—very clear, I must say."

The wait seems interminable. Grace is now also standing, staring out at the distant hills of New Jersey, beyond the sad construction sites that loom above the far shore of the Hudson.

Peiter Viser is tall, sports a designer stubble beard, and presents as if straight from GQ central casting. He dresses mostly in dark double-breasted suits (on the days when he is not creeping around the office in sneakers and jeans) is always direct, frequently passionate and often abrasive. A charismatic magnet to clients, one on one, it's difficult to get past the orbit of his ego. He is exhausting. He creates chaos. But in my judgement, he is also the best performing team leader and portfolio manager in the firm in terms of five- and ten-year returns.

"Before you two get started, I've got something to say," Peiter says, bursting into Miles's office, his South African accent sticking thicker than usual around his tongue.

Miles stands stock still. Imperceptibly, Grace somehow hunkers down and sways slightly as if she's about to return a serve. They both know he has trouble telling the truth. In fact, to him, as the old phrase puts it, telling the truth is the same as not getting caught in a lie.

"Whatever you've decided, you've rushed to judgement. The complaints have been withdrawn. It was all a big misunderstanding and I am prepared to let it go. Providing Ms. Corporate KGB here," Viser hoists a sardonic smile and winks at Grace, "gets off my back and apologizes."

Miles says nothing. Grace steps in. "Why do you think we asked you to come up here today, Peiter?"

"Pretty obvious, isn't it? You plan to fire me. Four weeks ago, you told me that you'd received a—" he wags his index fingers, "'serious' complaint from an employee about my conduct and compliance with company policy. But wouldn't tell me what it was. That you were conducting an investigation and that I should not try to find out who had complained. And then you had the nerve to ask me if I had anything I wanted to tell you. What a load of crap!" His arms are waving, his voice rises. The innocent outside the office raise their heads, curious about the scene that's playing out behind the glass wall. "Since that meeting I get nothing from you. Nada!"

"I've worked here for fifteen years. I'm the highest performing portfolio manager and team leader. I tell you: you guys would be nowhere without me and my team. I tell you seriously, the guys and I have been talking. Maybe we should just simply walk across to Goldman. This place is not what it used to be. I don't see why I should have to put up with this. Maybe I should simply take my options and get out. And maybe sue you at the same time!" Momentarily spent, Peiter rocks back and forth, heel to toe. Miles appears comatose.

"Thanks for that, Peiter." Grace is cold and focused. "Let's lower the temperature a bit." With that she sits on the chair adjacent to the sofa. Miles steps to the sofa and follows suit. Peiter, now standing on his own feels awkward, the wind out of his sails, and also sits, on the far end of the sofa from Miles.

"Let's go through this, Peiter." It's Grace leading the case for the prosecution. Since it's clear that Miles will provide no support, she feels she has no option but to play offense. "You are correct. We received an anonymous complaint, initially via the Compliance department. It pertained to portfolio managers making side income from doing personal investing outside the firm's portfolios. As you know, this is totally against our compliance policy." Peiter now sits like the sphinx. "This complaint was investigated jointly by Compliance and HR. You and your team were interviewed by Compliance about this. Right, Peiter?"

Peiter shoots back "But they didn't find anything." Thumbing his nose. "By the way, where is that Compliance guy this morning?"

Grace ignores the question. *But he's on the button, where is that snidely jerk from Compliance?*

Grace pushes her attack home, "Correct, they couldn't prove anything. During the compliance review we received complaints that there was often a hostile environment in the department and that certain individuals were frequently excluded from meetings and their performance..."

"Oh come on, Grace," Peiter shoulders his way in.

"...downgraded because of their sexual orientation. Others on the team complained about a lack of inclusion on the basis of their race."

"How many complained?" It is Peiter at his best. All front. "You look at my team. I've got all sorts from everywhere. Black, Queer, Gay, Proud. They can choose any identity they like. I welcome them all! I make an effort to be inclusive. They embrace themselves—you see I'm totally up with the lingo—and I am happy to embrace them all." He says this ironically, since he relishes his reputation as a womanizer. "On the other hand, Grace, you push me to recruit different sorts of people and then it turns out that you have handed me a ticking bomb because some of them are complainers! Look, I tell you, they are all welcome provided they perform and want to be part of the crew. Which analysts complained?"

Grace ignores the question. "Language used by you and your portfolio managers on the team was complained of as being demeaning, with frequent use of the F-bomb and references to the female anatomy and other sexual remarks that I won't go into."

"Good God, what are we running here, a kindergarten? All this is fucking bullshit!"

For a moment the air reverberates as the expletives fall slowly to the floor. Grace says nothing. She simply stares Peiter in the eye.

"I'll continue. Upon further investigation we found that there is indeed a pattern of behavior that is clearly against company standards of management conduct."

"Not true," Peiter says, looking at his fingers.

"None of this should be a surprise to you, Peiter. The results from the last climate survey showed your team to have the poorest morale in Investments."

"Corporate bullshit. So, what is this?" Peiter turns to Miles whose bulk is larding the far end of the sofa. "All a highly distorted setup. My guys may not always be a happy family but look, just look at the results we turn in. The clients love us."

"I know," Miles sympathizes. It sounds as a moan that issues from deep within him.

"The numbers are there. Not a single month in the last fifteen years when we have not met or exceeded the portfolios', specifically my portfolio's, benchmark. I challenge you to find any other in-house shop on the street that can put up that record."

"True," Miles says. He has become a one-man Greek chorus to the tragedy.

"This is not just about portfolio returns, Peiter." Grace is on her own. "It's about your leadership and the climate you have created. The compliance and reputational risk you represent to the company!" She is St Joan. She has visions. Unfortunately, the English are running the company.

"If you let me get a word in edgewise, here are some additional facts for your report, Grace. Ken Harding has resigned. He called me last night. Told me that he had said some things about me to the company that were a bit exaggerated. That he had been mad at me because I hadn't included enough of his ideas in the portfolio and that he was resigning with immediate effect, to take a job in London near his boyfriend, partner or whatever it is these days."

"Also, last week, Friday to be exact, we had a bit of a team meeting. People were very direct. Got some things out of their system."

Grace is shaking her head.

"I heard what they said and yes, to be honest, maybe I should have been listening for a long time. So, I will try to be better. Keep my mouth shut a bit more. But look, it's difficult to run a team with so many personalities. And to use your term Grace, 'preferences'." Peiter looks to Miles. "In fact, we would like to ask Grace to run a diversity session for us to put all this behind us and get back on the right track. And I say again, there is not a shred of evidence that has been unearthed that any compliance rule was broken. What do you think, Miles?"

"Interesting, Peiter. These things are serious, you know. We brought you up here today thinking I might have to fire you, given what was reported to me." Miles's tone is complicit and supportive.

Grace cannot believe what she is hearing. She is furious with Miles. He is totally blindsiding her and off-script.

"Yes, but that was before you heard what I had to say. I mean, if we were off the rails and the guys and I have straightened ourselves out, we must be good, right? I own, I suppose, that we may need some guidance and advice. Like with Ken. Or Jen as he used to be..."

"Well you..." Grace makes a valiant attempt but the game is up.

"How am I supposed to deal with a situation when a girl decides to be a boy and expects everyone else to overlook that he is wearing a pair of jeans today but was wearing a dress last week?" Peiter is smiling. It is, after all, a joke.

"You make this sound like some childish game, Peiter. As a manager you are obligated to create and operate a fair and non-discriminatory environment. Not to threaten or intimidate. You know we have policies and principles." Grace hears herself begin to parrot corporate speak.

"It's not like when you were coming up through the ranks, now everyone is so much more aware." Grace knows she's lost it. The situation has gotten out of hand, she has broken the cardinal rule. Communicate the decision. Limit the conversation. Execute the separation process. Instead she has got into arguing the case. And is losing it.

He's good, Grace thinks. *Without Ken Harding and the proof of the trading infraction, I'm just left with lousy management behavior. A dinosaur who is a jerk who should be fired because he's totally breaking all our values. And creating a highly toxic climate. But he's been smart enough to have closed the door on instant dismissal. Likely the staff in the department won't stand by what they said previously. He's done an end run. At least on this one.*

Disconsolate, Grace turns to Miles, who says, "Well Peiter, you've shed some new light on all this. This is what I am going to do. Grace, I want you to visit with the Equity team and take the temperature and provide me with a series of recommendations around what needs to happen to close any gaps we may have. Peiter, you've come very near the edge here. Grace, anything to say on this?"

She is done. "To me this is very serious. My job is to make sure that what's on the wall in terms of our values is actually happening on the shop floor. I will meet with your team members as Miles directs, Peiter. I'm also going to reach out to Ken. The guys over at Corporate may also have something more to say."

Miles looks at her. *Yes, she wears her inexperience like that Chanel scarf she's got on.* "Excellent. Then we're all good then. Let's get back together in one week." Miles hauls himself to his feet.

"Smart call, Miles. Good meeting and outcome. Great we can all work our way through these things. Thanks for your input, Grace. Always helpful to get some feedback. Very good." And with that said, Peiter is out the door and back to playing the market.

CHAPTER TWO

My family is a cocktail of secrets and ambiguity that I seldom drink.

It's eight and a half minutes, if it's a straight shot in the elevator, from my office at XelFunds to the one-bedroom apartment I lease in Battery Park City. At about 7:30 I step through the door, throw my black leather tote bag on the coffee table and collapse onto the couch. It's been one hell of a day. Wound tight, I lie in the fetal position, my arms wrapped defensively, staring blankly across the room. My heavy eyes are soothed by evening glowing in chalky shafts of light between the half-closed blinds that I fastened to the window last weekend. Looking at it, I can see that my room, sparsely furnished with the sofa, coffee table and chair I ordered online to rent from West Elm, says it all about my life outside the office. I have no life. The Egyptian carpet that my grandmother gave me is the only furnishing I own. I cling to it with my gaze. It anchors the space and my emotions.

The barely audible moan of the West Side Highway, distant sirens and intermittent thud of apartment doors percolate the apartment walls marking the return of my unseen neighbors. My look returns to the carpet, triggering memories of sitting at the kitchen table in the trim post-World War II ranch house on Long Island that was once my home. When I listen hard, I can almost hear my mother's thickly accented voice saying to me, "You know Grace, you have done so well. We are so proud of you. My journey here was not easy."

And so, as has become my habit recently, as refuge from the deranged circus of my work, I rehearse the gauzy myth that is my ancestry.

It is Cairo, Egypt, June 1954, two years before Colonel Nasser will nationalize the Anglo-French Suez Canal Company. Political tension with Britain, France and Israel is as pervasive as the heat.

The setting sun casts long swarthy shadows; it is nearly time for Friday Maghrib prayers, the fourth prayers of the day. Heat scythes across the streets, and dust stings Jenna's eyes. She walks with her head cast down towards George's black Oxford shoes which are coated in dirt, her slight hand gripping his.

Bicycles, together with a tangled mass of recently introduced Japanese mopeds, pour by, almost liquid in the acrid, exhaust-laden heat. Morris Oxfords, Ford Pilots and trucks packed with workers jostle down Saliba Street. Donkey carts trot alongside buses bristling with passengers. Men in shabby dark suits wearing the fez amble towards the mosque, quickening their pace to avoid the streetcars. The delicate smell of mango and ginger suffused with the pungent stink of the Nile seeps through the fetid air.

As if in some Broadway musical, a policeman standing at the corner, wearing an off-white uniform, directs traffic which eddies through the intersection. A scrawny man in a grimy thawb and kaffiyeh, limping determinedly across the dusty road, stumbles on a slab of concrete into the path of an oncoming truck. There is a sickening thud and terrifying scream as the truck careens to a halt. Instantly a crowd gathers in a noisy gaggle of sweat over the man's body.

Jenna is pulled away and around a corner by her adoptive father, then on past the Metro cinema, and the pair enter the block of rambling, dimly lit apartments which has become her home.

On entering the block Jenna climbs the darkened stairwell behind George to apartment 5C, where he knocks three times on the door. There is the sound of a lock being turned and a bolt being thrown. The door is opened slowly by Prisha, Jenna's ayah, a diminutive woman of about fifty. The pungent aroma of curry hangs in the air, rice steams on the cooker in the cramped kitchen. The child falls into Prisha's arms. She loves Prisha and these crowded rooms which have been her home since she left Durban two years ago. She gently releases Prisha and skips the couple of paces to her tiny bedroom. She throws herself on her bed and gazes through the open window across ragged brick-strewn rooftops towards the sky, which drips golden through the droning call to prayer.

"How was today?" Fey takes a step into Jenna's room, holding a rag doll. She is gaunt and wears her thirty-five years in a permanent frown that most interpret as disapproval.

"It was good." Jenna's voice has a sing song musicality and is heavily accented, betraying her native Durban.

"We have news for you." Fey is tenuous and still not well practiced in conversing with her adopted daughter. She hands the doll to Jenna, sits on her bed and rubs the back of her neck. "We have to move from here."

"But we only just arrived. Why?"

"We had a message to say that our work here is done. So, we have to go home."

"Can I go back to Durban and my mother then? Is Prisha coming with us?"

Fey is cut to the quick by the child's words. She is profoundly saddened that she and Jenna have found it so difficult to form any real bond of affection. "No, you must come with us to America. Prisha has to stay here in Egypt." The child bursts into tears and uncontrollable sobs. Fey scoops her up, rocking her back and forth, but Jenna remains inconsolable.

"Why must we leave?"

"We have been told we must leave. We only have a short time to pack up. Then we must go to the port and take a boat to America. I am very sad too." Fey is still reeling from shock. George has just told her they are to be expelled from Egypt. They have forty-eight hours to gather what belongings they can carry and get themselves to a cargo ship bound for Liverpool and then transfer to another vessel bound for New York.

Jenna had been born in Bombay into a family of lawyers. Brimming with ambition and the expectation of inheriting his grandfather's law practice in South Africa, Jenna's father moved his young family to Durban, when she was an infant of six months. A bright child, she attended an excellent private kindergarten run by Coptic nuns. The law practice had never done particularly well, owing to the irascible nature of Jenna's grandfather who built his business around the many small enterprises owned by the growing Indian community. Jenna's father slowly fell out of favor with the old man, who paid his junior partner a pittance, and it eventually became clear that it would be years before Jenna's father would inherit.

Gandhi brought the plight of the Indian community in South Africa to international attention, beginning in Pietermaritzburg where he was thrown off a train for refusing to move from a first-class compartment. Years later, unlike the lauded Gandhi, Jenna's father remained an unknown, and died of tuberculosis at a time when he too was involved in an action on behalf of the Indian community, this time against the Pegging Act.

Jenna's mother found herself in an impossible situation following her husband's death. She had no money of her own and was eventually made destitute by her husband's mendacious grandfather. Desperate for help, she turned to the sympathetic nuns who ran Jenna's school; they in turn suggested she should contact a young couple, the Reverend George Rutler and his wife Fey, who were Presbyterian missionaries stationed in Durban.

It was a long shot. Almost miraculously, it seemed to George (two parts enthusiasm and one part compassion) and his wife Fey (equally constructed, but rather more selective in terms of who was worthy of compassion) the couple adopted Jenna as their only child.

The adoption proved to be a laborious bureaucratic process which entailed obtaining legal custody from India, a relatively discretionary procedure rife with bribery. Fortunately, after much wringing of hands and Jenna's grandfather reluctantly putting in a fix with the Indian consulate, Jenna was issued a new passport and the necessary papers to support adoption. The American consulate was sympathetic and processed the required visas in minimum time.

Although welcome, the adoption was not an easy experience for the Rutlers personally. Beneath the surface their marriage was in tatters. George, his head so often buried in the sand, was passionately in love with his call to the ministry, to the exclusion of all else. Fey, her two feet planted firmly on the ground, hair tied in a tight American braid around her head, longed for something other than the itinerant life they had scratched out on foreign fields for the past several years. They both felt, however, that Jenna's arrival was an act of providence, a Hail Mary for their marriage.

Soon after the family received adoption papers, the Rutlers were once again relocated, this time to Cairo. Leaving Durban was deeply imprinted on Jenna. She stood for hours at the stern of the cargo ship the family boarded for Cairo, straining to see if her mother or grandfather were at the docks to bid her farewell. No one came.

For Fey, each day in the heat of Cairo was a struggle. The romance of travel was long gone. Her compassion spent, measured out in the grimy teacups of daily living.

On Saturday evening, the muezzin calling out the Adhan warns of the coming night and is the ever-present soundtrack to conversation. Prisha is in her quarters at the other end of the apartment, sewing, and Jenna is asleep. George leans against a wall in the kitchen. Fey sits at the kitchen table sipping something from a teacup. A throbbing pulsates from deep in the apartment block.

"I can't believe we're being kicked out." George walks to the sink and turns on the faucet. The pipes judder as brown water issues from the spigot. He slowly washes his thin hands. "I managed to get hold of the Ruling Elder today to see if there could be a last-ditch attempt to keep us here but he said the best thing was for us to get out and to do it as soon as we can."

"I've been fasting you know. I've given up bread." Fey says this as if not hearing him.

"I feel alive out here." George wipes his hands on the grubby towel hanging on the back of the kitchen door.

"I did it so I could spend more time thinking about God." Fey hears herself but not him.

"I know you've never felt my sense of mission." George speaks to her but does not notice she is not present.

"But all I do is spend more time thinking about bread," Fey mumbles.

Their words run by each other like trains in the night. They both hear the rhythm of words but neither picks up the other's meaning until one of them derails. They live in foreign countries of their own making and have lost the passports required for entry to the other's territory.

"How's the packing going?" George asks as he seats himself opposite Fey at the mean kitchen table.

"We're done." Fey's words are loaded with finality.

George doesn't pick up Fey's meaning but begins his interrogation. "Did you manage to get anything for the farewell at the church?"

"What did you have in mind?" Fey says, with more than a tinge of sarcasm.

"Well, we've been here such a comparatively short time. There are only twelve of us that meet. I feel so sorry for them. I'd love to give them some remembrance of us—that we care about them." He is the good shepherd of the ninety and nine. Not of Fey.

"Perhaps a dozen roses; one each?" Fey replies on George's behalf her voice cracking with bitterness.

"You can sound incredibly cynical," George says.

"Me, cynical? Whatever can you mean? Why should I have any reason to be cynical?"

"I know it's been rough on you," George's voice softens a little.

"You think?" Fey's back arches as if to pounce at him.

"Look, what I'm trying to say is, we'll get through this. This is only a setback, not our story. We've got to eat our own cooking. We have to endure, believe." Says George. "Remember Ephesians 3:30 Fey,

He is able to do abundantly above all that we ask or think.

We are on a journey. You'll see this is just the beginning of the adventure!" George's tone is that of the fresh-faced priest, full of zeal addressing his congregation, not his wife.

"You heard the one about the chicken and the pig? Henry over at the market told me about it this morning." Her voice is tired, listless, more the barmaid than the Sunday school teacher.

"What's that?" George asks, reluctant but playing her game.

"Well," Fey says, as she rises shakily from her chair, no longer wishing to have her head level with his. "The chicken and the pig are walking down the road one time early in the morning. The chicken points to a sign which reads 'Breakfast'. The chicken says to the pig 'How about some breakfast?' The pig looks at the sign then at the chicken, scratches his head and says, 'Chicken, I'm not so sure that's a good idea—for you it's a contribution, for me it's total commitment!'"

"Oh yeah. I remember it now." George remembers the gag but sees no connections.

"I'm sure you do. Because that is how it feels to me right now." Fey is leaning over him. Her hot breath bathing his face.

"What do you mean?" George's expression is blank.

"You really want me to spell it out?" Fey's voice is tremulous and rising. "First, we are off to the lovely Congo. What a model colony that was! Don't you have fond memories of the Mouvement National Congolais, George? You remember the good old MNC and dear old uncle Lumumba before he got famous? And you must remember the lovely night out we had. Just you and me and those lovely guys with the knives and machine guns. And of course, George, don't forget those over-friendly Russians."

"None of that was my fault." He is Pilate, as he washes the guilt from his soft white hands.

"No, none of it was your fault. But next time you take a woman out on a dark night, George, and abandon her on the road with a bunch of drunken nationalists while you go off to get gas, don't be surprised if you come back to find her raped and nearly dead."

"You've been drinking." George is all disdain.

"Indeed I have. What else is a girl to do to on her last Saturday night in a hellhole?" Fey raises her teacup as if to toast.

"You promised you wouldn't get back on that stuff." He slaps the table hard with the flat of his hand.

"And you promised to take care of me. Was that taking care of me, to have me raped and then whip me out to Durban for some R and R? Do they know, George? Did you tell them?" She will have nothing of his show of anger. It energizes her.

"Tell who what?" he asks.

"That I was raped in the jungle?" she screams at him.

"Of course they know," George says. It is a throwaway line. A defensive hand going up.

"And as a reward they send us here to Cairo?" Fey says. It is her final evidence of his and their cruelty.

"It was a fresh start. You are out of it. Drunk." George is on his high horse. He will not come down.

Fey looks at George with a sadness her words cannot express. "Yes, and now I'm getting out of this stinking country, thank God!"

"This has been our mission," he capitulates.

"No, it's your mission. Your life we are leading. Your calling. It is truly all about you!"

"That's not fair and that's not how it used to be when we started out."

"When we started out, I was..." Fey's head is not straight as she searches for the right words. "...a naive child. Seeing this all out here, the infighting and petty squabbling in the Mission." She feels strangely unsteady on her feet. "How you have to suck up to the powers that be..."

"But..." George tries to break in but Fey will not have it.

"The hostility of the locals, the poverty... Oh, seeing those poor children every day. The stink of that damn Nile. Rape at knifepoint. It's not what... You can't see that?"

"What you went through," he is quick to answer, "was unimaginable and I will never forgive myself for putting you in that situation, but let's be real, that's not the whole story. You were in love with the idea of being a missionary. You longed for the romance. To be out there. A bohemian lady bountiful. In a New Look dress with violin music. Did you ever have a real call?"

"Oh, that's rich. You bastard. And you, you just wanted to be needed by all. George Almighty dispensing his pearls before swine, as usual the center of attention. You called me, George. You called me! I loved you! But you had me raped, George. You had me raped! I'm not mad with God, I am mad with you! It's you, you are God, George. You are the high and mighty, the divine!"

He knows instantly that he can go one of two ways. Anger and frustration outweigh love. Exhaling, his words come down as a hammer. "Fundamentally, you are a real bitch." George is also standing; they are head to head. His nostrils flaring. His eyes bulging. His hands clenched, ready to strike her.

"Ah. Now we're getting real..."

Jenna wanders into the kitchen rubbing her eye. "Are we leaving yet? I heard yelling. Are you angry with me?"

"How could we be angry with you? You are our very own princess." George scoops Jenna up in his arms and she puts her head against his reddened cheek. "Come on, let's get you back to bed."

Fey falls backwards onto her chair, then forwards across the table, her shattered life spilling like her loosened hair across the kitchen table.

The Rutlers returned on a tramp steamer to Babylon, with only Jenna as a reminder of their more exotic, divinely ordered days. Babylon, twenty-five miles from New York City, dating back to 1689, founded on harvesting sea salt. A town named by a Mrs. Cocklin, to reference its bawdy reputation as a stopover for travelers on Long Island's south shore. Babylon, home of the first black professional baseball team. The family reluctantly moved into a stark 1950s-style ranch home. George, eager to start a new work, immediately embarked on a six-week US preaching tour, waving a brief goodbye from his black Ford, departed his desolate wife leaving her marooned, with no close family, little income and Jenna their adopted child.

As Jenna progressed through the school system she was, as a practical matter, fatherless. The periods of George's absence grew longer and his relationship with Fey increasingly strained. Nevertheless, Jenna proved to be a bright student with a particular facility with numbers and landed in time at West Babylon High School.

A school report from this period reads, 'Jenna is an excellent student who is eager to learn. She has a particular interest in English literature, mathematics and music where she has progressed well beyond many of her peers. When called upon in the classroom she indicates strong reasoning ability. She is very diligent in her studies at school and spends much of her time outside of the classroom in the school library. Physically, Jenna excels at running, and gymnastics. However, she has not shown great interest in mixing with other pupils and as a consequence is somewhat personally isolated. There have been two instances where Jenna has been reported by other children to have been the subject of bullying by other girls and as a result apparently suffered some physical abuse. These instances have of course been followed up by the staff but at the time of writing, Jenna has shown great reluctance to cooperate in our investigation, which is still in progress.'

At school and frequently at home, behind her dark eyes, deep in her imagination, Jenna walks down Mohammed Abodou towards the El Hussein Hospital in the heat of Cairo. She follows the dusty footprints made by her adoptive father's black Oxford shoes, now so distant and cold.

On a summer afternoon she sits in the bleachers on Salt Field three rows back from the front for the commencement ceremony. She is proud to be graduating. She sits erect, intensely focused on Sabrina, the valedictorian, hanging on her every word.

"The journey to achieving a goal is more important than the accomplishment."

Jenna is scissor-sharp. Her silky jet-black hair is pulled back into a ponytail which emphasizes her almond eyes. Her arms are folded.

"Make a difference in the lives of others. It is time for you to make a mark on this world."

With or without her father, Jenna is determined to break out of Babylon and is done with crying.

The bland bank in Babylon where she takes an entry-level job is not Jenna's idea of freedom. She sits caged, disguised as teller two. But it's there that she encounters Scott's broad smile as he cashes a check. Scott, the eldest of five sons from an Irish family, laconic, a lover of music, and emotionally as solid as a rock. He has recently started to teach math and gymnastics. Scott and Jenna marry a year after their first meeting. Grace is born two years later, waving a fist and screaming at an unsuspecting world.

The conversation that I had one evening with Fey, at her house, just before I was about to leave home for orientation at university, floats into my recollection. My grandmother and I were sitting on her bed, rummaging through boxes of old photographs, when we came across a fading monochrome print of my grandmother, and my grandfather George. The photograph showed the couple sitting in an ancient Land Rover, parked by the side of the road, under a stand of fever trees.

"It seems like yesterday," Fey said. "We had stopped to take a break. It was hot and the sun was almost set, so the light was very dim and we couldn't really make out what was in the shadows." She turned the photograph round so I could see it properly. "It was noisy. Not the noise of the city, but of being in the middle of Africa. Crickets, frogs, crows, things moving around in the bush, the bray and call of who knows what, they have those birds over there, you know, nightjars, they have this kind of rhythmic call." I remember thinking it was as if Fey had been transported back to what she was describing and that somehow Fey and I were both there. "George had been warned that there were some pretty bad characters robbing people, and worse, along the road. But George and I were young and on a mission as we saw it, and besides, we had a driver, his name was John, who knew his way around. I remember his rifle, sitting next to me on the back seat. After about ten minutes John tried to start the car but the engine wouldn't catch. He tried again and again but it just would not go. We were stuck. We had a long heated argument about what to do."

"What did you do?" I asked.

"It's not like we could hitch a ride with a passing rhino." When Fey smiles her face wrinkles like a week-old peach. "We reckoned that we were about two miles from Maai Mahiu, the village we were making for. So George said it would make best sense if he walked to the village. We had been told that the Mission had a school and ran a surgery there, and in fact that's why we were headed there." Fey seemed anxious to provide details of the incident as if under cross-examination. I became concerned that she was so agitated and placed my arm around her shoulders. "So off George goes and we see his silhouette getting smaller and smaller in the car headlights as he disappears down the road."

I remember saying to her, "You must have felt scared, being left on your own?"

"No, not really. I was pretty used to fending for myself. But it was then, after George had been gone for about an hour and a half that I began to smell cigarette smoke. John smelled it too. I began to feel that we were being watched. I could feel John getting nervous. He came around to the back of the car and took the rifle from next to me. 'Going to see who that might be, Missus,' he said, and a moment later he'd disappeared into the bush."

"You must have been terrified!" I was totally caught up in my grandmother's story.

"Yes, I certainly was. I got out of the car and went and tried to hide myself behind the fever trees. I remember it clear as day. I didn't want whoever was out there to find me alone. I remember leaving my bag open on the car seat hoping that whoever it was would see the bag and be content with taking it. Three guys came out of the bush. Two were armed with a kind of machete, a 'panga' they call it in the local Kiswahili. The other guy had some sort of long stick. They had been watching us. They shouted in my direction for me to come out from behind the trees I suppose. When I stayed put, they came over towards me and the guy with the stick started poking it around so I had no choice but to come out. They stank of drink. I knew what was going to happen."

I remember being shocked and very quiet.

"It was like being hit by a truck." Fey closed her eyes as she related what came next. "They started to push me from one to another and then the first guy, I remember the pigment on his forehead was blotchy and grey, ripped my clothes off and did his worst. I was screaming and pleading for them to stop. They were just laughing." Fey didn't cry as she spoke, rather she seemed in a trance as she stared beyond me at the wall, totally absorbed in her story.

"It couldn't have been long. Just long enough for the first one to penetrate me. I didn't feel him. I just felt torn. Numb, as if somehow out of my body, looking down at myself. It was then that George came back with I can't remember who now, from the village. I just remember the noise of a truck and the sound of screams, my own I think and gunshots."

"Oh Granny, what happened?" My eyes closed as I gripped my grandmother, trying to control my own tears.

"They took me to the village. I just curled up in a ball." Fey wiped the back of her hand across her eyes as if to wipe away her memories. "I knew I was pregnant. I could feel the baby inside me and when I did, I never felt love. Only hate for the stranger who raped me. I kept living it again and again; I still do."

"What did George do?" I asked.

"He'd bring me hot tea and we would just sit. I didn't want him to touch me. We both knew we were broken. Nothing much was said. There was a single policeman in the village but the guys were never found. We stayed in the village a week then headed back to Nairobi. When we got back to base, no one discussed the incident. I don't think anyone could handle it. People knew I was depressed. I got a lot of sympathetic looks and was left on my own. George would leave for the day; I would drink a little at first. And then a lot. Sometimes I would throw up. Frequently he would come home to find me on the floor. It was hard for him, I guess. We were kids, how could he know how to handle trauma like that?" Fey looks at Grace imploringly and after a moment continues, "I started to show a little. I couldn't deal with it. I would sit for hours, desperately trying to work out what to do. I was guilty, frightened. I thought of killing myself. One afternoon I took half a bottle of codeine with whisky but then threw up."

"So you had the baby, Granny?"

"No, Grace. I had an abortion." Fey says this, her voice flat. It is a statement, not a confession. "I found a person to take care of it through a British nurse. It cost me fifty dollars."

"And George?"

"It was like nothing happened. We have never discussed it. He obviously knew I was destroyed. That I blamed him for everything. If I had loaded an abortion on him, I think it may have killed him. He is a self-centered man, but not an intentionally bad one. He has spent his life working to make believers but I'm not sure he has ever asked himself who he is. I basically broke down after the abortion and we were taken out and sent to Durban. When George brought Jenna into our lives, she was my salvation. She was my reason to live. She couldn't save our marriage but she saved me."

"And you and George?" I asked, eager to understand.

"Well, you know he travelled a lot. And eventually life went by," Fey said with resignation.

There was a long silence between us as my grandmother stared at the photograph and I stroked her hand. "Granny, why did you tell me this tonight?"

"I don't honestly know, darling. I think because you are going off and I want you to know what life can do to people. To know though, that whatever happens you can survive it, however terrible it is, if you can hold onto something; for years I held onto my bitterness and hated George for leaving me that night, and that nearly destroyed me and your mother, Grace. But now I'm holding onto something else, and that is forgiveness. And through all life's circumstances, that comes from a God who loves us. And I want you to know too that wonderful things can happen after bad things, Grace. Although I was dead inside God gave me Jenna and now you. And because of that I am, in my own kind of way, at peace."

I remember walking home that night in the realization and shock that for years my grandmother had carried a burden that I had no idea existed.

Startled by the sound of my alarm, I gather myself for an evening's work at my computer and prep for my regular 7 am breakfast with Al Jiminez at Corporate. Mindful of my mission.

CHAPTER THREE

The City of London skyline juxtaposing the grace of Wren and the cynicism of the Shard looms over the conference room through the rain-spattered panoramic windows. It is well into a depressingly damp evening. The consulting team has left the black conference room table strewn with presentation binders, half-empty pitchers of iced water and plates of sandwiches which are hardening in the air conditioning.

We have been winding up towards this conversation all day. Since his arrival at our London office mid-morning, my boss, Christian Purvis, CEO XelFunds, has taken to lying on a desk set to the side of the room which just accommodates his long-boned frame. A white terry towel has been rolled up and placed behind his neck, his knees are bent as he studies an iPad that he holds with both hands unsteadily above his head. I notice that in place of his usual highly polished Oxford shoes he is wearing a pair of black Nike trainers. As the day has worn on, the various pills that Christian has been taking, far from improving his mood, have made him punchy and irritable. From his occasional grunts and twitches he appears to be agitated and I think, preoccupied with the sales data coming out of Europe.

To any outsider coming upon the scene we would look ludicrous, like a stage moment from the farce that played for years at the Whitehall Theater which is just around the corner. Indeed, from time to time I've had difficulty in suppressing laughter and surprise myself by uncharacteristically confiding in my wife Cait by text, 'You'd love this, bizarre scene, think The Fall of Nelson on the deck of the Victory at Trafalgar. In dread of Christian crying out "Kismet, Hardy!"'

I'm ashamed to say that I've quite enjoyed the guilty pleasure of watching the various expressions on the faces of the consultants and staff presenting at the meeting as they have entered the conference room. No one knows whether to acknowledge Christian or ignore him. Christian will occasionally ask a question and have to repeat it, as a confused presenter will first have to detect whom they are addressing, since invariably his words are muffled by the trajectory of his speech. I'm half-expecting someone to drop their pants as if in pantomime and shout, "I say, I say, I say, a funny thing happened to me on the way to the conference room!" and for Christian to respond by jumping to his feet as he bows and shouts back, "Thank you very much! I thank you very much!"

It would be easy for you to think that I am a cynic or disengaged when it comes to the way we do business. As Chief Investment Officer, I take my role seriously. It is not that I don't care about what is at stake. It's that I can't help but see the comedic side of what is happening. My reaction is perhaps a kind of defense mechanism. A way of me avoiding commitment I suppose, after being in one company for so long. Or even boredom.

I sober up, divert my eyes and ask Christian if he is feeling any better.

"Not much. It's the same issue I had last year before my neck surgery." He grimaces, as he turns towards me. "Must be the sitting on the flight over here from JFK or maybe carrying that damn flight bag."

"Still painful?" I say, trying to show some empathy.

"Guess I should have listened to the doc," Christian replies, as he turns his head awkwardly towards Barry, who is seated across from him at the conference table. Christian's warm brown eyes, usually polished bright with wit and an infectious energy, look dull and hollow. His smooth Southern intonation is lacking its customary warmth. "Let's get on with it so I can get out of here. I asked you two to stay behind after the presentations because I want us all to be on the same page, be sure we have a meeting of the minds."

I hear the statement with skepticism. *Meeting of the minds? That would be telepathy then, since we have never discussed this topic before in any depth.* But of course I don't voice the thought.

"Barry, when are you sending a copy of the findings presented today to Pompton?" Pompton Financial, by the way, is our parent company: a big financial services conglomerate with global reach, where we don't fit. But more of that later.

Barry is not sure if he should leave the conference table and stand by Christian to answer his question but after a moment's hesitation decides to stay where he is. "I view you as the primary client, Christian. You hired my firm to provide you with a competitive analysis to bolster your business case for making acquisitions. My understanding is that we will present the report to Pompton jointly?" This is a kind of half-truth because although we are paying for this particular assignment, Barry's firm does a lot for Pompton, and ultimately his loyalty is bound to be to them.

"Well, after today it feels more like you've kicked a man when he's down, Barry." Christian chuckles but in so doing it seems his pain intensifies and he winces. "Far from bolstering our case, your report is in fact quite negative, if not outright derogatory. You've put us in a real bind, my friend. I have told Frost that he can expect a report recommending that Pompton makes a substantial commitment to our long-term growth." All this is now addressed to the ceiling as Christian has returned his head to its former position. At this point you should also know that John P. Frost, the perfidious Chairman and CEO of Pompton Financial Services, is undoubtedly one of the major villains in this story. But back to that evening in London.

"Christian, we were hoping that you would find our analysis helpful. It does indeed seem to us that XelFunds is facing multiple, heavy challenges." Barry's cultivated Indianlish accent has a phonetic authority. His manner, acquired primarily from his father who sits as a judge in New Delhi, combines an intense accusatory wit with self-deprecation. I find it difficult not to like him, despite his frequent references to his professors at Harvard Business School and his penchant for needing to be the smartest person in the room. The latter perhaps acquired from Birla Public School as a child or as a student at New College Oxford (which he frequently reminds people has connections with India dating back to 1579). He's even got me trotting his background out. But you have to admit he is impressive.

It's time I got in on the act. "But aren't you being a little pessimistic, Barry?" I counter from across the conference table, beginning to feel that the conversation is getting a bit out of hand.

I am visiting London for my monthly review of European Investment Performance and Fund board meetings. I speak with the restraint you'd expect, conscious of my British diffidence, from behind the defense of my steepled hands. Between you and me, I've found this apparently laissez-faire manner can be quite devastating to my opponents in a fracas of the type about to be played out.

"Not at all, Fen. As Chief Investment Officer you know that based on current performance trends and competitive positioning there is a real question as to whether XelFunds can sustain required growth in the long term."

I reply, "There is of course another rationale." And shoot him a 'don't tread on me' look. I always have an aggressive rejoinder when performance is questioned. It's an involuntary reflex. "Yes, there have been a few near-term gaps in investment performance and sales growth, I will give you that. But as you have analyzed the shortfall Barry, I'm sure that you will agree that this is a consequence of market changes that were truly black swan events."

Barry jokes, "So you are arguing Taleb? Only we consultants are supposed to read about black swans!"

Right—I tell you these consultants can be really smug at times. "Seriously, we recovered and thrived on change." I've trotted this out dozens of times. It is an opening stanza to a 'they done me wrong' meme of my creation, Christian just laps it up, when he's following the conversation, that is. Sometimes I think this canned soliloquy would make great lyrics on some country and western riff by the Stones.

"We have come through a lot of history. I would argue that in many ways, certainly in terms of recovering investment performance, we are stronger than ever." I hear myself croon. You have to admit that is a pretty good opening.

"Indeed, from my analysis it's not unrealistic to think that we can double our assets in four years and realize a pre-tax income north of two billion dollars in year five." I'm a bit surprised by my passion as I hear myself saying this. It feels more performance art than truth-telling. Nevertheless, my intuition, honed by innumerable conversations with Wall Street analysts and consultants of one sort or another, tells me to soldier on. Provided, that is, that I can maintain focus.

And after all, isn't it my job to be a good soldier? I ask myself as I hear my voice ramble on. "We've an impressive brand reputation, real brand dominance in several products and are known for delivering great value to investors." Now for the coup de grâce. "More, our investment strength is almost uniquely combined with a deep distribution network that is second to none!"

Why am I so defensive? I play with the thought. *Because I need to be. Barry is in truth mostly correct; the report is a real indictment of Christian, and indeed me and the rest of management.*

"Sure, I hear all that, Fen, and I get that from the inside it may look like that. But you hired our firm for an objective view. And I tell you..." I find the gentle pitch of Barry's voice strangely soothing and silently admire his delivery technique which slices the patient open while they are lullabied. "... having conducted our study, our view is that the business is in a very fragile position. To turn things around, you are going to need to do a radically different job..." *Cheeky bugger! Those who can do, those who can't teach, Barry!* "...in terms of defending your core sales channels and expanding into other domestic and overseas markets through current products and diversification. And all that implies substantially strengthening investment capabilities, Fen."

Fen Morgan. Yes, that's my moniker. "Indeed, my point entirely, Barry. We need to defend where we are now and grow. To do that we need the ability to acquire."

"But by doing that—growing without addressing fundamentals, you may just be making your problems bigger—sure, you will divert activity for a while, but eventually your core business problems will come through." Barry has a habit of shaking his head from side to side when he really becomes passionate and this is one of those moments. "You need to generate many more customer insights and build out truly market-leading products. I just don't think that as things stand you have the organizational capability to do that." Barry's balletic movement is interrupted.

"Andrea! Andrea!" Christian is screaming for his assistant into his iPhone from the table that has become his plinth on the sidelines.

"Yes?" Andrea's disembodied voice crackles a reply over the phone from the New York office.

"Can you send me the latest version of the US net flows we just got from Finance?"

Barry and I exchange glances. "Sorry guys—carry on." Christian has awakened like the kraken and raised his iPad above his head and is once again interrogating the sales stats.

I say, "Christian, it's essential you are with the conversation on this."

"I am, Fen, I am." Christian makes another attempt to turn his head towards Barry but quickly thinks better of it as he rejoins the conversation. "Yes, there are several bumps in the road. But generally, the company is in great shape, Barry. We just need you to help us articulate that. You know, put a little shine on the penny."

I am sure that the great London cockney line about not being able to tell shit from Shinola is going through Barry's mind, but he's too much the professional to voice it. "Perhaps it will be helpful for me to walk through our rationale again."

And so it goes back and forth, mainly between Barry and me, with periodic, increasingly incomprehensible, but authoritative mutterings from Christian. Thankfully Christian concedes to my suggestion that we should retreat to The Ivy for dinner.

These days The Ivy has hacked about its traditional menu and rebranded itself as a 'modern British' restaurant. I order Cornish fish soup and grilled Dover sole; Barry, knowing no better, falls for the squid salad followed by roasted hake fillet with saffron; and in typical form, despite his gammy back, Christian falls for the seared foie gras and a 340-gram Bannockburn rib-eye on the bone. I decide to order a bottle of good French sauvignon blanc, while Barry orders a glass of moscato, and, predictably, Christian sticks with a series of glasses of Midleton Irish whiskey.

We chat about how the UK has changed, the cost of real estate and the likely impacts of Brexit, then Christian, in a better mood after a whiskey and a half, returns to the fray.

"So, we are racing to the bottom, Barry, is that it?" Christian says appearing almost supine, like a basking seal splayed against the cushion recently supplied by a very attentive Italian waiter.

"Our analysis indicates that the company is underperforming against competitive benchmarks, however good you are feeling internally. Look at the data set we just provided. All the indicators, with the exception of some key equity funds managed by Viser, and distribution in some segments, are neutral or in the wrong direction." He spells it out. It is clearly a labor of love. But I can tell, deep in his soul he knows he is beating a dead horse.

"Client and stakeholder expectations of investment performance have changed; there is increasing competitive pressure on your previously deep client relationships." Barry, as if playing a pungi to entice a couple of cobras from a jar. "Fee compression is accelerating as automation lowers the cost of transactions, hurting your margins." I feel mesmerized by the words tripping off Barry's tongue, each a drop in the bucket of evidence proving the company's incompetence.

Barry raises his hands as if pleading; he speaks softly as if trying not to disturb Christian. "Your competitors are investing in new technologies. But you are not. Your product innovation is faltering. The competition is consolidating, which weakens XelFunds' dominance..."

I want to applaud and say "Bravo!" Even with the smallest of audiences, Barry drives each statement home relentlessly, like not-so-subtle stabs into a torso. I file the technique away for future use under 'pseudo-dramatic situations'. Truly, I feel badly that I can't take this conversation more seriously, but essentially I'm untouched by what Barry is saying. The company certainly has business issues, but the conversation so far has skirted causation.

Feeling puckish, I can't resist saying, "You like us that much, Barry? Apart from that, how was the show, Mrs. Lincoln?" Thankfully, Barry laughs.

I notice that there is no sound across the table from Christian other than his steady breathing. I suspect he has fallen asleep and add this to the list of embarrassments that I'm compiling for eventual inclusion in my memoir, which, like Muggeridge, I will title Chronicles of Wasted Time.

"If you want the most blatant instance of what I am saying, take something you are both quite familiar with." Barry is still using 'both' despite Christian's apparent escape to the Land of Nod. "Your initiative started last year," he says, "to build a global brand based on creating a superior investor experience..."

"I know it was not our finest hour." Bingo! At last something that Barry is saying begins to resonate with me. You should know that I am in no way a proponent of leadership theory (indeed I have detested the old chestnut 'Are leaders born or made?' ever since I wasted hours on the topic at a leadership program when I was at Cranfield years ago, where I was made to clamber up ropes and kayak down rivers in the Brecon Beacons). I remain firmly unconvinced that leadership theory is really what XelFunds needs.

"...and failure to get managers and employees across the firm to own the effort. Bottom line, you've lost critical time and millions of dollars. I've known you both a while—Christian?" Barry looks appealingly to me as he speaks. He reminds me of my dog. Christian is still out.

Smiling, I say, "I guess he's been called away."

Barry's manner grows even more intense. Weary, I close my eyes as if bracing for the coup de grâce.

"Fen, I'll be direct." There really is no stopping him. "The core problem is that the leadership team, or Group as you call it, has failed... Purpose... prioritization... deep culture problem..." I am looking straight at him but I wish he would speak in terms that will connect with Christian.

Here's the thing: I accumulate private collections. Mostly in my head. I collect theories, ideas about everything and shards of poetry or sayings and dates for this and that. But also gather stacks of old books, together with sketches by artists from the interwar period, gramophone records from the Fifties and even, for a while, vintage wines from Burgundy. On rare occasions I will also collect people, but frankly I am much more circumspect in my enthusiasm for that. I can live in my head for hours, rooting around in the attic of my memories. In the house I share with Cait and the children, I have files and closets full of papers and pieces that I will sit and contemplate in the early hours when the house is silent and only our dog, Fred, shares my lonely reconnaissance.

But back to the plot.

As you will have gathered, there is something within me that is highly resistant to including the systemic business thinking about people organization and culture that Barry is espousing in his pantechnicon of theories. As I process Barry's assertions, it seems to me that they are like a collectable that may perhaps be valuable. But that in the final analysis, his theory is of unproven provenance.

Glancing over at the cadaverous Christian, I observe, "Looks like this conversation is very much between us now. Truthfully Barry, aren't you being a bit overly dramatic?" As I say this, I remember the Ring Rot song our Romanian nanny was playing last Saturday in the kitchen of our home in Brooklyn. My head goes off on a ridiculous rant.

'You are quite fantastic
Up there in my attic
Inside out this traffic
Your worms in my head
You squirm girl
Your worms in my head'

"Truth is an interesting word, Fen. Do we ever get to the whole truth? I honestly don't know."

"What is truth?" At last an opportunity to move the conversation to something interesting.

When in spate, Barry takes on a pedantic academic tone where he clips his words. I bet that as he hears himself speak he knows he should tailor his delivery more, take his foot off the gas, but often he just can't bring himself to resist the temptation of proving himself right. At these moments some might call him a shade arrogant.

"Unfortunately, these conversations you have amongst yourselves don't seem to distill into strategic intent or execution..." He's still running on. "Senior Leadership Group... infighting, lack of diversity of ideas and people... pattern of deteriorating performance." Barry has apparently written all of this down and been practicing for months. It is a performance of which his father, the judge, would be proud.

I sit back in my dining chair and cross my arms as Barry's soliloquy continues to wash over me. I glance out of the window at the end of The Ivy at the night sky, now cast like a black velvet cape about the London skyline and see that the rain has diffused into a mist which blurs the edges of the proud buildings opposite. It's getting late. I suppress a yawn. As Barry continues to gesticulate and argue his point, I recall a line from a book on Confucius that I thumbed through.

'If you are the smartest person in the room
then you are in the wrong room.'

And continue to dismiss what I am hearing with more than a little self-justification.

Barry is not picking up on my cues, "I'll make a further point, Fen. In a business which is predicated on turning risk into profit, I find it surprising that there is little real comprehension on the part of the SLG that poorly managed risk can destroy a business at the speed of a click." The lecture continues, "This is of critical importance because aggressive risk-taking is regarded by this culture as gutsy and a key competence."

"Many would argue that that is what we are paid to do," I push back, but how much longer can this go on?

Perhaps Barry is a bit drunk, his accent and distemper is increasingly apparent. "Your current risk management systems seem poorly devised and staffed, and the leadership team expedient and focused on short-term returns and the size of the bonus pool."

I'm a bit buzzed myself. "There are indeed tensions with our parent, as you know, and yes, the friction gets worse when they perceive us as taking too much risk. But your analysis is incorrect. The core point of contention is that they want to use us as a cash cow, rather than invest in us as a business."

"I get that Fen, but you are blowing past the point I am making."

"How so?" Somewhere in the conversation the connection between Barry and I unspooled. I can see that we are talking past each other. Barry is trying to deliver what to him is his most important message. I am at some level deliberately not hearing it, as I wrestle with what seems to me a disjointed conversation about culture and company performance.

Next, I catch Barry saying something like "This is bad news, Fen, because the Senior Group—you call it the 'Senior Leadership Group', correct?"

"Right. The SLG."

"The SLG has unconsciously created the conditions where the business is caught on a knife-edge, a potentially lethal cycle."

"Come on, Barry. Lethal means killing people."

"All right, downward spiral then, where the company is led by people who act like 'heroic firefighters' or manage up to the next level to accumulate power and influence like 'courtiers'."

"Sanskrit to most people," I reply. It's become a slanging match and quite out of hand really.

"You still talking guys? My mouth's incredibly dry." Christian has resurfaced. "Are we any further along?" Barry and I are silent.

"Your very expert opinion is that our leadership team is inadequate and, by implication, that I am deficient?" The question Christian asks would be ironic if he was not looking distinctly groggy and beginning to haul himself upright and gradually sliding off the side of his chair.

"Shit, that hurts!" I have not seen Christian this angry in a long time. He had been listening to the conversation after all. He makes a further effort and stands, holding the side of the table, his grey pallor deadening his features as he glares at Barry.

"I think you may be taking what Barry is saying too personally, Christian. Let's hear him out."

Someone has to take the heat out of this. Whatever I think of Barry's hypothesis, I don't want him running back to corporate rubbishing Christian and me. They think badly enough about us already.

Christian lowers himself carefully onto a chair and looks at his Rolex. The party at the table opposite have stopped their conversation to look at us. I feel embarrassed.

"Look, I am trying to offer honest feedback, Christian." Barry says, his voice lower. "It is not my intention to cause offense." Barry instinctively lowers his head slightly as he speaks and breaks eye contact with Christian.

The tension in Christian subsides somewhat. "All right, Barry, run it by me."

"As I've sat with you through your management interactions, I've observed the SLG to act very differently collectively than they do individually. Here in this workplace they have a tendency to lack personal and collective authenticity."

"Authenticity?" Christian repeats the word, rolling it round on his tongue like an unpleasant vintage.

"The management climate they create is mercurial. The SLG as a body often seems to be consumed with the politics of power. They manage up to you, Christian, and have become individually and especially collectively so much less than they might be."

Christian is letting Barry run. Despite his initial indignation I can see that Christian, as a former military man, is beginning to admire Barry's courage to push back under fire.

"Individually, they harbor the fear that they will be excluded from decision-making and that they are personally vulnerable to the politics of the day."

I say, "From time to time everyone feels a bit insecure."

"Perhaps," Barry says, "but disconnected as they are from each other, they operate most of the time independently within their own organizational tribe."

"Yeah I read that 'Tribes' book too," I say, wanting to flash my literary bona fides.

"Life in the orbit of the SLG is a series of transactions that they win or lose. Courage is in short supply and compassion is viewed as weakness." *He's really quite Churchillian*, I think. "They don't seem to see themselves as accountable for creating a vision and strategy that their people are able to own. They are not glued together in any way by sharing values they think important."

I hear the words 'power' and 'politics', 'vision' and 'values', feeling them register on the vague periphery of my consciousness, as my mind wrestles with the challenges everyday life poses for my daughter, Rosie.

You've not met her yet. Rosie is my eldest. She is a special kid. She's always in the back of my mind. I have sort of fleeting glimpses of what the world must seem like to her. When I hear Barry talk, I find him hard to follow. Not because I'm thick, but because his language and worldview are foreign to me. I am left having to pull the pieces together, just like Rosie.

"Just look at the verbals in the employee survey. Because weak cultures are unattractive places to work in, staff turnover is at a record high." Barry is right on that; in many departments the company is a revolving door. "Many employees have confided in me that they feel that the first casualty of their work experience has been their loss of personal integrity. My true opinion is that without fixing the culture, shareholder, client and employee interests are continuously crucified on a cross of self-inflicted despair. And that is a bad place for you and the business to be in." Barry has gone too far and he knows it.

Christian does not respond.

Neither do I until my words tumble into the awkward silence. "Some might take your assessment to be a little harsh or even naive. If we are indeed suffering from a deficient culture and climate," I avoid the word 'leadership' and play the politician, "what do we do about it?"

Barry has a prodigious intellect. From previous conversations, I surmise that mentally at this moment he is riding his latest hobby horse, the Dunning-Kruger Effect.

Last week he called me up on my cell phone, typically at the crack of dawn, as I was in an Uber hurtling across the Brooklyn Bridge en route to the office and told me I should read a piece in the Harvard Business Review on the Dunning-Kruger Effect. So when I got to the office, before I got inundated I looked the article up. It turns out that what Barry was talking about is a cognitive bias in which people of low ability have illusory superiority and mistakenly assess their cognitive ability as greater than it is. This springs from the inability of low-ability people to recognize their lack of ability. There is a similar phenomenon that occurs in teams where individual team members may be off the charts in terms of individual brights but collectively the behavior of the team can border on the imbecilic. This was when it dawned on me that Barry's true thesis is that XelFunds has developed a culture of lies and is mired in office politics, personal ambition and prejudices of one kind or another. I was not surprised really. I had heard already from a colleague that he once confided that from a team perspective he thought our leadership group was as thick as pig shit. You can see that my knowing this colors my opinion of Barry. *But there again,* I tell myself, *he is probably right on the money.*

Barry takes a breath. "Fen, I think you, Christian and the entire team need to ask yourselves two simple questions: What is winning? And how do we win?"

In my cab back to my hotel, 45 Park Lane, I text Cait. 'Miss you. Will call in am. Assessment back on Rosie yet? All grim despair here with the consultant.' I look up at the illuminated statue of the Duke of Wellington as the cab rounds Hyde Park Corner. 'A real Balaclava J.'

CHAPTER FOUR

Another life, retold now. It is a fable I barely remember. Perhaps people can only truly recall their lives as legends and grow into the lore they have created. This is the story I tell myself.

North London. Early morning. Mist rising, light cascading between the beech and oak. The night has been unseasonably cold.

I lie with my back flat against the wooden park bench at the bus stop, my hands held aloft to frame the angled sunrise seeping between the branches in what's left of the ancient wood. When a child feels small, small things matter, and I am curious. I gaze at the world within my hands. The pattern of ragged leaves brushing against the mist and muffling the distant drone of traffic beyond the spinney and reservoir.

Curious, I conjure with the light and force my eyes to lose focus and refocus while my ears are still are buzzing with a poem I read by flashlight, beneath my bed covers last night.

'Faster than fairies Faster than witches,
Bridges and houses, hedges and ditches;
And charging along...'

I lose the thread, then recall another fragment... 'The horses and cattle...' then the rest of the poem, something about flying and whistling, is a jumble in my head.

I sit up, cough involuntarily and brush the dust from the back of my grey flannel shorts which float above my thick woolen socks. I am uniformed and half-child on the cusp of adolescence. My upper body is dressed as a miniature adult. Blue school blazer; cream cotton shirt; blue and grey striped tie, knotted tightly below my shirt collar so it can slip over a boy's head; brown leather satchel, my name 'Fen Morgan' written inside its buckled flap. Hair parted to the right; blue school cap, pulled down to the left above my grey eyes. My cap is embossed with a crest, a white insignia 'ST' superimposed on the letter 'A'.

I pause to listen. The air hangs dank. An engine murmurs, foreshadowing a red London Transport bus heaving around the corner. I see this is a Leyland ACE Routemaster and meticulously note damage to the front panel of the vehicle in a small black notepad that I fish from my jacket pocket. The pencil I use is gnarled with my teeth marks. I love the taste of wood and lead.

I rise from the bench, eager to board. A couple of adults shamble up alongside me to form a queue as only Londoners can. One, a plain-faced woman, wears crochet black gloves and scuffed shoes. The other, a thick set man wearing a mackintosh is sweating as he carries a battered case which has seen better times. There is a sullen feel to the tableau we form. No one speaks. I feel into my blazer pocket and a sense of unease.

Cross-ply tires slosh through the pools of acrid water in the curb gathered from last night's rain, as the bus lumbers to a halt. Eager to distance myself from the adults who laboriously settle in silence for the lower deck, I scramble onto the open platform, grab the handrail and haul myself to the upper deck of the bus and down along to the front seat. I use the back of my cuff to clear the condensation on the bus window and peer down at the street below my perch.

The aluminum frame of the bus shudders, exhales diesel toxicity from its six cylinders and gathers momentum as it hauls us along the indifferent tree-lined street which unwinds to run downhill.

"Mornin' Fen" the conductress's smiling face blooms without warning above me. She somehow took a shine to me and one day asked my name. There is more than a hint of tobacco on her breath which warms my face and a London Transport badge on the cap she wears to one side of her head. I know her well and love the way she presides over her passengers with what I take as a real sense of pride. Her aging gunmetal ticket machine dangles across her breast on its jaunty black leather strap as she leans, legs akimbo, to steady herself against the motion of the bus. It reminds me of the silver colored toy Colt 45 revolver I sometimes wear in a black leather holster when I play in solitude at home in the evenings.

I sense the conductress is kind, but take care not to look her in the eye.

"Hello Mavis!" a woman wearing a brown jacket seated somewhere behind me greets Mavis. It seems as if they are old friends. "First day back on the job since the strike?"

Mavis wipes a hand across her nose and looks up past me and the face that I have drawn in the newly formed condensation which streams down the bus windows and smiles. "That's right, dear. We all went out over pay on May the fifth." The bus jiggers sideways. Mavis goes with the motion and turns her attention back to me. "And a lot of good it did us. All that time out, I ask you." It is not a question but a statement.

Saying nothing, I place two coins in Mavis's palm and count the six tin buttons on her conductress's jacket. She prints out a smudged ticket on her Gibson ticket machine. I like to add up the numbers printed in blue ink on the bottom of the tickets I collect during the week. The numbers are bigger and more difficult to add than those on the old Bell Punch tickets.

Mavis sways away back up the aisle, pulling the bell cord running along the roof of the bus twice to instruct the driver to pass the next stop, and pauses to chat to the familiar passenger who greeted her earlier. I strain to hear her from my perch commanding the front of the top deck.

"When you've got something to do, you're content." Mavis's voice is loud and unfiltered and in retrospect, without introspection. She lives on her outside. The red scarf at her throat, that I've seen in the window on sale at Woolworths for ten bob, says that. "Yes, when you're busy it don't seem so bad." I try to decode what she is saying but am not sure what she means. "But it's all that talk of dying that gets me. What with Mother and Joan. And all that bad news and saying goodbyes." Even now I remember the sudden sadness in her voice.

"It seems one thing after another. Big loves, little loves. And all that union trouble down at the depot during the unofficial strikes." Words flow from her as from a water fountain. "The Workers Party, Socialism, you'd think they'd be over it by now. And what with all those riots in Ireland and those poor people shot dead in Derry and that new musical..." I've just been introduced to Shakespeare and some of his plays and have learnt that actors sometimes recite soliloquys and decide this is one of those... "What's it called? That's it, Hair, still going on despite all the outcry. I ask you, all that nudity!" I can feel her words more on my tongue than in my ears and then they are gone leaving me senseless except for the feeling of them passing through me like condensation dripping down the bus windows.

"It's all change, innit? I've got to work out what to give Bill for dinner tonight." She drones on, her voice slipping out from between her fascinating ruby lips. "Still I can't stand here talking to you," she says to her friend abruptly as she disappears to the lower deck.

Passengers at the back of the bus are smoking. The accumulating fog, wafting around the side of my head, aggravates my throat and makes me cough. (A cigarette stub will make me retch and have to bend over to stop throwing up. If I have to go into an ABC teashop with my mother, I can't sit at a table that has one of those silver ashtrays sitting at its middle.)

A passenger thuds down next to me as the bus fills. He is wearing a grubby grey overall with frayed cuffs and heavy shoes. He sweats, emits the vague odor of urine and holds a newspaper that has blackened his nicotined fingers. The headline 'Freddie Starr Ate My Hamster' makes me laugh out loud, and then feel uneasy, as I read a much smaller headline about continuing hostilities in the Middle East near the Jordan. *That's a river in the bible*, I think to myself. *What were British soldiers doing there?*

My mind drifts to my imprisonment at Sunday school last week.

I am one of eight roosting uncomfortably on a circle of wooden chairs in the dingy deacon's room behind the church hall. There was a funeral

Saturday and the odor of white chrysanthemums is still pervasive. A faded print of Jesus robed in white sitting amongst children is askew on the wall. It is labeled 'Suffering the Infants'. And I wonder as usual what Jesus or the infants can be suffering from.

Mrs. Hancock, her rotund fifty years dressed in a flowery skirt and woolen sweater, stands in front of an ancient flannelgraph which has been progressively pinned to a large easel. She points skywards, and then towards the floor and then us, the motley crew of children and squeaky adolescents in the circle. Her face is expressionless, except for the oval of her thick-lipped mouth which fascinates me as it continuously changes shape.

The flannelgraph depicts a cliff. Green scaled crocodiles thrash in the River Jordan and look up in eager anticipation at the figure of a young man descending on a brown hemp rope from the cliff top. Above, lions pace restlessly and peer over the edge of the cliff at the escapee who narrowly avoids being eaten. There are dark caves in the cliff wall and white eyed snakes are beginning to slither out of the void, also towards the young man.

"The river Jordan. Not a safe place..." I mutter to myself. I have these magical inner conversations continuously. I process ideas quickly. They always lead to the next iteration of thought and the next, like cards being dealt staccato. Each thought linked by a thread of ideas that has its own permutation. The ideas pile up until I feel overwhelmed and lock up. It's a bit like riding on my fixed wheel bike. The pedals go faster and faster with the wheel until it all gets out of control and I go flying.

We, the suffering infants, form a resentful crocodile, and are led back from the Sunday school room into the sanctuary, to join our parents who are listening to a talk on missionary work by the Reverend George Rutler. He says something perhaps about sacrifice and lost souls in Africa and Egypt; oddly, his name has lodged in my memory. The Minister looks old, worn and for no apparent reason, disappointed. I am more convinced than ever that the world is not only a very dangerous place but also quite boring.

"Stapleton Hall Road next! Stapleton!" Mavis's disembodied voice distills into two girls who clamber onto the bus. They brush determinedly past the conductress up to the rear seats on the upper deck. "Mornin' ladies."

The elder of the two children turns her sullen head over her shoulder in response but does not reply.

And so, the bus snakes forward, hissing and weaving, stopping and starting, until it is packed with a rag tag mix of suburban humanity. Teenagers chatter while sour superior faces gaze silently. Random portraits skewered serially to the wall of the morning commute.

I squeeze past the riders on the upper deck, down the stairs, off the bus and through the black iron railings that fence St Adrian's School.

As I enter the building, I feel my mood darken. End of term, yet the corridors still smell of fresh paint and disinfectant newly added to years of distemper and floor polish.

The air is already uncomfortably thick and damp. The school hall is full for assembly and noisy, giggling conversation. The chatter fades. The headmaster steps up to the podium to command the assembled students and staff.

I avoid my surroundings by studying the back of my hands and thinking about how the figure on the rope could drop past the crocodiles into the river and out to the safety of the other side of the riverbank.

We are ranked like cadets before the head, seated on creaking wooden chairs. I sit in the third row from the front of the assembly allocated to 1CC. At the end of my first year at the school I have done just enough to confirm my apparently less than average ability in almost everything. My mind trips from topic to topic. I am at once interested in everything and nothing. No one attempts to decode me as I attempt silently to decode everything. I feel like the wallpaper in my bedroom. Flat, anonymous and grey. I sometimes walk home from school with Terry to avoid the gangs of other kids waiting at the bus stop. Terry and I talk about cricket scores and football but mostly about buses and trainspotting. He is the only real friend I have. But one is enough really.

The pungent odor of sweat permeates the assembly. Teachers stand or sit around the walls of the school hall. They too wear a uniform of sorts. The men all jacketed, and appropriately taciturn, trying to look stern and interested. The occasional eye wandering towards the women. The women, a few painted with supine mouths, look at their shoes. One or two furtively touch their hair.

The head wears Harris Tweed and an overbite. He is thin, with the appearance of a gnarled stick much polished over the years. His white collar clings snuggly, moist against his neck; his tight blue tie has the effect of thinning his voice.

His name is Stephens. In 1919, deprived of a good war, he returned from Germany to resume life with his mother amongst the antimacassars of New Southgate. Behind his back we call him 'Inky Stephens' after the fountain pen factory in Enfield. No one is certain of his story. He is ancient and perennially tight-lipped as he navigates the school hallways, with his tripodal gait, looking at his pocket watch and avoiding eye contact with any of us.

The loudspeaker at the side of the hall is blaring out 'Good Vibrations' by the Beach Boys, a gesture by the deputy head towards modernity. This morning as he begins to address the school, Inky's manner is even more tentative and remote than normal. His upper frame begins to inflate, his brow glistens above his oval wire-rimmed spectacles. As he launches into his soliloquy, he gradually uncurls his body and lifts his head as his opaque green eyes sweep over the assembly. He has learned some trick, enabling him to stand taller in the mind of a child for years to come.

"Young ladies and gentlemen," his intonation is standard and English yet oddly menacing. "It is my task as your headmaster to bid you all..." His words slide out from tight white lips overseen by a pencil mustache. He pauses, the corner of his mouth curls as he inhales.

I am in the tunnel of my thoughts. I try to remember how to spell words. "Minute, that's spelled 'minute' or is that 'minite'?" I look at my

Timex watch. "How many minutes more of this?" I ask myself. "How do I spell jewel? Is it 'jewle' or 'jewel'?" I look anxiously at my watch again—there it is on the watch face: twenty-one jewels. "That's it!"

"Good Morning," he says. For a moment it seems Inky is floating behind the podium from which he is addressing us. He sways imperceptibly, apparently suddenly light-headed and perhaps, I speculate, feeling himself to be walking alone under a brilliant sky. He looks above and beyond us, towards the translucent stained-glass windows at the end of the hall, where his thoughts are lost amongst the abstracts boiling in the glare of the morning sun.

Inky's mental sirocco is broken by a cough from somewhere to his left. He gathers himself "As we part on our last day of term, I am struck by what the great poet Keats wrote,"

Do you not see how necessary a world of pains and troubles is to school an intelligence and make it a soul?

He peers over his spectacles at us in the serried ranks, looking perhaps for recognition of his brilliant opening. He finds nothing but our blank stares.

"Remember, you are all capable of being extraordinary young ladies and gentlemen here tutored in the three Ls: learning, leadership and life." He says 'life' with an odd lilt. His words fly forward and fall flat against distempered walls. "The three Ls are a form of esoteric knowledge that many outside this institution crave. You may feel that what you have been schooled in this year has caused you painful effort. But to you, girls and boys, what you have learned is the very stuff of food and drink for your intellect and soul." Has the word 'drink' made his mouth dry?

A large wasp, enthused by the warm air we have generated, has entered the assembly hall and some of us are following its angry meandering.

I eye the exit door and am ready to run.

"You are here because your parents have seen the opportunity and advantage that a good education in the three Ls can bring to a young person." *Obviously, you have not met my parents*, I want to tell him.

"In a sea of sameness, you have been chosen." *I have heard of the seven seas but never the sea of sameness.* I look around and can see everyone else is thinking this too.

"In a world obsessed with the transient and mediocre we will give you a lifelong education that will enable you to become proper members of society, not victims of your uninformed passion."

I look across at Jenny. She lives down the road from me and I can see that she is giggling.

"Remember, always be teachers." I am not at all sure I want to become a teacher and look in confusion at the staff who are also looking dismayed as Inky rambles on.

"Know your worth and you will become valuable to others. To quote the Bard..." And with this he opens his arms and palms wide. His raspy voice engulfs his audience such that many of the children cower.

"'We few, we happy few, we band of brothers.

They shall think themselves accursed they were not here.

And hold their manhoods cheap, whiles any speaks

that fought upon Saint Crispin's day!'"

It is suddenly silent. Nobody moves. Now no one is sure what the head means.

Both speaker and audience are awkwardly silent.

I sit quite still, not sure what I have heard or what to do.

It is as if the air is leaking ever so slowly from Inky's chest. He is punctured. His body deflates, folding back into his peculiar physical imprint. He turns slowly, beckons to the deputy head and walks with great intent from the podium out of the hall towards who knows what.

"Thank you, Headmaster." The deputy wears an odd grin as he steps forward to fill the void left by Inky. He speaks with a mountainous Welsh accent. "Let's build upon..." His voice winds up, as if reaching for some peak, "that framework, shall we?" His voice winds down. I think someone has told him to use his hands when speaks. He opens his fingers, he is a conjurer, "Let's talk about..." up goes his voice, "our plans for the summer holidays." And down again into the valley.

Inky is admitted later that afternoon to Friern Barnet Hospital, an asylum for the mentally ill.

Years later, sitting in a pub near my apartment in Muswell Hill, I learned Inky's backstory from a friend distantly connected with Inky's family. It seems that somewhere in his past, there was his comfortable life as an only child of an architect in the shrubbery of the London suburbs and then, bright and solitary child as he was, the private school that flung him at Oxford, where to his utter surprise he fell in love with Jessica. He managed to read English Language and Literature without surrendering much to the seduction of intellectual or emotional curiosity until he discovered her in the library, where she was working away, obsessing over Keats.

Unlike Inky, she was raven-haired, her skin shot through with alabaster. She introduced him to the Pre-Raphaelites. They moved into rooms on the top floor of number one Moreton Road. What started as a Keats romance soon became a Keats tragedy when Jessica was hit by a city bus one evening when she was riding her bike home to their tiny flat. Inky was devastated. In anguish he felt his newly awakened consciousness interred with her one rain filled morning in St Sepulchre's Cemetery, Oxford. He had nothing but the word 'Loved', her name, and the date of her birth and death inscribed on her headstone.

Visiting the Laing Gallery later that year with an Aunt who lived in Newcastle upon Tyne, he sees Holman Hunt's painting of 'Isabella and the Pot of Basil'. He knew this to be a Joycean epiphany; his life will indeed, like Lorenzo's head, be entombed in the Majolica for good. Jessica, like Isabella, was so abundantly beautiful and yet so manifestly a curator of the dead.

He took up teaching against the background of the late Twenties' boom and bust, and an Education Act that raised the school leaving age to fourteen. He landed a couple of jobs as assistant headmaster and found he possessed a gift for schedules, administration and structure.

He walked through the following years alone and with indifference. Disappearing into middle age, he became frustrated by what he saw as the frivolity and inconsistency of women other than his beloved Jessica. To him, like to Keats after the death of Fanny Brawne, women became, 'As children to whom I would rather give a sugar plum than my time.'

His mother, of course, became the exception. His childhood home with its panes of Victorian leaded stained glass each side of the oak front door in New Southgate was an easily accessible and safe refuge.

He threw himself once again into teaching and rose to headmaster. This time, even further removed for the warmth of relationships, his only certainty the holiness of his heart's affections towards his mother, who by that time was long dead.

"It's a sad story," I say to my friend, as we leave the pub to pick up an Indian takeaway to eat in my apartment.

CHAPTER FIVE

Saturday afternoon, in November. Fonthill Road pushes against Finsbury Park and is the armpit of three deprived North London boroughs.

The bottom of the street anchored by the Duke of Edinburgh Pub runs into Seven Sisters Road and the Astoria Theatre. Opened in the 1930s, the Astoria was one of the largest in the world. This was the venue where Jimi Hendrix first burned a guitar on the opening night of the Walker Brothers tour; the 1968 Beach Boys album 'Live in London' was recorded, and earlier audiences flocked to hear Johnny Dankworth and Sarah Vaughan.

To the north, the street of oppressive Edwardian buildings is capped off by Tollington Park Road, where the nineteenth-century preacher Charles Hadden Spurgeon would thunder his message into the foggy Sunday air. Three minutes' walk up the street from the Edinburgh, the Fonthill Tavern beckons, filled with its elderly florid-faced women in black dresses drinking stout. Around the corner in Lennox Road the Elim Pentecostal Church sits behind iron bars topped by barbed wire. The odd dilapidated car litters the dingy street which serves as a busy thoroughfare for red London buses and lorries, where few wish to linger beyond the kids kicking footballs between the traffic. Behind the brick and cracked plaster edifices life plays out with the smell of the sewer and alcohol and the occasional sound of a sobbing woman. Some of the buildings are being renovated and the sound of the Rolling Stones and ska from Jamaica throbs from open windows. The Edwardian walkups are accessed by flaking staircases and stairwells that lead down into seedy basements. No one is sure who owns these properties but are all too familiar with the trilby-hatted rent collectors who bang on doors each Friday.

My mother brings our aging family car to an abrupt halt and we spill out on to the dim street. It's around four in the afternoon. We are here to visit Mrs. Roffey and her son Andrew.

"This way." My mother ploughs forwards and up the staircase to the yawning entrance of the building which stands dark, dank, foreboding and filled with the musty odor of urine. I follow her as she walks determinedly across the hall and up creaking stairs to the third floor. She knocks gently on the door. Knocks again and the door cracks open. "Hello Mrs. Roffey, it's me and my son Fen. I've brought some shopping for you and have come to see how Andrew and you are coping."

"Oh, come in. I've been wondering if anyone would come around today." Mrs. Roffey beckons us in as she speaks with a thick cockney accent. "Come over here, I'll put the kettle on." Dressed in a purplish house coat, she walks to the greasy cast-iron gas stove, which skulks below a grimy window. She stands with her back to us, seemingly staring at a bloated sad pigeon interrogating the windowsill.

No one speaks as the grey metal kettle cracks and hisses as it heats above the flames. The air in the room feels damp and I begin to shiver. There is a muffled moan from the next room which startles me. I move closer to my mother. "Don't worry Fen, that's just Andrew," my mother says.

The kettle is beginning to pop as a prelude to whistling. Somehow, we have been standing since entering the room. Mrs. Roffey motions, "Do sit down," and the three sit around the kitchen table which is covered by a worn yellow tablecloth. An awkward silence descends. Mrs. Roffey, eyes cast down fiddles with her fuchsia house coat. We drink tea, me very reluctantly, from cracked china cups which sit unevenly on chipped saucers as I debate with myself as to whether I will now catch some horrible disease.

"Would you like to see Andrew then?" Mrs. Roffey asks as she stands and then opens the chipped bedroom door off the scullery. "Not such a good day for him today, I'm afraid."

We enter Andrew's room. Andrew does not stir. In the dim light that filters in between the curtains, he looks like a dying fawn. A skeletal form, below hollow eye sockets turned towards the dark wall. His hair is sparse and greasy. His fragile arms are covered by what looks like grey down. Death is consuming him like a shroud as it slides across his skin. There is a sweet pungent smell to the room that I cannot place. There is no sound, just Andrew's labored breathing and occasional gurgling as a spasm triggers a flick of his arm.

I squeeze my mother's hand and whisper, "I need to go to the toilet."

"It's down the hall son, one flight up at the end of the corridor," Mrs. Roffey says as she smiles at me. I know then that she is kind but somehow broken.

I reluctantly leave my mother's side and walk warily from the squalid flat into the darkened hallway. A shaft of light slants across the stairwell. The house groans heavy with years of unspeakable sorrows. As I mount the stairs and traverse the long passageway to the toilet at the end of the corridor, I feel the hair on the back of my head rise. I am aware of some dark presence behind me. I dare not turn around to see who or what it may be.

My heart pounds, as I enter the stinking toilet closet that serves the entire floor. I slam the door behind me to keep whatever is pursuing me out. An electric light bulb shines above me revealing feces that mire the toilet bowl. Newspaper has been torn into ragged strips and stuffed behind the pipe that runs down from the cistern to the toilet bowl. A rough piece of string has replaced the toilet chain. I can remember retching several times, steadying myself against the grimy plastered wall, opening the door and fleeing helter-skelter back down the corridor and stairs, the terrifying sense of someone behind in pursuit of me spurring me on at lightning speed. A door to my left opens and I catch a glimpse of a bald-headed man wearing a vest. Seconds later I am back in the sad rooms that constitute the flat, panting and still shaking from the shock of my encounter with the house. More is said between my mother and Mrs. Roffey, but my anxiety and nausea block out the words. All I can do is hold my mother's hand and look down at the ripped and pitted linoleum on the floor.

"We'll be praying for you. I'll be back in a couple of days to see how you both are. Bye for now then," Mother says. There are no hugs or handshakes. The door to the flat closes behind us. We descend crumbling steps and cross the pavement which now glistens moist in the chill of early evening, and board the haven of our black saloon.

"Let's go to the ABC, Fen," my mother says. So we sit quietly in the ABC teashop on Seven Sisters Road, as I recover from my education and watch the red London buses pass by the teashop window. "Her husband works in the sewers, you know."

I look at my mother as she looks at me earnestly and continues to speak. "Sometimes she has to be nice to men to get enough money to live." She speaks to me confidentially, as if I am an adult. "She's really got her hands full. How she copes, I truly don't know."

"What's in the sewers?" I ask my mother.

"All the bits and pieces people don't want and all the mess that goes down the toilets."

"Is it dark down there?" I say curiously.

"Yes, dark, smelly, and full of germs and rats." I wonder at my mother's knowledge of subterranean engineering.

"Why does he work there then?" I am forever curious.

"So they have enough to eat, Fen," my mother says.

The thought of food and the mess that goes down the toilets makes me feel queasy again.

"Do you have to be nice to men too?" I ask.

"Yes, but not in the way that Mrs. Roffey does," my mother replies, a half-smile on her face as she sips her tea.

"How do you have to be nice to men, then?"

"Well, often I have to listen to them, Fen, even when they are talking nonsense," my mother says.

"At least you don't have to get money from them."

"If only that were true, Fen. If only that were true," my mother says, getting up to go.

My recall of my childhood is like the rambling Victorian house that I grew up in. Full of rooms and memories which are rarely entered. I can remember the morning when I heard the moan of a siren warning of the arrival of an ambulance that had come to collect my grandfather and take him to the asylum. That morning he had left me two and sixpence. "There's a half crown for you in my bedroom on the chess set. Don't remember me like this, Fen. Remember the happy times we spent together." A moment of clarity in the depleted consciousness that was my grandfather's later life.

I accompanied my mother on a couple of her visits to the foreboding Gothic asylum. First we discovered my grandfather in a locked ward that was a bedlam of noise where I couldn't make out what was happening, other than that my mother was desperately sad. And then on a later visit, when my grandfather sat hunched motionless with another patient, on a bench next to a brick water tower in the asylum gardens. My grandfather's eyes were milky, and half-closed, the corners of his mouth white with adrenalin-infused spittle. I slowly recognized the other patient as Inky Stephens. Stephens, seemingly unconscious of me and my mother, was addressing my grandfather incoherently but with great urgency. My mother and I stood silently looking at the couple for a while, then walked away slowly towards one of the locked gates guarded by an austere nurse.

A dozen years later, I am watching The Sweeney or Battlestar Galactica on TV and am only vaguely conscious of Tottenham Hotspur winning the FA Cup. Even the political chaos presided over by Margaret Thatcher, the Conservative prime minister, goes right over my head. Neither am I protesting or angry. While Britons complain about the dull weather and cricket matches being rained off, I am playing a different game. I am earning great money as a jobber's assistant at the City firm of Cam and Donaldson, and living in a flat off the Old Kent Road that I share with friends who work at my office. On weekends I am cruising around in my almost new blue Ford

Cortina, to the sound of 'Intruder', from Peter Gabriel's new album, with the blonde-haired and eager-to-please Denise at my side. Life is a lot of fun.

The City of London in the early 1980s is a crucible of change. The gentlemen brokers, stereotyped as public school louts from Harrow or Eton, and jobbers seen as loud, brash and saucy cockney boys, are dying breeds. The sudden deregulation of the UK's financial markets, known as the Big Bang in 1986 provided me with new career opportunities. As the years pile up, I am confident and optimistic and quickly gain a reputation for being quicker and shouting louder as I fight aggressively for each transaction. I love the sheer sensation of the market where my natural facility with numbers places me to compete ahead of my colleagues. I have also developed a quality beyond audacity. I am able to take the helicopter view. I have the knack of being able to elevate above the immediate field of play and to see market trends and emerging opportunities. I am, if I may say so, an excellent soldier and analyst. But I am also an outstanding strategist.

I rise as the market turns towards pairing risks on the basis of options for the future, combined with trading in related assets and instruments: derivatives. I'm frequently promoted, yet still junior enough to make the leap from the sell side to a buy side firm and land a job as junior equity analyst covering European stocks at the London office of a major global bank based in New York.

I marry Denise with abandon on a sunny spring morning at St James Church in Muswell Hill in North London. A few friends attend the ceremony. Family on each side is limited. Yellowing photographs of the wedding show my parents looking on with evangelical dismay and standing well back from others in the wedding party.

Our marriage quickly becomes a turgid romp that's almost over before it's begun. The not-so-happy couple live in rooms off a shared landing in an Edwardian house, situated at the end of Kings Avenue, Muswell Hill. There are immediately arguments about money, the cost of the new water heater I bought, a pair of shoes she splurged on, the vacation we can't have and can't afford. I am stressed out working as a junior analyst and also completing a part time master's degree in finance at the London School of Economics. Denise trudges into the City each day but spends more and more evenings 'out with the girls'. Our arguments get longer and louder and by December, in fact on Christmas Day, Denise and I decide to part.

I keep the flat on, but it is a hollow existence. I finish my degree program, am again promoted, and by the age of thirty appointed a portfolio manager.

My life is my work. I am utterly absorbed by the market. My fund has a string of brilliant years, but I do not. I have a few close friends and start dating again. Weekends are spent in flashy country hotels with a series of attractive women with whom I enjoy great sex. But I always feel that these women and I are together alone, an orthogonal phenomenon, as sometimes put to one of the few who may understand me.

My mother is dead. It is the evening following her funeral. Shattered, I decide to walk home from Highgate Cemetery. The befouled London air is suffused with diesel fumes. It starts to rain, and the chill of deepening February twilight rises through my shoes. As I walk, I attempt to analyze my life. Apply a bit of my technical skill on myself. And for the first time in years I begin to take stock. My mind returns to my childhood and that day one November when my mother took me to the slum in Finsbury Park. She was trying to show me something of who she was and what she believed by what she was doing. I never thought of that previously. I feel an overwhelming sense of sadness and exhaustion. It's as if a pit has opened up out of nowhere. As I walk, my chest feels tight. I feel a sense of panic as I step between the pools of orange light cast by lamps that glisten in the early evening rain. I begin to cry. Then hear myself sob and wipe the sleeve of my black double-breasted overcoat across my face.

"So, God, why?" I hear myself mutter. "Why?" The question comes from out of nowhere. This question and God are not in my lexicon.

Suddenly, I have an intense desire to run. So I begin to run, down Muswell Hill Road, like the child I once was in the house in Finsbury Park.

The darkness of Highgate Wood broods to my left. I have a flashback to that man standing in the doorway. The rain falls heavily now and lashes my head. I push myself on faster and faster, legs akimbo, arms waving, hands grasping at the air. In what feels like a void, my left shoe slaps an uneven paving stone and suddenly, I am in flight across the unforgiving flagstones.

For a moment I think I may have broken something. I am aware of blood seeping slowly from my left temple. I lie very still on the slab of granite pavement. I am vaguely conscious of the snake of traffic as it hisses along the road around the red 3 Series BMW that is parked five feet from my head. "Are you injured?" I look up into the concerned face of a woman who is bending over me.

"I'm fine." I push myself up onto one knee. My left trouser leg is shredded and bloody. "Bit grazed, I think; that's all. Dignity damaged more than anything else." I probe my leg gently and feel the rawness of my skin which is broken and bloodied. I pull myself up. My head hurts like hell. I feel tipsy and sway a little. Instinctively it seems, the woman takes my arm firmly and steadies me. For a moment we stand, a Kodak moment in the evening murk.

"How did you do it?" the woman asks.

"I was running. Got a bit out of control," I reply.

"I'd say." Her accent is from South Dublin, perhaps. "Do you think I should take you to the accident department?"

"No, I'm fine," I say, playing the martyr.

"Are you sure?" she says.

I feel calmed by the smooth music of her voice. "Yes, I'm fine. Nothing broken. Just a few cuts and a ruined suit."

"Have you far to go?" Another question from her. The rain is pelting us in earnest now.

"No, just a mile or so up the hill to Kings Avenue," I say, sensing she is good at asking questions.

"Have you been drinking?" I feel that somehow, she has taken charge and is interrogating me.

"I wish. Maybe I should be," I reply defensively.

"Drugs? Did you pass out?" she enquires.

"No, I was just running." *Perhaps she is with the police?*

"Medication of any sort?"

"No, I was just running. Quite silly. Must have caught my foot."

Satisfied she asks, "Well why don't I give you a lift up there?"

While calmed, I feel uneasy. I don't like to acquiesce. "Well okay. But I really am fine." She holds the passenger side door open for me and I make an awkward transition to the car.

"You can see all right? I don't like the look of that bruise on your forehead," she says, inspecting me again in the dim light inside her car.

"What a terrible night." She switches on the ignition. The wipers begin to make a slopping noise, the only sound as the car moves away.

"Look, this is very nice of you. Take the fork ahead, turn left and it's the first road on your left," I say as the red taillights liquify on the windshield before us.

"Nearly there now," I say as she slows the car.

"Are you sure you are okay?" she says.

"Yes, honestly, I am fine." The car has been brought to a halt outside my flat. "It's been a hell of a day. Great way to end it. Do you live around here?" I ask her.

"Not far, over in Highgate. You caught me on my way home from work in Finchley."

"What do you do there?"

"Oh, I work at the hospital."

"In that huge Victorian nightmare of a place? Wasn't Jack the Ripper supposed to have been hospitalized in the asylum?" I ask, proud of my architectural prowess.

"No, that's another place entirely." It's her putting me in my place, but nicely done. "The asylum at Friern Barnet. That was turned into luxury apartments in the Nineties and is full of boy bands. I'm at Finchley Memorial. We go back to twenty beds in 1908."

"Look, I know this is awkward, but would you like to come up for a drink?" I ask. "It's the least I can do to say thanks."

"Well, it's not my habit to go picking men up. Quite literally this time. But okay, I'll come up for a quick drink. Provided of course that you're not an axe murderer or something."

"Come in." Since I parted with Denise my flat has become less of an oasis and more a canister for my depression. Denise took the pictures from the walls so that the overall sense of the rooms is of drab emptiness. We move into the sitting room where we both stand dripping. "Let me take your coat."

"Thanks," she smiles. "Have you got a towel or something?"

"I'll hang this over the bath and get you a towel." I take her black Burberry and hang it over the bath alongside my own, one flight downstairs.

I return with the towel.

"Odd place this," she observes.

"Well, you get to the point fast," I say admiring her forthrightness.

"I just mean that it seems a bit weird that your rooms aren't connected."

"I know. But the natives are reasonably friendly and it seemed like a good idea at the time we moved in."

"We?" she asks.

"My ex-wife and I."

"Not work out, did it?" she enquires, in her back-to-front way.

"No. No, it didn't." There is an edge to my voice that I did not expect.

"Well, come on then. Let's have a look at you." I'm disconcerted.

"I mean, let's see what you did to yourself." She smiles disarmingly as she pushes me gently.

"Oh." I sit awkwardly on the sofa. She examines my wrist and unceremoniously rips my torn trouser leg and examines the gash in my leg.

For the first time I notice her green eyes and the way she has tied her hair. She stands over me, inspecting the abrasion on my forehead.

"This is really thoroughly nasty but doesn't need a stitch. You should take a couple of aspirins tonight. And be sure to clean and get some antiseptic onto the wounds."

"Look, I'm going to get a shower then. Can you stay around a while?" I ask.

"Well, all right. Do you have any food? I'm starving."

"Couple of eggs in the fridge," I tell her.

By a process of elimination, she finds the tiny gaunt kitchen. The sink predominates, flanked by an evil looking gas stove and a fiberboard counter. Someone has squeezed a table and two chairs next to the wall. The room's only redeeming feature is a large window which takes up most of a wall and looks onto the street. She calls out to me, "This absolutely is a quite depressing place. You appreciate that?"

I am back, my wounds dressed and looking more human. "You don't varnish your words, do you?" We are both hungry and make a vigorous attack on the eggs and toast she has made.

"Lived here long then, have you?" she asks.

"About five years now," I tell her.

"And what is it that you do when you're not at home?" It is my life not my body that she's examining now.

"Oh, I work in finance." For some reason, with her I feel a bit ashamed about this.

"Doing what?" She is questioning. Always questioning.

"Managing other people's money." It's my standard answer. And usually no more is asked.

"And how do you do that?"

"Well, we develop investment ideas and hope they work out," I reply nonchalantly.

"And do they?" There is the light of humor in her eyes.

"Most of the time, or I guess they would fire us."

"And have any of them fired you?"

"You ask a lot of questions."

"I've been told that."

"And what about you?" I ask, with more than a little curiosity.

"I'm a pediatrician."

"Dealing with children, not feet then?" I reply, proud of my comeback.

"Ha! It feels like that sometimes."

"Where did you train?" I ask.

"UCL."

"London. You like it?"

"Yes, it's challenging but can also be satisfying to see just one of those kids recover their health. Well, that makes all the aggravation worthwhile."

"A lot of hours?" I enquire.

"Can be fifty or sixty hours a week and some on call at quite awkward times."

"Doesn't give you much time for a social life?"

"True. But it's important not to weaken!" She smiles and looks me straight in the eye. "There are also other things going on. I got involved in the Women's Liberation Movement that started with that conference, at Ruskin College—you know, demands for equal pay, equal education, jobs, free contraception. Don't know why I'm talking about that!" I perceive a deep sense of optimism in her, like a sudden glint of sunlight. I feel my depression ebbing away.

"And what about you, why were you really running like that tonight?" she says disarmingly.

"I was screaming at God. Asking 'Why?'"

"Do you do that often then? Running around the streets screaming at God? You think he exists then?"

"I don't think much about it at all." I will tell her everything. I will have no secrets.

"Then why tonight?" she probes.

"I was running from my mother's funeral."

She reaches for my hand across my mean-spirited kitchen table and touches my face with her other hand. We stay that way for a long time.

Her name is Cait.

CHAPTER SIX

Three months after Christian, Fen and Barry met in London, I sit isolated in my glass office eating a spinach salad, waiting for the weekly XelFunds Leadership Group teleconference. I scroll earnestly through endless texts, email and most heavily trafficked social media sites. For now, I'm ignoring my large screen desktop, which is divided to display six segments, in favor of my iPad.

Yes, as you may have gathered, I have a fast track gloss but I am also very much aware that I have something of, how shall I put it, a mixed reputation amongst my more seasoned 'hairy-arse' colleagues. The word around them is that I come over as appearing academic and simplistic when presenting ideas or arguing my corner. That I lack business savvy. Of course, I know this from a conversation I overheard while crouched on a bathroom stall. Not from any direct feedback. After all, how else would I know what people think of me in this place where no one really wants to speak their mind? They don't see this but I will tell you that I also suffer from a fight-or-flight reaction to interpersonal conflict where I know I can appear highly aggressive and inflexible on some occasions and at other times a pushover. I've also learned that I need to be very cognizant of what they think of me over in Corporate. That's how I got this gig, making an impression with a few of the right people.

"Hi Grace. Mind if I join you?" John French asks me, as his portly form fills the doorway to my office. "Better than me sitting and going through this alone."

I look up. "Sure, help yourself." I turn my screen towards him so he can view it.

"Seems ridiculous for us all to sit in our separate offices for these meetings."

John says this as he shoehorns himself into a chair a little too close to me at my desk.

"Yes, I know. Somehow, they got into this routine and now it's just become the way things happen." John has recently joined the company, is garrulous and awkward in his interactions with us. We direct our attention to the other images popping up in Zoom format as they gather for the meeting.

A few offices down from mine, Cynthia Browne, XelFunds' sharp-elbowed general counsel, (a bit of a dresser, in her smart black blazer), huddles with Tommy Richter, the head of Distribution, a twenty-year company veteran. I've sat in with them before. They will be forking down Chinese food, I bet. A bit of a legend, Tommy has deep roots in the Distribution organization and has seen it all before. He is hands-on with a very high need for structure and control. He continually laments the quality of investment performance and pushes for the product portfolio to include products manufactured outside of the company as a means of boosting sales and lessening reliance, as he often says, "on those bloody arrogant jerks in Investments". He revels in provoking confrontation and wears both the scars from his time in military and internal wars to prove it. He jibes well with Cynthia who, imported from Australia, has had a lot of experience in dealing with "arrogant jerks".

Steve Tremblay shoots a relaxed smile at the screen from his office in Phoenix. "There she is," Steve says in his Canadian accent. I'm not sure which of the women on the team he is addressing. Me or someone else? Steve has the air of a man who has fallen on his sword but missed. No one responds. So Steve continues to smile and stare. I am not sure that he can see us. Unquestionably, we have to help him with his presenting skills. Odd that the guy who is the Chief Digital Officer is so awkward using technology!

"Now then, is everyone dialed in?" Christian Purvis has a green box around his image on the screen and is obviously in a hurry. On first impression his broad smiling face, silver hair, firm handshake and smooth Southern tones ooze warmth and confidence. He is renowned in the industry for his deep network of relationships. If there were to be an award for glad-hander of the year, he would win it. Straightforward to the point of appearing simplistic, he sees life in monochrome, not technicolored ambiguity. People, including even me, often underestimate his tenacity. We fail to understand his worldview and complex personality, which was formed by training as a Marine and his service that followed. His story is classic XelFunds. He joined as a trainee in sales and rose through the ranks by persistence and a knack for survival. He has been the safe, rather than imaginative leadership choice and as such, so far, attractive to our risk-averse parent who is focused on maximizing near-term profits. Having achieved more than he ever dreamed, like many a general, he has adopted an unconscious strategy of digging in and defense, which colors much of his reasoning and conduct.

"Good," Christian leads off, his voice jovial as ever, calling from the corner of floor forty. "We've been using our monthly meetings to focus on the big issues, the big picture strategy and goals. So, I want to use these weekly sessions as an opportunity for us to dialogue, check in, have a good exchange about what's going on and driving results." His sentences tend to run on. "So, as we agreed..."

As I sit with John, my eyes roving the images on the screen, I notice that John is chewing with his mouth open, tumbling his food as he eats. *That's the last time I'm doing this with him!*

"I want to address three things today. Did everyone get the agenda?" Christian says.

"Yes I'm here, Christian. Let me tell you, pretty lousy flight again overnight." Fen is once again visiting the Investment team in London, as he advised the Group last week—pushing for aggressive returns and putting in place 'the winning philosophy and people capable of delivering it' a phrase that has become his mantra. I suspect that he frames what he says to the

Group in this way because he feels this is the kind of assertiveness that will sustain our confidence in him. Unfortunately, his pitch is generally perceived as code for a demand for more compensation for the investment professionals who frequently treat the rest of the company with disdain. In common with many Brits, Fen affects diffidence and excessive politeness as a way to hide an incisive edge. He would have you know but never mentions that he has tremendous intellectual agility and more than a touch of sophistication around the arts, especially literature. Yet below his bluff exterior it's pretty clear to me that he frequently feels insecure and out of place with his more extrovert and Ivy-educated colleagues. He would never, I am sure, acknowledge to anyone the pressure of playing to his self-image of infallible strategist and flawless manager of investment processes that is so far distant from his roots as a trader in London.

"Okay. Good you got there, Fen. As I was saying," Christian gets no further.

There is an anonymous muffled, "Hello? Hello? Can you hear me?"

"Abby, is that you?" Christian replies.

"Hello? Hello?" Abby Kent, the Chief Marketing Officer, always in a hurry, is calling in from a train bound for Washington.

"Abby can you mute your phone, please?" Tiffany says, ever the detail-oriented Chief of Staff.

Abby responds, her voice fading in and out, "Oh good, you can hear me then. Yes, sure. Hi everyone."

"So, Let's get down to it. What's the batting order, Tiffany?" Tiffany Smyth Davies is an import from the London office. She's as slippery as a glossy magazine covered in molasses and clearly on her way up. She can be an ally sometimes and speaks with a crisp Cheltenham accent. "Lucas is first up with the proposed Compliance scorecard."

"Right then Lucas, over to you." As he introduces Lucas, I can see on screen that Christian is texting while he talks. Probably his wife, who has messaged him yet again, about what I know Christian regards as their excruciating monthly excursion to the opera.

Lucas Aiello, the newly appointed Chief Administrative Officer, today, as on most days, regards all-comers with suspicion. He has already earned a reputation for lurking in his office on floor thirty-eight and always demanding people meet him there on his territory at ridiculous hours. His career has been an extraordinary litany of survival. His biggest talent is exerting discipline through personal intimidation. He attaches himself to power through budgetary control and regulatory requirements (none of which he truly understands beyond the policy headlines) as a means of pressing his own agenda. Lucas is seen by many as ego-driven and focused on stepping up to be the next CEO. But I know him to be cunning, and careful to cloak his motives. Meeting him initially is to be impressed by his openness and sincerity. He puts on a show of having rigid personal principles. But in truth is a snake in a suit, who takes particular pleasure in telling lies. But perhaps I am too hard on him, perhaps for him lying is a compulsion. Whatever his mental state, he believes that John, Steve, Abby and I report to him, which is causing a lot of confusion.

"Thanks Christian," Lucas says, his hooded eyes locked onto his screen. "So, if you all direct your attention to the pdf I sent out, you can see that I've drafted a scorecard that will drive accountability. Ownership and accountability for results. That's what I'm after…"

As he presents there is an unusually authoritarian and aggressive edge to Lucas's tone. I sense this immediately offends the collective Group consciousness which is altogether more passive aggressive in nature. We are also increasingly uneasy with Lucas and instinctively trust him even less than we trust each other.

The fact is that the Senior Leadership Group is not a happy family, and people are quite disconnected from one another. This latest bureaucratic idea from Lucas produces a sense of collective dread. Confusion about our mission, who owns what and who is accountable to whom is the cultural norm. The only thing certain in terms of management process has been that the mostly benign but mercurial Christian dabbles in everything. The game to date has been focused on keeping Christian happy, and ensuring that he makes decisions in favor of whomever is trying to influence him. Christian, by making Lucas COO, has handed him a loaded gun, and clearly Lucas intends to shoot whomever he can at the earliest opportunity. Christian, of course, appears to be unaware of these tensions and also of the rumored series of lunches that Lucas has recently enjoyed with John P. Frost III, the parent company Chairman and CEO.

"As you can see from page one," Lucas continues as the chilled atmosphere goes way over his head, "I am defining the balanced scorecard as an organization-wide management system."

"Say what?" Cynthia chimes in.

"Sorry?" Lucas is confused.

"Is this thing you are describing a Compliance scorecard as just advertised by Christian or a balanced scorecard?" Cynthia asks pointedly.

"The balanced scorecard is a management system. It's a way of looking at our entire organization that focuses on progress against big picture strategic goals and helps choose the best things to measure against those goals. It also links up to Corporate."

"So, Christian misled us then, Lucas?" Cynthia shoots back with a droll smile into the video link.

"Well, we may have got our wires crossed, Cynthia. Lucas and I did talk about this briefly last week." Christian decides to assert some control. The avuncular Christian Purvis, promoted for his assumed sales and financial competence five years ago and now fortified by his new executive coach has become a glad-hander extraordinaire. Ask Christian a question, if you can get a word in edgewise, and he will always tell you what he's been up to recently or share a complaint about Corporate (especially the way they treat his compensation). The glass has until recently always been half full. However, the market has been less kind over the past several quarters and the cracks are beginning to show, leading to speculation that things for Christian and the company are uncertain. This is making life something less than fun for everybody, and Christian unusually cranky.

Lucas continues, "It's this focus on high-level strategy and low-level measures that set the balanced scorecard apart from other performance management methods."

"Lucas," I enquire, "so how will this fit with the performance management system that we're just launching?"

"Well look," Lucas replies, "using the scorecard takes your big fuzzy strategic vision and breaks it down into specific actionable steps to take on a day-to-day basis."

I decide to take him on. "Okay. I know a bit about this from having worked scorecards previously. But specifically, how do you see launching this with the other programs that we've got on deck?"

"Yes, that's a good question, Lucas," John says, from next to me.

"I will provide you both with direction on how we will structure and integrate programs for implementation as the plan is rolled out," Lucas replies with an edge to his voice. "I'll continue. As you will see from page four, we will build a culture of information-sharing. The measures we will use will be investment process effectiveness, internal business process efficiency, learning and growth, client and financials. And we will view all these in the context of our vision and strategy."

"Hey Lucas, Fen here from London. Each decision is an act of faith, Lucas." Fen, as everyone on the team except Lucas and John Purvis knows, loves to throw around quotations, especially this one by Jacques Derrida. "Since you are so keen on a culture of information-sharing, don't you think it might have been an idea to share your plan with the Group prior to today? I don't see that focus on a scorecard is at all orthogonal to building our business."

By his expression I can see that Lucas has no idea what Fen means by 'orthogonal' but, undeterred, he ploughs on sourly. "Fen, I sent this to you last week. Unfortunate you didn't get the time to read it."

"Look", Lucas continues, "this is going to be a journey, but it has to be a disciplined march."

"Guys!" I see that Steve Tremblay is waving from Denver.

"A march to where, Lucas?" Abby asks over a crackling phone line.

"Towards what's dictated by the strategy," Lucas replies.

"Guys!" Something has gotten into Tremblay.

"And what's the strategy?" Abby piles on. "Simple answer to that. We don't have one."

"Yes, it seems that way to me too. We are putting the cart before the horse here." Cynthia is as articulate as ever. "We've got by pretty well so far on our traditional strengths. But things are changing. We're being hit by new technology market consolidation and the big boys are invading all those areas where we've been able to get away with being a niche player."

A disembodied voice cuts across Cynthia's. "Hey, stop!" It's Steve, unaccountably shouting and waving his arms at the screen.

Cynthia ignores him. "The stock price is going in the wrong direction. Against any indicator it looks like we have a problem. We don't need a bureaucratic solution Lucas; we need a strategy to get us out of this!"

"Bomb! Bomb!" Steve is now screaming.

"What?" Christian asks. "What's that?"

"We just received a bomb threat," Steve says, his face ashen.

"When?" Fen says, over the video link from London.

"Now. Bomb threat!" Steve shouts back.

"Who from?" Cynthia asks, her voice razor-sharp.

"Did you call the police? You should call the police," Lucas says, elbowing his way in.

"The police called me." Steve is looking petrified and sideways to someone off-screen.

"Precisely now: what is the threat?" Cynthia asks, her voice calm but severe.

"We are to evacuate the call center by 11:30 MST," Steve replies shakily.

"No more than that?" Christian asks.

"That's it. 'Evacuate the call center by 11:30 MST, there is a bomb.'" Steve replies.

"We can't do that; it will screw service!" Lucas says.

"To hell with that. Steve, you should get those people out of there!" I say.

"Yes, but what if there is a bomb in the parking lot?" Steve asks, a look of helplessness in his eyes.

"What do you mean?" I ask. Not thinking about the office layout in Phoenix.

"Our main exit is over the parking lot!" Steve replies.

"I say we go," Tom Richter sounds authoritative. "You don't want to leave those people in there!"

"What's that noise?" John asks from his seat next to me. We can hear the sound of sirens over the link from Phoenix.

"How many people are in today? What did the police say?" Christian asks, rapid-fire.

"I'm getting them out" Steve says determinedly. He moves out of shot while we all wait glued to the screen which shows only Steve's vacant chair.

There is the sound of clattering feet and muffled voices.

"Hang on!" It's Cynthia. "Steve?" No response. "Steve!" her voice is so loud, I can hear it simultaneously down the hall in my office and through the video link.

"Yes, what?" Steve is distant unseen and clearly panicked.

"What time is it there?" Cynthia's question hangs in the air.

"11:32," Steve replies.

"Too late then." It's a simple statement on Cynthia's part. But it takes a moment for it to sink in.

There is no bomb. If there had have been it would have detonated by now.

"I have to go," Steve says.

We are all stunned, except perhaps for Lucas, who I can see is busy on his iPhone. I close my eyes, horrified by our collective failure to make a decision.

"Well?" Christian asks, ignoring or perhaps unaware of our collective fright. "Where were we?"

By the silence, it is clear no one wants to continue, but seemingly oblivious to the chaos that has just occurred, Tiffany has leapt into the fray, her voice tinkling with enthusiasm. "Next agenda item. We've specifically crafted the off-site next Wednesday to address the strategy issue and how we can be better aligned to deliver our goals."

We've discussed the off-site before as a team. Tiffany and I are driving the event. Some are too apathetic to care very much but most, though they don't like the idea of a couple of days talking to each other about planning, will not openly oppose the idea which Christian has uncharacteristically embraced. "Don't forget to do your pre-reading!" Tiffany chirps.

Everyone other than Tiffany and I are distracted and doing something on their phones to communicate what just happened in Phoenix. We can hear what sounds like dozens of phones ringing around the building.

"Well, that was some meeting!" For the time being, Christian has stopped texting. "A lot said." This is what Christian does best, it seems. Just carry on regardless. "We are almost out of time. Lucas, it's clear that we need to do some more study before we take on the scorecard idea. Tiffany is on target, there are connections here with the strategy. You've done a great job in putting this together, Lucas, great job, but I hear a bit of blowback. We're dealing with a bit of a Venn diagram in terms of issues." Heads are nodded although no one is entirely sure what Christian means. "Let's you and I talk further and come back to the Group with some ideas. Clearly we need to tighten up our disaster readiness."

Christian gives no specifics, for which we are all thankful until Lucas volunteers. "Leave that to me it's a control function issue."

"Of course it is, Lucas." Cynthia's words are just audible.

"Very good everybody. Good meeting. Let's reconnect at the monthly board." Christian reaches forward to shut down his machine; a collective sigh of relief is almost tangible.

"Wait up!" It's me pleading for attention. "I know it's inopportune..." I can hear my voice sounding juvenile but I can't help myself, "...but I'd like to raise the issue of inclusivity training—we began to talk about it at our last meeting, but we ran out of time." Juvenile and irrelevant.

Several have already gone off-line. "Oh yes," Christian says, in the circumstances showing considerable magnanimity "I did not anticipate such an impassioned debate! Very important topics for the Group. Look, would you mind if we table that for this week, Grace. We'll get to it next week?"

"Okay Christian. Understood. Would you mind if I drop by to see you later this afternoon, a couple of other issues have come up?"

"Sure, I have a risk committee meeting this afternoon so come by around six." I can tell Christian is not thrilled at the prospect of a meeting with me. But what can he do? He has to play the game, particularly given the state of relations with Corporate. He'll just have to show willing.

"Great, see you then." I am perpetually in enemy territory, poorly resourced with no line of retreat and often, it seems, irrelevant. I smell blood in the water—hopefully not mine.

And with that the Management Group moves on.

It's 6 pm. The floor is empty and quiet. The hiss of the white noise pumped in to deaden the sound of voices during the day is barely audible. The sun sits low over New Jersey, painting the Hudson an oily blue and gold. Christian sits undefended at his desk. I approach the throne.

"Come in, Grace. What can I do for you?" There are three monitors presumably with their screens open on Christian's desk; his eyes slide between them as he motions for me to sit.

Seated, I hesitate. Christian looks over to me, "Shoot!"

"We have a problem." I carry a lot of stuff, the 'dead weight of bureaucracy', as Fen once put it. Consequently, I'm perceived by my clients, as a sort of hind tit that they have to drink at to do their people stuff. But every now and then there is some sort of crisis, where they need me as a partner. In my bones I know this is an inflection point.

"Prefer solutions, Grace. Prefer solutions," Christian says, his attention back with his screens.

"Peiter Viser." I say the name making Viser sound like 'Vicer'. It is somehow satisfying.

"What about him now?" Christian asks, guardedly.

"You heard what happened from Miles?" I ask.

"Of course, Miles was here just now for the Risk Committee meeting. Seems things are not as bad as you thought." Christian emphasizes the 'you'.

"I'm afraid that they are a great deal worse."

"How so?" Christian says. I have his attention again.

"Well, as you know, we have been conducting an investigation." As I speak, I am thinking about Christian's use of the 'you'. "Compliance had some concerns about Viser and his portfolio managers investing personally outside of the fund: using ideas and research generated during their work on the fund for personal market bets in other accounts."

"Yes, I heard that. That would be strictly against the code of conduct. But Miles tells me that that is a misunderstanding on the part of Compliance. The compliance review found no evidence of an infraction."

"That's true. But it smells to me."

"You of all people should understand, Grace, that we go on the basis of facts and data here. No infraction was found."

"Yes, well that's not my only point. We also uncovered a lot of employee issues. Mainly around gender and a general climate of intimidation. The old boys' club writ large." When I say this, I immediately know that it is a misstep.

"Look, I know we have to have a strict policy around all this sexual politics stuff these days: 'Time's Up' and all that. And I want you to know that I take the need to provide a good employee environment very seriously.

But again, Miles tells me the employee issues look like they're fixed—you need to do some follow-up, but it doesn't seem that we've got a problem."

"Christian. I'm a grown-up." I am on thin ice here. I can feel the ice cracking beneath my feet. "I don't need handling. It's a bigger issue. Jade Edwards is alleging Miles demanded sex in exchange for her promotion."

Neither of us speaks. This is a stillness that we both know precedes the storm. A yellow water taxi is glinting in the evening sunlight; it skims across the Hudson that has turned to a purple ribbon, far below Christian's office window.

"Edwards told me that she and Miles met at a party when she was working at another firm. They started dating. Miles offered her a job as a Portfolio Manager—leaned on Peiter Viser to create a new position. And then when she joined the company their relationship got messy. What was a fling became seriously uncomfortable for Edwards. She alleges that Miles would call her over to meet him for dinner and they would often end up in his bed. I asked her for specific dates but she was vague." I pause.

"There's more, I suppose?" Christian sounds weary.

"Regrettably, a lot more. Edwards says the sex was always consensual but that she felt that she couldn't refuse. Especially when Miles created a job as head of US equities reporting to him. She says she complained to Fen Morgan but that she has been ignored. As you know, recently her portfolio performance has suffered a bit. She puts this down to mental stress. She's been talking to her shrink about the situation and he has advised her to take a leave. She is concerned that if she does take some time off, Miles will retaliate."

"You know, she's got real talent. Great performance up until now. And everybody loves her." Christian's tone is wistful.

"Well, now Miles has created a monster. She is threatening to bring the house down. She doesn't feel safe working here with him. She wants to report to someone else. And a lot more I suspect."

"Has she confided in anyone else?" Christian asks.

"She says not," I reply cautiously.

"What have you told her?" Christian is beginning to push me.

"That I will investigate her allegations and will get back to her. In the meantime, I have told her that she should not mention this to anyone else."

"And what do you intend to do about this?" There it is from Christian, the 'you', the distance.

"Well, as I look into it, I'm bound to shake a few trees. The company has to be extremely careful about what we have here. We have to be objective and fair to all parties. This may all be in her head and not at all real. Frankly, I can't really see Miles doing something like this. Though he can be a bit of a creep."

"Where's Fen in all this?" Christian ignores my snipe.

"I've kept him out of it so far. He was out last week and in London this week, so I've not had an opportunity to brief him," I reply.

Christian takes his time processing what I've told him, then says, "We have to be airtight."

"I'm going over to see Al Jiminez, in corporate HR, about this tomorrow morning." Christian looks at me as if I am being disloyal.

"All we need is for Jade to add retaliation to her list of complaints. One way or the other this is going to be a real shitstorm." There never was much trust or intimacy between Christian and me. I guess what little there was just evaporated.

I'm sure Christian's wife is going to be furious that he will be late for the opening act of Aida at the Met. Despite blaring trumpets, I bet Christian will be dozing, along with serried ranks of other comatose husbands, by halfway into the second act. His half-sleep is likely filled with images of the grand gate of Thebes, the raging Amneris, and most dramatic of all, Grace Edwards shaking her raised fist.

I am not looking forward to breakfast.

CHAPTER SEVEN

Floors forty-nine and fifty in Tower Two are organized as a duplex. There is a perennial joke that if management were fired and the space let as a tourist attraction the stock price would instantly triple.

Floor forty-nine contains executive offices and an opulent reception area.

Floor fifty houses multiple conference rooms, a substantial executive dining room and numerous private dining rooms, the latter of which are used for client meetings and meetings between senior staff. The accommodation on both floors has spectacular views and art which luxuriates on the internal walls. The architectural strategy and decor are designed to impress and, as appropriate, intimidate.

It is difficult for me to work or be present on either floor without feeling a sense of vague hostility. A hush of intense passive-aggressive courtesy coats most interactions. Voices are rarely raised. Middle-aged brown and black service staff, dressed in crisp monochrome uniforms, stand as silent witnesses to the appearance and disappearance of the mostly white male mighty. They serve with a wry smile, apparently content with their lot.

To buttress my confidence, I have poured myself into expensive designer pumps and a black dress from Akris that is an essential part of my work wardrobe. My black Fendi tote bag is tucked securely under my arm as I walk up South End Avenue through the cool morning air towards Tower Two.

As I ride up to floor fifty alone in the glossy express elevator, I check out my makeup and shaggy jet-black hair that, as my stylist said, subtly emphasizes my bone structure and reinforces my assertive look. (I wish.) Self critically I inspect my complexion, reassuringly burnished almond, as my grandmother says. My walnut eyes look to me clear and perhaps a tad sharper than I would like. *Still how else would I penetrate their egos?* They will remember the way I hold my head, not my aquiline nose, the vague trace of a scar on my cheek or the slight misalignment of my right eye. *You can do this,* I tell myself. *Don't doubt it.*

I clasp my discreet gold antique wristband. *It's a bit self-indulgent I know. But who else is going to indulge me?* The elevator decelerates and my stomach sinks.

"Hi Tony. Good morning!" I say cheerily, as I exit the elevator. I am off to the races and full of vim.

"Mr. J is waiting for you in room three, Ms. Rutler." Tony the receptionist smiles at me and nods up the hallway. Al Jiminez is on his cell gazing across the Hudson as I enter the intimacy of the private dining room. He waves at me and holds his finger in the air. "Come in, come in, sit, sit." The room is flooded with the rich light of early morning. It's a thing with these buildings. They are light but cast long shadows.

I study the menu at my place setting which has been printed in fine type. Then remove my iPhone from my bag as I check the time on the black Swatch on my left wrist.

"Sorry about that, Grace. I hate to keep the guys in Asia up late. It seems like this time of the day is best for them, though. So, how's business?" Al is looking at his menu as he addresses me.

"Pretty brisk as always, a lot on. Both sales and assets are up so everyone is getting excited about the year."

"And the crew over there?" And this is how most of their meetings go. Al as EVP and Chief People Officer for CMG Financial Services maintains a loose hold on status at XelFunds and makes it clear that my role is to ensure that he's not blindsided.

"Know what you want?" Still looking down.

"Sure," I reply.

Al presses the remote that sits next to his plate and instantly Johnny appears.

"Hey, Johnny, how long have you been here?" I watch Al perform.

"Fifteen years, Mr. J. Fifteen years." Johnny has learned to respond to questions like this with just the right mixture of deference and humor.

"Incredible!" To Johnny, and then to me, "What's your pleasure, Grace?"

I want to respond, *That's a loaded question, Al,* but decide not to provoke him quite yet. "I'll do the oatmeal please. Low-fat milk and coffee. Thanks Johnny."

"Perfect, perfect. And I'll do the same, Johnny, but also some rye toast please." As Johnny exits Al asks me, "So, everyone is good? How's she doing then?"

"Who?" I know perfectly well who he means but I'm not going to give him an inch.

I quite like games, especially dangerous ones.

"Natasha of course, Natasha," Al says, his jovial air embracing us both.

"Oh sorry, you mean Natasha Frost, the Chairman's daughter? Okay, I think. Frankly, I don't like to ask, given it's a glaring breach of our anti-nepotism policy to have her working in Equities."

Al, defensively, "It's all perfectly within guidelines, given we got a waiver from the head of corporate compliance."

"Do you think she might have felt a bit under pressure to do that?" I ask.

"Grace, some would say you're treading on precarious ground with a comment like that." Al is a father chastising his daughter.

"Dangerous or not, it makes me feel uncomfortable that the policy is being breached. There could easily be some sort of insider trading situation, if she were to tell her father that the fund was going to do something and he were to front-run by buying or selling."

"That's not going to happen Grace. Frost isn't unethical. He's much too smart and too rich to do anything like that." He keeps repeating my name as if he is going to forget it.

"Well, okay. I'm not saying that Frost or his daughter is unethical. I'm just saying that they expose themselves, the company, and for that matter everyone who knows about this, to speculation. Also, it must feel like they have a spy in the camp to those guys on the Equity team."

"I hear that she's very smart and charming." He has a smirk on his face.

I leave it at that. Even I know when to stop. For a moment there is a taciturn silence between us.

"Not too much acquisition talk?" Al ventures.

"Well some, yes. Not openly, but there's speculation. Always has been. It's almost like a self-fulfilling prophecy," I reply.

"How's Christian holding up?"

"He's not taken me or the team into his confidence. So, he doesn't know that I know, if you follow. The main focus right now is the upcoming planning off-site on Long Island."

"Who's running that for you?" Al asks.

"COMPACT. They are a group of consultants out of Boston Consulting. Very smart guys."

"Yeah, know them. We use them too," Al says, matter-of-factly.

"They have a business simulation where they model the company, we plan to use it as a practice field for decisions and get a better perspective on the future of the business." There is another awkward silence. "Christian's got other problems." I surprise myself a bit by blowing the whistle so early.

"Meaning?"

"Well, we're drifting. There's a strong feeling in the team that we need a better sense of direction. And we've got this new guy on the team: Lucas. You interviewed him; true?"

"Yes," Al says, knowingly.

"Well, he's turning out to be more than a little aggressive and also something of an oddball. So there is more than the usual infighting." Al is not a skilled father confessor. I am not confident of him. Ours is a strictly business relationship. We both know we would dump each other at the slightest provocation.

"Grace, we've had this conversation before. Look, I'm totally on your side but you have to pace yourself. Take my advice, don't push back on Lucas. You never know how people are connected or what might come up next."

My antennae go up. Why should Al say this about Lucas? I hesitate but decide to swim to the deeper end. "Also, we've got a couple of worrying employee issues." I tell Al as his expression darkens. "I've been dealing with a problem with Peiter Viser. You know, the team leader for International Equities. We had what looked like a major compliance issue."

"He's the key guy there, isn't he? He's going to be a must retain." Al is unusually emphatic.

"Well, essentially it looked like there was something going on around his personal trading. Now you know why I was so sensitive around Natasha. Anyway, upon review, he had a kind of explanation and Compliance dropped the investigation. But the review also uncovered a truckload of employee concerns about his conduct and the climate in general. Again, he scrambled and put the fear of God into the team and the upshot was that one of the people with the biggest complaints resigned and moved to Europe."

"So, you are telling me that you had a problem but now you don't?" Al says, it seems to me, irritated and deliberately feigning confusion.

"No, I'm telling you the problem's gotten worse," I say.

"How so?" Al replies.

I shoot right back at him. "We have an additional team leader, Jade Edwards, down there, who is accusing Miles McCarthy and by implication, Fen Morgan, of trading promotions for sex."

Al exclaims, "You're shitting me."

Quaint language, I tell myself. Al does seem genuinely worried. "No sir. Edwards came to me independently claiming that she's consistently been paid less and been refused promotions because she's not been prepared to sleep, or I should say, keep sleeping, with McCarthy. She says Fen knows but has refused to do anything about it," I say with an edge to my voice.

"This is serious, Grace." *Thanks Al, that had slipped right by me.*

"Right," I reply, as innocent as day.

"You've got to put a lid on it somehow. There is a lot going on and something like this could throw us way off track. We need to get with Peter Hudgell. You're going to need some help on this one." Al is decidedly panicked.

Al and I sit in the Law Department library waiting for Hudgell to arrive. Al sits at the far end of the table. I sit in the middle in splendid isolation. The room is windowless. The dark wood-paneled walls and table feel distinctly funereal, or maybe it's just me calling *May Day! May Day!* from inside my entombment.

Hudgell materializes like an apparition. He is tall, his tight sallow skin bound in a white shirt and grey pinstripe pants. He enters the library wearing patent leather loafers and accompanied by a younger man.

"What exactly have we got here then?" It seems he is relishing the moment, like a police officer finding a turd on the sidewalk. He has taken the seat at the end of the table and placed a Mont Blanc pen on a yellow pad on the table in front of him. The younger man sits to his right. The seating arrangement is decidedly off. I feel the same sense of disorientation as I did in Miles's office.

"Grace, you lead off on this one," Al announces with a proprietorial air.

That's it, Al, I think, *we are a circus act. You are the organ-grinder and I am your monkey. This is a crock, go right ahead, hand it to me.* But I say—my tone, I would argue, surprisingly rational—"We have a senior vice president, Jade Edwards, diverse woman, five years' service, aged 48, heads up US Equities. Excellent performance, has come up through the ranks superfast with us. Was previously an assistant portfolio manager with Alliance."

The guy with Hudgell is taking copious notes on his iPad.

"Edwards has made a formal complaint about her boss, Miles McCarthy, who is CIO Equities."

"Yes, I know McCarthy," Hudgell breaks into my flow.

"Edwards initiated a meeting with me where she said she wanted to make a formal complaint that she was being harassed by McCarthy. Her story is that McCarthy got her into the company via his bed then their relationship got messy. What was a fling became harassment for Edwards. She alleges that Miles would call her over to meet him for dinner to discuss investment ideas and they would often end up in his apartment." I am on a roll now; my head dizzy. *And now ladies and gentlemen, Henry the Horse!*

I continue. "Edwards says the sex was always consensual but that she felt she couldn't refuse. Especially when Miles created a job for her as head of US Equities reporting to him. She says she brought her concerns to Fen Morgan but that she has been ignored. Recently her performance has suffered a bit. She puts this down to mental stress. Bottom line, she wants Miles's head and probably Fen's too. The situation would look great on the front page of the Journal."

"Okay, I get it." Hudgell's bloodless pencil lips are wrapped tightly around each word. "What are your thoughts, Al?"

"Well, Pete," (I have not seen Al suck up quite like this before), "things are looking pretty shaky over there right now. Handled the wrong way this situation could impact both planned leadership changes and the acquisition negotiations. The last thing we need is for this situation to turn into a pretzel."

I am beginning to analyze Al's vocabulary with renewed rigor—'pretzel'?

"Agree. Handled the wrong way this could be kryptonite." Hudgell pronounces this like some character in a DC comic. Maybe the guy with Hudgell is Clark Kent? "Grace, you need to ride herd on this."

I am thinking, *Oh, we are back in the circus then? Get a grip, girl!*

Hudgell barks, "You need to follow up with this woman..."

"Jade Edwards," I volunteer, as Al hangs on my every word.

"...so she understands that you are on the case. We need to buy as much time with her as we can. And we also need to start thinking about an end solution. Tom here..."

Ah, so he's not Superman! I can't help what must look like a bit of a derisive grin as Hudgell nods to the man at his elbow who continues to take notes.

"...will be your liaison with Corporate. Also, I think we need to take this up the line to John. Tom, will you get the four of us on John's calendar asap." This is an order, not a request.

Tom, mute, nods.

"Guess that's as far as we need to go for now. I'll see you later, Al." And with that Hudgell picks up his notepad and vanishes. I think I can detect a vague whiff of sulfur.

"Good to meet you, Grace. Tom Dawson." Tom speaks with an Australian accent and extends his hand across the table, smiling. "Looks like we will be working together on this one. I've just texted you my info. Let's connect so we can strategize."

I look at him squarely in the eye wondering if strategy is all that is on the menu. "Right, I'll give you a call when I get to my office," I reply.

Al and I are left sitting alone. "What's going on here, Al?"

"Alright Grace, I'm going to bring you into the loop. This is serious stuff," Al says.

I can almost hear a drumroll. "Sounds like it," I reply.

"XelFunds has a suitor." Al performs the reveal with as much poise as a very bad male stripper. "If the current talks go well, we should get to due diligence in about three weeks. From the corporate point of view, the deal logic is excellent. We've had a deal team on the project for some weeks. In essence we..."

I process this, gradually putting together the implications. *You really mean Pompton Financial, Al. XelFunds will be eviscerated.*

"...will have a substantial stake in the new entity and a couple of seats on the acquirer's board. It also de-risks our earnings volatility and releases capital that we can redeploy towards international growth of the core business."

"Is there a lot of overlap between XelFunds and the acquirer?" I ask innocently.

"Yes, mainly in the back office, and of course, staff functions. The deal will give the acquirer enhanced distribution and massively improve their fund lineup. In terms of people, they plan to merge the two leadership teams—pick the best athletes from both entities," Al says.

I wonder where this ridiculous sports imagery comes from. "Sounds as if there will be a lot of downsizing." Stating the obvious with some feeling.

"Yes, inevitably. I can't emphasize enough how confidential and sensitive this all is." Al loves this part, where he has the keys to the kingdom.

"Understood." Sounds as if the world and his brother know about all this. Everyone, that is, except the poor schmucks at XelFunds.

"The most crucial part is that to prepare for the change we need fresh leadership. We plan to replace Christian. Christian is dead in the water."

Here it comes, "Replace Christian? With whom?"

"Fen Morgan," Al says, as if he has found a cure for the common cold.

"I see." It feels as if I'm drinking at a fire hydrant. "Is Fen the likely long-term successor? Or is this an interim arrangement?"

"That depends on how all this shakes out. Fen could certainly land as the CIO of the new entity or maybe Vice Chairman or something. But that's speculation that's not useful at this time. The critical thing is to manage Christian's exit."

"What's the timing for the change?" I ask.

"Next week."

"That's the week of the strategy off-site." More to myself than to Al.

"I know. Tom's been working with your CMO and Chief of Staff, Tiffany..."

"Tiffany Davis." *So that's Tom's story. He's a plant. Good to know.* I say to myself.

"That's right, so we have a good grip on timing," Al says. "Essentially, we have to exit Christian, sign up Fen, and then communicate the change to the entire corporation without turning off the acquirer."

"That's going to be quite the trick." Sarcastically, I can't resist it.

"Agreed, you and I have to be joined at the hip through this." Al is not only jolly, he is positively relishing the thought. "Oh, and one other thing. We plan to put Lucas Aiello in as COO with all functions other than Sales and Investments reporting to him. Fen Morgan, Lucas Aiello and Tom Richter will form the Office of the President."

"That's going to be an accident waiting to happen!" I can only see looming disaster.

"Why do you say that?" Al asks.

"Earlier Al, I told you earlier," I reply. "He's already proved himself to be a highly political, unpleasant jerk!"

"You have really connected with him, then?" *Ah, so Al is capable of a comeback too!*

"He is a disaster. Totally what the group does not need," I say, involuntarily shaking my head. "He will kill us with bureaucracy and paralyze us with even more infighting than we already have."

"Well, you need to know, Grace, that he is extremely well connected. In fact, good friends with Frost."

"So, let me play back what just happened." I feel myself winding up to some kind of breakdown. "We have a major employee relations issue. Bad enough of itself but this comes at a time when the corporation is negotiating the sale of the company, to be facilitated by firing the CEO, promoting an investment guy with little leadership experience into the top job and layering almost everyone in the leadership group with a guy thought of as incompetent, who nobody, and I mean nobody, except apparently the Chairman, trusts or likes. Did I leave anything out?"

"You have a way of putting things, Grace. Let me reframe this for you," Al says, pleased with himself. "There are some serious changes coming down the pike. You can be helpful and do your part to make what's happening a success, or you can leave. I'd prefer you to stay because I think you are the best person to help the corporation and your colleagues through this. But if you can't step up you should probably start thinking of stepping out. Am I clear?"

The phone rings. "Sure. Sounds good. We'll be up."

"The Chairman wants to see us in his office now Grace."

I have this joke about people doing the perp walk when they leave the company, and everyone stares at them. That's how I'm feeling now as I walk with Al up one flight of internal stairs towards the Chairman's office.

Al and I are greeted by the 'lovely' Angela (why the 'lovely' no one knows. It perhaps refers to the reputation she has of filling the Chairman's ears with the latest pernicious gossip) in the Chairman's suite, who makes eye contact with us both as she stands like a robotic sentinel, smiles and asks, "Can I get something for you? He's just finishing up."

"No, we're set thanks, Angela." Al speaks for us both. Strange that everything gets so formal and staged up here. Not Angie but 'Angela'.

As we wait, the sound of an orphan phone calling its owner with a muted vzzzt stirs the oppressive air. The late morning sun blazes a last scarlet gasp against the windows, as it disappears into the hulking clouds that brew over the towers of Jersey City, on the far side of the Hudson. My mind still racing, I find myself mesmerized by miniscule dust particles that float and collide in shafts of light which, like the clouds, march dejectedly across the grey carpet.

Angela raises her mannequin head. "Please enter. He's ready now."

Frost is standing behind his desk in conversation with Hudgell, who stands, shoulders slightly rounded, before him. Frost breaks off, "Come in, come in. You must be Grace. I've heard a lot about you." He has a soft, genial Southern accent. Atlanta maybe, where he played football?

"All good, I hope," I say, smiling and keeping it light.

"Very much so, come sit." Frost beckons our trio to sit an arm's length from each other at his conference table. Frost's office walls are festooned with photographs. Frost, one of four good-looking African-American men in evening dress with the President, who has autographed the picture. Frost, years younger in American football gear holding a trophy. Frost golfing with Tiger Woods. Frost robed, receiving some kind of academic honor. Frost, standing at a podium somewhere in the tropics, the fonds of a palm tree framing the scene, half of a banner with the word 'Smash!' visible over his right shoulder.

There is a grey cabinet behind Frost's desk, full of plexiglass awards inscribed with 'Best' and 'First' and the number 'One'. I am immediately struck by a single image which dominates the cabinet's middle shelf. Frost, as ever in a business suit, stands beaming with his arm around a young woman who is graduating. It's the only object in the office that strikes me as not entirely about him or staged.

I take all this in and am instantly struck by Frost's knavish charisma, which sparkles from his dark eyes. In his late fifties, he is tall, looks athletic and wears a crisp open-necked white shirt with generous cuffs, stapled to his wrists by silver links. He exudes an air of pugnacious confidence, perhaps gained through his years as a junior lawyer and staffer for a senator before he entered corporate life. The other two men in the room appear to shrink and sit back from the glass conference table.

Frost sits with his back to the sun, his face difficult for me to discern. "Grace, if you were going to the moon and you could take three people from XelFunds, who would they be?"

My first reaction is that the question is some sort of joke. Instantaneously though I realize it is serious. "In terms of leadership, Cynthia Browne our general counsel, Abby Kent, and Fen Morgan."

"Two out of three women, looks as if our diversity and inclusion programs are working then?" Frost shoots me a puckish smile.

"They are the best minds and most committed people." I stand my ground.

"What's your assessment of Fen Morgan?" Frost has become the counsel for the prosecution.

"He's very driven. Has turned in consistently good investment returns, so has a solid reputation as an investor. Is passionate about the centrality of the investment function which in his view must be at the core of all strategy and decisions. He's facing a lot of issues, especially around reining in the Equity Team, some of whom don't have much respect for his investment experience." I speak in a rapid, deliberative monotone. "Despite being a bit cold, in general I'd say he's largely open to new ideas and innovation. Can be outgoing but more often gives me the sense that he feels that people are a necessary interruption. Highly analytical and an incredibly quick study. Dives into details and constantly follows the markets." I am surprising myself at what I've observed unconsciously. "As you would expect, is entirely work-obsessed and is regularly in the office at 7 am and leaves around 8 pm. Quite international in outlook, not surprising given he's a Brit. Married to a very bright Irish woman. Closer to his own team than to his colleagues. Is ambitious, and although he has come late to management, having arrived would probably like to be CEO someday. A bit of an autodidact. Came up the analyst route, master's degree earned part time from the LSE." My aria delivered, I rest.

"What happens if I put Fen in the CEO slot?"

I punt, "Depends on the circumstances."

"Meaning?" Frost leans forward.

I prevaricate. "Well, if it's an orderly transition and Fen gets the proper mentorship, I think he has great potential. If he's put in overnight in the context of major change, it's a high-risk strategy."

"Because?" The word is slung at me.

"He's never had this scale of challenge previously and it's unproven that he will be able to manage large-scale change." A statement of the obvious, obviously stated. *Am I a disappointment?* I ask myself, returning to my earlier image of being in the circus. *The tattooed lady rather than the prancing pony?*

"And?" He is voracious, he wants more.

"In addition, the leadership team needs a lot of work," I say, glancing at Al who is expressionless.

"Is he loyal?" Frost uses the word 'loyal' as an offensive weapon. His eyes scrutinize and prey upon me as I feel him probing.

"To whom?" I will have him know that I am not a pushover.

"To me." And there it is at last for the four of us to see, as 'me' menaces above the conference table.

"I can't answer that." I meet Frost's gaze. He is trying to undress me.

"Peter here," he nods at Hudgell, "tells me we have a tricky employee issue. How worried do I need to be?"

"As yet undetermined, but it should be on your radar if you are thinking of a lot of change."

"What's your assessment of this Edwards woman?" Again Frost fires rather than asks the question. *Come on,* I say to myself. *Focus, do your stuff!*

"She's angry. She's volatile. And very possibly telling the truth."

"And what is truth these days?" Frost has a sardonic streak. I want to spit at him, he is so self-satisfied. I leave the question unanswered.

"Well Grace, we are counting on you to get us through this." Frost is no longer scopophiliac but more impresario, the ringmaster demanding his tricks. "I believe Al and Peter here have sketched out a game plan with you. It's going to be an interesting couple of weeks." He stands, the others follow suit. "Thanks for coming by. Look forward to staying in touch."

Al, who has said nothing, and I walk toward the door. Dismissed like a couple of refugees, I have more the sensation of running than walking.

"Peter, can you stay a few more minutes? I'd like to talk further." It's an unspoken rebuke to Al who avoids eye contact with Frost as he leaves his office.

We are almost through the door when Frost calls after me, "Oh and of course, how is my Natasha doing?" Natasha. His darling. Natasha who laughs out of the photograph at the center of his cabinet while Frost ogles her contemporaries.

Still in motion I reply, "Fine, I think. On balance, I guess we will have to think about keeping her on." *Yes, live dangerously,* I tell myself. *In the circus of the damned, my virtuosity as a performer is unmatched.*

We co-conspirators have little sense of victory as we enter Al's office.

"Okay, so this is how it goes." There is something very different in Al's demeanor.

He issues me an abrupt order, "You get with Tom Dawson and interview Edwards."

"I am set to meet her this afternoon, actually. I'll pull Tom into that meeting."

"I want a detailed written report of what transpires. You'll also need to chase down anyone else who is involved in this, including of course Fen and McCarthy."

"It's okay Al, I've got this. Are you feeling alright?" Al is distinctly grey and slumps in his chair, starts reading email and ignores me.

"I'll be on my way then."

The elevator falls earthwards, a stone shooting me through fifty floors, that have been stacked by architects and construction workers, who have no idea that they are building a theater of the absurd. I step out at the lobby level into the jostle of workers impatiently grabbing expensive coffee and cake.

CHAPTER EIGHT

Outside, the temperature has reached a rabid 89 degrees. Sunlight beats without compassion, hammering the simmering waters of the North Cove Marina, which thickens the heart of Brookfield Place. The pocket-size harbor of 32 slips is packed with craft paying 6 dollars a foot per night, New York's best kept secret for the billionaire owners of the ponderous yachts that boast opulence, jostling for a berth in the inlet. The restless adjacent waterfront plaza is thronged with perspiring tourists covered in an emulsion of bleached urban dirt, and a scattering of office workers surfacing for coffee who blink their pink eyes nervously, like rabbits in the dazzling sun.

Inside the tower block it's a constant 71.6 degrees Fahrenheit. Cooling and heating systems have been carefully placed at the heart of building design and construction. The same is not true for the human capital that occupies these shiny office floors and marble-coated halls. This is a habitat of unremarkable days for most, boredom and dreams for others. But for the afflicted few it is the venue for ambition, self-aggrandizement and above all, power, where psychological volatility and festering conscience is the natural stuff of daily life. These are the snakes in suits who slither into the body politic when no one is looking. Some might say Lucas is one of them.

The Art of War, a Chinese military treatise dating from the Late Spring and Autumn Period is attributed to the Chinese military strategist Sun Tzu. The popular book it inspired has thirteen chapters which detail strategies to enable commanders to calculate their chances of victory. The book explains the economy of warfare, why attack, strategy, alliances, armies and cities are critical to winning. There are many philosophies expressed in the book but for Lucas there has been no greater organizing principle for his career than taking advantage of opportunities which arise from openings caused by the relative weakness of the enemy. Lucas, while not greatly endowed with abstract intelligence, has great native cunning and insight around his associates' weaknesses.

Abby and Tiffany are working jointly on the agenda for the upcoming strategy off-site and are briefing Lucas and John on the session's goals and related logistics. Lucas is still chagrined over the debacle that he experienced at yesterday's SLG meeting. He leans back from the round conference table, his nose flaring and mouth shut.

Tiffany walks the meeting through the planned agenda. "We've developed this format in conjunction with Barry and his team from COMPACT, the consulting firm that's helping us facilitate the event. Day one begins at 7:30 with dinner, a quick review of the business environment, latest competitive research, market metrics, that's Abby, and top-line financial projections, John you have the ball on that. And yes, Grace is going to provide some quick feedback on the employee climate—you know that chart she has about employee engagement. She wanted to be here for this conversation but has some kind of employee issue going on."

"Are they any good?" Lucas asks as he sniffs.

"Are who any good?" Abby says.

"We think so, Lucas. Barry has been working with Christian and Fen on a few things and they seem to like him. He's got a lot of competitive insight and industry experience." Tiffany's response is even.

"I've got good people. Frost knows them too." Lucas appraises the women from beneath his heavy eyelids.

"That's very useful, Lucas. Perhaps you can send me a note of who they are so we can bear them in mind?"

Lucas makes some sort of grunt.

John asks, "Are people going to be able to get there by 7:30? The conference center is on Long Island, right?"

"Yes, I think we will be OK. Some will leave midafternoon by car. Christian, Fen and Tom are set to helicopter in from the seaport." Tiffany continues. "Day two we've planned something different. Abby and I are going to run a SWOT analysis session. The meeting will break out into four subgroups and brainstorm strengths, weaknesses, opportunities and threats. We'll conduct a report back and analyze themes and that will lead to an afternoon discussion of future strategy."

"This is a small meeting for a breakout." Lucas leans back from the table as he speaks.

"What we're going for here, Lucas, is to create some shared understanding of where we are now and where we need to go over the planning horizon. By talking in smaller groups, we think we can have more candid conversations." Abby makes this statement avoiding eye contact with Lucas. Her comment is like a red rag to a bull.

"I've been hearing that the trouble with this place is that people want to get along and go along." When Lucas speaks, he makes statements and rarely asks questions.

"Is that true?"

"You tell me, Abby. What I hear from my people is that we need more ownership and accountability. We need metrics and reporting that ties in with SEC regulations. Scrutiny on 12b-1 fees. I hear we need to review policies and procedures for potentially conflicted activities and better valuation processes. From what I gather the investment team can roam the range and totally ignore risk guide rails. They view any pushback from the control functions as a speed bump not a stop signal." He has learned to look at an audience but there is something in his look that feels to those on the receiving end that he is looking through rather than at them. "I'm told we need standard workflows to handle stale pricing. In other words, ensure that we address the most frequent advisory fee and expense compliance issues identified in the SEC's risk alerts. These are just examples of how our everyday work needs straightening out. If we do that all this strategy stuff is more likely to resolve itself, because the swamp will have been drained." Lucas gurgles a bit like an agitated river. His monologue sounds superficially coherent but carries all sorts of flotsam and jetsam before it which accumulates as he speaks. He babbles on. "Rule 22 E-4 boiler plates will not be effective; the front end should result in a more effective LRMP ..."

Abby breaks into the diatribe, "I'm not absolutely clear on what you are saying, Lucas. I'm sure you're right, we need excellent administration and control but the purpose of this off-site is to close the key gaps we have as a leadership team—'If you want to go fast, go alone. If you want to go far, go together.' A quote from the Walking Dead season nine I think, or perhaps, Hillary Clinton or maybe even an African tribe somewhere. But do you get my point, Lucas?" By his raised brow it's clear that Lucas does not.

"You know a technique I've used before," John raises his hand as he speaks, his voice tenuous, "is to simply ask people to write down the company's mission anonymously on a slip of paper, in not more than thirty words. Someone reads out what people have written. It's an amazingly powerful tool for articulating whether or not people are on the same page."

"Thanks John," Tiffany presses on. "Perhaps we can work with that idea. I'll talk to the consultants." John is delighted with the recognition. "Day two, will wrap with a dinner Q and A session with John Frost. Day three will focus on refining the mission statement and creating three or four strategic priorities that can be owned by the Leadership Group."

"So, thoughts?" It's Abby again.

"Lacks structure," Lucas says, his voice brusque. "You need to put together a specific timetable with clear deliverables and timings. As it stands, some might say you've built a boondoggle, not an agenda. If you hand over the organization of the meeting to me—I'm sure you have a lot going on—I can get one of my operations guys to work on it a bit. Input the ideas you've just been explaining."

"And you, John?" Abby battles on.

"Well, I've been part of these things before and I can see what you're trying to get at. Maybe you can firm up the agenda a bit as Lucas suggests. Redraft it with timings and explicit outcomes for each session?" As John says this he wriggles slightly in his chair, anxious above all things not to offend.

"Good thoughts, gentlemen. Thanks for your input. You've echoed what we've been going for—a combination of getting at the big issues but with the discipline of working within the framework of a well-articulated plan. Don't worry, I'll redraft and circulate for comment, Lucas. I want to get this to Christian for approval by Friday. Back to work then!" Tiffany rises with a weak smile and exits with Abby.

With the two women gone, Lucas engages John. Instinctively, Lucas knows that John is a soft target. "Thoughts, John?" Lucas says, leaning towards John across the conference table.

"Good meeting I thought, Lucas. They took on board a lot of what you said," John says, beginning to rise in an effort to distance himself and exit the room.

"Perhaps so. Been meaning to ask you. What's your view of the strength of our financials?"

Lucas throws out the question. John sits down.

"Well, things are looking a bit tricky. My guys just worked up the quarterly indicators. I haven't released them yet. Distribution is doing okay but it looks to me as if we may be buying sales by dropping margins. Also, some of the new investment products we've been launching are simply more costly to build and deploy, so in terms of pretax income we are on a declining trend that..."

"That's my analysis too, John. Put that together with an admittedly loose attitude on compliance and risk issues... I agree with you, the company is in real jeopardy." Lucas says.

"I wouldn't necessarily say that we are in jeopardy. It's just that..."

"Yes," Lucas cuts John off, "highlighting these gaps as you're doing is critical. Can I count on your support, John, as I begin to tackle these issues?" This is not a request from Lucas. It has the tone of a directive.

"I think Christian undoubtedly understands the business dynamics. It's just that..."

"He is failing to get a grip? Yes? I think many will agree with you there."

John places the flat of his right hand across his mouth as if wiping away is words "But I'm not saying that Christian has lost his grip. I'm saying that..."

"Oh, I know, I think a lot of people would agree with you about that too. We need some changes. But can I provide you with a bit of advice, John?" Lucas says, a vague smile on his face.

"Sure, what's that, Lucas?" John replies, a slight tremor about his mouth.

"Don't push things too hard. Going against the CEO when you've just arrived can be a risky business. Work out your strategy then act when you've got your ducks in a row. You're certainly ambitious." Lucas raises his brows, expressing grudging admiration.

"Wait up, I think you've misunderstood me," John replies, panicked. "I'm not trying to undermine Christian. You asked me what I thought of the strength of our financials and I merely pointed out that we have got some negative trends that need to be addressed. There is a lot of good stuff going on too."

"It's okay, John. You can be honest with me. This conversation is totally confidential. You can trust me. Will you shoot me those latest results? It would be good to study them so I can support you when you make your points at the next leadership meeting." Again, this is not a request by Lucas but an order.

"Yes, I can do that." John says, his head bowed like a submissive child to a playground bully.

His domination complete, Lucas looks at his watch with a half-smile; he always enjoys breaking them in. "Well I can't stay talking all day. I've got a brown bag lunch meeting with my reports. We have a book club going—keeps the team sharp. My reports are reading The Art of War. Have you read it?"

"No," John says, his shoulders slumped forward.

"Thought not. You may want to get a copy and join us. I'll catch you later."

John remains in the room. He knows he has been had and somehow co-opted by Lucas but doesn't have a clue how to manage his situation forward.

Lucas chews on a handful of nuts and raisins while his direct reports graze skittishly on boxes of pizza strewn across the conference room table. He the boss, they his caporegime and soldatos. "Right guys, let's have it, what's going on?" This is the weekly meeting Lucas conducts to interrogate his direct reports. "Top things you are working on. What you got done. Roadblocks and what you are going to do to resolve them. Adam, you are up." Adam is Lucas's consigliere, unquestioningly a believer in Lucas's authority and always anxious to prove himself. He has served Lucas previously and moved with him from company to company. He knows intuitively what Lucas wants and has great skill in persuading others that it is unquestionably in their best interest to agree with Lucas too. He is also very effective at working his personal agenda while representing his boss. For many to encounter Adam is to encounter a threat. At the same time, he has a shrewd sense of how to run interference with Lucas's colleagues and frequently talks Lucas down from his more extreme positions.

"The main focus this week has been on driving adoption of cloud migration. The objective here, though I need remind no one, is operational scalability at lower costs. This is all about enabling on-demand storage and enhancing processing capabilities and advanced analytics. Amy, you take it from here." Amy is a bright AVP reporting to Adam.

"A good example of the opportunity here is where advanced analytics can capture all kinds of structured and unstructured data to improve decision making—investment insights from news reports, analyst reports and social media. Advanced tools can even sense change in the sentiments of company managements and analysts by analyzing earnings calls. I tell you, the younger guys in Investments are loving this."

"What about the middle-office priorities?" Lucas interjects.

"Well, that's where we get to roadblocks. A lot of people on the street are hiring data scientists and we need a lot of collaboration to execute between new-age, tech-enabled people and old-school industry vets. We are stuffed full of vets who don't really want to change. That's the frustration."

"Hey Amy, did you read The Art of War this week?"

"Yeah sure, you told us to, Adam. How does that connect to this?"

"Attack, strategies, alliances, armies and cities, Amy. When you are out there you've got to be aggressive about pursuing our goals. You've got to view every interaction as an opportunity to defeat the opposition. You have to think strategically, make friends of people, or enemies if necessary, but you have to invade their space. Take the initiative."

"Adam's right," Lucas says, "there is much too much inertia. People in this place are stuck. They all need changing. If people won't adopt our ideas, we have to go right through them. There are just too many people around here who refuse to take ownership and accountability." He is almost shouting. "Working here has to be about winning. And how we win is to drive for results and take no hostages. Do you get it, Amy? Because I need to know you get it? Too many people fucking well don't get it, Amy. This place has got to change." His mood has turned dark. He glares around the conference table but meets no other eyes except Adam's. Everyone else has their eyes down.

The phone rings. Lucas picks it up. "All right, the party's over. I need the room."

"Good afternoon, Mr. Aiello. I have the Chairman for you."

Lucas sits erect in his chair, his hand running through his short silvery buzzcut.

"Hello Lucas. How are things going?"

"Pretty much on target. Some resistance to getting change done but we've talked about that before."

"And Sofia and the children?"

"All good, thanks."

"Let me get straight to it. We are going to move on Purvis and manage his exit around your meeting on Long Island next week." Frost's voice is thick and honeyed "He will be called back to head office and informed of his departure with immediate effect."

"That's going to be a big surprise at this end." Lucas can't help smiling into the phone.

"Don't doubt it. I have more work to do with a number of board members but the logic is unassailable. I simply can't afford to have him in place as we negotiate the sale of the company."

"Is there anything you want from me?" Lucas playing the supplicant, begins to sketch a hanged man on his notepad.

"I am going to need you to be my inside man, Lucas." Frost slides the components of the role he wants Lucas to play, like a card shark. "My eyes and ears and an advocate for my actions with the senior leaders there. I've decided that Fen Morgan will succeed Christian and that the staff functions and operations will be consolidated under you. That's Legal and Compliance, Risk, Technology, Marketing, Finance and HR. They will all have a dotted line back up here to Corporate but day to day you will need to pull everything together. Distribution, Investments and you and that woman Tiffany will report to Fen. You will have a new title, Chief Operating Officer and Vice Chairman, XelFunds. The Senior Leadership Group will continue as is but as a practical matter, Fen, the heads of Distribution, Investments and you will form the office of the CEO and call the shots."

Lucas, ever aware of the dynamics of power, asks, "Who else knows about this?"

"A handful of people up here: Peter Hudgell, Ella Keegan and Al Jiminez and, as I said, key members of my board."

"Is Fen aware?"

"No, not yet. I plan to get to him over the weekend when he gets back from London."

"Are you worried about Fen, Lucas?"

"To the extent that he may not be reliable, yes."

"Lucas, you worry too much."

Lucas is all business. "Who is going to succeed Fen as Chief Investment Officer?"

"We have been planning on Miles McCarthy. However, a potentially hazardous employee issue has cropped up. So that blows a large hole in the plan. If McCarthy is a no-go, I will move up Peiter Viser."

"Who's on the case?"

"Grace Rutler from HR and one of Hudgell's guys from Legal."

"Do you want me to weigh in and handle it?"

"No, not right now Lucas. We have the situation boxed. What I need from you is to let me know if you can see if there are any gaps we need to cover. And of course, keep me informed around any issues that you think I should be aware of. I needn't stress that this is absolutely confidential. I'm counting on you Lucas. Lucas, you are my watchdog. Keep me posted at all times."

"Got it." Lucas immediately resents the designation but keeps his head. "It's going to be quite something. How does this impact the acquisition negotiations?"

"Clearly the acquisition is a big driver of everything right now. If we can pull it off it will be transformational. In essence it's going to be a heavy stock transaction. The sale will substantially de-risk Pompton, enable us to focus on the core and deepen what we do best while still giving us a significant holding in a global investment business. We will have three seats on the new entity's board. I will hold one of the seats. The others will go to Fen, for now and Hudgell. Conceptually, there will be a lot of back-office integration but investments and distribution will remain more or less unchanged in the new entity post sale."

"Who will be the CEO of the new joint entity?"

"I've not resolved that yet; the negotiations may not be successfully consummated. The deal was brought to us by an investment banking company who sees synergies but there is still a lot that is ill defined. Neither side has got into due diligence so we're wholly unsure of what's behind the curtain on their side. Realistically, if things go well it will be another ninety days before we get to due diligence. If we get through that and any related regulatory issues it's likely to be a further six months before we close the transaction."

Lucas is silent for a moment as he processes what Frost has told him. "Lucas, you still there? I have to run but you've got the measure of this, right?"

"Oh yes, sure," Lucas says.

"Quite like the old days, Lucas, when you got it done for me at City Life, right?" Frost's voice is all esprit de corps.

"Yes, that was indeed a ride. And it sounds as if this one will be quite a ride too! I'm still your attack dog John," Lucas says. He knows how to ingratiate himself with power.

"Indeed you are, Lucas. Stay vigilant. Stay vigilant."

Lucas sits for a moment. He feels elated but somehow strangely inflamed, never the partner, always the dog.

Lucas exits his car service limo on West 41st Street at 7:10, then checks his phone for messages as he walks across the grey street that has been spritzed by a passing cloud burst. He has chosen this restaurant because it resonates with him—old school service, masterfully prepared steaks with all the trimmings and darkly lit private tables and banquette seating. He feels good here, a contender. No, a winner.

Natasha is waiting for him, drinking a martini that sits before her next to her phone. The scotch on the rocks she has ordered for him glints an icy sweat.

"Fancy meeting you here!"

"Small world, I guess." It's their usual greeting as they begin their evening dance.

Lucas leans in, kisses Natasha slowly, then slides alongside her in the curved booth. They sit, their thighs touching. The back of his hand wanders down to her leg. She crosses her ankle over his beneath the crisp white tablecloth. Nothing is said for a moment as they both feel the tension building.

"What do you see on the menu?" Lucas asks, his appetite piqued.

"I'm not actually hungry. At least not for food." Natasha brushes back her lustrous black hair, exposing the dark skin of her shoulder.

"Maybe we should move up the agenda then?" Lucas says salaciously, reading the menu.

"Sounds good to me. Let's eat light." Natasha replies, her tongue tapping on the 't' in light.

Lucas orders the light Riesling Natasha likes. They sit waiting for Chinois chicken salads they have both ordered.

"How was your day? God, that sounds so pathetically domestic." Natasha leans into him.

Lucas smiles. "It really does."

"Sorry."

"To answer your question—a few things brewing that could be interesting. For both of us maybe. Yes, on balance today was a bit more interesting than normal," Lucas says, beginning to simmer with satisfaction.

Their wine and salads arrive and punctuate their conversation which has become restrained, meandering around work and vacation destinations until it slides into intimacy.

"This always feels so deliciously illicit." Natasha says, her fork poking at an errant lettuce leaf. "Meeting in an anonymous place. No one knowing. What would those prudes say if they ever found out?"

"Yes, that would be more than awkward." Lucas is more than happy to play her game. But also wary. "We have to be discreet. No Instagram entries about the food or us taking selfies."

Natasha laughs.

Lucas pauses. "You look amazing. I see you all the time but I can't say anything. It's killing me."

"Well at least you know where I am if you want me." Natasha teases.

"I want you all the time."

"And how long will that be for?" Natasha's tone has changed as if caught in a squall of resentment.

"Right now, it feels as if it will be for a very long time." Lucas attempts to calm her.

This sounds all too practiced to her. *How many other women has he used this on?* "And how about your wife and daughter?" Natasha says, brandishing her irritation at him.

"We've got a good understanding. I bring home the bacon. She doesn't ask: I don't tell."

"Tonight, for instance. What's your story?"

"Business dinner. Early start. Makes sense to stay in town. Why are you asking me about Sofia?" Lucas pushes back, away from the table, suddenly feeling the physical distance between them.

"See, even her name, it is so different from mine. What attracted you to her?"

"I thought this was about us. Why do you keep coming back to her?" Lucas knows himself to be brass-knuckled and no good at this girl talk.

"Oh, just curiosity. Wondering what's going on in your head. What you're telling yourself when you're fucking her after you've fucked me?"

"You love doing this, don't you? Seducing me then trying to make us both feel bad because you've got a conscience or something?" Lucas says, with an edge to his voice that he rarely shows to her.

"It's not a bad conscience. Sure, I feel guilty but I think we both know that what's between us is more transactional. It suits us both. You're an attractive man. I like your body. You seem to like mine. We use what we have. It's admittedly satisfying. But let's be honest. It also sucks. Doesn't it feel like a bit too much effort sometimes? After all, you must be fifty or something?" Natasha's taunting him.

"You can stop this any time you like, you know. No hard feelings from me." There is a bitter, sullen tone to Lucas's voice.

"That's my point, Lucas. There are no hard feelings on either side. There is a lot of desire, even passion, between us. We get hungry for each other. We are both great traders in lust. But don't you crave something more? Or maybe you have all that with Sofia. Don't you get tired of living for these surreptitious date nights?" Natasha says wistfully.

"Why have you gone all philosophical on me? I thought you were good with what we have. I'm a very practical guy." Lucas scratches his nose, looking at the check quietly slipped to him by the maître d'. "I need stability. Someone who will launder my shirts that I can turn to when things get tough. Someone who will be part of my family. A person my mother will like. A person who will like me. A person I can have a good conversation with, who understands what a wife does."

"And you also need someone on the side," the matter-of-fact Natasha says.

"Yes, someone on the side," Lucas replies coldly.

"How many have you had—on the side?" Natasha asks, inching away from him.

"I need notice of that question. And you?" Lucas replies.

"Give a girl a little dignity," Natasha says brazenly.

"You know, I've never had such a frank conversation as this before," Lucas continues, enjoying her provocation.

"Maybe it's a generational thing. A 'Me Too' moment?" Natasha says, grinning.

"How times have changed."

"Indeed they have. You are becoming an exotic breed, Lucas."

"Just look around you here," Lucas says with a nod. "I'd say there are at least ten years between the men and women eating here. Most of them up to what we're up to. It's the major pastime in places like this. You ready for a change of pace now? I'm booked in at the Andaz around the corner. It has a great vibe. We can continue the conversation or maybe start one that's more interesting?"

As they leave the restaurant for the Andaz, there is some kind of melee across the street. People are arriving and the press are shouting and taking photographs.

***

Lucas sits in his white hotel robe on the side of the bed in room 624, his head still thick with alcohol, reading the note that Natasha left him around midnight as he was sleeping.

Lucas Darling,

Thanks for another lovely night out and fun conversation.

I wonder what Daddy would say!

Love Natasha.

p.s. no Instagram post! :)

For him, this is a moment of rare introspection. Maybe Natasha is right. This life is all wrong. Distorted. Lucas leans forward eyes closed, his head over his knees, riffling through the garret of his memories. Turning up his mother's smile here, a day with Sofia and the kids there. His mind's eye shuttering on an afternoon on a beach in Florida, the sun setting over the sparkling ocean. They have no money but he is happy.

He feels indescribably sad and alone. Beached on the failed logic of his life and fleshy consumption, he longs for more. Out of nowhere he begins to sob uncontrollably. Wailing like a child. He holds his head in his hands, rocking back and forth, feeling tired, very tired. A fragment from a song he learned in childhood forms in his mind. He fumbles for it, a distant memory just beyond his reach. Then it comes to him. He plays the memory of his grandmother humming softly,

'There is a fountain filled with blood,

drawn from Emmanuel's veins;

And sinners plunged beneath that flood,

Lose all their guilty stains,

And sinners, plunged beneath that flood

Lose all their guilty stains.'

He says aloud, "I'm weirding out." He wonders if she gave him something in that joint they smoked?

Lucas's phone rings insistently. "Hello?"

"It's me. You didn't call last night," a woman's voice says.

"Things just went on," Lucas replies.

"Are you all right, your voice sounds off?" the woman says.

"Think I picked up something, a cold maybe." Lucas's voice sounds arid.

His choice of words is not lost on the caller who says, "As long as it was just a cold, Lucas. I thought I was going down with something myself yesterday."

"The negotiations went late. My bad," Lucas replies, his torpid voice depleted of all energy.

"Negotiations often do. Are you home tonight?" the woman says.

"Yes, usual time," Lucas replies.

"Good. The kids are asking for you."

CHAPTER NINE

I observe her through the glass wall of Interview Room Two. She sits alone at the grey wooden table, fretfully riffling through her purse and perhaps her torrid memories. She fishes out her phone and sets it before her on the conference table, parallel to a black leather-bound notebook and a white envelope, face down. Now very still, she closes her hazel eyes and breathes deeply, her hands at rest on her thighs. Her perfectly curated hair frames her feline face, accentuating her cheekbones. She wears the immaculately tailored suit and white silk shirt recently recommended, I am sure, by her stylist. Even at rest, she has a cultivated magnetism that demands to be reckoned with.

I tap on the door. She is instantly alert and has the appearance of someone ready to pounce, her shrewd eyes evaluating the intruders for threat.

"Good morning, Jade. Thanks for meeting with us," I am-business like and continue without pause, "Let me introduce a colleague of mine: Tom Dawson."

"Good morning, Grace. Pleased to make your acquaintance, Tom." Jade's face tells Tom wordlessly not to waste her time. "So, where do we go from here?" Jade sits erect, pronouncing each word staccato as a brittle stiletto. As she once explained to Miles, she has worked hard to rid her speech of 'infection from my hometown' as she described it—the grimy street accent of her parents, with its suggestion of mahjong parlors, street markets and counterfeit jewelry.

"Jade, I'm trying to get up to speed here. Could you just run by me what you've told Grace?"

Jade is wary, her voice thin, "Where are you from, Tom? I've not seen you around here before."

"I work in the legal department, helping the team on sensitive people issues."

"So you're a sort of headbanger tough guy?" Jade has sanitized her accent but not her unvarnished directness.

"No, my job is to help resolve misunderstandings."

"Look Tom, I don't think we need to take your time over this." She is as sharp as a whip. Her rapid-fire continues. "I have given full account to Grace. It's pretty much clear that: 1. This is case of discrimination on the basis of my sex, 2. I have been retaliated against by my manager, 3. I have been treated totally against company policy, 4. The company operates a policy of systemic discrimination. That's it, Tom."

I asked Tom not to attend this meeting with Jade. I feel he is conflicted, but he insisted. Before I can interject, Tom ploughs on.

"Yes, Grace outlined that for me. But humor me. Just walk me through what's happened that's got you so upset".

"Upset? I'm not upset. I am not some deranged woman." She continues as if clipping her sentences out of the Huffington Post. "The company brought me here and then made my life hell. I'm not some 'Me Too' hashtag. Some object. There is a big problem with the men in management in this company. Someone has to blow the whistle. It just happens to be me. Oh, and, by way, I have pictures to prove it." Her dark eyes bore into Tom's. She is highly analytical and superficially as hard as nails.

I attempt to lower the temperature. "Jade, we are not here to contest this with you. To argue the point. We really do need to understand what happened so we can determine how to address your concerns."

"I want to see my personnel file."

I answer, "I can arrange that for you. You will need to read it in the office with a person present. Look, Jade, I know you are frustrated but can you run through your concerns one more time for us, please?"

"We keep going around." Jade apparently capitulates. "I will tell you one more time. I met Miles at a party when he and I were working at Petra Bank. He left to come over here. One day I am walking down Pine Street. I run right into him. He is very nice. Very warm. A bit shambling, as you know, but I like him. Seems genuine type. At the time I am an analyst. I know I am brighter than my job. We meet for a couple of drinks then one time while I'm drinking an espresso martini he's bought me he offers me a job as junior portfolio manager. So I throw in my job at PB and start over here. Turns out he leaned on Peiter Viser to create a new position. Soon after I join things get messy. He takes me for fancy dinners. We end up at conferences together. He calls my room. I pretend I'm out. He's at my hotel door late at night. He looks so sad, I ask him in. Months go by. It's on and off. I decide it needs to be off. What was a fling, a bit of fun and glitzy, gets to make me seriously uncomfortable. For me it's over, you understand, but he keeps calling me, calling me. Same thing every time. He calls me for dinner, I go with him to some nice place and we end up in his bed."

"So again, Jade, when was it that all this happened?" I am taking careful notes.

"Between when I joined as portfolio manager to when I got promoted to Team Leader US Equities."

"Promoted?"

"Yes, as you know. He moved me up from Portfolio Manager to my current job."

"There's more, I suppose?" Tom asks, with a hint of resignation.

"You tiring of me, Tom?" Jade clearly dislikes Tom but continues. "Yes. So whenever we meet, it's consensual. I'm not saying he raped me. Although in a way he did because I did not feel I could say no. Especially when he promoted me. So, I get sick of it. He tells me to come to his office for a meeting. This time he is all formal. Hands me a performance evaluation. Tells me that my team and I are on a downward fund performance trend and that if we don't improve we could all get fired. I tell him this is ridiculous; that for a couple of quarters' trend, whole market is suffering. If you look at three-year performance, not one year, we are still doing good in second quartile. We go back and forth. He is waving his hands, like he is going out of control, losing temper. It's embarrassing. People are looking up at us wondering what's going on. I tell him 'What, you say this to me because I won't sleep with you now?' He tells me to get out of his office. I get very worried. Here is someone trying to get at me for the wrong reasons. Then I go and complain to Fen Morgan."

"Tell me about the meeting with Fen. Be specific," Tom says, as he leans forward.

"Well, I always think Fen is a nice guy. So I go see him confidentially. I tell him in my own way what's been going on but I don't think he wants to hear from me. He starts talking about my performance and his concerns over the past couple of quarters and wondering if I have the lost plot, gone off the boil and stuff about portfolio style, the team and all things like that. I tell him I am stressed out. That my doctor..."

"Doctor?" Tom asks.

"Yes, my shrink has advised me to take a leave. I tell Fen I don't want to take a leave. I want to stay in the game. I tell him if I take time off Miles will take the opportunity to retaliate. To fire me." For the first time her voice wavers.

I ask, "And what did Fen say to that?"

"He says it's not retaliation I should worry about, it's my performance—he doesn't want to hear me."

"So what happened then?" Tom is now unsure if he is playing good cop or bad cop.

"I don't hear anything from anyone. Radio silence. I call Fen but his assistant says he's out—Asia and then London. And Miles just sits there brooding in his office. I'm waiting for axe to fall, feeling sicker and sicker. Doctor prescribes medication. I don't know what to do next. I go and see a big shot lawyer to find out if I need protection. I show her some of the texts Miles has sent me, a few of the pictures I took on my phone of us having a good time. She writes this letter to give to you today, Grace."

Jade reaches for the envelope that has until now been lying innocently on the conference table as if it is a mahjong tile and slides it over to me with a firm finger and vague smile.

"Thanks." I carefully place the letter in front of me.

"It demands that the company conduct a formal investigation into harassment and the other matters I described today."

I open and read the letter as Jade outlines the content. "It notes," Jade says, "that I am not the only person who has recently complained of adverse treatment within the investment division. Management must be instructed to cease harassing behavior and that appropriate disciplinary action must be taken. Training must be provided so that employees are treated in accordance with company policy. Any negative action with regard to my employment duties, status, location or compensation or future promotion or discipline will be regarded as retaliation and subject to action under the law and that I should be assigned to report to the CIO who can provide impartial supervision." Jade's manner and tone change as she recites the letter's contents. She is confident and astringent. Like any good mahjong player, she is cunning, focused on tactics, observant and adaptive. She forgets nothing.

There is a brief silence, broken by Tom. "Is there anything else you want to tell us, Jade?"

Jade opens her black notebook and ticks off several items. "No, I think that covers it."

"Very well. You've given us a lot to absorb. I must instruct you not to divulge our conversation today to anyone in or outside the company other than your legal advisor or therapist. We need to confer. I will contact you by

Monday morning at the latest with the next steps in our process. Any other questions, Tom?"

"No."

"Well, thanks for being so clear with us, Jade. We'll talk Monday."

"You'll call me, Grace?" she says, addressing me.

"Yes, I'll call you Jade."

"This is confidential, right?"

I reassure her. "Yes, what you've told us is strictly confidential to management for purposes of the investigation."

Tom and I look at each other after Jade leaves, the sound of her heels striking the marble corridor floor as she retreats.

"Well, that went well." Gallows humor from Tom.

"You are a master of understatement, Tom." We both laugh louder and for longer than Tom's observation merits. It is a bit of light hysteria. "She sure has her act together."

"May I see her letter?" Tom asks.

I hand it to Tom's well-manicured left hand. "Well-crafted as an opening salvo. The law firm sounds familiar but I can't altogether place them. Oh yes, Scott, Anderson and Wilson. They are very active employment litigators on the street. Handle mergers and acquisitions mostly and high-profile individual cases. I wonder how she got hold of them?"

"Of course, that's where I know them from," I say as Tom waves the letter at me. "We did a lift out of a sales team a couple of years back. I remember the team had retained them to act for them to negotiate their exit."

"It's obvious that they have coached her well," Tom replies. "This is clearly a first move on her part."

"Listening to her, Tom, it seems to me that a lot of this could be true. But of course, it may be all 'he said, she said'."

"Whatever the fact-base this is unlikely to end well for the company. Especially in light of the likely public perception of something like this." My brain is saying, *In spite of Tom talking like a litigator, I could get to like him.*

"Well, it's clear that we've got to see McCarthy asap and also Fen Morgan." When I think of all the work involved in all this, it's really the last thing I need at this time of year. "Hopefully we won't get into having to chase down a whole cast of characters beyond them."

"This is truly time-sensitive," Tom says. "We need to stop this dead."

"How, is the question." I leave the interview room wondering how Miles will react to all this.

CHAPTER TEN

There is a steel-faced clock above the door and a whiteboard on the wall. The room is windowless and cramped. Two plastic chairs flank the grey plastic table. Tom and I sit on one side; Miles, recently arrived, is seated opposite us. Harsh electric light falls upon us from above, bleaching our faces. There is a stack of old computer monitors in the corner.

Miles wheezes a bit from the pollen allergies that aggravate him at this time of year. "Twice in one week, Grace. I am privileged." His complexion has lost its natural tone and is sallow, apart from under his reddened fatigued eyes where his skin has swollen to form darker bags. It looks to me as if he's had a hard night drinking.

"Must be in our stars, Miles. Let me introduce Tom Dawson. He's a colleague from Corporate."

I feel as if I'm introducing a fellow member of the gestapo.

Miles ignores the newcomer with a cursory, "Pleased to meet you, Tom," and continues to focus on me. "Well what's up, Grace? What's all this cloak and dagger? Why did you need to see me here in a meeting room outside the investment floors this time?"

"Let me get the door. Miles, we've got something that we need to talk to you about." My voice is conciliatory. Come to Mama.

"Tell me something that's not obvious." But he is no fool.

"It concerns Jade Edwards." I toss him the grenade.

"Jade? Come on, first it's trumped-up issues, out of all proportion, with Peiter, and now it's Jade. What is this, some kind of a witch hunt in Equities?" Miles is clearly quite rattled.

"I am going to come straight to the point. Jade has made a formal complaint that you are sexually harassing her..."

"What! That's totally outrageous!" Miles interjects, crossing his arms over his chest. From the corner of my eye, I can see immediately, that Tom also judges Miles's response to be contrived.

"...that you have promoted her in exchange for sexual favors and that you have been marking her performance down because she won't cooperate with you sexually."

Miles is now ashen. He lowers his head unwraps his arms and clasps his hands in front of him on the conference table as if to adopt a position of prayer. Moments pass. When he looks up the corners of his mouth are white with saliva and he is breathing rapidly. His speech is unfiltered. "That woman is poison. That is a total lie. I will sue her. She is a real bitch for doing this."

I press him further. "So there is no basis to her allegations?"

"None at all."

"Why would she be doing this then?"

"Because she wants to see me gone, to get my job. Get revenge of some kind. Who knows what's going on in her head?"

"Miles, whatever has gone on here is going to come out in the end. It would be best to be candid now. Walk me through your relationship with her from the start."

Miles's entire upper body is restless. He unclasps, leans back and again crosses his arms, as if to protect himself before speaking. His words tip out awkwardly onto the table as he organizes a ragged defense. "Clearly she is trying to put up a smoke screen here to obscure her failure as a team leader and investor."

"So how was it that you brought her into the company?" Tom gets in on the act.

"We met years ago when we were at Petra Bank. She was a bit of a rising star. There was a general buzz that she was on her way up. As a managing director there, part of my job was to keep an eye out for talent. We had a couple of drinks a couple of times. We probably commiserated with each other a bit because I was on my way out the door and my marriage was on the rocks and she had some boyfriend problems, I think. When I landed here, I could see that we needed to inject some new talent. It seemed obvious to reach out to her."

"So, you created a job for her?" I ask casually.

"Yes. As you well know, Grace, we have had a policy of identifying external talent and then creating entry-level positions to bring them into the organization."

"It wasn't unusual for you to do this?" Tom probes.

"Unusual, yes. In line with company policy to recruit exceptional talent? Yes."

"We could find other instances where you have done this in the Equity Department—that is, created a new position specifically for a talent hire?"

"Well, we may not have always accounted for recruitment in that way, Tom."

"Did you sleep with her?" I am sharp, to the point.

"Is it a crime if I did, Grace?" It is fight or flight. Miles will fight.

"To be specific. Did you sleep with her when she was reporting to you during your time here at XelFunds?"

Miles looks down as if sensing the floor is about to give way. "Do I need a lawyer?"

"I can't counsel you on that, Miles. We are not the police and this is not a criminal case. All Tom and I are trying to do is to clarify the situation and protect the company and its employees."

"Yes. I did sleep with her once or twice." Miles is defiant, contemptuous of our questions. "But it was while we were at Petra Bank. We had no reporting relationship and it was a couple of years before we ran into each other again."

Tom sticks the knife in, "So it would not be unreasonable for her to construct a theory that you had created a job for her to win a sexual favor? Or that her promotion and performance evaluation was contingent on, shall we say, being nice to you?"

"That is not how it happened!" Miles's face is purple; he looks as if he is going to strike Tom, who leans back from the table. "Yes, I've fessed up. Years ago, we had a brief affair. But that was before we had a business relationship here. At no time since she was employed here have we had anything other than a strictly business relationship."

"Miles," I speak softly, he is done, I have him. "Jade says that you have evaluated her performance unfairly?"

"No Grace. That's not true. Just look at the numbers. Performance has slipped. And it is counter to the prevailing market sentiment. The problem is that instead of getting out there meeting with companies and attending conferences and generating fresh ideas for the portfolio, she has been staying back here and politicking. I have tried to coach her. I have engaged Fen in the effort too, but she simply won't hear any advice. We had a major blow up about this just last week when she reacted to me writing her up—I felt it was only honest for me to give her a formal heads-up that if she didn't get on the road to improvement she would be out. The other thing about her performance is that she's been swinging for the fences—pushing the risk parameters. If she doesn't modify her style, she could do real damage to the fund and indeed, the company."

"Fen would corroborate what you are saying on the performance side?" I ask.

"Absolutely. In fact, he's been pushing me to confront her."

"Jade indicated that she had emails from you and some pictures that will support her claims of harassment?"

"I don't know what she might come up with but there will be a satisfactory explanation, I can assure you. What is it she wants out of all this?"

"It's quite the list, Miles." I continue. "That the company conduct a formal investigation into harassment within the investment division. For management to cease harassing behavior and that appropriate disciplinary action be taken. Training to be provided to managers to ensure they understand and properly administer the company's policies for people. Protection from retaliation of any kind and that she should be assigned to report to Fen."

Miles rubs his now reddened face with both hands, exhales and sits motionless. "Where to from here?"

"Is there anything else we should know about this, Miles?" I ask

"No. This is very embarrassing," Miles replies to my final question.

***

Miles is long gone but the distress he emoted remains in the room.

"Thoughts, Tom? He has corroborated a substantial amount of her story," I say, looking at my notes. "Even if their sexual relationship didn't continue when she joined the company, their history put her in a very difficult position—no pun intended!"

"I disagree. I can't think why she would want to be here unless she could see an opportunity to exploit their relationship to her advantage."

"Wait up! That's utterly unfair to her. She really got under your skin, didn't she? Perhaps she came here believing that it would be possible for them to work together. She might just have been perfectly naive." Why am I not surprised that Tom takes this line? He, like all the others, seems congenitally incapable of understanding what it is like to be a woman in the workplace. They simply do not get the dynamics. How complicated and subtle it all is.

"You can think that, having spent time with her? She seems like an incredibly smooth operator to me. Manipulative is the word I would use. She knew exactly what she wanted. Just look at the contrast between them. She's a very attractive woman in her early forties, quite out of his league.

Clearly been around a bit, has a shrewd understanding of how the world works. He's a guy ten years older than she, easily flattered. Lonely, a lot of money, bored perhaps, and she provides the ideal opportunity for him to get back in the game. Yes, she knew exactly how to manipulate him."

"It's hopeless," I say under my breath. I had expected better.

"What's that?" questions Tom.

I decide to tell him "Women are always judged more harshly than men. Any display of assertiveness or emotion is seen as negative."

"Simplistic," Tom replies.

"Maybe, but it is the truth," I say flatly.

"It's never that clear. People at work are a kaleidoscope of genes, race, gender and, I dunno, intellectual capacity. And I should add environment and personality. To see everything framed in gender terms really doesn't do it. I am surprised that you see things in such traditional terms."

I must say that I had not credited Tom with this depth.

"Yes of course I have to agree with you. You are right. But that doesn't negate my point. The first reaction men have, and they are still in the overwhelming majority in most power positions in business, at least in the States, is to hear women as shrill and judge them to be too emotional."

I find that I am, ironically, getting quite emotional myself as I say this.

"Well maybe you frame things as you do because, although you are still young," Tom beams at me as he says this, "your views are still over-influenced by the whole Women's Movement thing. It's sort of subliminal in your head maybe?"

"Perhaps, but what are you saying?" I am genuinely curious.

"Simply that while you may have been absorbed in fighting the old gender wars, many have sat through a different movie where they have seen much more prejudice in different ways. If you are not..." Tom leaves the thought hanging.

I am not going to push him. "Instead of speculating," I say, "let's for argument's sake go with your assessment, give Miles the benefit of the doubt. He hires her because he thinks she's a talent. She sees it as an opportunity to leverage her career through him. But in reality there is no involvement between them beyond appropriate workplace interaction. Where does it put us?"

"I'm not saying he didn't sleep with her. I said she was manipulative." Tom is a lawyer. He dissembles.

"Right. But don't you think we should stick with unwinding what occurred rather than playing the psychologist and trying to figure out their motivation?" My retort is a bit rough but serves to get us back on track.

"Well, from a strictly legal point of view, if no infraction occurred in the workplace there is no liability. However, as a practical matter, given the facts as we understand them, no matter who is manipulating whom, it seems to me that the situation is untenable." Tom's logic is ambiguous. I look in his eyes. He is younger than I thought.

"Agreed," I say, for the sake of moving forward. "She has to report to someone else and that is not at all practical, given the nature of her job and how her funds are tied into the overall structure of our Equity funds."

"Surely she must understand that?" Tom has begun to type something into his iPhone.

"She's on a kamikaze mission. One or the other has to go," I say flatly. "Either way this will likely end both of their futures with XelFunds and probably elsewhere. Certainly for Miles. What a mess."

"Indeed." Tom piles on, "And given the likely intervention of Jade's lawyer and no doubt Miles's, this is potentially a very expensive and high-profile case for the company to litigate."

I check my phone also. "Well, I'm still trying to set up a meet with Fen. Want to join when I do?"

"Wouldn't miss it for the world! I think we should get back with Hudgell and Jiménez following that. I will shoot for getting on their calendar at six this evening."

CHAPTER ELEVEN

The 3:45 Virgin Atlantic flight back to JFK from London Heathrow is the usual grind. A half-drunk Australian across at the bar in Upper Class is having some sort of conversation with a flight attendant for the first hour of the flight and then collapses onto his flatbed in a fitful, gurgling sleep across the aisle. The seats to my left are thankfully empty.

I have four rules for long-haul business travel: travel alone if you can; work on outbound but not inbound flights; if possible, avoid airline food; drink only water.

As usual, I have transgressed my fourth rule and am enjoying a good glass of red.

Tonight, my agenda is simple: solve the London Times crossword, catch a movie, essentially get my head out of work for a while. And yes sleep, for which, after many years of air travel, I have formulated a well-rehearsed, sleep-inducing routine.

The crossword dispensed with, I flip through the available movies but quickly become bored.

Confidentially, and I don't tell even my closest about this, I keep a notebook I call my Book Of Wisdom in which I jot down odd quotations that I've remembered from my childhood (it started by learning by rote in Sunday school) or picked up from a book or an article or fragment of overheard conversation. Graffiti I come across on the walls of city streets while on business trips is also a favorite source for my entries. But somehow those to which I return come from an earlier era.

I have memorized the reputed year when the author of the quotation died and interrogated each of their meanings. I use this as a bit of a diversion to help me de-stress and also, at night, sleep. Especially on long-haul flights. Understand, to me, it is like walking down a familiar road where quotations stand like a maze of buildings, forming the meandering streets of my memories. I have taught myself the trick of closing my eyes, as in my imagination, I stand before each structure and ponder its inner meaning. Sometimes I hurry past one or another and linger at random. Each structure carries its own mental imprint.

The habit has become so ingrained that in moments of tension, I know that I now tend to default to vocalizing a quotation rather than forming an original thought of my own making. A bit like a literary form of Tourette's Syndrome. As a result, I am aware that I have earned something of a reputation amongst my staff and even my family, of being abstruse.

Tonight I have caught myself staring out of the Airbus 330 cabin window for a long time. Physically transfixed, and a bit soused, my thoughts roam untethered like the cumulus clouds drifting about the azure Atlantic spread over the infinity below. Suddenly weary, I put on my Bose earphones, close my eyes and drift into a dreamy labyrinth of internal dialogue filled with familiar yet vague images where I am both protagonist and audience.

In my dreamscape, I stand before an English country cottage with a thatched roof at the bottom of a hill covered with luxuriant green grass. There is a message neatly painted on a stone in the middle of the cottage garden.

'Men do not change, they unmask themselves.'

Madame de Stael, 1807.

The message is familiar. An inner voice, perhaps an emotion, speaks from somewhere deep within me. *You are always waiting for me, always warning me to question. Verify before trusting. How right you are. And what are your instincts about Frost and Hudgell and that new character, Aiello? Beware of them, Fen. Beware of them. And what about you, Fen—what's under the mask?*

I find myself answering, *Pass on that one this evening, I think*... I smile to myself, vaguely aware of a flight attendant bending over me and removing my empty wineglass.

My imagination takes me drifting through my unconscious to an ornate Victorian townhouse which has recently been meticulously painted. There is a blue plaque on the wall.

'There are no uninteresting lives, just inadequate ways of looking at them.'

G. K. Chesterton, 1905.

A voice says, *Typical of you, G. K., to put the onus back onto Fen. Some of these guys you work with are quite dysfunctional you know. They have the narrow corridor of their work but no exits to interesting places. Or again, is that just you not being able to see beyond yourself Fen? No, perhaps that's unfair. Some of them are just plain boring! And by the way, is the quotation accurate or distorted in some way?*

I wander on through my dream and pause before a Georgian townhouse. Carved into the lintel above the door are these words,

'If we do not find anything very pleasant, at least we will find something new.'

Voltaire, 1778.

Voltaire—love it! says the voice. *How many times have I had to tell you that Fen, just to keep you from going insane with all that mind-numbing routine you have to endure and look, this one's a condo!* A flag flutters in the breeze that Fen feels on the side of his face. It is inscribed,

'The perfect is the enemy of the very good.'

Voltaire, 1778.

True Voltaire, but so hackneyed. The voice mumbles, not wishing to give Voltaire offense. *And look, here comes the fire station.* The voice has taken on a female tone and something of a county accent.

'Above all, don't lie to yourself.

The man who listens to his own lie comes to a point when he cannot distinguish the truth within him, or around him,

and so loses all respect for himself and for others.

And having no respect he ceases to love.'

Dostoevsky, 1881.

Can't remember who this is. My goodness it's prescient though. Relativism.

Images riff and begin to flash like shell bursts against a blackened sky. Soldiers in the Great War being wrung from trenches, blasted and flung through the air, limbs akimbo. Gaunt refugees fleeing on carts down sodden tracks. Faces: Kaiser Wilhelm, Marx, Lenin, Malenkov, Churchill, Hitler, Stalin, Eisenhower, Einstein, Nixon, Kennedy, Trump, St Peter, St Paul. The frames freeze into a marble floored hall. Two figures, eyes locked, stand in a circle of brilliant light.

'What is truth? Pilate to Jesus.'

Gospel of John, 18:38.

From the shadows, my inner voice speaks. *It's as if the world never heard him answer that question. We wander around like sick puppies, we do. There's a contagion of lies, it permeates everything. Come on now Fen, no wallowing!*

'Rather than love, than money, than fame, give me truth.'

Thoreau, 1862.

Ah, now you're talking. Another voice deeper within me speaks. *But what is truth, Fen, to you, really? Is there absolute, ultimate truth? Dangerous territory, Fen. Why this question tonight, Fen? Somehow this question sounds very related to the existence of God, is it not? If God does exist, what would he be like? I tell you Fen, this is a dangerous conversation. We have been here before. But that was years ago when you were a child. Come on, there must be other much more interesting truth-or-dare questions. Look, here's the pub.*

The public house looms before me from out of the mist. Inside it's packed with the noise of voices which drown my inner conversation. Through the haze of cigarette smoke, I see a gnarled man in a dark suit wearing a bowler hat. The man suddenly transforms into a circus master in a bright red jacket and black top hat who yells questions into a microphone that crackles and cracks his words, which seem to mesmerize the crowd who turn to look at me.

What are you most self-conscious about?

What is the most embarrassing picture of you, Fen?

What would you do if you were the opposite sex for a month?

Have you ever let someone else take the blame for you, Fen?

Have you ever cheated or been cheated on, Fen?

What is the scariest dream you have had, Fen?

Have you ever been loved but not loved in return, Fen?

Come on, let's get out of here, Fen!

I push back through the crowded pub and as the din recedes am conscious that my heart is racing and that I suddenly feel weak. The air outside is cool. Rain is cording the ashen sky. I am possessed by a sudden feeling of terror, as I enter a large public garden and sit, then lie, on a bench, in a small wood which feels vaguely familiar. The sound of traffic moans in the distance. These words are carved into the back of the bench,

'The repentance of the common man is for his sins;

the repentance of the elect is for his heedlessness.'

Dhul-Nun al-Misri, 859.

What a great name, says the voice. *I have wrestled with you before, al-Misri. Certainly, it's the story of my life. Like lying on this bench and drinking this third glass of red on an empty stomach. Oh, and I love these words Fen—Look, they are written on a banner being hauled by a biplane across the sky!*

'To dare is to lose one's footing momentarily.

To not dare is to lose one's self.'

Kierkegaard, 1855.

Never were grand convictions were they, Fen? No, you are always listening but never hearing. At last, here come the Tolstoy buildings. A series of black blocks materialize, chalked up with a single quotation,

'I sit on a man's back, choking him and making him carry me,
and yet assure myself and others that I am sorry for him
and wish to lighten his load by all possible
means except by getting off his back.'
Tolstoy, 1910.

Go on, pile on the agony—Yes Fen, that's you I'm talking about. Remember
you picked that quote up in London in Trafalgar Square on a red flyer during an
anti-war demonstration? True, you struggled across the square trying to escape
down the Mall, the seething crowd shouting angrily for peace. You were wearing a
blue Navy greatcoat at the time. The rain spat at you like spittle from the mouth
of capitalism. Now, where did that come from?

The shapes of the buildings are becoming vaguer to me as they distil
into mist. I see them only dimly now. *Oh no, you are not leaving until you get*
to number 15, Fen. Words are daubed like graffiti on a brick wall.

'Parting is all we know of heaven and all we need of hell.'
Emily Dickinson, 1886.

It is everyone, isn't it Fen? You and me and a cat named blue. We want to
leave but there is no exit sign. Everyone is in this temporary state, this transition
towards God knows what from who knows where. It all feels so bloody pointless.

My eyes fading, I glimpse number 21. It is a coffee shop which has a
neat card in the middle of the window.

Everything but the Girl
Name of some kind of group I think, Fen.
Who does a man love more, the woman he lies to or the woman he lies with?
Can't see the number of this house, Fen.

I suddenly wake to the noise of the crew announcing the flight's arrival
in New York. My mouth feels as dry as the Sahara. My head throbs. I have a
vague sense of arousal. I am unsure of what I have dreamed. I only remember
the sound of retreating feet echoing down an intricacy of quotations.

I sense the attitude of the Airbus adjust for landing and hear the
undercarriage lower. Sharp crosswinds buffet the plane and as I peer through

the cabin window it appears to me that the aircraft is flying sideways onto the runway. I hear the familiar sound of the engine's thrust and hydraulics moving the flaps to de-crab the plane. Moments later the we land with a loud thump and decelerate to the cacophony of reversed engine thrust. As the plane lumbers down the runway, like a duck on tarmac, I check my voicemail to the disembodied sound of the purser welcoming everyone to New York, the local time being 6:35 pm. We are an hour late.

The clogged highway into the city from JFK is miserable. The combination of a Mets game and rain has reduced traffic to a crawl, like rats in a drain. I spot my limo waiting curbside across from baggage claim, throw my suit sack into the trunk and climb in. "Thanks, Henry. How are you doing tonight?"

"Good, Mr. Morgan. Good. Least I was till I came by that accident on Ocean Parkway. Sorry I was late for the pickup."

"No worries. I just got through immigration. And how are the kids, Henry?" Unaccountably, I really like using Henry's name.

"Doing well. Doing well."

"Your eldest, Peter, he's going to City College this fall, right?"

"Yes Mr. Morgan that's right—you've got a good memory." A yellow cab cuts in front of us. "You know, I've been driving limos for the past twenty-five years and I swear that I ain't seen anything like what's been going on these roads lately."

"It's the same everywhere. The infrastructure's shot and overloaded."

"That's right, and the drivers are just too tired and overloaded too, if you ask me." We both laugh, sharing the joke.

"Too right." As he speaks, I scan my messages. Fifty or so have accumulated in my email since I left London Heathrow and another dozen calls and texts are demanding attention. I dispose with most, rapidly consigning them to trash and retain four messages which demand immediate attention.

The first is from my eccentric assistant, Pierre. I know I should fire him but quite enjoy his subversive and random humor and having him around despite his considerable administrative shortcomings, many of which are illustrated in the random message I have just received.

No Fires. Please note, I am out from this afternoon through Tuesday.

1. Grace Rutler wants you to call her urgently. If you don't reach her she will be at your office at 7 am Monday
2. Christian wants you to stop by his office at 7:30 am Monday
3. You have a call with John Frost at 8:30 am Monday his office will call you on your cell—no indication of agenda
4. The materials for the 11 am Audit committee Monday are in your electronic board book
5. Lunch Monday at Yanni's at 12:30 with Denis Parker from sales and the Norwegian client
6. Russel Reynolds called to reschedule your 2 pm Monday interview with the candidate for Growth. It's now TBD.

Enjoy the weekend!

Pierre Poste

I am disturbed by the tone of the next message from Grace, who in my experience is one of the more even people I work with.

Fen.

Important we connect as soon as practical.

Employee issue discussed previously is now acute.

Grace

Two other messages are also demanding. The first from my son Joe.

Dad Need to solve math problem for homework tonight...

$(X-1)/X$ can this be simplified further?

Joe

The second, from Cait, is unusually austere.

Call me when landed!

Cait

"Hey, it's me." I've put Cait on speaker so I can hear her better above the drumming of the car's tires on the glistening highway.

"Thank God." Cait's voice is fraught, her Irish brogue unusually strong. "Why didn't you call me earlier? Where are you?"

"In the car. What's going on?"

"It's Rosie. There was an incident." Cait's voice oscillates with tension.

"Incident?" I repeat.

"At school. There was a shooter drill. They sounded the fire alarm. The kids were evacuated into an instrument closet. Evidently there was a problem with the lights in the closet. Someone outside in the corridor turned them off in error. The kids were freaked enough by the drill and the noise of the alarm but they all screamed when the lights went out. Rosie kicked and slapped everyone she could make out in the dark. They said she just went wild. Started beating on the door. By the time they got the door open she and several other kids were covered in slap marks, some were even bleeding..."

"Shit. Is she okay?" I say, interrupting Cait's flow.

"For pity's sake, let me finish, Fen!"

"Sor... shit... call's dropped," I say half to myself half to Henry, who I know is listening from the driver's seat.

"Hello, Fen?" Cait has called me back.

"Yes, sorry. Call dropped. What was that again?"

"Shooter drill... The other kids were taken back to their classroom but Rosie refused to let anyone touch her. Fortunately, after they called me... You still there, Fen?"

"Yes, but it's hard to hear you," I say.

"I got around there in record time, because I happened to be at home this afternoon. Rosie was sitting all alone on the ground with her knees pulled up to her chin and her sweatshirt pulled over her head. She was still shaking and had blood on her shirt and her knuckles were raw. It was bad, Fen. She looked so bereft."

"Hello? Are you still there, Cait?"

"Yeah, I was just taking a moment."

"So, what happened?"

"I eventually got her out of there and on home. At first, I was going to take her to the emergency room but decided that that would probably just add to the trauma. I felt like punching someone out over there. What was the school thinking?"

"Where is she now?" I ask.

"She's up in her room, curled up on her bed," Cait says.

"What should we do?"

"I called Eileen. She suggested I stay near Rosie tonight and take her over to see her tomorrow."

"I know Eileen has been seeing her for a while now, that she's a good psychologist, but does Rosie need medication for this to keep her calm, or something? Do we need trauma advice?" Casting around for some way I can say something that will help.

"No, I think what Rosie needs most right now is a little space. And to know that you and I are here for her. When are you going to be home?" Cait asks.

"About another half-hour."

"I am so angry with the school!" Cait says.

"You would think that they'd understand that doing that to a kid with Asperger's was bound to trigger that kind of reaction. Unbelievable," I say, resonating with Cait's anger.

"How did Joe react?"

"He knows that there was some sort of incident but I've played it down."

"Okay, we've got a lot to talk about. Sounds as if you did a brilliant job in managing the situation," I hate myself for sounding so condescending.

"I don't need handling, Fen." I can hear the exasperation in Cait's voice as it courses down the line. "I need you here working this through with me. I'm getting tired of being Mom the lone ranger with these kids. You are never here when it matters."

"Look," I simper, "I can understand that you have been under a lot of stress this afternoon but that is wholly unfair. You make it sound as if I am uncaring. As if you are the one that does all the heavy lifting."

"I am." Cait's voice, ice cold, slices into the cloying atmosphere in the car.

"You know that that is not true." I speak with equally icy precision, now embarrassed that Henry is party to the entire call.

"You tell that to the kids. When was the last birthday where I didn't do the leg work? Who runs the logistics on this place, the house, the beach house, the dog, the vacations? Such as they are. I've got my own career you know. And that's a laugh, taking the back seat as it does to yours. It is fucking well true. I do the lifting. You are a fucking tourist."

"And that makes you Mother Teresa, does it?"

"Fuck off, Fen." The cell goes dead.

"'Temper is a weapon we hold by the blade.' J. M. Barrie, 1937," I say, half to myself and half aloud as I remember Henry is driving the car. We ride on in silence.

At 9 pm the black limo carrying me pulls up outside our recently purchased brownstone in Brooklyn Heights. I am struck by how the windows shine from the house like long golden lanterns cut into the dark façade which glistens in the rain. I take my black leather suit sack from Henry and mount the stoop to the mahogany framed front door. I can't resist pausing to peer into the house hallway, looking for Cait before opening the door.

The tableau waiting as I enter the new polished concrete and stainless-steel kitchen consists of Cait, her face flushed, chopping red peppers on a wooden board; Alina, our Romanian Nanny cum Housekeeper, bent over the sink (generally, the results of Alina's efforts are so intangible that no one is very sure what she does all day, but somehow, despite our constant complaints to one another about what she does not do, our family has become entirely dependent on her); and Joe, sitting at the island intensely focused on his Apple notebook. And of course, Fred our Golden Retriever, who lies asleep, sprawled across the floor.

"Evening awl!" I love to affect a cockney accent. And do it even tonight despite the awful call with Cait.

"Oh, hi Dad. Thanks for the solution to the math problem. It's cool. How was belle Grande Bretagne?" Joe says, looking at me up from his computer.

"Her Maj sends her regards." It's a game I play with Joe. We both enjoy the routine and the secret smiles we give one another as we play it out.

"Good efening, Mr. M," Alina says, looking at me over her shoulder.

Cait continues to chop wordlessly as Fred slowly drags himself up and lumbers over, tail wagging, to greet me.

One hand stroking the dog, I open the fridge. "Where's Rosie?" I ask

"Upstairs. Got one of her moods on," carps Joe.

Cait looks up. "That's not fair, Joe. She's just tired and had a rough day."

"Don't see why she gets all the sympathy."

"Hey, come on Joe. What happened to all that Save the Earth, Save the People stuff you were talking about the other night? Doesn't charity begin at home? I'll go up and see her."

I tap on Rosie's bedroom door and enter to find her curled up on her bed asleep.

Her computer glows with a screen saver of Fred rolling in mud. Rosie is breathing deeply. I pull a blanket up over her shoulders and whisper to her "Sleep tight little one." I bend and kiss her tenderly on her forehead. As I look at Rosie's peaceful face, I am suddenly conscious of my tears, drawn from some cistern deep within me, rolling slowly and uncontrollably down my cheeks. They collect on my chin and fall silently from my face onto the grey bedroom carpet. I feel as if have been kicked in the stomach and am instantly sick with exhaustion. I stand stock still waiting for my sense of bewilderment to subside, my mind empty of everything but the vision of my daughter, terrified and imprisoned in a dark, hostile room. I become conscious of a presence behind me and turn as Cait extends her hand to my shoulder. She gently kisses me on my cheek and brushes back my hair.

"She is so young and confused. Will we ever reach her Fen?"

I have no answer and silently reach past Cait to turn off the bedroom light. We exit Rosie's room leaving the door ajar, then stand silently in the hallway, staring into one another's eyes, the space between us a gaping infinity waiting to be filled by an embrace or touch that does not come. I search for words but my lexicon is unequal to the moment.

My mind races for a quote to capture my emotions until, like answering a Jeopardy question, I say, "The heart has its reasons of which none knows." I even add the author. "Blaise Pascal."

"For God's sake, Fen."

"I'm serious, Cait, I don't think we will ever figure her out. We can only love her. I am so sorry."

My phone goes off, chirping Ode to Joy. Demonstrating the sensitivity of a dead sheep, I take the call, "Fen Morgan."

"Fen, John Frost here. We were set to talk in the morning but I'm hoping you might have a moment now. I hope I am not calling at an inopportune time?"

"No, not at all John. Could you hold the line for a moment please?" Surprised by the call I put it on mute and point at the phone with my free hand, "Cait, it's the Chairman. I need to take this."

"You are a child, Fen. Fuck off." And with that, Cait walks away.

I run upstairs to my home office, followed by Fred who has appeared from nowhere. "Sorry about that, John."

"Not a problem, Fen." I'm surprised by the warmth in Frost's voice which is unusually oleaginous. "I'm calling because I'm going to make some changes and I want you to be an important part of them. I'm going to ask Christian to retire and plan to appoint you as his successor."

I'm hearing this, but thinking of a line I've heard, stretching for who might have written it.

'Restless he longs for storms as though in storms there is rest?'

"Fen, are you there?" Fred has collapsed on the floor and is licking his front leg.

"Yes John. Just trying to absorb what you are saying."

"Fen, are you ready to step up?

"To CEO XelFunds?" This feels unreal to me. As if from a dream sequence.

"Yes," Frost replies.

"Where does the board stand on this?" I ask.

"To be frank, there were some reservations. But everyone has come over to my opinion that we need change in leadership, especially in view of the likely transaction."

"John, I don't want to appear slow here, but I'm confused. Surely if we are in the throes of a transaction, and by transaction I assume you mean sale, why would you want to change horses mid-deal? Christian has been in the seat for years. He has all the relationships. Knows where the bodies are buried—the firm's dynamic. Aside from any personal feelings people will have, aren't you taking a huge risk in putting me in the seat? Or indeed anyone else at this critical moment?"

"Yes Fen, there is some risk. But weigh that against the alternative. The deal negotiations are still in process. We are not sure of the eventual structure. I understand that there has been an assumption that the proposal is a sale. However, as we have got further into the negotiations it's become clear that if we position it right Pompton can exchange XelFunds for a substantial minority holding in the acquirer, together with some cash. This way we de-risk Pompton but retain the upside of being a substantial shareholder in the new entity."

When Frost wants to turn on the charm, he often enthralls his prey by flattery, with the pretense of sincerity and personal vulnerability designed to create an atmosphere of mutual admiration and dependence. He is compelling and once lured, the bait is sweetened by the offer of some kind of incentive exquisitely crafted to the target's appetites and vulnerability. Once captured, the target is throttled into servitude. I know instinctively that I am no match for Frost's perfidious scheming. I can feel Frost's coiled attention on the other end of the line. The ticking of the clock in the crocodile, and suddenly I am Peter Pan, naive and malleable under a spell and up for taking orders like Captain Hook.

"The market will love it. At last we will have an Investment guy at the helm." Frost continues full blast, his logic pressing upon me like a heavy rain. "There will be many manufacturing and distribution opportunities both within the acquirer's existing channels and between the acquirer and Pompton. It's a big win. No doubt the acquirer will rationalize operational capabilities but for the most part XelFunds investment management and distribution capabilities and its brand presence should be greatly enhanced by being part of the new entity. There is a lot that is unresolved as yet and the fact of the matter is we may never consummate the deal. But I want to be ready to execute this deal if it works out, or be ready for the next opportunity and ensure we continue to grow the current business."

And I am thinking, *Yes, and I've seen how these grand plans have worked before. Our type of buy side investment firm is all about culture and that's always the first casualty when a firm is absorbed into the bureaucracy of a behemoth. I don't think this guy has got a clue about what he's doing or what's at risk here.* But I say, "So, do you have a sense of the post-acquisition structure?"

"Yes, as currently envisaged Pompton will have three seats on the new entity's board. I will take one of them, Peter Hudgell another and you will have the third. Conceptually there will be a lot of post-acquisition back-office integration at XelFunds but Investments and Distribution will remain more or less unchanged. When you replace Christian the staff functions will be consolidated under Lucas Aiello who will become Chief Operating Officer and Vice Chairman XelFunds Funds and report to you."

"That's legal and compliance, risk, technology, marketing, finance and HR under Aiello?" I see it now, that worm Aiello has somehow got in on the act. My gut tells me that is going to be a big problem.

"Yes, they will all have a dotted line back up here to corporate but day to day Lucas will manage the flow. Distribution investments and that woman Tiffany will report to you, along with Aiello."

"So John, you want me to double as Chief Investment Officer and CEO?"

"No. You step up to CEO, we put Miles McCarthy in as Chief Investment Officer. That's what the succession plan says. Yes?"

"Correct. Except John, we have a few issues that we're trying to clear up with McCarthy right now."

"I know. They relate to his relationship with Jade Edwards. Your woman Rutler is on the case. If McCarthy is an issue you should fire him and promote Peiter Viser. One way or another this needs to be resolved quickly. It could sour everything if left to fester."

I'm quite shaken that Frost is aware of the issue with Edwards, but keep schtum.

Frost continues, "The Senior Leadership Group will continue as is, but Tom Richter, who will continue as head of distribution, Aiello, and whoever is the new CIO and you will form The Office of the CEO and call the shots."

"That's a lot, John. Sounds as if you have been working this for a while. Who else is in the loop?"

I may as well get familiar with the politburo.

"My staff, key members of my board. Time is of the essence, Fen. I understand that you have a planning off-site on Long Island next Tuesday. I plan to deal with Christian next Wednesday morning. I am traveling between now and then," Frost says.

"So, what should I be doing, John?" My sudden expression of fealty surprises me.

"Fen I need your commitment. Your loyalty."

I am silent, conscious, of the obsequiousness which cloys my throat.

"You have to be prepared to step up Wednesday. Communicate what is happening to the XelFunds team when I call Christian away to meet with me," Frost says. "Then get yourself back to the New York office and raise the flag there as CEO. You also need to resolve this issue with Jade Edwards. Do what it takes to shut it down Fen. That woman Grace Rutler from HR seems bright. Work with her. If things get tough bring Aiello into the loop too, he's got good instincts in a case like this. Call me Monday as planned. You will have determined a path through all this by then. Have a good weekend Fen. This is a big moment for you. Regards to your wife. She is going to be proud. Very proud."

Frost has forgotten my wife's name is Cait. It is unimportant to him.

CHAPTER TWELVE

My cell is silent. I sit in my home office staring at the photograph of Cait that sits on the right side of my desk. Cait is walking across a cornfield somewhere in upstate New York, her red hair tied back, she looks exuberant. She holds Rosie with one hand and Joe with the other. Rosie has placed her free forearm across her brow; her expression is full of questions.

My mind is racing.

'We saw the swallows gathering in the sky,

And heard them noise.

We had not to look back on summer joys,

Or forward to a summer of bright dye.'

George Meredith, 1910.

I run the fingers of my right hand across the polished surface of my desk. Then pick up one of the rocks in the collection I keep beneath my computer. It is a shard of flint, honed in ages past to a crescent of sharpened stone. Too large for an arrowhead, it is perhaps a knife and has an edge sharp enough to skin a rabbit or scrape a Neolithic horse into the hillside at Uffrington. The light of the English summer when I found the implement comes flooding back to me.

Cait and I are hiking to Wayland's Smithy, a Neolithic tomb, over chalky grasslands. I am looking up at the enormous white equine figure that quelled troops, upset kings and hosted pagan rites across the ages. Cait and I are ebullient. I am working near the stock exchange in the City of London. We rent an apartment near Blackfriars Bridge which affords a view of the river

Thames. These are the first months of our marriage, each day an allegro of demanding work, our evening adagio ended with a coda of warm and fervent embrace and frequently more.

In my mind's eye we walk to the soundtrack of skylarks that pitch and dive on the late afternoon air. Recalling the image of Cait walking in front of me, I lean my forehead on my desk, close my eyes and rehearse George Meredith's 1881 poem, The Lark Ascending, set to music by Vaughan Williams just before the outbreak of the Great War.

'He rises and begins to round,
He drops the silver chain of sound,
Of many links without a break,
In chirrup, whistle, slur and shake.
For singing till his heaven fills,
'Tis love of earth that he instills,
And ever winging up and up,
Our valley is his golden cup
And he the wine which overflows
to lift us with him as he goes.
Till lost on his aerial rings
In light, and then the fancy sings.'

Now as then, I am filled with wonder at her loveliness. Yet imprisoned in my orphaned heart I have become mute and cannot bring myself to disclose the depth of my feelings. I can only trust that in some way Cait will find and rescue me as she did those many years ago as I lay bereft on a pavement in Highgate.

At about 1 am I find myself awake; my mouth parched. I gather myself slowly, my body feels wrapped around me like a crumpled paper bag. I walk, drained, to our bedroom.

The house is quiet now; there is only the dull moan of traffic from beneath the Promenade a block from the house. Cait is asleep, curled tight beneath the sheets, facing the wall like a chrysalis refusing to pupate in my presence. I undress silently to the steady rhythm of Cait's breathing and slide beneath the cool sheets. Not touching her, I stare at the chinks of light that stab into the darkness from beneath the blackout drapes, like the perseveration of thought that stabs at my medulla. My last thought before falling into a long dark sleep is of Christian and of a fragment someone had scribbled in the margin of a copy of the Financial Times I picked up in the departure lounge at the Heathrow.

'Conscience is a fashion,

It changes every year'

Josef Skovrecky, 2012.

I wake late to the sound of Alina's voice singing above the vacuum in the hallway. My phone is fat with dozens of messages which I delete wholesale, sitting half-awake, on the toilet. Entering the kitchen, I find Cait sitting alone at the concrete island. She is reading the New York Times, her red hair tied back ready for business. Fred sleeps below the long kitchen window.

I extract orange juice from the fridge. It is chilled like the atmosphere between us. "Where are the kids?" I attempt an amateurish lightness.

Cait's head remains inclined toward the newspaper. "Took them over to their karate classes. Maybe you can pick them up at eleven?"

"Sure." The silence between us feels impenetrable. "Frost called me last night."

"Apparently," Cait says, her skin tone very white against her red hair.

"Look, are we going to carry on like this all morning?" I say standing opposite her.

Cait drops the paper. "With all that's happening here with your children, the first thing you want to talk about is work. You literally are self-absorbed, aren't you." It's a statement not a question.

As ever with her, my reaction is fight or flight? Uncharacteristically, I choose to fight. "OK, so I missed the main event yesterday. Sorry. I failed you and Rosie. I am an uncaring, evil, absent bastard. Oh, and I should throw in ambitious, avaricious, sexually frustrated, potentially promiscuous, selfish, self-satisfied jerk. Is that enough for you, Cait? You're the one who has self-sacrificed. You are the one who put your career on hold and followed me here. You are the one who keeps having to glue this family together as we fracture. You are fucking perfect, Cait. Enough masturbation before your selflessness?"

"Feeling better now, are we?" Her face is flushed. Her Irish accent is strongest when she is angry. She walks silently away through the doorway.

I pick the kids up from karate, their faces shining with sweat. Savoring the grip of their hands on mine we walk to the deli. Then sit at the deli counter eating ice cream from paper cups. Joe asks me, "Do you know where numbers come from?"

"That's an interesting question, Joe. What do you think, Rosie?" I say, trying to engage her.

"Dunno." Rosie is absently counting the lights on the ceiling.

Joe volunteers, "I asked Alexa on Mum's phone and she sent some websites I didn't really understand."

"Well, I think numbers came from a very long time ago," I say, my arm round Joe's shoulder. "Different groups of people had different sorts of numbers. But ten got to be the most popular in India and they spread to the rest of the world from there in the sixth or seventh century."

"So how do people know numbers are true?" Joe says, looking up at me.

"What do you mean, Joe?"

"Well for instance that three is three and that four is four? We made the number system. Some scientists think that if we made contact with aliens their numbers would be different," Joe says this between shoveling chocolate ice cream.

"That's an interesting point, Joe. Where did you get that from?" I ask.

"Oh, I was just watching some program but it seemed interesting. And on Dr Who there was a whole episode about the number seven. There were Cybermen in it and everything. I like Dr Who. People don't appreciate how complicated it is. Like Cybermen are not real robots, they are organic beings that become robots. As opposed to robots, that is."

Rosie says, "Why do you always have to talk about robots, Joe? Why do you love robots so much?"

"Because they don't talk back like aggravating sisters."

And at that Rosie jabs Joe hard in the neck with her index finger. Joe shrieks in pain as he is prodded sideways on his stool and, uncharacteristically, begins to cry.

"What on earth did you do that for, Rosie?" I am genuinely appalled by Rosie's savagery.

"He's always making fun of me. He's very annoying," she says, her eyes suddenly burning with rage.

"Why must you ruin every outing, Rosie? Come on, we're going home." Furious, I drop a twenty on the counter, grab Rosie by her arm and march her, struggling, towards the door. In the street Rosie kicks me hard in the shin. Whatever the rules, I am sorely tempted to smack the child.

"Right, you little bugger, you're going straight to your room when we get home."

"Don't care. You can't frighten me. Who are you to tell me? You're never home. Don't fit."

"I'm not trying to frighten you, Rosie. You can't hit people and think you will get away with it!"

"I don't give in to threats." Rosie is standing with her head bowed, her hands over her ears as she rocks slowly back and forth.

"It's okay, Dad. I'm okay. It's just her way." Joe takes my hand as passersby glare and avoid the melee on the sidewalk. Sad, we begin to walk home, Joe leading me by the hand and me dragging Rosie by her arm as she screams in protest behind me.

By the time they clamber up the stoop to our brownstone I am mentally exhausted but Joe, resilient as ever, runs off to play with Fred.

"Go to your room now!" I am filled with frustration.

"Will not!" Rosie says, intransigent.

I tower over the girl. "Upstairs now!"

"Not intimidated. Don't give in to threats!"

"What's going on?" Cait appears, descending the stairs.

"Rosie hit Joe." I feel like a child myself now, my dignity left somewhere outside in the street.

"Rosie, what were you thinking?" Cait steps between Rosie and me, and squats so she is slightly lower than Rosie. She says softly, "Go to your room as your father says." Rosie hesitates then turns and slowly climbs the stairs to her room muttering, "Don't give in."

Later, when the kids are upstairs asleep, Cait and I sit, uncomfortably closemouthed, scanning the Times' supplements. In the harsh modernity of our kitchen, we are alone together, mute islands of misunderstanding in an ocean of unexpressed emotion.

I break first, "This is pointless."

Cait lowers her paper but not her guard, "Meaning?"

"There is a lot going on."

"Yes, there is a lot going on. A lot of things getting lost and broken, Fen."

I struggle against what feels like the unrelenting tide of resentment that flows between us. "I don't mean to be like this."

"I know. But it's the way you are. And it hurts to be on the other side of whatever's going on in your head, Fen."

"So, tell me what's happening to us?"

"It's called life. We can either get through it together or apart." Sometimes her words have the quality of a razorblade in butter.

I am taken aback by the starkness of her statement. "So now we are in a therapy session?"

"More like a sort of desperate self-help I think." There is no longer an edge to her voice. Tears begin to flow down her face. "Why is it that women are the ones who cry?"

"Because they get more lost and broken?" I reply.

"No, it's because they know what's lost and broken. And that breaks their hearts."

I feel a compulsion to quote Tolstoy.

'Everyone thinks of changing the world but no one thinks of changing themselves,'

Leo Tolstoy, 1910.

But for once I muzzle my Tourette's. "So, what's most broken about us then?"

Cait's answer comes crashing back at me like an eager. "We have a kid who is broken in ways neither she nor we understand. The two of us live in separate worlds, our best communication is in the sex we no longer have. You are never here and when you are you are always online to someone else." Her pent-up rage beats at me mercilessly. "We have few friends, a lot of acquaintances and none of them talks genuinely about what's going on with them. The culture here is interesting but essentially alien. We have a ton of money but no time to spend it. We are wildly successful professionally but personally we have no real idea who we are, no ambition to discover life. We live in a time where no one tells the truth and no one cares if they do or don't. Oh, and I forgot to add, in a country where every year more people die from addiction and shooting each other than in a major war. Oh, and yes, how could I forget, we wrap the whole shit situation up in racism and a sulfurous climate. And we are in it all alone, Fen. Absolutely alone."

No longer able to contain myself I step over to her, then draw her up to me from her chair as she sobs uncontrollably in my arms. Surprising myself, I too begin to break down. For once I have no quotes, no knee jerk, smart arse comment. All I can say is, "I am... I want... I've been so absent."

My phone goes off, but for once I ignore it. I know I love her.

We walk upstairs to bed.

***

I have brought her tea and a digestive biscuit on a small tray. The 6 am Sunday sunlight streams through the window, infusing the room with a warm golden glow. There is a stillness to the house which is free from the weekday murmur of jostling traffic.

"Good Irish breakfast tea," I say.

Cait grunts as she surfaces from below the white duvet. The dog has followed me into the bedroom and is snuffling at our bedside after a piece of the biscuit. "I got a call from Frost last night."

"I know." I sense Cait's disappointment that this is the first thing I say, but I plough on. "He wants me to step up to CEO."

"Well, that is news. What's happening to Christian then?" Cait goes right to my pain.

"Christian doesn't know. At least I don't think so," I say, knowing in the pit of my stomach that I have betrayed him.

"This stretches your loyalties a bit, doesn't it?"

If find it difficult, but an enormous relief to get my words out, "Indeed, puts me in a lousy situation. Frost is a real snake. This latest acquisition bid is looking serious, so the whole company could disappear. Although they will need me for the transition. I was also talking to our HR woman by phone yesterday and she tells me we have a giant problem with Miles. And to cap it all Christian is really losing his grip, regardless of this latest Frost move."

"All sounds a bit Elizabethan."

"Yeah, a cross between Julius Caesar and Hamlet; everyone ends up killing each other. Makes me just want to walk, especially after last night— 'It's easier to find men who will volunteer to die, than to find those who are willing to endure pain with patience.'"

"Is that Shakespeare?"

"No, it's Julius Caesar," I reply smiling. "Whichever way this all goes, I think I'm screwed." Our laughter is a bit louder than called for.

"Do you have any options in taking the job?" Cait asks.

"Not that I can see. I feel I owe something to my people, if not the corporation. I am..."

There is a piercing hammering on our front door, shattering our intimacy. It startles us both "Who the hell is that? It's loud enough to wake the entire neighborhood," Cait says, with a frightened look on her face. The insistent hammering sounds again, louder than previously. Fred barks excitedly. Instantly, Rosie and Joe have scrambled out of their beds and are suddenly running into our bedroom.

Rosie halts at the bottom of our bed, her arms across her chest, rocking silently. It is Joe who speaks as he stands next to her clutching a bear and looking terrified. "What's happening, Dad?"

I beckon the children to me. "It's okay. I'm going down to see who it is."

With great apprehension, I descend the stairs and approach the door with Fred growling at my heels. The dark form of a heavy-set man looms through the plate glass, poised to strike it again. "Hold on, I'm coming," I shout as if to ward off pandemonium. I yank the door open, the baseball bat that I keep at my bedside in my right hand. "What the hell's going on?"

For a moment I'm fazed. "What the heck are you doing here at this time of day?"

"We need to talk." The intruder stinks of beer. "I've been up all night."

"You'd better come in."

Cait shouts anxiously from the bedroom, "Who is it, Fen? Are you okay?"

"It's all right, everyone. Panic over. It's someone to see me from work." I reach down for Fred, who has started to jump up excitedly at the stranger.

"You look like crap." And he really does.

Without ado, I lead the way to the sitting room. "Take a seat. Can I get you a coffee or something?"

"Coffee would be good."

"You got it. Sit, sit," I gesture. "I'll be back in a trice." I exit the sitting room and vault back up the stairs to Cait who has the children either side of her in bed. "It's bizarre. It's Miles McCarthy."

"What does he want?"

"No idea. He looks in awfully bad shape. He's in the sitting room. I offered him coffee. I'd better go and see what's up."

Minutes later I return to Miles with two espressos drawn from our extravagant Italian machine. "So why the drama?" I ask.

"I'm in deep shit, Fen." Miles has chosen to slump into one of the deep black leather armchairs that sit ponderously each side of the sofa. His disheveled mass fills the cushion like an unruly bundle of burdened conscience. He looks utterly defeated, as if he has lost something precious, his usual stolid appearance now a caricature of anxiety. His eyes are a tortured red, his cheeks oddly hollow. There is a desperation about him, as if he has become untethered in some way.

"I'm listening." We have always got along. Miles's unimaginative, plodding but reliably risk-averse investment style, allows me to float above the daily grind, knowing that he has my back. Miles, his ambition drained, is mostly content to let me lead and to keep the bureaucrats off his back, providing he is allowed his many personal eccentricities.

"You asked me a while back if there are any personal issues between me and Jade, after she brought you a complaint about me. I told you not to worry. That it was sour grapes on her part and that in fact..." Miles is sweating and moves his bulk uncomfortably as he leans forward, "...to put it politely, her complaint was a ruse to divert attention from her performance which has been slipping over several quarters." He has not stopped moving. His eyes rove over the room.

"Yes, I remember the conversation well." I feel my gut tighten.

"I lied," Miles says. As if to dramatize the moment, the air is suddenly filled with a truly malodorous stench. Fred, who has been oddly interested in their conversation, slinks sullenly from the room as if greatly insulted. Neither of us acknowledges that the other has farted.

"About which part. The relationship or the performance?" I ask.

"Both. One colors the other," Miles replies.

"You've been screwing her, then." I say this as a statement of fact, my tone even.

"She wanted to end it. I didn't. I pursued her. I tried to pressure her. Her performance is no better than average. She occupies the job rather than excels. But she doesn't deserve the way I've been trying to destroy her." The smell of whisky reaches out at me from his chair. Miles inclines his head forward as if focusing on the carpet. I think that he's about to throw up or perhaps fall into an inebriated slumber. His lips are moist. Spittle has accumulated at the side of his mouth.

I say nothing as I absorb the implications of what Miles has told me. And then Madame comes seeping into my mind,

'Men do not change, they unmask themselves.'

Madame de Stael, 1817.

I mutter something to myself as Miles stirs from his reverie. "There is more. There are pictures. Selfies taken by us and pictures I took of me that I sent to her. I am finished, Fen."

I remain speechless, struggling with how to formulate what should come next.

Miles keeps on firing the bad news, playing out the sick joke he has brought to ruin a Sunday morning. "It's been over between Jessie and me for years. Monday to Friday she is in Boston, with the kids her family and her prissy friends. I am down here to live the monastic life. She doesn't ask any questions. I don't tell her any lies. Now this is going to be everywhere. I've thought of ending myself."

The comment shakes me out of myself. "Look, as I see it there is a lot of alignment here between the company and your interests." I am desperate to find something, anything that will bring him some hope.

"How so?"

"If you go down. If this gets plastered all over the media, the Street is going to have a reaction. This 'Me Too' stuff is kryptonite." Suddenly, having Miles in such close proximity makes me feel as if I am going to throw up too.

It's as if Fred has shit on the carpet. "For your sake and for the company we have to put a lid on this."

"That woman from HR, Rutler, is in hot pursuit. She's already taken a statement from me. She's a real ball-breaker."

"Yes, well, whatever advice she has to offer may or may not be taken. Let me think about this overnight. I'll come by your office tomorrow before noon and we can sort through it then. In the meantime, why don't you go home, have a shower, get some sleep and lay off the whisky?"

I stand and motion towards the door. "Shall I call you an Uber?" Suddenly there is an urgency within me to have done with him. To cast him out.

Miles stands uneasily, his hands shaking. "No, I'll walk for a bit. You know, there are days when I honestly hate Jade. She is a fucking bitch. And there are days when I love her so much that I feel I can't live without her. I used her, Fen. But she's using me now. She wants to crucify me."

I stare after Miles as he shambles heavily down the stoop and onto the empty sidewalk. Frantic for something to say I call after him. "Chin up Miles—'Cry havoc and let slip the dogs of war!'"

Miles half-turns for a moment and looks back up at me from the sidewalk, his face contorted into a grim smile. The saddest smile I have ever seen. I will not forget it. I muse, *Poor bastard, he's being carried away.*

'A leaf upon the brook of time,'

WH Auden, 1973.

He has no idea what's hit him.

The entire interaction between Miles and me has taken no more than ten minutes. A slice of time I now carry indelibly etched in my memory.

CHAPTER THIRTEEN

Quiescent as a cadaver, Miles lies prone in the hallway of his apartment in a pool of vomit he threw up just before he passed out. His cell phone programed to 'anticipate' rings and vibrates in his jacket, repeating a rising musical scale. At first he does not stir, then as the insistent ringing persists, consciousness seeps slowly into his skull. His body begins to register pain. His head throbs as he begins to haul his 270 pounds from the hallway over to the sofa where he collapses, panting from exertion. The cell rings again, sending its disturbing tones flailing towards his beleaguered ears. Then the phone stops, leaving the room vibrating with silence and the subterranean pounding of his heart as the air pressure blitzes his eardrums.

His black terrors of the previous evening suddenly reignite, chasing ruinously though his imagination like a wounded animal. He whimpers into the crook of his arm, covering his eyes. His turmoil resolves into a question that is grabbed like a lifeline by his intellect. "What's the point?" The question stands stark above the reach of his emotion which ends its churn. "What's the point?" He is suddenly stone-cold sober. The analyst in him ingurgitates the decaying inventory of frustration and disappointment which is his life. "Kids gone. Brother gone. Job gone. Marriage gone. Mom gone." There is a certain order to the drivers of his despair. It is as if he is in a process of deconstruction. "Health gone, bloody diabetes." For a moment he finds himself laughing, "Red Sox gone."

He feels himself disconnected, sinking physically and emotionally into a blackness, a hideous absence of soul, where he is left with only his appetites.

His addictedness to consumption. His yearning to consume alcohol, food, weed, sex, sport, cars, anything that he can experience, anything that he can hold, anything that will be certain, that will fill the absence of things that matter.

Then there is Jade. He sees her standing in the half-light of his room as she had years ago. She was beautiful to him then as now. Admiring of him. Accepting. He wanted to give her the world. She was fun. Alive. His secret love. He wanted to consume her and be consumed by her. It was more than just the sex. It was a compulsion that riveted his heart to the out of control engine of his passion.

And then on the nights when she did not come to him, he would constantly check his messages like a teenager. He had to have her attention. Attention he never got. His addiction for her turned to anger, and anger turned inwards to depression. His days became a long, jejune slog relieved only by an occasional visit with his kids or a game at Fenway Park followed by a fumble with some random admiring woman he picked up at the bar of the Boston Ritz Carlton.

For an instant he wonders if there might be something more. Something outside his submission to the ego-god he has created. From somewhere beyond his understanding, he barely senses a voice he has so long repressed, flickering like a crack of light beneath the knurled door of his darkened soul. For a moment he strains to hear it. He can feel his spirit lift. Then it is as if the possibility of change is extinguished through his tsunami of self.

"Enough!" He says out loud. "Enough!"

He sits up. His head is suddenly clear. He has resolved on a course of action. He showers, feeling light-headed and mildly joyous. Standing naked before the mirror he blow-dries his hair and sprays it admiringly into place. Then dresses in a crisp white shirt, dark blue tie, his best suit and an expensive pair of black wingtip shoes that he has been keeping for a special occasion.

The wall safe opens without protest. It contains a passport, 500 dollars in cash, the key to a deposit box, a picture of his two children and a stainless-steel Smith and Wesson Model 60 revolver, together with a box containing 5 rounds of .357 Magnum ammunition. He has always been fascinated by the gun, particularly the smoothness and high quality of its finish. And as he wraps his fingers around the black plastic grip it feels solid and at once makes him feel calm and secure. He places the revolver in a black leather briefcase and makes for the door, carefully side stepping his vomit which is sinking slowly into the hallway carpet.

By the time his yellow cab rattles up outside the Financial Center, the West Side Highway has assumed its familiar Monday morning roar. He pays the fare with his Amex card, leaving a twenty-dollar tip. "Thanks, Ahmed."

"Thank you, sir!"

He surprises himself by saying a weird, "Have a blessed day," as he exits the cab and steps onto the sidewalk. He pauses, cranes his head back, and looking up wonders why he has never noticed the amazing architectural achievement of the towers that surround him. Entering the Financial Center, he stops off at the Financier Patisserie to pick up a double espresso and a cranberry scone, a combination long his favorite. As he waits for his order a fragment of conversation between baristas drifts by him on the tawdry coffee shop air.

"But Ryan, it's the difference between the ice melting and the ice being there."

He is unsure if this is a discussion about frozen mocha or climate change. Either way the sliver of conversation strikes him as strangely profound. He is the ice. The difference is that shortly he will not be there. "Problem solved," he says to himself.

Holding his building pass and the coffee and bag containing the scone in his right hand and his briefcase in his left, he awkwardly navigates the entrance turnstiles to his office on floor forty. There is an x-ray machine for visitors but he passes through the lobby with his revolver undetected.

By 6:30 Miles is standing at his desk, his immaculate suit jacket hung neatly behind his office door, and begins his daily ritual at his Bloomberg terminal.

His mind is crystal clear. His bloodshot eyes brighten when he sees futures are up twenty-two percent on Friday's close. He sips his espresso, sad and yet strangely content. He walks slowly to his office door, takes his jacket from its wooden hanger and removes two white envelopes from its inside pocket. The first is addressed to his two children, the second to Fen. He lays the letters on his desk, perfectly aligned one above the other, dons his jacket, being careful to pull down his shirtsleeves so his gold cufflinks are just visible, and exits his office.

By 7 am the sun has ascended to scorch the city. The orb hammers at the Hudson as it slithers, as if a shocking brass serpent, between the Manhattan and Jersey skylines. The Investment floor is hushed as if exhausted, awaiting the morning confrontation with the market onslaught. Grace and Fen sit opposite each other at his desk, their heads bowed over copies of the report Grace has prepared on her interviews with Jade Edwards, Miles McCarthy and Peiter Viser. The report headed 'Prepared for Attorney Review, Attorney Client Privilege' is brief and in bullet point format. It outlines the allegations that Edwards has made concerning McCarthy, McCarthy's response, and also Grace's finding on her investigation into Viser, and allegations made by his staff around compliance and employee relations issues.

Fen looks up and is met by Grace's deep burnished eyes. "As I said to you on the phone Grace, it seems to me that there are two quite separate issues here. The assertions made by Edwards and the concerns you raise over Viser." Tom also sits with them around Fen's conference table but chooses to listen rather than contribute.

"You could view them as separate, yes." Grace chooses her words, not sure where Fen will come out having read the report. "But both of these situations occur on Miles's watch and are related to his management. Jade has inferred that she is aware of complaints other than hers, so it's easy to see how both of these situations may come to light as related to each other—they are both evidence, if proven, that the company is enabling a hostile work environment through at best deficient and at worst corrupt management, that it is breaking employment law and financial regulations."

Fen says to himself as much as to Grace, "You can avoid reality but you cannot avoid the consequences of reality."

"Sorry?" Grace is bewildered.

Tom fires off, "It's Ayn Rand," and looks pleased with himself.

"Just a quote, Grace. What's your take on what Edwards told you?"

"Before we go down that rabbit hole Fen, can you corroborate any of this? What do you know?"

"You want to know how far I am implicated in this mess, is that it?" Fen refrains from saying what he is thinking, *Sometimes you may be a bit too smart for your own good, Grace.*

"Well it must be clear to you that you have a pretty vital interest in the outcome of all this. The players here are ultimately under your purview. To be complete, I need to have a statement from you on record as to what you knew and when you knew it."

Fen smiles. "Let the punishment fit the crime..."

Tom sits back, thinking—*You are right, Fen—This is all getting to be a bit like a farce from Gilbert and Sullivan...*

"Here's what I know." Fen's voice is steady. He'd make a good witness. "Edwards was recruited by McCarthy. She has been an excellent hire—so a wise choice on McCarthy's part. Yes, per her statement, she came to me several weeks ago making allegations about McCarthy—mainly that he was being too critical of her in terms of her performance. She also alluded to the fact that their personal relationship was strained. I pointed out that her results and those of her team had indeed been below par over the past few quarters and that she needed to focus on getting out to meet with companies and understand better what is going in the market. I told her that she had great analytical strengths, and stressed several times, as I said, that in order to do better, in addition to digging into the numbers she needed to get out of the office to conferences and clients and broaden her breadth of investment ideas and vision. That numbers can take her so far but that to keep winning she needed to hone her investment instincts. In addition, she needed to engage her team more. I told her that the feedback that comes to me is that she is a driver and not an enabler of her people. She needed to communicate with them better, clarify their roles more and have conversations with them about expectations. It is not that she is not tough—the problem is that she is too tough and that there is no sense of joy in working with her. I also suggested to her that she might want to connect with Dean Harris over in Fixed Income—he is a great leader and from an investment point of view has seen it all.

She said that if she needed a mentor it would need to be someone who knew equity investing and active management. I didn't have the time to argue with her so suggested that we update in thirty days to see how things are going."

"Did you write the conversation up?"

"No, Grace, I didn't write the conversation up. This was not a meeting concerning her performance. It was a meeting initiated by her."

"So, she didn't raise the harassment charges?"

"As I said, she alluded to the fact that their relationship was strained. I heard her, but at the time it didn't sound too serious—not at all a 'Me Too' in the making."

"And that's it?"

"Unfortunately, no."

"You interacted with her again?"

"I had a brief follow up conversation with McCarthy where we agreed to keep her performance under review. I felt uncomfortable instinctively about what she had said regarding her relationship with McCarthy and asked him outright if there was anything going on between them. He denied it, saying anything that she might say about their employment relationship was probably sour grapes, and I didn't push it. When you told me that Grace had made a formal complaint, he called her charge a ruse to divert attention from her performance which has been slipping over several quarters. To answer your question, I have had no further discussion with Edwards since the interaction some weeks ago that I just outlined."

"So, the allegations she is making in her statement are new to you?"

"Not as of this weekend, no."

Tom jumps into the conversation. "Meaning?"

Glancing over at Tom, Fen adds, "McCarthy came to see me yesterday. He told me that he had had a long-term relationship with her, that he'd been screwing her. She wanted to end it. He pursued her, pressured her. He said that Jade didn't deserve the way he'd been trying to get at her."

"Shit."

"Shit indeed. He was in a really bad way. In fact, I was up half the night wondering if he is ok. I tried to reach him on his cell but there was no response."

"This is bad."

"Indeed, this is very bad, Grace. A real Balaclava."

"And what about Viser?"

"Give me some space here Grace. Let's try to defuse one bomb at a time. Look, I've got to go over and meet Christian then I'm tied up till this afternoon. Let's meet here again at two."

***

The route to Jade's office from his takes Miles through the middle of the new biophilic workspace the company has deemed optimal for investment productivity. As he traverses the natural light, plants and organic colors, it strikes him ironic that in practice, the intentionally calming environment provides the jungle of nooks and crannies for the tribalism that consumes the portfolio management teams. He feels the reassuring handle of the pistol in his bulging pocket as a couple of the younger analysts pass him, saying "Hi." He responds with a warmer than usual smile as he reaches the elegant internal glass and steel staircase and walks purposefully around it into Jade's office.

***

Christian is standing, looking out of the window. "Years ago, before my first wife died, she and I saw a yacht named Cunning Linguist while we were sailing off Cape May. She found this hilarious. So, at certain times, I'd whisper to her that she's my little cunning linguist. She couldn't stop laughing." Fen stands next to him as they both stare out towards The Battery. "They want me out, Fen." Christian is tanned as usual from his weekend sailing Long Island Sound. Fen is silent. "It's been in the works a while, I know. Anne says I should just walk but I'm damned if I'm rolling over for a shark like Frost."

There are helicopters hovering over the vicinity of Governors Island. Two more marked 'Police' pass the Tower, flying like wasps towards the others, their dull roar penetrating the window. "The board won't let him ditch me. He's obsessed with the idea of selling us. What a jerk. He's done nothing since he got into that job." Christian gurgles on, his words lost on Fen who has heard it all time and time again. "It's not as if we haven't been winning; assets are up, sales are up, investment performance is up. Sure, we might not be growing as fast as some may wish and sure, margins have declined a bit, but we are still a tremendous buy." The less Fen speaks the more Christian's feelings overflow, a cascade of accusations, fears and regrets. "I really don't know what the bastard wants other than complete control. All of them sit up there in Corporate but have no idea how a business like this is run. They all grandstand. Say nothing when we are doing well but are the first to drop all kinds of shit on us when the going gets tough. Then there's the way they are always trying to interfere in pay and bonuses. Now he wants to be informed if we make any major hires or fire any of my direct reports. This is becoming a bureaucratic nightmare. And the bastard lies all the time. He quotes facts which are flat out not true in meetings with the board and expects me to back him up. Then when I do and he gets caught out by a board member who has actually done some analysis on the board book exhibits on performance, he accuses me of providing him with bad information." Something causes Fen to look away from the window to check out the TV screen in the hallway visible from Christian's office.

The bloody red headline running across the bottom of the screen---SHOOTER INCIDENT TWO SHOT ON GOVERNORS ISLAND NEW YORK---STAY TUNED FOR MORE NEWS---Fen turns back to the window remaining silent, aware but not attending to Christian's words.

"And then he's parachuted all these people in. Basically, Aiello is a plant. This new CFO is so shit-scared of his own shadow I have no confidence that he will represent things in the right way. Grace's loyalties are very much questionable too, in my book. I think Tom is pretty solid—we have a sales camaraderie given all those years here in the trenches together. But it's really you and Cynthia that I trust, Fen. You are a supporter, Fen, you are on-side, aren't you?" Christian touches Fen lightly on the arm. "I said, you are on-side, aren't you?" Fen's stomach turns.

The flurry with the helicopters appears to be over as the choppers peel off to the south and west towards Newark Airport.

Fen decides to use diversion as a way to avoid Christian's question. "The situation with McCarthy and Edwards is looking problematic." Fen continues to look out of the window rather than at Christian as he speaks.

"I feared that it might come to this. Grace briefed me when you were in London. One way or the other this is going to be a load that lands at my door. You see, Frost will use this against us, specifically me. It's not as if they are actually paying me for this. My bonus last year was way off. Compared to the guys in the other divisions I'm plain underpaid. When I think of how I have built this place. To be expected to deliver as I have year on year and never to be recognized for it, it's disgusting. I've built this place basically single-handed. And to be told that our return on capital employed is unacceptable is—unacceptable! Who thought of that measure anyway? I tell you: those guys upstairs are full of it. You know, for years we basically kept this entire organization afloat with outstanding returns—shoveling in revenues, building assets, grabbing share and generating cash with the float. Life was fun, the business was full of possibilities. Now is any of that good enough? No! Now we're told that we've got to focus on combining capital and operational expenditure—it's all about whole-life costing. Between that and the regulators choking us off, things are simply less interesting. Fen, have you any idea what it's like to spend a day with Frost and company explaining how we developed a system for measuring the effectiveness of our asset management systems?" It's a rhetorical question, but Christian is by no means finished. "In the old days..."

Fen tunes Christian out as he raves on. Fen is seriously conflicted. He feels a great deal of empathy with Christian's profound isolation and vulnerability that drives his ranting, but also guilt that he has accepted the thirty pieces of silver offered by Frost. He respects the man personally but sees Christian as essentially incompetent as a business leader. *Or is that just my way of justifying betrayal?*

"Why are you holding on, Christian?"

"Holding on to what?"

"Your job, Christian. Why take all this?"

"It's who I am, Fen. I came here twenty-five years ago. I am this place. I breathe and sleep this culture."

"But can't you see yourself as doing something more?"

"Oh, you mean a round every morning and watching reruns in the afternoon? It would kill me, Fen."

"So, you will never let go?"

"Not till they pry the place from my dead hands," Christian says with a smile. "That was Charlton Heston, wasn't it?"

"Yes, 'from my cold dead hands' I think—'I'll give you my gun when you can pry it from my cold dead hands.' He also said. 'There are no good guns. There are no bad guns. Any gun in the hands of a decent person is no threat to anybody except bad people.' And how has that worked out for everybody?"

"You're funny, Fen. Always got an angle, always got some sort of quote."

The air is suddenly splintered by a loud alien crack followed instantaneously by something screeching for a millisecond like a fingernail on a blackboard. The piercing stills time. Fen and Christian are frozen to the spot. Silence fills the sudden void around them like a bewildering shroud. A moment later a horrendous wailing scream rends the air.

"No! No! No!" reaches them as they still stand transfixed.

"That was a gun." Christian is flinging his office door open and running, pursued by Fen, towards the sound of a woman's voice wailing. Christian, ahead by a few feet shouts, "It's from down on thirty-nine." Both men clatter down the staircase, throwing themselves headlong towards the sound of sobbing.

What's left of Miles is slumped across Jade's desk. On entering Jade's office, Fen is immediately struck by Miles's empty right hand, which is dangling from the edge of the desk, almost imperceptibly twitching. Jade is spattered with blood and pieces of brain and is cowering as she convulses with primeval whimpering, her back against the bookcase behind her desk. Her hands pushing at the air, her fingers spread wide, as if by pushing she will ward off Miles's body. The office is like a scene from a profane Netflix police procedural, except the blood which seems to be everywhere is a glossy reddish brown and already congealing. Fen notices that the blood dripping from one of the framed posters on Jade's office wall is obscuring the Mandarin characters for 'crisis'. His head goes off on a rant about how many people have misunderstood the etymology—"Not danger plus opportunity," he says to himself, "the Kennedy speech and Gore got the trope wrong. It means a point where things change."

While Fen is standing rigid with his relentless abstraction, Christian has stepped around Jade's desk and is supporting her as she slumps in his arms. The acrid smell of the gunshot hangs on the air.

"He just came in here. 'This is for you, Jade' he said, and put that gun in his mouth. His eyes were locked right on mine. Why does he hate me like this? Why does he hate me?" Later, Fen will recall the pallor of her skin and thinking that she also had the look of the deceased, as if something in her soul had been extinguished.

Employees attracted by the pandemonium have gathered outside Jade's door and stand transfixed like Fen. One of the cluster is retching in reaction to the harrowing scene, another simply runs away, screaming hysterically. Someone has broken the glass to the fire alarm which is now blaring and flashing an angry strobe light across the ceiling.

Christian gradually leads Jade around her desk and past Miles's prone body. "Get back. Give us space, will you!" He guides her to a chair in the shared workspace a few yards down the hall.

Fen kneels by Jade and finds himself saying, "It's okay, Jade. It's over. You're safe," and placing a gray raincoat that someone has passed to him around Jade's shoulders. Instantly the coat takes on traces of spattered blood from Jade's dress and hands and face. Fen wants to vomit but instead grips Jade's arm tight.

Christian leaves Jade with Fen and returns to Jade's office and carefully closes the door, entombing Miles's corpse, which remains visible through the blood-spattered glass wall. The cacophony of sirens arriving at the building competes with the fire alarm which continues to beat mercilessly at the lurid air.

"Everybody!" Christian shouts commands against the hysterical din of the fire alarm. "Gather in the elevator hall till the emergency services get here. Is there a fire warden here?" Someone waves over to him. "Treat this like one of the evacuations you've practiced. Sweep the floor then keep everyone in the elevator hall until the responders get here." The floor empties itself of terror-stricken employees who comfort each other by the elevators. Christian and Fen stand over Jade who is still convulsed by the trauma. Christian takes Jade's hand and squats beside her. "It's not your fault, Jade. It's not your fault. It will be all right, Jade."

The world seems to stop for Fen. He stands with his eyes closed, arms folded tight across his chest, his head inclined towards the floor. He feels as if a rock is pulling him to the floor. His head throbs as if he has been hit very hard in his face. His hearing feels impaired. The alarm sweeping over his senses makes him nauseous. But above all he feels as if he is in a movie where everything is oddly unreal. He has moved from a state of reality and consciousness into some horrific alternative version of the world that has totally sapped his resilience.

After what seems like interminable deafening noise, the alarm stops. A fireman appears, together with a security officer who is nervously carrying his gun.

"Over here!" Christian waves. Moments later the floor is swarming with emergency personnel and police. Jade is taken off on a stretcher, accompanied by Christian's assistant, whom he has called down from the floor above.

"Come by the elevator, Andrea," Christian tells her over his cell. "Don't use the stairs." Christian, who has remained perfectly calm and self-possessed through the entire incident, has made a number of calls. To Grace, to invoke emergency procedures for employees; to Lucas and Tiffany, to handle the operational response to the evacuation; to Abby, to initiate PR readiness; to Cynthia, for legal purposes; and to inform Frost. He has also called an emergency meeting in his office with the Senior Leadership Group for noon.

Christian is high on adrenalin and addresses Fen, "Fen, you'd better get moving on this too." Fen, at first pacing outside Grace's office, now sits on the edge of a chair in the hallway with his head in his hands, a few feet from Grace's door.

"Sorry?"

"You need to provide some leadership to the Investment team. Get the team leads together. Tell them that there's been an incident. Invoke whatever procedures are required on trading etc., so we continue to manage the portfolios."

"Yes. Okay. Sure, Christian." And with that Fen wanders, listless and in shock, back to his office, where he paces up and down, feeling suddenly cold.

The morning's sudden trauma has bifurcated the two men. Christian is invigorated, his years of training in the Marines resurfacing to provide him with the clarity and confidence that has been for so long absent. He is in his element. Ordering the tangible.

Fen by contrast is driven into the night of his mental labyrinth where everything is uncertain, particularly what to do next. His mind is blank. He keeps rerunning the sight of Miles across Jade's desk, and Jade making odd motions as if to push Miles's corpse away. He is sickened by the thought of Miles pinioned to the rigging of his life, feeling that each day was filled with the carnage of wrecked dreams. He picks up his cell. "You've reached the voice mail of Dr Cait Morgan. Please leave a message and..." He keeps trying but she does not answer. On his fourth attempt he sees that she's calling him from her office. "I thought you weren't going in today?"

"What's going on, you sound frantic?"

"It's Miles."

"Miles?"

"He's dead."

"My God! Dead. What happened?"

"He shot himself."

"What?"

"He shot himself. Blew his head right off in front of Jade Edwards." As he hears himself speak, he realizes how utterly unreal it sounds.

"Did you see it happen?"

"No. Christian and I heard a shot and we ran down to her office and there he was. Blood everywhere. She was hysterical."

"Did he say anything?"

"Who?"

"Miles."

"No, he was dead at the time."

"I meant did he make any comment. Leave any note explaining why?"

"Pretty obvious isn't it?"

"So, you and Christian found him?"

"Yes."

"What happened to Jade?"

"She's gone to the hospital with one of the staff but physically she's okay. Didn't suffer any injury. Other than being covered in blood and the blast."

"No other injuries?"

"No. A lot of people are going to be traumatized."

"And what about you, Fen?"

"Had better mornings."

There is silence. Cait knows that he is processing and says nothing as she thinks, *His mind works like the rotating SPOD on a computer screen— spinning pizza of death in this case. God, I'm becoming more like him!*

Fen speaks uncharacteristically slowly, guilt weighing on his every word. "How did I not see this coming? He was right there in our house but all I wanted to do was to get him out of the door. He needed me and I failed him."

"You are not God, Fen. There are limits on what you can do to fix things, you know."

The line is silent for a long time.

"Guilt will crush you Fen."

Silent for a long minute he replies, "But none of us wants to take responsibility do we Cait? We spend our lives avoiding ownership because ownership might threaten our survival." His head is pounding. He is desperate.

"You're talking about big things here, Fen. You are in shock."

"It feels as if it's all connected, Cait. Christian was unloading on me this morning. He has no real idea of what's coming or how I am involved in it and when it comes out that one of his closest friends has been part of the plot to get him out, he is going to feel totally betrayed and he is going to be right. I am the Judas who has betrayed him. It feels like Miles is in my head. As if I'm shooting dead any kind of integrity that I have left." He is standing, his back to the door. The sun has climbed well clear of the grasp of the surrounding buildings.

"You are going to need to forgive yourself for this, Fen."

"Cait, sorry. I will have to call you back."

Grace has entered his office with Tiffany. Grace speaks first. "Are you all right Fen?"

"Yes, just absorbing it all." He sits in his chair, his right hand over his mouth and his nausea as he stares at Grace. She notices his left hand is shaking. He senses her glance and moves both hands beneath his desk.

Tiffany pushes on like a hydrant. "I've activated the DR plan. The Team Leads and Trading have got the portfolios in hand. We've directed everyone who wasn't already in the office to work from home today."

Grace adds, "So everyone is working the alternative work plan routine. The police have cordoned off this floor and thirty-nine. I understand that it will be out of use for a few days, treated as a crime scene."

"Yes, I got a call from a Detective Brose. They are going to want to interview you and Christian and everyone who was in the office when the incident occurred."

Fen is very slowly recovering himself. He is numb, shell shocked, his emotion still gripping his intellect. As Tiffany speaks Fen feels himself to be dislocated from his body. Tiffany is talking but he is not absorbing her words, rather, he is struck by her efficient grasp of mechanics and total lack of emotion. It is clear that she is unaffected by Miles's death, that a man has killed himself a few yards from her office.

"They have asked that you remain in your office until they come by to see you, Fen." Tiffany looks at Fen, not entirely sure what to make of the hand over his mouth and his closed eyes.

"I reached out to our employee assistance people and they're going to get a team down here for trauma counseling. You all right, Fen?"

Fen hears Grace from somewhere near and makes an effort to swim out and up through his devastated senses towards what she is saying. Grace repeats her question "Are you all right, Fen?"

"Oh yes, very good. Fine, Grace." Recovered a little, he begins to find these questions about his well-being uncomfortably intrusive. And wonders what it is about his demeanor that is eliciting these questions? He has no idea that his body language is so fetal.

"So, you will dial into the ten o'clock emergency staff meeting?"

"And what about the two of you?" he says, pushing back at the question.

"Grace and I are good, Fen. Christian asked us to make sure his directs are contacting their reports just to make sure they are good too."

"OK, got it," he says as they walk out of his office.

Fen is off walking too. Walking over to Parliament Hill Fields across the sandy void of Hampstead Heath. There is a slight breeze. His feet traverse a thousand cavities and pits in the turf as he follows the broad track between the limes and dark firs mixed with beech trees that fringe the Heath. It is mid-year an ocean of summers ago. He has walked with Cait up from Wentworth House where Keats had walked with his fiancée, Fanny Brawne, up to the lip of Parliament Hill. London is three hundred feet below them, shrouded in a panoramic haze as the sun sears off the early morning mist. He and Cait stand in awe of the view.

"Why would we ever want to leave this, Fen?" Cait is leaning on his shoulder.

"Why indeed," he murmurs in response. As they stand in silence, he remembers the words engraved on Keats's gravestone.

'Here lies One whose Name was writ in Water.'

John Keats, 1821.

He drifts back to the present, *strangely apposite*, he says to himself. *Miles, your name is indeed water now, quite liquidated and erased. Except perhaps for a guest appearance in a confession to a priest or tale to a stranger on a flight to Asia.* He smiles a bitter smile.

Reluctant to emerge from the maudlin yet healing balm of his reverie, he procrastinates further. As he does so, gazing out of his office window, his eyes fall upon the dark of the Hudson sliding stealthily below in the shadow of the towering office blocks. He remembers a verse from his childhood.

'Darkness was upon the face of the deep
and the spirit of God was hovering over the face of the waters.'
Genesis 1:2

He savors the juxtaposition of the face of the deep, the emotions, terror, torment and loss he has just experienced, with the idea that God is somehow near to lives writ in water.

"But where is God when you need him?" he asks himself.

CHAPTER FOURTEEN

I am back at my desk on the other side of the yellow tape that now serves as the boundary of the crime scene. Post trauma I feel myself to be shut in, and focus on my computer screen as I work through the mountain of electronic messages and chat which is demanding my attention. As if trapped in some bizarre remake of Groundhog Day, I pause for a moment and wipe a hand across my face, trying to repress images of the morning's events and those from previous days which keep winding through my head. Apparently, remarkably in control of myself and the situation as I activated the disaster recovery plan, only the set of my jaw as I clenched my teeth will have betrayed the stress I was experiencing. But no one will have been watching me.

My phone rings.

"Grace Rutler."

"It's Tom."

"Hi Tom, can I call you back?" *I'm drowning. I'm not sure I can hold it together. The last thing I need right now is a session with a corporate lawyer.*

"I think it's a matter of urgency that we talk now, Grace. In fact, I think it's vital we meet in person." Tom's voice is cold, any intimacy we shared has dissipated.

"This place is like the little shop of horrors, Tom."

"I can imagine." He has little empathy. "Can you come over here to the law library? Hudgell wants to see you asap."

It is as if another great weight has been placed about my shoulders. "Okay, I will come over as soon as the police are through with me. I have to stay in my office now until they have interviewed me."

***

The dull buzz of the restroom's fluorescent light is suffused with the whisper of air-conditioning and odor of sweet, superior grade, industrial freshener, which flits into the brooding air with a hiss, marking every ninety seconds. A deep-buttoned red leather couch sits pretentiously opposite the vacant toilet stalls.

Standing before the large silver framed mirror, which looms over four wash basins, I lean forward and bow my head as I push the palms of my hands against the stark white marble sink top adorned with a single red rose. The rose droops in a small crystal vase.

The pit in my stomach draws the heaviness of my forehead and aching shoulders down towards the cold slate-tiled floor. Quite suddenly, I am utterly exhausted, isolated and alone, floundering breathlessly as if hermetically sealed in a web of emotions totally beyond my control.

Grasping for the surface of my senses, I force my head up and gaze at my face in the mirror. My dismayed eyes peer accusingly back, as tears begin to make their way slowly down my cheeks. I observe this, somehow separated from myself, as if I were a stranger. I am angry, furious with myself, with Miles, the weakness of Fen and all the fucking men that surround me. Exhausted and nauseous, I debate the merits of falling to the floor and curling up against the wall.

Not here, not now, get a grip. Pull yourself together.

My mind is crowded with the many times and places before this when I have felt the same sense of desolation, where the cost of my career has been to me like a hunting knife carried dangerously close to my heart, compelling me to cut to the core of any deep tendon that threatened to be a loving relationship. For a moment, rational thought tops my emotion, I speculate as to whether my absorption with climbing the greasy pole of career, business priorities, petty crises, status, and money has compromised my capacity to think, or connect emotionally. As I look upon my reflection, I know myself to be desirable, yet simultaneously, in a moment of self-knowledge, I know myself to be spiritually unformed. My mantra of working like a dog, having a good time with friends and traveling to exotic places is the kick, is the reward. Getting ahead is the prize. This morning, the mantra feels cold. As cold, unappealing and dead as Miles's corpse.

I rinse my face with tepid water and begin to fix my makeup.

My image in the mirror draws me towards her. *Well if you are so smart, you tell me what was the alternative? Stay on Long Island? Do the two kids and a mortgage thing and lose my mind? Or break out. Get a life, compete, be somebody. And why shouldn't I have that? What's wrong with that?* The eyes that stare back at me are heavy with sadness.

There had been Peter. I unfold his secreted memory. Peter, who has haunted my dreams for a decade, the phantom troubadour from the life I might have had. I met him on Corfu. A summer junket with the girls, and then suddenly Him. I see him now standing on a wall above the beach at Palaiokastritsa, his boyish grin challenging me from under his battered panama. The kaleidoscopic synesthesia of days that followed are hardwired into my memory. The hours of light chatter in a cool taverna, drinking cheap ouzo. Walking up the rocky path to the monastery teetering on the bright white promontory high above the cobalt sea, we wander amongst the last orgasm of blazing wildflowers, orchids and butterflies. The caw and wailing of gulls as they whirl around our heads, a fresco of grey and white painted into the neon blue sky. And then the nights spent in the ecstasy of finding one another and the earnest conversation that followed. His broad Australian accent softened by years of study at medical school has retained its edge. He is direct and subversive as his eyes sparkle with humor. We talk of the endless war and of the refugee camps in Lebanon where half a million languish. Of his work as a doctor with the UNRWA. Of the guilt of my cosseted life in the US. He taunts me, 'This is not real. Your easy life in America is not real. In the camps, that's where it's real' Listening to his voice I am intoxicated by desire. Desire for him, for the life he represents, for escape from the mundane. He writes his contact information in pencil on a piece of ragged paper and hands it to me with a lone wildflower as he is leaving. 'Come see me in Lebanon. We eat proper food there!' We lock eyes as he powers up his ancient rented Vespa and dissolves into the warm lethargy of a Mediterranean afternoon.

***

Summoned to the meeting by Tom, I am trying to divine Hudgell's intentions as we sit in opposition to each other, across the conference table in the Pompton Financial Law Library. Hudgell is flanked by Tom and a half-dozen other male flunkies who sit like the chorus in a Greek tragedy, apparently charged with taking notes. It seems as if I have entered an alternative universe. I am Alice at the Mad Hatter's tea party. As Hudgell broods amongst his minions, he reminds me of a large snapping turtle I once saw in shallow waters under the arch of a bridge in New Jersey. It waited, like an ancient dinosaur, reptilian jaws biting viciously at the swirling eddy that surrounded its gnarled wagging head. The Archelon was deliberate, cold, hard and dangerous to the feet. I want to scream but think better of it. Although I have been around corporate bureaucracy for years, I smell the sense of unfamiliar panic in the room. The atmosphere is out of balance, like the seating at the table. There are no introductions. Those present know who I am. It is apparently unnecessary for them to be introduced to me.

Hudgell, who has been instructed by Frost to get things under control, is presiding over a hurriedly convened inquisition. My inquisitor in his stiff exoskeleton, is adorned by his customary white button-down shirt, blue striped tie and customary grey pinstriped suit. His skin is drawn as tight leather across his expressionless face. He peers from his hooded eyes and resumes his questioning.

"Continue." There is an arrogant edge to Hudgell's voice which he has honed to menace.

"Continue?" I repeat refusing to play his game, meeting his gaze as I sit isolated opposite my antagonist.

"With your account," he says sourly, as he waits to devour my words in the watery current of mistrust that flows between us.

Perhaps my body language conveys distaste, signaling, *this guy is on a real power trip*. Nevertheless, I compose myself and address the question at hand. "That's about the sum of it. We knew Miles was under pressure, but we had no idea that he would do what he did."

"So, you are not aware of any previous behavior in the workplace that could have reasonably led you to believe that he was a danger to himself or anyone else?" Hudgell demands of me.

My antennae are up. "Peter, what are you trying to get at in this conversation?" I glance at Tom who sits, with his eyes down, taking notes, reinforcing my sense of quarantine. *Hello stranger, fancy meeting you here!*

"I am establishing a fact base, Grace, while all this is fresh in your mind," Hudgell replies.

"So, the conversation is about liability?" I ask.

"No, but clearly there is a lot of exposure here," Hudgell replies impatiently.

"I can see that. But it feels awfully like you are trying to apportion some kind of blame."

Hudgell ignores my comments and snaps out another question. "You think the situation is contained?"

"No guarantees. I've no idea what the police will turn up, what story the press will tell and perhaps the real wild card in all this is Jade Edwards."

"Where is she now?" Tom asks.

"She was released from the emergency room and taken to her home by Christian's assistant Andrea." Our eyes meet with my reply. I am beginning to think that he may not be on my side.

"Has she been told not to talk to the press?" Another question from Hudgell.

"No, we didn't give her a briefing on how to deal with the press as she stood soaked in blood and brains." Sarcasm drips between us. My instinct cuts in. *Don't go too far, girl. Stay focused!*

"What's the status of business operations?" It is clear that Hudgell is working down a checklist.

"We have implemented our disaster recovery plan. Investment and administrative staff here in New York are working remotely. Trades are being conducted as required. The operations center in Phoenix is not impacted—other than by the obvious emotional impact of hearing someone in New York blew their head off," I say, loading my reply with scorn.

Hudgell shifts in his chair. "How is the management team reacting?"

"A few of us were impacted directly because we were on the floor at the time of the incident. Others were informed and have been focused on getting things done." I find myself asking, *What do you want me to say, 'All present and correct sir!'?*

"And Christian?"

"He's really stepped up to it, taken control and has called a meeting for noon." Saying this I take an ostentatious look at my watch.

"Interesting. And Fen?" Hudgell says doggedly.

"Fen? Fen has taken it hard. He has done what he needs to. But he is at the center of this. Miles was a longtime acquaintance, if not friend, as well as a subordinate so he's confronted with the crisis at several levels." As I say this, I try not to betray my sense of deep disappointment at how Fen has been essentially absent from required action, leaving all the operational complexity caused by the suicide to me and Tiffany. *He is a nice enough guy,* I opine silently, *but essentially he's an introvert, incapable of leadership in this type of crisis. Beyond this I find myself intensely frustrated by and critical of his self-absorption. Harsh criticisms, I tell myself. But accurate.*

"What's Lucas Aiello doing?" Hudgell asks, pushing me further. I sense that my assessment of Lucas will be taken as a measure of my loyalty to Frost and Hudgell.

"I've called him but he was in late today so I've not spoken to him directly." I decide on a new tack. "Peter, I very much appreciate your interest and support in all this. But it's important that I get back over there to stay on top of events. We have a management meeting planned for noon, as I said, and there are going to be a thousand questions that need answers. And by the way, why isn't Al here?"

Uncharacteristically, Hudgell hesitates, then issues a curt instruction. "Can you give us the room please, gentlemen? I'll catch you after lunch. Tom, you can stay." The Chorus troops out unsmilingly in an awkward silence.

"We have something of a crisis on our hands up here at the corporate level too, Grace." Hudgell's tone is different. Factual rather than challenging. I sense that he needs something from me.

I exchange looks with Tom and say under my breath. *No shit, Sherlock.*

"A number of events are converging to make this critical," Hudgell says.

At this point John Frost enters the room unannounced and sits at the far end of the conference table. Frost and Hudgell exchange nods. Frost is imposing, in full executive suite battle dress, tailored white shirt with Windsor collar and red Hermes necktie, Amedeo Testoni antiqued leather Oxford shoes. His hair is newly cropped short, he looks crisp, fit, and to me very sure of himself, as if he has just walked off the shoot for the July cover of Black Enterprise Magazine, that featured him as the Most Powerful US Black Executive.

Frost chimes in with his genial southern tone. "The men who just left are lawyers from our investment bankers and the law firm guiding us through the XelFunds sale. What just happened is obviously a major threat to the transaction. In addition, you should know that Al Jiminez is no longer with the corporation." He is warm and conspiratorial, and not at all the voice I expect. It is as if we are old intimates meeting after far too long. "You've done well, Grace. I'm counting on you to do more. You've got to hold them together." It occurs to me that he has been listening in on the meeting. "Fen is the key here. You have got to ensure that he comes through this with flying colors. We can't let these events put us back. I still plan to move on taking Christian out later this week. The logistics remain. We execute the leadership change this Wednesday."

I touch my temple with my left hand then reach for the tray of cut-glass tumblers on the middle of the table. "I see." I pour the effervescent water into the glass, hoping to conceal my surprise.

"And Grace," Frost beams at me, he is almost cherubic, "I am expecting that this will go well. It's my legacy. And I'm expecting you to do well." He pauses as if the thought is new to him, "Should I conjure with your name as a lead candidate for head of corporate HR?"

I think, *He is playing me. You have to hand it to him: he knows just how to manipulate.* "I guess you have to decide that for yourself," I say this as Frost rises from the table and steps towards the door.

Frost turns and again smiles at me, his face half-lit, half-dark, in the seduction of the late morning sun.

The noon meeting called by Christian is cancelled. He has too much to do. He texts the Senior Leadership Group. 'You must row own boats until we can catch up at the off-site Wednesday. Call me if you need.'

Later, I walk by Fen's office. Eyes closed, he is still sitting at his desk after his interview with the police. I imagine he is constantly replaying his conversations with Miles and the sight of his ruined body across Jade's desk. There is a book open before him. I pass his office again fifteen minutes later and see him determinedly pick up his phone and then appear agitated as he speaks to someone.

An hour later I return. Everyone has left for the day. I enter Fen's office and see the book on his desk is open at The Second Coming, written by Yeats in 1919.

'Turning and turning in the widening gyre
The falcon cannot hear the falconer;
Things fall apart; the center cannot hold:
Mere anarchy is loosed upon the world,
The blood dimmed tide is loosed and everywhere
The ceremony of innocence is drowned;
The best lack all conviction, while the worst
Are full of passionate intensity.'
W. B. Yeats, 1919.

CHAPTER FIFTEEN

They have stumbled out of their beds at some forsaken hour, hauled themselves out to the Glen Cove Conference Center on Long Island, to talk strategy. The dinner planned for the meeting kick-off was cancelled in the chaotic days following Miles's suicide, the balance of the meeting truncated. The meeting room, which is uncomfortably large, is chilled like the atmosphere between the members of the senior leadership team. In the middle of the conference room a U-shaped table sits like three adjoining coffins shrouded in a white sheet.

The events of earlier in the week loom over them. No one wants to talk about what just happened. The individual interviews conducted by the police into the circumstances of Miles's suicide still reverberate around their heads.

The questions asked of Fen in his office by Officer Brose, a young black police detective chewing gum, seem relentless. They sit at his oval conference table late on the morning of Miles's suicide. Brose peers accusingly at him over her black-rimmed eyeglasses. Her braided hair pulled back stretches the skin over veins which protrude on her imposing forehead. She notes what he is saying in a black leather notebook using a pencil. Her fingernails are short and well-scrubbed.

"What is it you do here, Mr. Morgan?" Brose's voice is pitched low and pugnacious. Fen immediately feels he is the accused.

"I am the Chief Investment Officer," he says with some diffidence as he feels his insides scream, *I confess, I am guilty.*

"That makes you Mr. McCarthy's boss, right?"

"Yes."

"How long have you known Mr. McCarthy?" Brose is wearing a creased green linen jacket that is losing its composition, and a 'Pride' rainbow lapel pin.

"We've worked together for seven years," Fen says, looking uneasy.

"How would you describe your relationship with Mr. McCarthy?"

"We have, I mean had, a good working relationship."

"You were confident in his abilities?" Officer Brose asks.

The inevitable internal rant begins in Fen's head, *Miles's abilities to do what? Hold himself together? See the point in living? Stay off the sauce? To understand why he was drowning? To reach beyond himself?* Deadpan, Fen replies, "Yes."

"Where were you earlier today?" Brose inquires.

"I've been in this building this entire day," The questions Brose continues to ask are walking towards the inevitable examination of Miles's weekend conversation with Fen until they tread where Fen fears most, "So, Mr. McCarthy contacted you over the weekend?"

"Yes," Fen answers.

"Was that usual?" Brose says, looking at her notebook.

"It was not unusual for him to call me at any time over a business issue. It was unusual for him to arrive unannounced at my house."

"Did he seem changed in any way when you met with him?" Fen is hardly listening to the officer's questions, he is back with Miles hearing his voice, seeing his hands shake.

"He was very upset. One of his team had made a complaint against him. And he was clearly terrified about what was likely to happen."

"What sort of accusation?"

"That he had been harassing her."

"What is the employee's name?" Brose asks.

"Jade Edwards," Fen replies.

"And it was in Ms. Edwards' office that the incident occurred?"

"Yes," Fen answers.

"Was the accusation true?"

"He said that he had been pursuing a relationship with her. His marriage was over, it was complex." Fen notices that Officer Brose has traces of a scar on her left cheek. The skin is flattened and darker in tone than the rest of her face. Evidence of a knife or bottle wound perhaps? "The company has been conducting an investigation into the matter. He had been questioned by HR recently."

"So, what did you do?"

"I listened to him. Gave him a drink. Told him not to worry." Fen is looking down at the yellow pad of lined paper on the desk before him, trying to concentrate on counting the number of lines. Perhaps if he concentrates hard enough Officer Brose will leave, along with the pain of what he must recall.

"Not to worry about what in particular?"

"I felt that he was overthinking the situation. That the situation would probably be resolved somehow."

"Was that realistic?"

"I was also concerned that..." Fen's voice fades as he again focuses on the pad of paper, on which he has written MILES in block capitals.

"Concerned that what, Mr. Morgan?" Brose says, closing off Fen's retreat.

"That he might get overwrought if I didn't try to calm him down. He had obviously come to me to get some sort of reassurance."

"And you gave it to him, knowing there was an ongoing investigation into his conduct. Was that wise, Mr. Morgan?"

"Is this an interrogation of my behavior or an enquiry into why McCarthy killed himself?"

"Why, do you think they are linked?" Brose says, her voice implacable.

Fen does not answer. *And there you have it, ladies and gentlemen of the jury. The officer believes I am morally culpable. I watched and purposely, knowingly, recklessly and negligently let Miles walk to his suicide? The foreman rises before the judge. Yes, your honor he is culpable.*

"And then he left? Mr. Morgan?"

Fen is lost in thought. "Sorry, I missed your question."

"And then he left?" Brose repeats the question.

"Yes, then he left. He was only with me for a short time, maybe twenty minutes."

"Did he threaten anybody at that time?" Brose says, her eyes remorselessly scouring Fen's demeanor.

"Don't be ridiculous. I have told you he was upset. He came to me for reassurance. No, he did not threaten anyone." Fen's mind goes back to Sunday and processes the chain of events. *Miles was certainly angry with Jade. But how could I know that he was so angry with himself he would take his own life? Had I listened. Had I not been so anxious to rid myself of him. Were I not so fucking angry with him for shitting on his own doorstep and mine, I might have seen what was going on with him. But what are you, Fen, a clinical psychiatrist or a money manager? Neither.* He excoriates himself. *You are a human being who has no fucking empathy because you are so self-obsessed.*

"Did he indicate that he was depressed at any time?"

"I am not a shrink. I can't pronounce on his mental state. I just told you he seemed terrified and I think very sad. Does that count as depressed? You tell me," Fen says, his voice petulant.

"Was he isolated?"

"I wouldn't have said so until now."

"Who was he close to?"

"Me. I suppose." There is now a hollowness to Fen's response. He is close to an emotional collapse. He is barely running on an orphaned mental acuity. "I wouldn't say he was close to anyone. I don't know."

"Had he ever complained of being intimidated?" Brose asks.

"He was too big for that."

"What was his family situation?"

Fen wants to say 'desolate'. "I just told you!" Fen's frustration is obvious. He is beginning to really dislike Brose.

"Did he have a history of mental illness?" Brose is undeterred.

"Not to my knowledge." Fen rolls his eyes.

"Had Mr. McCarthy ever used drugs?"

"How would I know?"

"Do you have a drug screening policy?"

"Yes."

"Did he ever test positive?"

"No, not to my knowledge," Fen says. His arms folded, leaning back in his chair. The emotion rolling over him has left him splenetic.

"Do you or your family use drugs?"

"That's ridiculous. My wife is a doctor. I am not going to answer that," Fen says.

"Have you ever seen drugs used in the workplace?"

"Obviously not. Are your questions about Mr. McCarthy or are you trawling, Officer?"

"Mr. Morgan, you may find these questions invasive but we often find that drug use plays a major role in workplace crime."

"So, you are treating this as a crime?"

"We have to cover all the bases."

"Had he discussed ending his life with you?"

"No." Every question now reverberates around Fen's head—*That is a lie, Fen. You know that's what he was really telling you! But he never actually said it outright did he, Fen? You are Jack Flash; you are clear on that one!*

"Were you aware of his relationship with Jade Edwards before she made her complaint?"

"I knew they were close. I didn't know how close or make it my business to find out." *You have me there, Brose!*

"Have you ever seen Mr. McCarthy in possession of a firearm?"

"No."

"Is there anything else that I should have asked or that you want to tell me about Mr. McCarthy or this situation?"

"No, you covered everything. How long is this process going to take?"

"We have to question management and everyone associated with the case so we will be around for a couple of weeks probably." As she stands to leave Officer Brose hands him her card. He thinks about saying something about putting her on his Christmas list. Brose says in a weary voice, "Call me if anything occurs to you."

"What about getting back into the office space?" Fen asks, drained.

"It will take a week or so to clear the area, after that you will have access. We will keep you informed."

Brose departs, leaving Fen to reflect on her questions. He feels as if he has been assaulted. He is numb. What does she think of him? In what other circumstances would their paths cross? He knows that she has got the measure of him. She is right to accuse him. He knows himself to be incapable of truth-telling.

Fen sits silently with the Senior Leadership Group at the conference table, their heads bowed in reverence to their iPhones as they engage in their morning devotional to electronic messages, the market and social media. Their names are written on tent cards which sit on the table, with binders containing a copy of the program for the off-site and required prework, together with yellow notepads and pencils.

Fen, sitting at the center of the table, breaks the silence and asks, "The funeral is a week today, is that right, Grace?"

"Yes, that is right, Fen; or at least that is what the family is planning on now. Timing is a bit vague given the body has yet to be released by the coroner."

"Seems a hell of a time since he died," Lucas says coldly.

"The police have been following their investigative process, I guess."

Fen adds, "Where is the funeral to be, Grace?"

"Just heard this morning. Concord, Mass, outside Boston. It seems the family has a plot up there and the cemetery is prepared to take him."

John asks Grace, "Any thoughts on who should represent the company?"

"I think that's an individual rather than a corporate decision, John. I will be going up. You too, Fen?"

"Yes, I'll be going up too and, I think, Christian."

Cynthia, seated to Fen's right, looks up from her phone, "How's the investment team taken it, Fen?"

"I'm not sure how to answer that. The people who were on the floor at the time are having the hardest time. The others have been working remotely since we've not been permitted access to the floor until the police are done so it's difficult to get a general sense."

"But as a practical matter," Lucas asserts, "performance has been unaffected, right?"

Fen, who has developed a distinct dislike for Lucas, responds, "Oh yes, Lucas, everyone is sufficiently unfeeling to ensure that performance is unaffected."

Tiffany asks Grace, "And what about Jade?"

"I've not heard from her. I understand that she is staying with a friend."

Steve, ever naive, blunders into the conversation. "She was having some kind of affair with him. That's the story, isn't it?"

"I don't think it helps to speculate on what triggered events."

Grace affirms Fen's response. "That's right, Fen. It's not helpful to speculate on what may have happened."

"Are you satisfied with the media reaction, Abby?"

"In all the circumstances I think it came off okay. The line that we took was expressing extreme sympathy and placing the incident in the general context of the sadness of mental illness. Institutional clients were concerned with succession, as were board members, but after the initial flurry things seem to have settled. The extraordinary win of the US soccer team at the World Cup, combined with another Middle East crisis, hasn't hurt either in terms of crowding out the story. Thankfully it seems we are just one sad story amongst many." No one challenges the truth or cynicism of her statement.

There is no energy in the room. What has become the normal atmosphere of antagonism when they meet is simply leaden.

"Great to see everyone. My name is Jerry." Jerry is short, earnest and several pounds overweight. He sports a carefully curated ginger beard which he hydrates, conditions and combs regularly with a boar bristle brush. "I am a consultant with COMPACT." He is half-leaning on the flip chart positioned in the middle of the space created by the U of the conference table. "And I am here with my partner Jonas." Jerry motions to his right where Jonas stands fit, silent, and smiling at the group from under his dark shaved head. "And let me also introduce Penelope our coordinator." Penelope, evidently the representative of Gen Z, waves seriously, as if to make clear that she has more to do than drink and take drugs. "Our managing consultant, Barry, has got caught up on the LIE, but will be here shortly. Good. Very good. In the meantime, you will know that we are a consulting company that specializes in managing change in financial services companies..."

"Where's Christian?" Cynthia is in a bad mood and even more acerbic than usual. She has been bitten by what she believes to be an Asian tiger mosquito and is scratching at the large red swelling up on her neck. Naturally she has taken an instant dislike to Jerry, who she has decided is a lightweight. *On the other hand*, she tells herself, *Penelope looks interesting.*

Jerry is unphased. "Thanks for asking that, Cynthia. Legal is always on the ball, right? Right?"

Cynthia avoids eye contact and studies her phone.

"Christian has been detained briefly and will be here shortly, Cynthia. I understand that he had a critical client interaction. Good. Very good."

"No, it's not 'very good' Jerry because if we don't have Christian's attention and engagement in this process, we are wasting our time." Cynthia wants to add, *The truth is that our dysfunction as a team is very much the result of the way Christian is managing. He is miscast, out of touch and plays the team off against each other.*

But thinks better of it.

Grace, observing, is horrified. She wants to howl 'Mayday! Mayday!' *Where the hell is Barry?* she screams to herself.

"So, let's set some ground rules for our session." Jerry continues to struggle. "What rules would you like to set for our conversation?"

"Don't waste our time?" It's Cynthia again.

Jerry repeats it, "Don't waste our time," as he writes it on the flip chart. "Nice one, Cynthia."

"Don't piss on my back and tell me it's raining." A ripple of laughter runs around the table.

Jerry reddens a little, "Thanks, Tom. Not sure I'll take that one."

"Don't beat a dead horse," Steve, his timing somehow off, can't resist getting in on the act.

Even Lucas joins in, "Never try to teach a pig to sing. It wastes your time and annoys the pig!" More laughter.

"Failure is not an option; it comes bundled with the software." Steve again. The tension in the room eases down.

Trying to help Jerry, but totally off point, Abby shouts, "Success is finding out what's wrong with your business before your competitors."

Fen rouses and also gets in on the act. "There's an idiot somewhere deprived of a village." Nobody fully understands what he means but the amusement continues.

Tom adds, "Eagles soar but weasels get sucked into the engine." He is by now roaring with laughter.

"The higher the monkey climbs, the more you see his backside." It's Cynthia again.

John caps off the flow with, "The wheels are turning but the hamsters are all dead."

The lightness of the moment bursts with the word 'dead'. It is a reminder that Monday's tragic events have not been addressed; they weigh like a dead elephant in the center of the room.

"What else?" Totally lacking sensitivity to the change of tone, Jerry attempts to plough on, almost pleading, "What ground rules?" The group is once again silent and lost. Many are checking their phones. Lucas gets up and goes to the coffee cart which is parked at the back of the room.

"You have to hand it to him, there is no stopping him." Tiffany has been sketching out a man hanging from a gibbet next to a shack in spidery black ink across her notepad and writes 'Abandon Hope All Ye Who Enter' above the door to the shack. Then 'FUCK UP!'

The farcical atmosphere is reinforced as the door to the conference room flies open. Barry has arrived. "I do apologize everyone. I flew in last night and made the mistake of staying in the city. The road was totally snarled."

"Yes, I found that too when I drove in at seven." Cynthia's voice drips with sarcasm.

"You are right to be angry, Cynthia. I can only apologize." Somehow Barry has instant command of the room.

Demonstrating uncharacteristic savvy, Jerry capitulates. "Okay, let's take a ten-minute recess. We will reconvene at 7:30."

Cynthia, Geoff, Fen and Steve join Lucas at the coffee cart and mutter darkly about what a waste of their time this is, and where the hell is Christian? Tom and John sit at the conference table intent on email. Abby, Tiffany and Grace withdraw with Barry and, as Abby puts it later, ripped him a new one, for allowing Jerry to be inflicted on the group.

Somehow the meeting is wrangled to order. The Senior Leadership Group, more sullen than ever, but surprisingly all present except for Christian, are arrayed before Barry. "When I met you one on one to plan this session you were very clear. You indicated a number of significant gaps." He steps to the center of the table and looks each member of the group squarely in the eye. "You repeatedly told me that there is a lack of vision. That the environment is highly political, in fact someone used the word 'toxic'. And that you are disconnected from each other and a sense of purpose."

The dull chuffing sound of a helicopter landing outside the conference complex penetrates the meeting room. It registers subconsciously with Grace who is trying to focus on Barry.

Barry raises his voice. "Sorry about the noise. They filmed a key scene in the classic Cary Grant movie North by Northwest in the library here. Maybe they are still chasing him!" The sound of the helicopter blades chomping begins to recede.

Barry ignores the distraction. "If you were going to spend valuable time at this session, I heard you say that it is imperative that we focus on articulating XelFunds strategy, clarifying the purpose."

Grace is thinking, "Okay start Barry, but don't fall into consultant-speak."

"Strategy can be defined as creating a unique and sustainable game plan. It implies choosing to run a different race, performing similar activities differently, or performing different activities from those of other institutions." Barry is quoting Porter, and pauses to let his comments sink in. "A unique value proposition compared to other institutions. A different, tailored value chain. Clear trade-offs, choosing what not to do."

Abby takes a furtive glance at her colleagues and thinks, Barry may have stanched the bleed.

Barry continues, "Activities fit together and reinforce each other." Abby hears him say something about "strategic continuity with continual reinforcement in realizing the strategy" and senses a change in the room.

Barry writes 'MISSION?' on the flip chart. "You will recall I know, that there is an ancient proverb that sums the situation up: 'Without a vision, the people perish.'"

Geoff Peach, bespectacled, portly, and self-satisfied as ever, has recently returned from sick leave. He leans back from the table. "Sounds as if you've got religion." There is some laughter. "Not to be cynical—though quite honestly, I always am—aren't you being a bit naive?"

"Thanks for your candor, Geoff. My point is this. It's been proved again and again that organizations that offer their people and clients a sense of purpose, a mission, are winning organizations. Here is the essence of what I'm going to argue over the next two days. When a transformational vision, empowered by shared values and ethics are at the heart of the business strategy, focus on client needs, creating shareholder value and healthy culture is a systemic outcome.

"Geoff, in financial services we turn risk into profit. But in the age of hyper-transparency, risk can destroy a business at the speed of light because the ferocity and speed of events can be overwhelming. Here's the thing, a high resilience culture can dramatically reduce vulnerability and people risks."

Barry stands in front of Lucas and says, "Organizations can be walled in by a lethal combination of tenuous leadership, errors and dysfunctional culture. You don't need me to tell you that life in a dysfunctional culture is miserable and dangerous and that often the first casualty is personal integrity."

Lucas does not like being confronted and moves uncomfortably in his seat. Barry smiles, "Not to pick on you of course, Lucas." Lucas and the others laugh, but knowing glances are exchanged. Word on how Lucas intimidates his team has become common knowledge in the Leadership Group.

Barry continues, "Because weak cultures are miserable to work in, they are at a serious disadvantage in the talent war. As I said: put tenuous vision, expedient tactics and systemic errors at the core and you get a weak culture full of anxiety. Conversely: put vision, ethics and accountability at the core and you get focus on client needs, a resilient culture, excellent reputation and high performance."

Tiffany looks around the group who seem to be engaged and exchanges a look with Grace which says, "Thank God for the cavalry."

John Purvis, ever hesitant, voices a question: "I don't think anyone here would disagree with you in theory, Barry. But this all sounds a bit academic for us. What are the practical implications of what you are saying?"

"Right, so let's get very practical. There was a consensus amongst you that the organization needs change. I want to engage you in a journey that will challenge you to enable culture change, manage growth and seize opportunities to engage employees as your partners. Will you suspend your disbelief and take a step toward creating purpose and vision of which you can be really proud?" Barry interrogates each face at the table. There is an uncomfortable silence.

"Well look, since we're here we are not going to say no—yet." As usual, it's Cynthia who speaks up in her Australian accent. "But as John says, what is it that you are asking us to do?"

"So, let's kick off then. Many of you told me that you have a feeling that what has sustained the organization so far is not sufficient to get the organization to the next level. The first question I want us to address is this, what is XelFunds' mission? Let's see if there is any consensus amongst the team."

"Last week we sent out a pack of pre-work so you could give some thought to the topics we will address during this off-site. Please look in your binder at section two, page twelve. This is where we asked you to think about how we should state XelFunds' mission in light of current business conditions and likely future challenges. You will remember from your pre-work that the notes on this page describe what makes for a good mission statement.

Please take one of the yellow pads and write down what you believe the XelFunds' mission to be in thirty words or less. And pass your answer to me over here at this end of this table."

At first there is silence and then the Group slowly complies. Steve Tremblay and Grace exchange surreptitious looks and begin to write. Off to a quick start, Lucas exudes his usual air of truculent intensity and appears to be scribbling paragraphs.

Tom Richter reaffirms his understanding of the task. "This is my version of the mission of the company in thirty words or less, right—do I sign it?"

"Right Tom. What is the company's mission? No, don't append your name."

"This is a big task from zero, shouldn't we discuss it first?"

"Thanks for the comment, Steve. Hopefully, you will all have been able to give this some thought prior to today. But the point of this exercise is to get your personal perspective—to provide us collectively with an idea of the range of perspectives and opinions that individuals on the team have around where we are now and where we need to be headed. Think of the exercise as a benchmark from which we can build dialogue, understanding and some agreement. Does that sound reasonable?"

There are some grunts to signify agreement, followed by silence as the group slowly complies with the requirement of the exercise. Abby and Geoff take their time to complete. Tiffany begins to tap her pen impatiently against the edge of the conference table as she waits for her colleagues to finish writing. Fen is withdrawn. Having quickly handed his submission to Barry he is sitting motionless.

"Okay, let's see what we've got here. Jerry, Jonas, Penelope will capture each statement on the flip chart as I read it, then post them around the room. Thanks."

Barry proceeds to read aloud each statement without attribution to its author.

> Consistently make money for ourselves and our clients through the wisdom of our ideas and the power of our people and culture.
>
> We are committed to outstanding standards of professionalism and entrepreneurship. We work hard to know and provide the highest quality investment products, services, and insights to help our clients reach their objectives through delivering consistently high performance, global, diversified portfolios that deliver superior risk-adjusted returns.

> Our mission is to drive sustainable growth and defend our strong industry position, enabling better financial returns than rivals through skillful managers, dynamic client-centered risk management, excellent sales capabilities and financial strength.

It's clear that the Leadership Group is all over the place. Barry presses on with his reading and at the same time tries to tease out themes and differences.

> Our mission is to make our investment expertise broadly accessible through prudent risk management strategies, effective distribution and marketing, to help national and global Institutions and Individuals achieve their goals.
>
> We enable our clients to thrive by delivering superior investment solutions, service and technology, based on our capacity to innovate, manage change and the genius of our people.
>
> Inspire clients with brilliant investment opportunities and service which outperforms the competition and results in a reputation of being good people to do business with.

As the process continues, by their body language it's clear that the team is hooked.

> At XelFunds we value our clients and will build strong products and services to meet their needs in line with our strategy. We aspire to be the best global player in investment management by leveraging our ideas, technology and people to sell the best products to the best clients at the best time.
>
> Be a great company to do business with, a great place to work and maximize shareholder returns.

The door at the far end of the conference room bursts open, and Christian strides in with a broad smile. "Good morning, sorry I'm late. Critically important client call—they were all over me about the incident and wanted reassurance. So, what's going on?"

"We are just into the process of sharing perspectives on what should constitute the company mission statement."

"We've got one of those, haven't we Barry?"

"Yes, it's in the binder in front of your tent card—page twelve. The question is, as we discussed in our prep meeting—is it fit for purpose and how can we engage the team around our purpose and direction?"

"Oh yes, got you." Christian sits, opens his binder, then fishes his iPhone out of his pocket as it vibrates and rings out 'anticipate'. "Sorry people, I have to take this." Apparently unaware of the disruption he has caused, Christian stands, then walks out of the meeting.

No one speaks. "I'll continue then, shall I? How are you doing with capturing all this, guys?" Jerry gives a thumbs-up and begins to post the accumulated statements around the meeting room's walls.

Barry continues the readout.

> Maximize returns for our investors by developing and deploying a product range and sales capabilities which deliver better than average returns and manages back-office expenses and risk, by taking advantage of corporate capabilities together with synergies with our Parent.
>
> We focus on creating and delivering an investment experience that helps clients to achieve their planned goals. As a major international player in the investment industry we are proud of our heritage and independence of thought and action. Everything we do is focused on the needs of our clients and delivering them value through our non-bureaucratic and innovative approach to business.

"There are a lot of great ideas to analyze here. I'd like you to form up in two groups of three and one group of four and list what you see as the main themes emerging from the statements. I'm giving you fifteen minutes, after which I will ask you to report back on your findings."

The participants break into the format Barry has described and start to break down the statements he requested. There is an excited buzz of conversation.

Moments later, ashen-faced Christian puts his head round the door to the meeting room. "Fen, can you step out for a moment please?" Fen hesitates then follows Christian through the door.

Grace's heart sinks. "So it begins," she mutters under her breath.

Despite the various provocations of Jerry's poor start, Barry's late arrival, Christian's entrance and departure, and the atmosphere of latent antagonism, the group is beginning to have some interesting conversations, and settling into the task of compiling themes.

Ten minutes later, the door opens again, revealing Fen, who asks Grace to join him outside.

Barry makes an intervention. "It looks as if there is some stuff going on that is detaining Christian, Fen and now Grace. Let's use this as an opportunity to take a break and reconvene in ten minutes."

Cynthia, Steve, Tom and Abby caucus around the coffee cart.

"What the hell's going on, Abby?" Cynthia is furious as she pumps what is now tepid coffee from a flask.

"I've honestly no idea, but obviously something big is up."

Moments later Fen and Grace, both looking grim, re-enter the conference room accompanied by the sound of a helicopter, this time revving up for take-off.

"Barry, can you and your team give us the room please?" Not looking surprised, but disconsolate, Barry files out with his entourage.

CHAPTER SIXTEEN

All eyes are on Fen. "Christian has been called to New York for an urgent meeting with Frost. We are to wait here until we get word about what is going on."

"What's happening?"

"I don't know yet, Abby."

"Are they going to fire him?"

"As I said, I was just told by Christian that he was recalled to the city and that we are all to sit tight here, Cynthia. It's going to be important that no one communicates to the staff or indeed anyone else what's going on out here until the situation clarifies."

"How long is that going to take?"

"I don't know, Lucas."

"What does Grace know that we don't?"

"I called Grace out of the meeting because I wanted her to have a few moments' start on thinking how we should handle this with Barry and his team, Geoff. I suggest we all take an early lunch. I will message you as soon as I get word of what's going on. And please, once again, no mention of this to anyone back at the ranch. If anyone communicates this outside this room it will be around the company like wildfire and then online and into the press. We owe it to Christian and our staff to keep this quiet until we are in a position to know how we should move forward."

"What are you going to say to Barry, Grace?"

"Thanks Tiffany," Grace says, sounding quite composed. "I'm going thank him and his team for their efforts. Explain that we have an important internal priority that demands our collective attention and that we plan to reschedule this meeting for a future date. I am sure that he will understand in light of all that we are dealing with right now. And also ask them to respect confidentiality about the change. Odd, but I thought he wasn't really surprised when asked to leave."

"Do you know more than you are saying, Fen?" Cynthia is suspicious and persistent.

"I'm going to brief Barry." Grace stands and walks to the door.

The meeting disperses without Fen answering Cynthia's question. Steve and Tom head for the conference center dining room, the others shuffle over to the bedrooms assigned to them which are some yards down a walkway from the conference center.

"What's happening, Tom?" Grace is calling Tom Dawson from her bedroom.

Tom is pacing in his office on floor forty-nine of the Financial Center. "Christian left Pompton's office about three quarters of an hour ago. He was very stone-faced as you might expect. He should be back with you in about another half-hour. Frost is calling Fen to instruct him on next steps. How are things over there?"

"Not so much shock as anxiety. My sense is that no one will be surprised by Christian being fired. But I think they will be shocked by the timing. When the other shoe drops about the possibility of XelFunds being acquired—then there will be major concerns."

"Understood. I've reviewed the draft of the internal organization announcement you sent and also finished the draft of the press release. I just emailed a copy of both to Fen for his review."

"Many changes?"

"No, I think we boxed it. I sent you copies too. Hang in there, Grace. We have to have a drink when we are through all this."

"I suspect that may not be for some time."

"Any word on Jade?"

"No. I plan to reach out to her this evening. Tom, can I get back to you? I've got Fen calling me by the look of it."

"Sure, let's touch base later."

"Grace," Fen says, "can you meet me in the parking lot? I just got word from Frost."

The rabid noon heat is being silently consumed by the automobiles which sit simmering on the black tarmac. It's the sort of feverish temperature that squeezes energy from the soul like toothpaste from a tube. As Grace approaches Fen she sees he is leaning back against his ancient Porsche 911. He looks haggard and is sweating profusely. He squints up towards the powder blue sky, searching for the glint of an approaching helicopter.

"Frost just called me. Christian is inbound. He should be here in less than twenty minutes." Fen is trying to adjust his vision but is finding it difficult to focus on Grace as she stands with her back to the sun.

"Any news on what happened?"

"Some years back, a helicopter that was meant to land here landed in the Russian Diplomatic Mission next door. It caused a major diplomatic incident." Fen rubs his right eye as if trying to erase what he is about to say. "He's out. I'm to step up to CEO and Chairman XelFunds. Aiello is in as COO and Vice Chairman with all staff functions and operations reporting to him. Viser is in as Chief Investment Officer reporting to me. Tom Richter will continue as Head of Distribution and together with Aiello and Viser will function as the Office of the CEO—my inner cabinet if you will. We will keep the Senior Leadership Group but it will be more of a communications group than a decision-making team."

None of this is new to Grace but hearing Fen recite the changes makes what had appeared theoretical to her horribly concrete. She feels nauseous and giddy. It feels as if Fen has just unleashed an attack dog on her. The fear and anger that she is repressing is difficult for her to control. But holding it together, she asks, "You know we have a major issue going on with Viser?"

"Yes Grace, I know that."

"And you are aware that Aiello is a power-obsessed, intimidating, pathological liar?" Grace says.

"Hasn't escaped my notice that he has his issues," Fen replies.

"You do understand that this will destroy the company and the Leadership Group?"

"Might you be being a little over dramatic, Grace? We are the same people. Doing the same jobs. It's just that the working format has changed."

"This is a really bad idea."

Fen is surprisingly sharp in his response. "That's as may be but it is what it is. I would not have organized it this way, but I was not given a vote. I'm just trying to get my head around what it all means. My instructions are to inform the group here of the change and to go back with you and Lucas to the office so we can 'raise the flag' and reassure the troops." Fen is still reflecting on 'raise the flag'; when Frost spoke to him, he had used the phrase with a sense of military triumphalism as if they were both atop Mount Suribachi during the battle of Iwo Jima.

"How does this impact the acquisition talks?" Grace is amazed that Fen is playing the part of such a good soldier. The phrase 'battlefield conversion' floats into her head. She had never imagined that he would succumb so quickly to Frost.

"So you are in on that too?" Fen remarks with surprise.

Grace says nothing.

"Well, the acquisition is a major driver in all this. Frost did not feel confident that Christian would be effective in representing the company through the acquisition process and that he was not up to the task business-wise."

"Are you going to tell the group about the acquisition talks?" Grace asks.

"Yes, I have got the go ahead to do that."

There is at first the vague and then the rising sound of a helicopter approaching. Fen and Grace, deep in conversation have not noticed Lucas walking across the parking lot towards them, followed by Cynthia, who is still scratching her neck, some distance behind.

"Congratulations, Fen!" Jubilant, Lucas breaks into the conversation, totally disregarding Grace. "Frost just called me."

"I see. Thanks, Lucas."

"We will have a lot to do." Lucas makes his statement sound more like an instruction than a comment. "You waiting for Christian? It looks like he is here."

Cynthia joins the gaggle as they are looking up at the helicopter which is now churning out air and decibels and beginning its descent through the light breeze onto the grass two hundred feet distant. "That's Christian back from the city then?" The lilt of Cynthia's Australian accent bounces upon the churning air as the chuffing helicopter rotor blades wind down into silence. Without pausing for a response, she steps between Lucas and Fen and continues, "Glad I caught you and Grace, Fen. I just heard from Jade Edwards' lawyer. She wants ten million dollars."

There is a dazed silence, accentuated by the absence of engine noise.

A lone figure has been released from the side of the helicopter by the pilot and is making its way unsteadily towards them as if a little drunk. He walks as if in defeat after being medivacked from some dug out during his service towards the end of the war in Vietnam. Indeed, as he has helicoptered back from the city following the weary track of the East River and then over the shimmer of Long Island Sound his mind has been full of the jangling memories of flying over the Mekong, his feet soaked from trudging exhausted through paddies. Then sliding further with his memories to the bottom of a B-52 bomb crater where his platoon is asking him "Lieutenant, what is that orange color in the water?"

Fen nods. "I need to talk to him. I'll see you back at the conference room. Grace, will you get everyone together please. I'll see you all there in fifteen minutes or so."

As Grace, Lucas and Cynthia retreat across the parking lot towards the conference center, a black SUV swings past them. The trio turns to see Fen and Christian get into the back seat. A limo driver gets out and paces off into the parking lot, lighting up as he walks. "Now I've seen it all," Cynthia observes, "a bloody confessional on wheels!" Grace and even Lucas guffaw.

"Cynthia, you've got to tell me where you get them from!"

"It's not the jokes, Grace, it's the way I tell 'em!"

"I'm done, Fen. It was an ambush. This place is not too different from the Asian jungle after all." Fen is listening intently, "One of the problems we had was resupply. So unreliable. Basic items like dry socks and salt tablets were never in supply. Most of all the chow was C-rations that came in brown cans and ran from disgusting to inedible. There was never any easy way to heat the food so we were always eating stuff that was congealed and sickeningly cold, straight out of the tin. Towards the end of our time there, we started using pinches of C-4 plastic to heat up the chow—some of the guys didn't do so well on that!" He smiles more to himself than to Fen. He looks through the window at the limo driver who is pacing around the parking lot, yelling what sounds like Russian into his cell phone. Turning to face Fen, Christian looks him straight in the eye. "You knew about Frost's plan to replace me, didn't you Fen?"

The question strikes at Fen with unexpected intensity. He instantaneously feels anemic, his emotions trapped in a microburst of claustrophobia as if he is choking under a tsunami of guilt. His worst fears about himself and his ambition outweighing his integrity are overwhelming. He has been too weak to resist the seduction of career and all that Frost offered and too cowardly to be honest with Christian. His life lived in a soporific cocoon of self-interest has led him to a place where he feels utterly empty. Intellectually he is on an oppositional trajectory. He is asking himself how else he could have survived had he not played politics in such a pernicious environment. After all, why play the game if not to win? If he had not served Christian's purposes for so long would not Christian have abandoned him in the same way that he had abandoned so many others over the years? The fragment comes to him "As you sow, so shall you reap". For a millisecond he is back sitting in the Sunday school circle on a small wooden chair, Mrs. Hancock standing over him in her floral-patterned dress, her ample breasts pressing down towards him.

She is saying, "The memory verse, Fen, the memory verse?"

Fen replies, "As you sow, so shall you reap. Galatians 6:7." Now he can't bring himself to say anything to Christian and breaks off eye contact.

"It's okay, Fen. It's nothing really. You are a trader. My stock collapsed and you had to sell. It's just that I trusted you. I thought you might be different from this."

Fen remains silent, trying to process Christian's words that have cut like a razor into his marrow. As usual, it's Fen's intellect that mouths off, leaving him apparently cold and unresponsive. *Why is it that as a culture we are far more interested in success and advancement than introspection? We all seem to lack any kind of concept of who we really are. Or could be. It's as if we grow into automatons devoid of introspection and unable to absorb anything beyond the mundane. We feel dead spiritually and such energy as we do have is directed towards...*

The silence that fills the space between them as they sit alongside each other in the limo is fjord-deep. Fen is torn from his reverie by Christian's voice calling to the driver and then saying to Fen, "I'm going home, Fen. I should have done it a long time ago." The moment remains sad and bitter between them.

"You're not staying to talk to the others?"

"No. I think the situation is past that. You broke it, now you've got to buy it Fen." He smiles ironically. "Watch out for the bastards. Don't trust Frost, and don't turn your back on Aiello for a moment. They will both screw you. No bad feelings between us. We went through too much together for that." He grabs Fen's hand and grips it. "A good man always knows his limitations. You're a romantic. You want to be an outdoorsman, Thoreau, on the efficient frontier of investing. A hunter ready to make a killing. But you are too soft, too squeamish. Not so soft, mind you, that you won't leave me here bleeding alongside the highway." Again, Christian smiles but the words are like a bitter prophecy on his tongue. "This is not your game Fen, you will be short-lived."

Fen is standing by the limo as it rolls out of the parking lot, half-afraid that, like the lieutenant's car in Dirty Harry, Christian's limo will explode on departure. He feels foolish as he waves farewell to Christian, who has tears flowing down his cheeks. "How the mighty have fallen," he mutters to himself as he walks back to the conference room, hyped by adrenaline. It surprises him that he is also weeping. He cannot determine if his tears are from joy, sorrow or merely the result of a high pollen count.

He stands stock still weighing Christian's words. "Was he talking about himself or me?" His face hardens as he pronounces his internal verdict. "He's a vulture without the balls to pull the trigger."

Having composed himself, Fen enters the conference room to the sound of raised voices. Heads snap towards him and the room falls silent. He wants to say 'Friends, Romans, countrymen, lend me your ears. I have come to bury Caesar not to praise him.' But thinks better of it as he reflects on 'the evil that men do lives after them'. Instead he simply says, "I need your help."

"There are three things you need to know. First, there have been some leadership changes. Christian has left the company and I have been appointed his successor."

Cynthia interrupts the silence that follows Fen's statement. "Did he fall or was he pushed, Fen?"

"How did he take it?" Tiffany is clearly genuinely upset.

"I think he was pretty realistic. Not shocked that he was removed but surprised by the timing."

"Do I need to set up communications around this, Fen?"

"I'll get on to that in a moment, Tiffany. Let me give you the full picture before we get into logistics. Second, you should also know that Lucas has been appointed as a Vice Chairman and that you will all now, with the exception of Tom and Tiffany, report to Lucas who in turn will report to me. Peiter Viser will step up to succeed me as CIO and will also oversee Equities until we appoint a replacement for Miles."

There is stunned silence as they take in what Fen has said. "Look Fen, this is positively outrageous. We all came to XelFunds so we could have a front-row seat, a place at the leadership table. And now you tell us we are layered and reporting to Lucas. No disrespect, Lucas, but you know shit about Legal," Cynthia says in full flight. "Besides, there are regulatory reasons why Legal should not report to Operations, given we are the watchdogs for what's going on in Operations." As she speaks, her breath is labored, her face swollen and red as she continues to scratch at her neck.

"Same is true of Risk. We should not be subject to Operations," Geoff adds with his usual curt pomposity.

"Yes, with respect, Fen, I can't see being layered by Lucas is going to work for us out in Phoenix." Steve Tremblay is unusually assertive. "The technology issues we are facing are jugular to competitive success. There needs to be continuous dialogue between all of us, not organization layers."

"I understand there are concerns but given what's going on we will need to have different structures from the past." The air is reverberating with anger and resentment. "Third, Pompton Financial is about to get into the due diligence process with a potential acquirer for XelFunds. We are on the block."

"How real is it this time Fen? We've had so many rumors and half-assed attempts to sell before!" As she speaks Cynthia is making an attempt to stand, her face is swollen and has assumed a sickly shade of crimson. "I need some air!"

"Cynthia, are you all right?" Fen rushes forward as Cynthia collapses across the table with a thump, and falls to the floor, scattering pitchers of iced water.

Instantly Grace is kneeling over Cynthia. "She was stung by something earlier. I think it may be anaphylactic shock of some sort. Call 911!"

"Of course I was bloody well stung!" Cynthia may be down but she is by no means out. Under protest, she is eventually carried out from the conference room on a gurney bound for the Emergency Room at Glen Cove Hospital. Her salty recriminations introduce a tone of dark farce to the afternoon as they echo down the corridor that is her route to the ambulance.

It takes an hour for the meeting to reconvene. They are possessed by a feeling that none of what is happening is quite real. Grace like Fen keeps rerunning the interview that she had with the police following Miles's suicide. She hears herself whispering it under her breath, *suicide*, as Fen begins to speak.

"I appreciate there are real challenges in our situation. We have to be real about where we are and get on with what we have been charged to do. So here is what is before us." Grace cannot but feel that there is something amiss with Fen. He is talking but these are not his mannerisms or words. "Abby, you need to call Tom Dawson in Corporate Legal and liaise with him on getting out a press release and an internal announcement about the management change. There will be no announcement on the possibility of a sale unless and until the suitor signs a letter of intent. Needless to say, discussion of a possible sale must not go beyond this room.

Grace, I want you to work with Abby on both the internal announcement and compilation of talking points for this team to use as the basis for communication about the organization changes."

Grace nods to signify her understanding as she makes some notes on her iPad. She silently speculates. *This is not like you at all, Fen. You are just not this directive or structured. How hard is Frost pulling your strings?*

"I'd like to work with them on that too," Tiffany says.

"Sure Tiffany, do that."

"I'm flying back to the office with Lucas and Tom to raise the flag there."

There he goes again, declares the voice in Grace's head. *He would never normally use language like 'raise the flag'. 'Wave a white handkerchief', perhaps, but never 'raise the flag'!*

"Grace, Abby, Tiffany, you should join us too. Grace has arranged temporary space for us away from the quarantine area where Miles took his life."

Ever the pedant, Steve asks, "What about Geoff, John and me?"

"You are going to have to take ground transportation, Steve." Fen's response is uncharacteristically sharp.

"And what about Cynthia?" Steve adds.

John raises a hand. "I will go over to the hospital to see how she's doing. I have my car here."

Fen smiles, "Thanks John. Maybe you can send me a text when you get a sense of how she is?"

"That's a good point. Some of us brought our cars here?" Tiffany asks.

"Like me", says Fen with a laugh. "I guess we are going to have to work that one out. Maybe you can drive someone's back to the city, Steve?" Then, "I want us all to get together in my office at 8 am tomorrow. Steve, I suggest you stay over in the city for this one—no more video calls!"

Lucas, nodding, adds, "Yes, and those who now report to me, should be prepared to meet with me following that meeting."

"I suggest that you delay that meeting, Lucas. The team will have a lot to do in terms of communications. Maybe your reports can meet with you at the end of the day tomorrow?" The group exchange glances. Clearly they are all surprised by Fen's new assumption of authority.

Lucas does not argue but his expression conveys his annoyance.

"It's going to be a tricky few days. In addition to the management changes and acquisition we have got to cooperate with the police investigation into Miles's suicide and Jade's accusations. Stay close. Let's get to it." Fen, having pronounced this benediction, rises and walks determinedly towards the door.

As the helicopter climbs into the sky out of the conference center, Fen looks down. Strapped into his emotions, his literary defenses low, the only thing he says to himself is, "Shit, was that actually me?"

Lucas obsesses, strapped into the seat opposite, staring at the cumulus clouds before the window, relishing possibilities as he plans his next moves.

CHAPTER SEVENTEEN

The Trinitarian Congregational Church in Concord, Massachusetts traces its history to its founding by the first settlers in 1636 and now sits, following its reconstruction after a fire in 1926, a dominating white sepulchre at the corner of Walden and Hubbard Streets. From inception, the church has been involved in issues of the times and today prides itself on compassionate concern. It has an air of abandonment during the week as if it is now fighting a rearguard action against the future.

At 10:30, an elderly man struggles to open the oak door of honor beneath the corner steeple, which thrusts against the brooding sky. A scattering of thirty or so people have filed into the hard wooden pews at the front of the church to memorialize Miles McCarthy, who has been cremated. A picture of Miles, hardly recognizable in his graduation regalia, has been mounted on a tripod to the right of the lectern that stands before the stained-glass windows dominating the front of the church. The new pipe organ breathes the music to The Mountains of Mourne, as three members of the clergy file in from a side door to sit before the congregation.

Grace and I have flown up from New York. On the forty-minute Uber ride to the church from Logan Airport neither of us says much. Perhaps for fear of expressing too much emotion. Perhaps because we feel nothing, as we ride past the saltbox colonial houses, checking our phones for messages and the latest on the markets.

As we enter the church, we recognize one or two others from the company, including Christian and his wife, whom I acknowledge with a taut smile.

Miles's wife Jessie sits flanked by her children and people who I take to be other relatives in the pews at the front of the church.

Grace and I sit a few rows behind Christian, as a sad silence broods about our heads.

I see Grace look down at the picture of Miles on the front of the order of service. Below it there are a few verses by someone don't know.

'I bless the night that nourished my heart
To set the ghosts of longing free
Into the flow and figure of dream
That went to harvest from the dark
bread for the hunger no one sees
All that is eternal in me
Welcomes the wonder of this day,
The field of brightness it creates
Offering time for each thing
To arise and illuminate
May my mind come alive today
To the invisible geography
That invites me to new frontiers
To break the dead shell of yesterdays
To risk being disturbed and changed'

I can't help but contrast the turbulent man I knew with the optimistic quietude of the verse.

Grace, I know, has other things on her mind. She has received a series of phone messages all laced with the same vitriol. A rasping anonymous voice, "Bitch, you got what you wanted. May you rot in hell for what you did to Miles." All the messages have the same tone but one in particular keeps coming back to her. "You may as well have shot him yourself, bitch. God will never forgive you."

As she has gone about her business, I've noticed her looking apprehensively in the faces of colleagues and staff trying to detect hostility.

It has not been a difficult task. She has become a magnet for negative feelings as she has pushed the organization to get back on track following the suicide.

Examining the order of service, I find it equally discordant and turn from the front page to the program. There is to be no other music.

The first of the clergy, a middle-aged woman with short hair and a desiccated face wears a black robe and rainbow-colored stole. I hear her begin to explain the order of service, say a word of welcome, that Miles attended Sunday school at the church when a child and that the church is a vibrant community of faith, deeply committed to nurturing something or another; and tune out as I gaze at the figures on the stained glass window.

Miles's daughter Pen rises to give a eulogy. She has a broad face with striking green eyes and the untidy look of an academic of some kind. As she reads, head cast towards the sheets of paper she holds in her pale hands, the timbre of her voice carries the same edge that Miles's did in his earlier days. "I did not know my Father well." At first she speaks deliberately, as if delivering a paper. "He did not know me well. He abandoned me for his work. I abandoned him for my life." She pauses in an attempt to quell the emotion that is beginning to roil her voice. "And yet I still cling to those rare magical days when I was a child and he would drive us over to Crane Beach and we would run into the water and shout at the gulls. And the evening he came to Brown and we ate out at an Italian restaurant. How he hated Italian food!" There is some mild laughter amongst the congregation, as Pen pauses and smiles, more to herself than to the congregation. "Typically, he had a glass too many and I must say I did too... I did not resent him, I loved him and still do, but we never told one another." Her final sentences are stark and feel like the slamming of a cell door against concrete. "He died alone and desperate. And has left us desperate too."

Pen raises her head, tears streaming from her reddened eyes, and returns to her pew.

As I hear Pen speak, I find it difficult to retain my composure. I resonate with each word. My mind goes back to the morning when I heard the gun shot that blew out Miles's brain. Sitting here I have an epiphany. *When I heard that shot, something happened in my head. Something happened in my heart. I am somehow changed.*

I sit within the circle of my thoughts, as Miles's son John follows his sister to the lectern. He walks with hesitation as if in discomfort from an injury of some kind, his large frame slightly hunched as if he is carrying a great weight. His hair is wild, face unshaven. He looks unrepentantly over the congregation. "In the end he was sick and we didn't know it. Depression, that was it, and the drink. This was not a close family. We don't like each other much a lot of the time. Dad was better with numbers than with people. He was better with other people than he was with us. But we loved him, didn't we, Mom? We loved him." John has the same intonation as his sister and father. His hands are gripping the sides of the lectern. His arms are rigid, his head leans forward, eyes closed, as he barely gets his words out. "And he loved the Red Sox. And maybe even someone else more than us, his family." John pauses a long time. "My life was cratered on dope but he never condemned me. One night he found me down by the harbor. I was totally stoned and I thought he was my dealer. I hit him in the face because I thought he was delivering late. Another day when he came to get me, I threw up in the car going home. Remember that Pen?" He waves at Pen whose sad green eyes are suffering through every word her brother is saying. "When I was found two years ago, when I changed, broke the habit, he was pleased for me. But he never wondered why I changed. He never believed that there could be good for him too. He never believed that he could be found. You see he was lost and no one found him. We talked in that apartment of his in the city. It had green walls. Neither of us could stand it for too long so I left early and took the train home. But I cried, Dad. I cried for what we didn't have. I cried for what we didn't say as I rode the subway. He was a good man, no matter what people will say. He was a good man. I am sorry he could not find a better way out. This changed me, Dad: 'Come to me, all you that labor and I will give you rest.' I think it could have changed you too, Dad. But you could not change, Dad, because your life made you crazy. Too crazy to live." John leaves the lectern and meanders back to his place next to his mother who is quietly sobbing.

I can see Grace is feeling raw. She can't decode John or his family.

I walk to the lectern. I look beyond the smattering of people at the front of the church to a woman seated in the half-light at the back below the gallery. I am acutely conscious of my British accent as it echoes up the church walls. "My name is Fen Morgan. Miles and I were colleagues, but I don't think I was a good enough friend to him. He was a brilliant investor. People trusted him with their money and they were not disappointed. People trusted him with their friendship. But we let him down." I glance at Christian whose does not react. "He was a great guy to go out with. He would always have a story or two and, when it took him, jokes." There is the smallest of laughs from the pews; it is as if people are desperate for anything that will defuse the tension. "When he was on, he could be the biggest raconteur in the room. He loved the Sox, was passionate about them. And he was always full of what was going on with his kids. Pen, how great you were doing at school. How the only other doctor he had in his family was Doctor John! Yes, he loved his crazy music too. He loved that Doctor John song, Right Place Wrong Time, and used it all the time. Often in the wrong places I might add!" There is another laugh that ripples down the aisle a little more strongly than the last. "John, he unquestionably regretted losing touch with all of you." I address this to Miles's family. "And Jessie, I am so sorry for your loss. I fear Miles's work took him from you but I hope you can remember him as we do, a remarkable man." I begin to lose it. I fear that what I am saying is becoming totally incoherent. "To me, the Bard captures something of comfort,

'Cowards may die many times before their deaths;
The valiant never taste of death but once.
Of all the wonders that I have yet heard,
It seems to me the most strange that men should fear death
Seeing that death, a necessary end,
Will come when it will come.'"

Walking back to my place next to Grace, I fear that I have totally failed to convey anything of my real feelings. Of my guilt. I turn my head to glance at the back of the sanctuary and recognize Jade behind a large pair of sunglasses.

I whisper to Grace, "Jade is here." Grace turns and meets Jade's distant gaze straight on.

The priest who was the second to enter the church at the beginning of the service, rises and stands behind the lectern. He is a young man with short cropped hair and wears a dark business suit. He introduces himself. "My name is Stephen Paisley, I am the Minister of New Life Church here in Concord."

He reminds me of one of my junior analysts.

"Two readings", Paisley speaks with a light Irish brogue, "one from the Old Testament, one from the New. The Old Testament reading from Isaiah 45 verse three.

'I will give you hidden treasure,
riches stored in secret places
so that you may know
that I am the Lord,
the God of Israel
who summons you by name.'

"The New Testament reading, Matthew 6:21, where Jesus says,

'For where your treasure is, there your heart will be also.'

"Risk Management. I understand that that is what Miles did for a job. He was a Risk Manager."

What an idiot. He's even got the bloody job Miles did wrong! I am unreasonably angry as my head fills with guilt and remorse.

"Now, I have so little money personally that no one needs to manage it. But it sounds as if Miles made a lot of people happy by managing theirs." This elicits a perfunctory laugh that rises from the congregation then falls flat.

"Yes, I know Miles's official job title was that of Money Manager but I'm inclined to think that he was managing risk of one kind or another

"In fact, it is easy to label people as this or that isn't it? To evaluate people by what they have accomplished in material terms. A butcher, a baker, a candlestick maker. A Money Manager. A good Money Manager. A bad Money Manager. We tend to look at people superficially. Evaluate them by mundane criteria. By how they have managed the risks in their lives to achieve prosperity or otherwise. To view their academic or financial record, their LinkedIn profile, or for those in financial services, the 10-K of their life, and determine if they are a success or failure.

"We tend to perceive people as living in a single dimension. But the truth is that we all know ourselves to be multidimensional, multi-faceted people. We are fathers and mothers, sons and daughters, lovers and haters, winners and losers. We are dreamers who sometimes have nightmares. We are children but often feel ourselves to be terribly old. We are fearful yet sometimes have great hopes. We want to do good but are capable of untold evil. As a species, hugely complex and stupidly simple. We love and want to be loved.

"But sometimes we get out of whack. We fail to manage the risk entailed in our lives. Sometimes things go terribly wrong. Sometimes we fall instead of fly. Sometimes we live our lives in a single dimension and forget, or fail to understand entirely, that living our life for stuff and for experiences alone, 'jumping for the jelly beans', as they say, creates the risk that we may miss the point. In fact, as someone once said, jumping for the jelly beans is the broad road that leads to destruction."

Craig Dinsell

As I listen, my mind wanders down the maze that is my memory. To the innumerable times when as a young man I repeatedly heard this sort of earnest pleading for my soul. It is like music played in a distant room. A long-forgotten summons to a purpose that has always eluded me.

"Money management, managing financial risk, was the work that Miles did, not the person that he was. Miles was a father who had failings. A father who left his kids feeling fatherless sometimes. But also, a father who rescued them when they were failing. Miles was complex. Life is complex."

The young minister's words wash up towards me like a tide of naivety that will never quite reach me. I feel listless, sympathetic, almost a yearning for my childhood home. Then, as if highly resistant to hypnosis, when I hear, "Life is complex" I want to shout back, "Kafka—The meaning of Life is that it stops!"

"In the end, Miles was his own harshest critic. Were his failings so great in his own eyes that he inflicted the harshest penalty upon himself that he could imagine?"

"So how should we feel towards Miles? Angry? Sad? Should we be outraged by him or should we have a sense of compassion? Should we judge him, or do the circumstances of his life and death stand as a judgment against us?"

The church is a cavernous void. I wrestle with the cloying atmosphere as it presses in upon me. I am weary of the torrent of the all too familiar, sanctimonious, regurgitated religiosity, unfolding in my ears. I want it to stop.

And yet, despite my contempt for the simplistic words, I am surprised to find myself being drawn towards what I am hearing. For me, it is like entering a cavern, long abandoned on the cold side of a mountain.

"Stay with me for a moment; let's go back to those verses I read. What are they saying to you and me? There is a lot of historical context around Isiah 45 but this morning, because of time, I will take the verse at face value. Let me read it again:

'I will give you hidden treasure,
riches stored in secret places
so that you may know that I am the Lord,
the God of Israel
who summons you by name.'

"God is addressing Cyrus, an unbelieving King. This character was probably the founder of the Achaemenid Empire. The first Persian Empire. He was prompted by God to decree that the temple in Jerusalem which had been destroyed should be rebuilt so the Jews in exile could return home. God is saying he will give Cyrus, a heathen unbelieving King, hidden treasure so that he will know that he is the Lord and that God's people can return home.

"Here's my question to you this morning. It's a bit audacious. But hear it all the same. In the teeth of this sad occasion, as you, maybe like many of us, are feeling so much sadness and loss and wondering why God could let all this happen to Miles and to us..."

I have become fascinated with Paisley's open face and the deliberation with which he forms each phrase. It is as if he is unwrapping each thought from white tissue paper. The concepts pile up, like the remembered transgressions of my childhood.

"What is the hidden treasure that God wants you to have? To be specific, how does God, in the face of all that's wrong with your life and with the world, want to restore your life?"

A more seasoned speaker, matured by years of not being listened to might have stopped at this point but the homily marches determinedly on.

"What is the hidden treasure that God wants you to have? Prosperity? Financial success? Material security? The good life? These things are perhaps legitimate, but we know they do not satisfy. They are obvious, they are not hidden. No, the riches God has for us are hidden in secret places. In the places many of us have ignored for a long time. If we want the truth God has for us we have to search for it, we have to seek it out. If you live for your ego, for the material, you will likely get what you want or be frustrated by not getting what you want. In either case, I doubt you will be fulfilled."

I continue to follow, but what I am hearing now is simply not making sense to me. The argument seems to be circular. Don't live for your ego, for the mundane, but rather find yourself in God. But surely if the point to life is finding oneself, isn't that the ultimate ego trip?

"You are multi-dimensional. Only hidden treasure will satisfy. So what is your life to become? The sad story of a search for the mundane? Slavishly traveling the road to those things that don't satisfy, or a story about the adventure of finding hidden treasure?"

The word 'treasure' triggers me to remember one evening, when as a child I attended a fair at my elementary school. I was about age seven at the time. There were various games to play that had been contrived by my classmates, but one in particular fascinated me. It consisted of a large map of an island roughly the shape of Australia. A series of locations were pinpointed on the island indicating mountains, rivers, a mine, a jungle, and a series of coves and sandy inlets. Offshore, a galleon was depicted sailing upon the open sea, flying the Jolly Roger. The object of the game was to identify the location where pirates had concealed buried treasure. Players were invited to stick a pin into the spot where they believed the treasure was to be found. I was overjoyed, when at the end of the evening I was awarded a book of collected poems for children. Later that night at home, I sat in bed reading by torchlight From A Railway Carriage by Robert Louis Stevenson and Jabberwocky by Lewis Carroll.

'Beware the Jabberwock my son!

The jaws that bite, the claws that catch,

Beware the Jubjub bird, and shun

The fumious Bandersnatch'

Lewis Carroll, 1898.

The caution in the nonsense poem echoes around my head.

"And what is that treasure? Jesus said, 'I am the way the truth and the life.' Jesus said, 'I am the resurrection and the life. He who believes in me will live even though he dies.' Jesus claims to be the source of spiritual life."

"Is the life that Jesus offers, hidden treasure, worth seeking? Perhaps even in the sad circumstances of this morning, he is calling to you by name?"

I further recall the following morning at school, when sitting on a bench, changing into my gym shoes, I came upon an elastic belt with an elaborate plastic buckle, in the shape of an astronaut, that had apparently been discarded. Rather than bringing my find to the attention of my teacher, I secreted the belt in my gym bag and took it home. The next day I wore the belt to school and was quickly accused of being a thief by a classmate. My parents were called to the school to be apprised of my behavior. Horrified by his son's misdeed, my father confiscated my poetry book. I remember my outrage and guilt arising from the incident. And wonder if the seeds of my love for poetry, obfuscation and anger directed at my father and authority figures in general stem from this childhood memory. 'Treasure' is not a good word.

I break from my childhood memories and am again aware of the sermon as it continues.

"I have come to know Jessie and her family well over the past several months, and I have been sharing in their journey and total shock and desolation over these past several weeks as they have wrestled with the grizzly fact that Miles took his life in the most terrible of ways."

And now I really want to scream. *Where is the call to acknowledge guilt?*— My personal guilt for letting Miles go unheeded to his self-immolation. And what of the devastation Miles has wreaked on others—his family, Jade, his coworkers and friends? I detest this Hallmark theology that tweets superficial answers—'Believe in my Jesus, he will save you'—and urges me to move on and accept the pap of canned solutions. I have a hunger for something I cannot articulate. My spirit is weak from malnutrition of the soul. I cannot self-soothe. I will not be soothed by what I cannot believe.

"There are no trite, easy answers, but somehow, still on these most difficult of days, we are holding on to the treasure of knowing Jesus and trusting ourselves into his strong hands as he holds onto us and calls us to follow him. Jesus says, 'Where your treasure is there will your heart be also.'" Paisley concludes his sermon abruptly, "How are you managing risk in your life this morning?"

Grace and I again exchange looks. I grimace slightly, but hold my emotions in check, tightly buttoned under my dark tie and white collar. Neither Grace nor I had expected remarks like that. We, especially me, are not used to encountering faith.

The memorial ends with a reading by the third priest wearing purple Catholic vestments. "My name is Father Tommy. I was a pal of Miles when we were lads at BC. This is a hard time for all. We share in your sadness, Jessie." He recites an ancient Irish blessing.

'May the road rise to meet you

And the wind always be at your back

And the rain fall softly on your fields

May God hold you gently in the palm of his hand.'

Father Tommy raises his hand, then pronounces a further benediction.

There are a series of greetings, a few hugs and tepid handshakes, then Grace and I are back in the Uber bound for Boston Airport. We don't speak much in the car as we process what happened in the service. We wonder what happened to Jade, who vanished immediately after the benediction.

CHAPTER EIGHTEEN

Logan Airport is the usual scrum around the gate to the Delta Shuttle where frustration reigns owing to two flight cancellations. Resigned to a long wait for the next flight to LaGuardia, Grace and I take refuge in a corner table in Vino Volo, since later flights are leaving from terminal E.

"Hardly Italy, but they actually have a great wine list here. Especially the reds." Once the server leaves, I continue. "That was not entirely what I was expecting."

Grace jokes, "The wine?"

"No, the remembrance" I reply smiling.

"Indeed. Very sad. I was expecting that, but not the 'come to Jesus' piece."

"The family is a complete wreck. In truth, I never really got that far into his private life with him. Miles would talk about his kids but it seemed to me that his relationship with Jessie was quite painful."

"What did you make of Jade being there? Do you think Jessie noticed her?" Grace is tracing a fingernail around her napkin.

"I don't think so. It was pretty murky back there. I am genuinely surprised she showed up."

"Yes, she has a lot of brass, as they would say where you come from, Fen."

"But why would she want to be there today? After what Miles did to her."

"Perhaps after all, she really did love him? Or perhaps she was curious about his family? Or, maybe she is just drawn into the drama of the whole thing, who knows?" I've not heard Grace talk with such depth before. How little I really know her.

The server brings our drinks and a few small plates with bread and cheeses.

"And how are you doing through all this?" Grace asks.

"Well, to be frank, I find myself quite distressed in a way I have not been for many years." I am rarely candid. Why am I opening up to her?

"About where your treasure is?" There is a new intimacy to our shared smiles.

"No, about the guilt I feel for not being there for Miles. He walked away from me and I didn't stop him." I immediately feel vulnerable for having shared my thoughts.

"I hadn't stopped to think about it that way. After all, he was a grown-up, making his own decisions, wasn't he?" I am grateful for Grace's defense of me.

"Yes. But had I seen his despair more clearly. Had I not walked by him on the other side, so to speak. Had I been more responsible, perhaps I could have prevented what happened?" This is my confession. I am relieved to get it out.

"Who's to say? I think people have to take responsibility for their own actions." It seems such an unsympathetic rejoinder from one so young but perhaps we can't see our fragility until we are on the downward slope. I wonder what it is in her background that has made her so hard. So possessed of the need to be right. She is a person of remarkable determination.

"My point entirely, Grace," I say as if to someone in a different tribe. We are on different pages. I wonder if she sees any culpability on her part, or if she just doesn't want to countenance acknowledging it.

"You ever heard anything like that preacher?" Grace says, inspecting my face. "It reminded me a bit of church when I was a kid on Long Island. What was your take on that 'where your treasure is, there your heart is' bit?"

"Interesting, perhaps, if it was in a different context. I was a bit too emotional to follow him closely." Maybe I have opened up a bit too much already.

"I think his point was perhaps that there is more to life than climbing the greasy pole."

I am thinking how odd it is that different people can hear different things in the same place. "As a matter of fact, yes," I say, "It's been like a treadmill, and I've not yet stopped to ask myself what I am doing with my life and who I am doing it for. But who does, I'd like to know, unless there is some sort of big trauma that causes that kind of navel gazing? I guess this is that kind of trauma."

"There is a price to pay for being in the game we play? Wow, this is getting heavy." Grace sips her chardonnay. I am not sure if she is serious or sarcastic.

"Yes, but not just that Grace. The price is proportionate to the goal. What's the goal?"

"Satisfaction, I guess. The satisfaction of doing a good job, accomplishing something."

I sense that Grace wants to say something more but she's not forthcoming. So, I say, "But who are we accomplishing it for? I'd like to think it's for my family. You know, for my kids, but the fact is that the nature of what we do squeezes everything else out. So honestly I'd have to admit that I'm doing what I am doing for the sake of my ego. Recognition, the security that I have when you have to listen to fewer people. And I suspect very possibly this has made me a much nastier and less interesting person than I hoped I would be."

"I think you are being too hard on yourself, Fen. I give up a lot too, but I also get back a sense of accomplishment and self-worth that my mother never had. She came here adopted into a family where her adoptive father went AWOL, leaving her to take care of her mother really. There was a lot of religion about but not much love. And my Mom and Dad were not rich people. Every penny counted. We lived on Long Island, but I felt like we lived on the moon. I couldn't wait to get out, to be someone else she was not."

"Sounds tough."

"And then being my color and a woman is not all show business either. No matter what your credentials, the sexual politics are different. You feel like the deck is stacked against you. And by the way, it is. But you've heard all this."

"No, go on," I say.

"Well, it's often like you are in a room and no one is listening. Sometimes I feel I'm there as a necessary appendage rather than a contributing partner. Not with everyone all the time. But it's just that the feeling of insecurity is there all the time. So yes, what drives me, if I'm honest, is a need for recognition and the need for personal financial security. To be on the same terms as everyone else."

"So no search for the hidden treasure?"

"Well yes, of course. I'm not a moron. I don't entirely jump for the jelly beans. I want to do something good in the world. I want to help people. Make the company a great place to be, help us return value to shareholders, make the world a better place, even pay taxes. It's just that those goals are aspirational. I don't think about them much, no one articulates living that way. I see myself as surrounded by people who want to get on. People who want power and that's a trip. I fear that if I don't assert myself, if I'm not as aggressive as they are, I will fail. And if I fail there will be no one there to catch me."

"We are all in the fear or greed game, like the market then?" I hear myself. The cynic.

"When you get down to the naked truth, I think so," she says, looking like a child orphaned by the truth.

"And what of the bigger things, what of integrity? What of love, even?" I ask this of her genuinely hoping to hear some kind of meaning.

"Integrity can be slippery in my experience. So much seems situational. We look at managing risk in terms of breaking rules, not in terms of doing the right thing."

"And love?" Here it is Grace, the big one. What of love?

"At the end of the day, when you have pounded through all that's on at the office, there is not much room for anything else. Maybe a one-night stand now and then." Her cheeks flush with embarrassment. The second glass of wine loosened her tongue a little too much. "But for love you have to connect with the right person, and I'm way past Tinder and all that. Or do you mean something different?" She raises her wine glass and hides behind it for a moment; she appears quite uncomfortable and surprised by the turn of conversation.

"Well, there is the love that is wrapped around sex. The thrill of the chase," I tell her.

"Then there is the love that changes into fidelity to a person or idea. It can be a passion for something. Something to live or die for. Maybe the happiest people have that kind of love?" I am the professor.

She plays the diligent student. "That all sounds very grand, as you would say. But as a practical matter, how would that kind of love have impacted what happened with Miles?"

"For a start, maybe I would have been more interested in him as a person." I refill our wine glasses "Maybe I would have been less worried about the inconvenience of his visiting me on the weekend. This is crazy, but that guy in church resonated with me this morning. I've never discovered who I am or what I am searching for. I have one kind of treasure, my investment portfolio, and logically my heart is mostly with that since I spend most of my waking hours thinking about it. I have another kind of treasure, Cait and the kids, and my heart is partly with them of course. But there is another thing going on here isn't there—what is the real value of those investments and what do they return?"

"I've been getting threats." Her words come right out of left field. Grace covers her face with her hands and quietly breaks down. Her body shudders as if being hit. My instinct is to hold her but I stay sitting opposite and extend my arm to place my hand on her shoulder. I can hear her gasp for air. Then quite quickly, her breathing becomes easier, as she takes control of her emotions and nails them down under her iron will. She will continue to be who I expect her to be. She will let herself show me the appearance of letting her guard down, but not reveal the darkness she feels in her soul.

"Wow, we are getting right out there now," she says, blowing her nose. To me she is near the edge, I can see she desperately needs to share her feelings. Perhaps the guilt she feels deeply for pushing Miles into oblivion? She whips out her compact and inspects her makeup and repairs the damage to her face as if I am not present. She is expert, it takes only a few seconds. It is a cloud that has passed overhead and now it has gone leaving her refreshed. Only the sadness in her eyes tells a different story.

"What sort of threats?" I'm not going to let it go.

"Nothing too specific. Just that I'm a bitch and will get mine in the end. That I'm responsible for Miles's death. Stuff like that."

"Have you informed the police?"

"Look, it's really no big deal. I'm a big girl you know."

"Yes, but even big girls need looking after sometimes." We are on the edge of something.

She brightens. "We were talking treasure?"

I laugh. "Indeed, we were. What is the absolute return on the lives we have spent managing other people's money?" We retreat from intimacy.

"Sounds to me as if it's time that you bought yourself a red Lamborghini like everyone one else who wants to avoid answering that one."

"What does it profit a man if he owns the whole world but loses his soul?"

We are both soused by now. "No, no Fen, you have it wrong. It's the game we are in. You have to win. Because if you lose now, we are all going to be in deep shit."

***

Six weeks have passed. I am sitting at my desk feeling distracted. It is as if I have landed in a foreign country where things are done quite differently. I wonder what LP Hartley actually meant by 'the levelling aspect of sinnerdom' as I stare listlessly at my computer screens, which I've set up as a kind of portcullis, permitting others only limited access to the fortress of my person.

The two Bloomberg terminals' six displays brim with multicolored tickers, data and graphs which gyrate hypnotically before me. I appraise the M&A deal data as I toggle back and forth between the deal and investment screens. The familiar list of securities I have selected on the basis of complex characteristics related to exchanges, sectors, indices, domicile, geography and other criteria provide me with a sense of continuity, even comfort. The time that I spend staring at these screens is cathartic. I can almost feel the endorphins trickling like morphine from my pituitary gland. I return again and again for another shot like an addict or an obsessive lagotto rooting for truffles. I think this may actually make me happy.

The other two screens on my desk show mail, instant messages, social media, calendar and news feeds pouring out the sly conspiracy of market views. This morning Peiter Viser is being interrogated on CNBC regarding the outlook for Domestic Equities. I have arranged my landline and two iPhones on the desk to the right of the terminal, together with a black notebook to fill the remaining gaps in my redoubt.

I now suffer my days as a stifling stream of meetings driven by urgent and unimportant issues that demand resolution. And the odd important interaction. Candidly, I feel myself drowning, in repeated conversations where people want things from me. My input. My opinion. My sign-off. But most of all, my attention. I have allowed myself, like Christian before me, to become the solitary spider at the center of a web of divergent interests and office politics that sap my energy to build a different future. It did not occur to Christian and it has not yet occurred to me that this culture of dysfunction might be capable of change. I still call Barry occasionally for advice, but most of the time I keep my own counsel.

Yet I have changed personally. At Concord I was shot, it seems, through the head and heart.

I sit in one-on-one meetings with my reports, affecting listening to them like a shrink. I have seriously thought of acquiring a couch on which they could recline during their sessions with me. I tell myself that this way I can let them meander through their time with me and I can watch the market unencumbered by them seeing what I am doing. Sometimes I am interested in the stories they are telling me; sometimes I look past them over their shoulder to the office outside my glass wall and long to wander freely around the halls and financial markets.

A couple of the people I meet with regularly, like Cynthia, are always fun to be with, her acerbic wit, intellectual agility and cynicism lighten my day. Others like Lucas are less convivial.

My mood darkens each time I am compelled to meet Lucas. For such interactions I have weaponized my unfailing courtesy so am able to fire off blisteringly sarcastic comments over the top of my Bloomberg machines towards Lucas, who sits at my desk, mouthing off instances where rules have been transgressed, scheming to discipline and fire people, issuing dark warnings about his colleagues and what I suspect are downright lies. Sometimes Lucas will drop in to see me unannounced. This typically occurs last thing in the evening when I want to leave the office for what is usually the sanctuary of my home. On such occasions Lucas will stand in my doorway and inevitably be angry about something. He will always drop into the conversation that he has been talking to Frost. "As I was saying to John on the phone last night... I'm not sure John would like that... John and the board are convinced that…" And I will nod and smile and wait for Lucas and his contrivances to disappear, perhaps with the smell of sulfur. Lately, these apparitions have become a regular part of my afternoon. On reflecting why, I have decided that Lucas is invariably looking for approval. The man, despite all his dragonnades, is desperately insecure.

When meeting me, Lucas will describe in detail how he has ordered his department and individual roles and summoned his team to staff meetings. He brandishes the agendas for such meetings and the goals that he has driven his people to formulate. There is something almost childlike about his tone. The more he craves approval the less I will yield it.

Lucas leads off, "I've made it very clear. First, I had my performance engineers set up role mandates for each person reporting to me. Then I had everyone send me their top five goals and related timeline for execution. It's been a hell of a few weeks, I tell you. Real culture change." He crosses his arms and smiles with great self-satisfaction, waiting for me to comment.

I say something like "I see", but Lucas does not believe me.

"Now I expect them to send me a list of deliverables each Monday. I sit with each of them with my secretary, so I get them on the record about their commitments. Then every Thursday we meet for a brown bag lunch. My reports and I sit at the table and various other staff sit around the walls of the room."

Beyond his need for approval, I cannot fathom why Lucas should want to provide me with this amount of information.

"Then I go around with their to-dos. I get a very clear view, and so does everyone else in the room, of who's taking ownership and accountability and who is on cruise control. I tell them this is active performance management. My staff bring a chart that shows if an area is up, level or down."

I am horrified. It sounds to me like the proceedings of the Star Chamber, deciding the guilt and punishment of people accused of violating the monarch's order.

"That Cynthia has only made one meeting and is already on the shit list, in fact that's what I want to talk about today. If not now, eventually, I want to fire Cynthia, that guy Purvis, and Grace. Make a few examples. Get the attention of the rest of them. They don't get it, you know. I tell them. No going along to get along!"

Being deliberately obtuse but also genuinely confused, I reply, "I'm not sure I get it either. To get a long, what?"

"Not get a long, what. Get along how!"

"How? What?" I crane my head to get a better view of Lucas whose face has reddened.

"They need to speak up and speak out!"

"I suppose that leaves... when?" I say looking hard at my inbox, trying not to laugh out loud.

"They don't get it."

"I see Lucas, but isn't that where we came in?"

"Some of it is outrageous."

"I have a Dalinian thought: the one thing the world will never have enough of is the outrageous." I say this half to myself, half to Lucas.

"What do you mean by that?" Lucas is suspicious that I may have insulted him in some way.

"Simply that whatever you feel right now it would be disastrous to break up the team in the middle of negotiating the transition and what a lot of people are seeing as traumatic change. We need to maintain momentum. I am sure that Frost would not want to do anything to slow us down. Don't you think the acquirer, the board, our clients and Frost would take a dim view if we lost half of our senior team within a few weeks of assuming leadership? You may want to think again."

"Well, I am not going to stop pushing them, or for change."

"As well you should not, Lucas, as well you should not." As I have been talking, I have been scribbling in the black notebook that sits on my desk. I tear out the page, fold it in two, "Well, if that's it for now, Lucas, we'd better get on. I will see you at the Senior Leadership Group meeting at four." Lucas rises with me as I come around my desk and walk Lucas to his office door, saying, "Thanks Lucas." I hand Lucas the folded paper.

Back in his office, I can see Lucas reading what I have handed him, through the glass wall.

> 'It is easier to build strong children
> Than to repair broken men.'
> Frederick Douglass, 1895.
> Executing the plan is important
> Who you become as a result is crucial!

By his expression I can see Lucas has no idea what I mean.

I am proved right. No one except Grace asks me how I am finding my new role or if I need anything from them. And, of course, at first it does not cross my mind to ask anything of any one of them.

There is a continual—and soon tense—back and forth between Frost, who is constantly dabbling in the acquisition process; his heavies, especially Hudgell, who is power hungry; and me, as I try to manage what I regard as assaults on the company's boundaries. No one has provided me with a playbook. My only mandate is to deliver the sale to the acquirer and keep the lid on XelFunds until the sale is consummated.

Acquisition meetings are full of statements by the acquirer concerning the strength of the deal logic and their conviction that the XelFunds brand, investment and distribution capabilities and culture will be a perfect fit with their portfolio of companies. But somehow the body language of the principals portrays a very different story. Every time that the XelFunds team and I sit down with the acquirer's team, I have the mental image of Isis fighters slitting the throats of hostages.

CHAPTER NINETEEN

I stand at Fen's office door. "Is this still a good time for our update?"

"Sure, Grace. Come in." He looks a bit apprehensive. I have heard from his assistant Andrea that, unlike Christian, Fen takes real pleasure in deleting his meetings on his calendar once they are done and that this subversive act is causing her a lot of confusion in terms of tracking. I noticed that he has three more meetings today; bound to put him in a bad mood.

"Fen, do you mind if we sit over at your conference table?" I'm all business.

"Sure." He drags himself reluctantly across the room.

"There are a ton of things I'd like to touch base on today; here's my list." I can see his heart sink; my update has twelve topics. "I know time is limited so if you don't object, I'd like to focus on item one."

"Employee relations? The phrase sounds embarrassingly promiscuous!" He's not changed. He will take every opportunity to make light of what he doesn't want to handle.

"I felt it prudent to keep the topic generic," keeping my tone serious.

"Miles and Jade, our favorite subject?"

"Yes."

"Okay," he sighs, "where are we?"

"At one level, with Miles we seem to be getting out of the woods," I say positively.

"You mean the medical examiner's verdict?"

"Yes, given that it's been ruled a suicide," I studiously avoid the word 'death'. "We are getting back to a more normalized routine. As you know, the work area is clear and Jade's office has been reconfigured; the crime scene, if you will, has gone. But I remain worried that there is still the possibility that someone may emulate Miles's suicide or be triggered in some other way. Did you know suicide is the number two cause of death between age twenty-five and thirty-four?"

"That's a depressing thought." I can see that he thinks I treat all that has happened as if it is some sort of standard exit process. In his head he will be playing a Monty Python tape in his British accent saying something like, 'Excuse me for a minute, will you? I'm just going outside for a quick suicide,' 'I'd prefer if you'd do it tomorrow, it's going to be quieter then and we won't have that group of visitors from the Japanese bank. And by the way next time can you make it less messy?' For someone who can be funny, he can also be very unfunny and childish.

"He was older than that, though. Between twenty-five and thirty-four years old, you said?"

"Age is not my point. My point is that it is a huge problem—that someone may try to emulate Miles. I've been reading about clusters that can occur like a virus." Since our conversation at Logan Airport, it has been awkward between us. I suspect we both feel we 'overshared', as some of my girlfriends might say.

"Is there anything we should be doing?" Clearly Fen has no idea what he means by saying this, other than it's the sort of thing he thinks he should be saying.

His eyes tell me his thoughts are drifting. Perhaps towards Miles and the instant they spent together in Brooklyn between when Fen opened his front door and when Miles walked away. Fen has told me that sometimes his memory plays their meeting frame by frame, like a sepia movie about to unspool. There is no soundtrack. Just the look on Miles's face and the sound of a pistol shot.

"I'm not sure. Obviously, we have a duty under the law to provide a healthy workplace, but this is tricky. We have offered counseling but no one took it. We have briefed managers on identifying stress and reinforced how to get help through the employee assistance program and hotlines and how to communicate up, if anyone has concerns. We have also strengthened surveillance and building security at all our sites. That's another thing, our managers are getting stressed out, not only about what just happened with Miles's suicide but also with the cumulative stress caused by the acquisition, and also what's going on with the world at large—mass shootings for instance." To emphasize my point, I lay both hands palms-up on the conference table. I am aware that there is a nervous edge to my voice that is unlike me. "I worry that as a team we haven't really debriefed. You know, discussed what happened to Miles in any meaningful way, our fiduciary responsibilities, or how we are coping as individuals and a team."

Fen picks up on my last point. It's as if he can only take so much and my last point is the one that interests him. "That's pretty private, isn't it Grace, how we are coping?" He scribbles something in his notebook, perhaps to avoid looking at me. The subtext of our conversation at Logan looms subversively between us.

"It is private at one level, but at the company level there is a leadership responsibility to create the right operating climate. How our colleagues feel about things personally makes being able to talk about it no less necessary?" I search Fen's eyes again as he glances up from writing.

"Different people take things in different ways, Grace." His ambiguity leaves me uncertain.

I persist "True. But there is no stigma to expressing feelings about this. How can the leadership help others if they themselves haven't got help?" *Is this conversation about us or about leadership?* I ask myself.

"Not everyone wears their heart on their sleeve." Fen glances up from his notebook. "Someone like Cynthia will drive right through this kind of situation. Someone like Tiffany might need more help."

"It's not about wearing hearts; it's about recognizing that people have them." There has been a role reversal from our previous conversations. It is usually Fen who is on the side of the angels.

"This is not the only thing happening, Grace. If we give the tragic more air, will we get more?"

"Can I ask you a question, Fen?"

"Sure."

"Have you changed your thinking from our conversation in Boston?"

"Regarding what?" He is at once alert.

"In relation to thinking through what we are trying to achieve?" I have fumbled the question and Fen will not help me retrieve the ball.

"Right now, I am just trying to figure out my job. I am beginning to think that part of that is setting boundaries." I can feel Fen's words pushing me away. He has become a locked box. He will not open up. Certainly not to me.

I return to less treacherous ground. "There is a fiduciary issue here. In France, they just put half a dozen people on trial, including the CEO by the way, for creating a hostile environment which resulted in people killing themselves."

"Some cases make themselves. Not everything needs to be so dramatic." It is his form of rebuke.

"I get that. But see what is going to happen here. Jade will say that she was harassed by her manager. She complained. Then in the most passive aggressive way possible, her manager kills himself right in front of her. And what does the company do before the event? Nothing. And what did the company do after the event? Nothing."

"I'm not saying do nothing, Grace. Do all that people engagement stuff you do. I am just saying be measured."

"Not unreasonable but the issue here is not policy. It is leadership." For a moment I can see he weighs challenging me on my inference but thinks better of it.

"And you actually think that a 'come to Jesus' session where we let it all hang out is going to change the behavior of the senior team?" Somehow we have both become angry and frustrated.

I've thought a lot about what I should say to Fen and what I want to hear from him. Night after night as I've clambered restlessly through sleepless hours, I've rehearsed what I will say at this point in our conversation. I tell myself that it's important that I'm pragmatic. I plunge in "No, I don't think a single session talking amongst the senior team about what happened to Miles will change a lot. But it could be an important start. Do we have a core issue here? Is our culture sick, as Barry would have us believe? Answer: yes. For years, we have all allowed ourselves to live a set of values that stink, so long as we have delivered the bottom line. It was our conversation at Logan that got me thinking about this. You were right about so much that afternoon. No one has wanted to rock the boat, because rocking the boat can threaten the stock price. And now Lucas is causing havoc and destroying any remnants of decency that we do have. And Frost doesn't care. Indeed, it seems to me, that he wants to promote dysfunction so it somehow gets him to a sale quicker. And by the way, most people see that we are in trouble Fen. Most people understand what is happening to us. We are compromised and probably the best thing that can happen to us is that we are sold." I am a bit breathless. Fen looks at me as if I have thrown up over the conference table.

Fen places his elbows on the conference table, steeples his hands and closes his eyes. Given our conversation in Boston I fear that he may utter some sort of prayer. But instead of genuflecting, he rises from his chair and walks to the window. "Let's say for one moment that you are right. From a moral point of view, what is our obligation?"

"What do you mean?" In my head I'm screaming, *That's right my man, you can do this!*

"Well, as we sit here, we are being paid. We are taking the money for what you say is abhorrent."

"Abhorrent is strong, but from some points of view, yes." Fen hardly lets me finish my sentence.

"No. From every point of view, if what you say is indeed true, we are enabling bad things to happen just by occupying the jobs we have. We are furthering the conspiracy to damage the shareholders, employees and customers for whom we are responsible."

Job done. I am already stepping back emotionally.

"Or is there a dilemma here? Is it more like Faust? Have we given our soul at least in part, in exchange for a belief that while the culture as a whole may stink, at least the piece that we live in can be influenced by the integrity we are prepared to live? This is what I've been thinking. Maybe this is an opportunity to change things. Perhaps we can play a different game? Perhaps we can put our soul in a different place?"

I don't really get it. I say, "What happened to Faust?"

Fen turns from the window towards me, smiling. "Oh, he was irrevocably damned because he preferred human to divine knowledge. In fact, in Germany throughout the sixteenth century he was vulgarized as a figure of fun."

"Isn't there a better model?" I now see now that there is a wasteland of confusion between us. I may have set him off in a direction that will end in confrontation with Frost, leaving me little room for maneuver. Fen is far more politically naive than I thought.

"I'm working on it. Seriously, if there is a way forward to save the company it's going to be a real Hail Mary. I don't need to say this, but in terms of priorities, the first thing we need to do is resolve the situation with Jade. If we fail to do that, end of story. We urgently need a settlement."

"Agreed." At least he hasn't lost the plot on that. "Cynthia and I are set to meet with her and her lawyer tomorrow. Her lawyer asked for the opportunity to put demands to the company before the company invokes mediation. We will need parameters from you on any financial settlement."

"Yes, and I will need approval on any big number from Frost. Second, I need to pull the crew together. It's been clear to me from the start that Frost imposed this ridiculous structure to ensure we are weak and that his man Lucas has a chokehold on everything that is independent from him. We need to build a new leadership team. A coalition of the willing if you like. I am sure of you Grace, Cynthia, John, Steve, Tiffany and Tom. But I am not entirely sure where the others stand and Lucas is a major concern." I feel guilty that he has come to trust me so.

"Is there any way that we can meet off-site with Cynthia and the rest?" I know that I am getting him further in but I can't resist it. "If they are in, maybe we can figure out how to manage through this."

"Okay, it's risky but let's try it. Why don't you very discreetly round them up for drinks at my place this Wednesday evening at 7:30. If the whistle gets blown, I can position the gathering as part one of a two-part get-to-know-everyone session where a second meeting will follow and include others in management. We also have to deal with the acquisition issues. As far as I read it the acquisition is a lot more complex than it had appeared initially and it looks as if it may be stalling. Frost is giving me hell hourly. Something doesn't smell right about it to me. In fact, from a shareholder and employee point of view, I'm beginning to think it will be a disaster. Bad for XelFunds and bad for Pompton Financial. We are a long way from consummation. There is a lot at stake for Frost in fact," Fen pauses. "Let's keep that till later."

Then he says, "To your point earlier, we need to address the employee climate. Put together a coherent and pragmatic plan to rebuild the culture based on high conviction, not shared greed!"

"Yes, and if it's not too consultant speak, this becomes part of a strategy for change which is owned and driven by the senior team." I can't help myself. I am a natural collaborator, a chameleon of loyalties.

"Frankly Grace, this is moving a lot further and faster than I intended. But we are between a rock and a hard place. None of this is safe. Are you sure that you are in?"

"You bet I am." Has he subconsciously detected something in me? The way that I have been looking at him perhaps. My furtive glances at his mouth as he speaks rather than looking him in the eye?

"Very well then. All's fair in love and war. Let's get it done!" He smiles at me and for a moment, without cynicism, I return his gaze.

When I return to my office, I see a dead wasp shriveled up on my mouse pad. I know it to be an omen. Of what I am not sure. From somewhere I remember the old Buddhist meme, 'Death ripens the result of birth.'

CHAPTER TWENTY

An article has appeared on page one of the business section of the New York Times. It is entitled 'The Search for Equality'. Where next? The piece bemoans the continuing problems experienced by women and minorities in the workplace and describes several cases of egregious conduct by individual executives and the companies that employ them. Of itself the story might be unremarkable, given the plethora of recent pieces on 'Me Too' consciousness. However, the story goes further and takes a new tack. The article refers to the Jade Edwards allegations of harassment and discrimination on the part of Miles McCarthy, the latter's tragic death and the question of XelFunds' accountability for creating the culture within which such events could occur. The focus of the story is that the public are greatly divided as to whether the 'Me Too' movement has created a climate where offenders are held appropriately accountable, or whether in fact the movement has gone too far, and created a climate of instant condemnation and persecution, where a rush to judgment and unproven allegations are ruining careers and even driving people to suicide.

The article causes a firestorm within Pompton's executive suite. Grace has been bombarded by frantic messages from Tom Dawson and Hudgell demanding assurances that she is on top of the situation. She has been working overnight with Cynthia and Abby on XelFunds communication strategy for the press and employees in response to the article and has drafted a memo to staff explaining the company's position. It reads,

Colleagues,

Many of us continue to be in a state of shock and are all deeply disturbed by the tragic events that occurred recently in the New York office. Our hearts go out to Miles McCarthy's family and all who have been impacted by this very sad and tragic event.

The accompanying press release contains our response to the assertions that appear in today's New York Times. Let me reinforce what that statement says: XelFunds does not tolerate harassment or abuse of our employees or business partners.

If you have a concern please speak up and bring it to the attention of your manager, HR representative, legal department or Ethics Hotline. Also, know that my door is open to you at any time. I assure you that all such concerns will be thoroughly and impartially investigated. I appreciate that you may have questions, but please understand that we cannot discuss the specifics of investigations.

I am excited by the opportunities that are before us as we move ahead and look forward to earning your trust as the new CEO.

Fen

Grace, Cynthia, Tom Dawson and XelFunds' external legal counsel, Andrew Miller, are set to meet with Jade and her legal representatives at the JAMS Mediation and Arbitration Office at 620 8th Avenue at 9 am to discuss her claims against the company. This is not to be a formal mediation or arbitration but has been proposed by Jade's counsel as the opportunity for an informal exchange between interested parties before they enter formal proceedings. XelFunds' external legal counsel has expressed concern that this may not be the most prudent approach to resolving the case and that it might indeed prejudice the legal processes but Cynthia has insisted that it is worth trying to settle the case quickly, given current business circumstances.

Simultaneously, Cait stands in her kitchen in Brooklyn, drinking coffee and reading a column by David Brooks in the Times, about what he describes as stumbling into the age of diversity, before she leaves for work. She is interested in what he has written about the way that political preferences are increasingly driven by age rather than race, sex or education. She jealously guards this time of day, between the kids leaving for school and Fen leaving for the office and her own departure for work, as critical to her mental health.

Cait turns to the business section of the paper and there, plastered across page one, is an article captioned 'The Search for Equality'. She reads the piece in some shock but with more than some cynicism, especially as the story features not only the sexual details of Jade's complaint but also, to her surprise, describes the physical effects of Miles's suicide in gory detail. The company has responded to the allegations in the story to the effect that it does not tolerate harassment or abuse of employees. If a concern is brought to the company's attention it is investigated quickly and thoroughly. It always ensures that such investigations are impartial etc. Its employee policies are proactive and designed to actively promote a healthy psychological and physical working environment. She nearly chokes on her coffee when she reads,

> Employees are encouraged to report any instance of harassment or abuse to their manager etc. The company has conducted a comprehensive investigation into the matters raised by Ms. Edwards. The matter is currently under review and the company cannot make any further comment at this time.

At the same hour, in the XelFunds boardroom in Tower One, Fen, with Cynthia at his side, is meeting with the leader of the acquisition team, Simon Alverez, together with John Purvis, Lucas Aiello and Peiter Viser, to review progress on the sale of XelFunds. Viser, who sits with a self-satisfied grin on his face, is clearly elated by his recent elevation to CIO, or as he likes to describe it to the Investment team, the peerage.

Simon Alverez, a thin, sleek, dark-haired man in his early forties who frequently wears a frown together with his dark jacket, blue jeans and white shirt, is clearly worried about something. Fen thinks this odd since it seems to him that Alverez usually has the bearing and sneering attitude of a fine sommelier at Jean-Georges. Simon reports to Abby who is too weak to manage him, so as a practical matter Cynthia has stepped in and regularly supplies his marching orders which, surprisingly, he follows with the contented agreement of a podenco.

Alverez speaks with a strong accent acquired during his childhood in Argentina. When he says, "We have hit a snag," Fen deliberately hears it as "We have it a snug!" And finds it hard to keep a straight face as he thanks the Almighty that he still has a sense of humor, then checks himself, remembering the many times he has seen others react to his own equally inaccessible British timbre.

"This is what I wanted us to hear, Fen." Cynthia's voice has a serious intonation that immediately signals bad news.

Alverez says, "It looks like there may be a problem with the ownership structure."

It's 9:45 in the ante-room at the JAM's office. Grace constantly checks her iPhone for messages from Cynthia who has been radio silent for the past hour. Grace fears further delay will antagonize Jade and decides that she should proceed with the meeting. She motions to Tom and Andy who are standing at the other side of the room chatting by the coffee cart. "Okay, we can't wait any longer, we're going in." Accompanied by Tom and Andrew, Grace knocks on the door and walks into the conference room occupied by Jade and her lawyer, Richard Vernon. Introductions are made and handshakes and cards are exchanged before Tom and Andrew seat themselves each side of Grace, across the conference table from Jade and her lawyer.

"My apologies for the delay." As Grace speaks, she looks directly at Jade, who is a wreck. Grace is shocked to see how Jade appears transformed. Her hair which normally shines in a bob cut framing the strong lines of her face is awry and now accentuates her reddened eyes, from which the light seems to have faded. It strikes Grace that Jade suddenly looks old. Jade does not reply.

Vernon takes the initiative. "We wanted this conversation to be outside the run of normal litigation because we would like to bring this matter to a close, without formality, for the good of all concerned. My client has no wish for publicity. She simply wants to get on with her life without further prejudice to her person or career. Let me cut to the chase." As Vernon speaks, he is careful to address all three of them across the conference table. His small black eyes probe the faces of his opposition, trying to weigh up who is likely to have the authority to make a deal. "My client has been the subject of devastating injury to her person and career. The facts are undeniable. My client complained confidentially to officers of the company about the harassment and hostility of her boss. The company did nothing about it. Indeed, it permitted the circumstances where the life of my client was threatened and she was subjected to horrific trauma that has destroyed her health and probably her career."

"As you know, Mr. Vernon, from our extensive correspondence, we dispute what you are presenting as facts and take a very different view." Andrew Miller addresses Vernon from behind his silver wireframed eyeglasses with quiet assurance. A man in his late fifties, he gives off a slightly resigned air, not altogether of boredom, more that he has heard all this before and is unmoved by the hearing.

"Well, we could let a judge decide that, but here is our offer. My client will consider withdrawing her complaint in exchange for," and at this Vernon begins to raise his fingers as he reads from a prepared list of demands scribbled on a yellow notepad.

"1. Fifteen million dollars as compensation for her distress. 2. Continuing with her current employment responsibilities but reporting directly to the CIO. 3. XelFunds management receives training in managing diversity in the workplace. 4. XelFunds issues a joint press release with Ms. Edwards to the effect that we have reached an agreement for an undisclosed sum and that Ms. Edwards continues as a highly valuable member of the firm. 5. In addition, Ms. Edwards is guaranteed a fixed-term contract for five years at the minimum of the current level of base pay and bonus."

The room is replete with a stupefied silence. A clock on the wall is heard ticking.

Andy smiles oddly as he speaks, as if suppressing a bad case of indigestion. "It was my previous impression that we were invited here today to see if there was a basis for settlement. These demands are outrageous and absolutely unacceptable to my client." Grace does not know Andy well and can't determine if his outrage is genuine or manufactured. "We need to take a break to discuss what you are offering. What you are demanding is not at all in the realm of possibility for us. But let us at least process what you are saying. Shall we reconvene in an hour or so?"

When Grace, Tom and Andy caucus in the adjacent side room, Grace says, "Andy, you have this ability to somehow make everything seem more comfortable than it is. Thank God one of us is staying grounded."

"In reality it's suppressed panic, Grace. My read is that they are overplaying it. To go up is simply a negotiating ploy. Will you take her back, Grace?"

"I really can't see that is an option for either her or us, Andy."

"We could be compelled to if this goes to trial, Grace," Tom says.

"Perhaps Tom, but I think this whole thing is out of proportion."

Andy asks, "What terms are you empowered to negotiate?"

Grace and Tom look at each other. Tom takes the lead. "The corporate intention is to make this disappear, and from a shareholder point of view we need to keep this under the radar."

"Do you have a number?"

Tom turns to Grace, "Your thoughts?"

"Well, our normal severance policy is a maximum of a year's total compensation. Her package is around three million including long term compensation. So, given the unusual circumstances of the case, it seems to me that six million would not be unreasonable and could be defended before the board."

Andy responds, "That's essentially half what she wants, I'm not sure that will cut it."

"I think I'd better call Hudgell to get a view."

"Do that Tom, and I will call Fen, although frankly, I'm no longer sure of who has the say so on this?"

"It's almost certainly going to be Frost," Tom replies.

Grace tries to raise Fen and Cynthia but there is still no response. Tom is more successful with Hudgell and they return to the negotiation with authority to settle for six million and no reinstatement, deciding to focus on the financial settlement and Jade's employment status and to deal with the other matters as secondary issues.

Returning to the negotiating table, Grace appraises Jade's body language as Andy frames the counteroffer. Jade is picking at the skin on the back of her hand and appears to be totally out of it and not hearing what is being said.

"Look guys, this is not nearly enough given what my client has been through," Vernon continues the negotiation dance, and so a couple of hours go by with breaks for both sides to consider the other's offer. It seems to Grace that Jade is increasingly fragile and near the edge of her composure. She remains silent through the entire discussion.

XelFunds have upped their offer to eight million dollars, excluding the value of Jade's stock holdings and have presented this as their final offer, following very reluctant authorization from Frost.

Vernon begins, "You know the gap is still too big," and begins to enumerate the wide range of issues that remain on the table, together with the abuse that his client has suffered.

"I take it!" Jade's lips are partly closed, the sound of her indistinct muttering is hardly caught in the flow of conversation.

Grace, alert to Jade's demeanor asks, "Did you say something, Jade?"

"I will take it. I will take the money. The eight million plus my unvested and vested stock. I take it!" Her muttering pitches up into something more like a scream.

"I can't live with it. I see his face. I hate that place. I will never go near it again. He did that to me, to me! I am a human. Not an animal. You think I want the money and that's all, Grace. It is not like that. When he kills himself, he kills me! My life is dead. I can never go back. And no one cares. I am inconvenient to you all now. An investment gone south. Well, I walk. I go with something of myself maybe. You think I am the bitch, the hard one. Don't you see? I tell you I hated him and I did! I wanted him for how he could help me. And he wanted me for a bit on the side, a nice fuck on a Friday night when his wife was in Boston. But then something happened. I felt him drifting away. It was like I was losing him. He was sliding out of sight and I could not stop him. So I hate him again because I hate myself. But I think I truly did love him, Grace. I take the eight million and go someplace. Someplace it does not rain. Some place that is not New York. And I leave you with the bitches, Grace and I leave you with these bad guys who are empty suits who want to fuck you, Grace." Jade stands unsteadily and leans against the conference table. "You fix everything now, Richard Vernon, and I will sign. I will sign." They watch her walk to the door. Emptied of her rage she seems frail, a half-person passing beyond them into her personal desolation.

They are all dumbfounded.

Vernon gathers his papers into his briefcase and leaves the room. "You will be hearing from me then, Ms. Rutler, gentlemen."

Andy, Tom and Grace also leave without much being said. Although there is a quiet sense of suppressed jubilation flashing between the three of them as Tom turns to Grace,

"Want to come for a drink?"

"No thanks Tom, I'm just going to walk a while." And Grace does indeed walk for a while and thinks about the bitches she works with and the guys in empty suits who want to fuck her and as usual, feels quite alone.

***

As Cait finishes reading the newspaper, Alina breezes into the kitchen. She is sweating from the exertion of walking up from the subway. "They are ridiculous, you know?"

"Who?"

"Those guys digging the road. You can't walk by for the whistles and shouts."

"You should be happy. You get to my age; you listen for the shouts but they don't come!"

"You are not so bad, Cait."

"Thanks for saying, Alina. I need the morale boost!" Smiling to herself, Cait rummages through her leather shoulder bag and pulls out her iPad, tempted, but avoiding the deceit of checking her makeup in the mirror.

"Was it different?"

"Was what different?" Cait is slightly annoyed because she wants to get on to her work and call Fen about the article in the paper.

"When you were my age?"

"When I was your age, Alina, dinosaurs still roamed the earth."

"Seriously, do you think it was that different or is it all the same?"

Unconsciously, Cait looks at her watch, then realizes that Alina is asking a real question. "Well, I am sure that it was quite different."

"I mean, did you feel under this constant pressure, almost like you are under constant surveillance?"

"Well, in some ways I did actually."

"You had the What's Up and Facebook and Tinder too?"

"No. But I had the nuns and Father Conroy and my Dad and my sisters. They were like the Nazis sometimes!" Cait leans back against the refrigerator and smiles.

"You see, where I come from we have this definitely weird history." She speaks like rapid fire. "I know my history, you know. Absolutely like the Lord's Prayer. We were like a big feudal quagmire. I like that word, I got it in my English class last week."

"Oh, I wondered where all those gems you've been using lately came from!" Cait says laughing.

"Anyway, like I was saying, Romania is old country but obscure. 'Obscure', that's another one. We are Transylvanians like Dracula, but as it turns out the Austrians then the Russians they suck the blood out of us! That is funny right?"

"Yes, I suppose it is." Cait is watching her. Why hasn't she seen Alina like this before?

"Then come all the big wars, a kind of weak dictator king, the Iron Guards, the fascists, Hitler, until we hit a brick wall, Russia, so we get occupied again, this time by the Soviets and Ceausescu the soviet puppet. You ask me how I know this?"

"Yes, I was wondering."

"I get it all from my grandfather. We are close family when I was kid. He teaches me all this. We are not stupid."

"I am sure."

"In 1989 we have a big revolution, get into the EEC and NATO and all that. We become good global citizens. Then everyone gets unhappy because the big dreams we had didn't happen. And now everyone forgets the Soviets and everyone is unhappy and protesting again."

"And you came here to the US, Alina?"

"Yes, I get out. I do not love my country. I was processed by it. I learned English as young as humanly possible. I watch MTV. I love American culture. I am not stupid at the university, I read Florenta Albu and Lena Constante. I see Natalie Portman at the movies. I find it hard to leave my mum and dad and sister but I have to get out. I make a whip out of shit. My aunt in Queens she gets me in here. You know there are ways. I make new family with them."

"But it is not up to your expectations?"

"You mean did the media sell donuts to us? I did not say that many things are not good here! But I am completely thinking as I am walking down the street that it's not so different here. Same big social media. Same big focus on having a good time at night and on weekend. Same work pressures. You know, with Adrian my boyfriend, he works in technology start-up like a dog. Twenty-four hours they have him on call. We live by Chinese food and Netflix, when we can stay awake to watch it. This is the life we lead. This is living the dream for us now."

"Yes, I suppose it hits us all in different ways."

"And for you, how is it for you?"

This conversation is going to a place where Cait is not comfortable. Its direction is a little too close to home to have with Alina. But despite natural caution Cait says, "Life gets complicated. Fen and I are immigrants too. We also have very complicated histories. We come from different tribes and find ourselves in this place, where the village and tribe are also very different. We are in a kind of bubble I suppose. I was saying this to Fen the other night. As I think about it, many bubbles within bubbles in fact. We are in New York. We are on the Heights in Brooklyn. We are in jobs that have their own bubble. We rarely burst the bubble to look at reality."

"Until someone blows their head off right on your doorstep. Right?"

It dawns on Cait that Alina has read the paper, this conversation is undoubtedly all about that. "Yes, it was a terrible shock."

"You think that as it says in the paper it was all about him feeling persecuted because of how he pressured her?"

"I can't say. I didn't know either of them that well."

"To be honest I don't think he should feel that guilty. Men are men. They do what they do. Like those guys in the street. They will always whistle."

"Only if we let them, Alina." Cait can't resist the opportunity to educate. "You asked me about growing up. My life was all about men of one kind or another. It was about the rules they created. No this. No that. No abortion. No weed. No infidelity. No fags. At least not publicly. We didn't know much about Islam or Islamic terrorism but we had nuns wrapped in their own kind of hijab and our own guys blowing up the Brits. We had abused kids locked in orphanages. A religion that sat on us like a graveyard. And predators peddling child pornography after the sermons they preached. We had a lot of anger and outrage. I had a lot of anger." Cait pauses for a moment. "And a lot of laughter and humor and a big diaspora living happily in London. And that's where I got to eventually. Sometimes it's difficult for people of my generation to understand why people of yours don't seem to value what we fought for. By the time I arrived on the work scene it seemed like all the spadework had been done. In '69 Bernadette Devlin was the youngest Member of Parliament; Miss World had been protested. My focus was learning about how the first UK Rape Crisis Network was formed and how I could promote women's and patients' rights."

As if not fully registering what Cait has said, Alina replies, "Oh I think we do."

"You do what?"

"Value what women of your generation did to make things better in this country. Not that I think about it, frankly. But, you know, all this stuff in the media has a kind of chilling effect. A date can seem like an interview. You have to be so careful what you say if you have a date. You feel apathetic— new word too, by the way. Dating is kind of exhausting. But you know, you take your heart in your teeth. First you go online. You hope to meet someone. You see their profile. You know it's mostly likely a con job like your own. Maybe you show up at some nice new restaurant you have found in a nice black dress. You know," she makes a sweeping motion with her hand, "you get that cool haircut, yes?" She nods at Cait who smiles and nods back. "And then you have a tense evening if you ever do meet the person who of course shows up late and with the wrong look, in a pair of blue jeans and a shirt that is too small for him. Is he allowed to touch you? Are you allowed to touch him? And do you pay for drinks or does he pay? And when you get out of the restaurant you look to see if he has a nice black BMW or better still some cool road bike, but it turns out he took the subway and lives some place you don't want to go, for sure. You tell him, like horses' Easter, that will never happen! If you do eventually go to his place it's a mess. He lives in a trash can that you know he will expect you to clean. And then the whole sex thing. We have all seen so much porn that it's hardly worth doing it so we just sleep a lot."

"You know that's so true; sleep really is the first sign of recovery." They both dissolve into laughter.

Cait sees that Alina is in her bubble too. They have not talked about what is in their hearts because their heads are full of shit? Alina is beautiful. She thinks of the small questions, the stuff of her life, of her survival, unlike herself who is still tormented by the tectonic plates of social policy and the ghosts of her childhood. "Well, I'm not sure we solved anything but it was great to chat. I definitely do have to go."

"Interesting conversation," Cait thinks as she walks past the men working in the road by the subway. For an instant, her mind wanders back to her idyllic childhood in Dalkey, and her unresolved feelings of guilt about poverty she witnessed daily on the streets of the Dublin. From somewhere she hears a whistle. She turns and looks a construction worker straight in the eye and he smiles.

***

"Very well, Simon. And what might those problems with the ownership structure be?" Fen asks the question and settles back into his chair.

Cynthia intervenes and scribbles on a pad as she speaks. "Before we get into this, let's be clear, this conversation is privileged."

All eyes are focused on Simon. "Well, on our side as we dug in we found there are very deep holdings by management in XelFunds."

"There is nothing new there, Simon. Our long-term compensation programs are designed to ensure that a good chunk of key employee net worth is tied up in the company. We have a pool of shares under the Equity Holders Agreement allocated to the employee stock program. How much is that approximately, John?"

"Fairly high, Fen. In fact, about twenty-five percent of the equity."

"And how much of that is outstanding, John?"

"Almost all of it."

"It's not that portion of the equity that I'm referring to." Alverez uncorks and starts to pour. "When we got into the remaining equity, the Pompton corporate holding, we found that two individuals hold a significant portion of the stock."

Fen sits forward in his chair. "Mr. Frost and Mr. Hudgell."

All eyes are focused on Fen, who steeples his hands before his mouth.

"And what's the other shoe to drop, Simon?" Cynthia asks, her voice unusually restrained.

"Indeed, as I told you," Simon speaks as if describing a very fine and expensive vintage; he swills his answer around his mouth savoring the moment, then spits out his reply. "We researched the major equity holders of the acquirer and to our surprise found that Frost and Hudgell are major stockholders in that corporation too, through a hedge fund where they have a controlling interest."

"How very quaint," Cynthia mutters as she types something into her iPhone.

"Were you aware of this, John?"

"No. As we've moved through the acquisition process, I've been finding a few odd things in the financials, but frankly I never thought to look at it in any sort of analytical way." His body language becomes very defensive as he crosses his arms. "I'm still new to this to a great extent."

"This is not necessarily strange to me, Fen."

"You think not, Lucas?"

"Not necessarily, no. I think we need to ask clarification from Ella Kagen in Corporate Finance. I am sure she will give us the right guidance," Lucas shoots back, trying to summon some kind of authority.

"From a deal perspective then, are you saying that Frost can essentially approve both sides of this deal, Simon?" Peiter Viser asks this question with an incredulous tone.

"Well, I am saying nothing for sure." Simon now sounds as if he is not confident in the wine he has poured. As he exchanges glances with Lucas, he appears uncertain as to whether he should stick with his recommendation or apologize for the wine being corked. "There may not be any conflicts when we understand the whole story. We came across what look like some interesting facts and reported them to Cynthia, who thought I should surface them."

"Right. Let's not jump to any conclusions here. It will be prudent for us to keep this conversation between ourselves. Lucas, I think this is a matter for me to bring to Frost, so I would rather you did not discuss it outside this room for the time being. Simon, who knows about this in your team?"

"Two senior analysts."

"Very well, tell them to keep quiet too. I will get back to you when I am clear on the impact of this information following discussion with Frost. Thanks for bringing this to our attention, Simon. Great progress! Let's get back to work."

As the meeting breaks up, Fen asks Cynthia to stay and asks, "What do you think?"

"Sounds like a shit show to me. There is clearly subterranean stuff going on."

"Surely the auditors and the board must be aware of this?"

"Stranger things have happened. Those two guys…"

"You mean Frost and Hudgell?"

"Those two guys are going to make a ton of money if this transaction is consummated."

"Could it could be that the board knows about the XelFunds side of this and views that as an appropriate part of Frost's compensation?"

"That would be odd but I suppose maybe it's possible. But I bet they don't know about Frost's holdings in the acquirer and if they do that's a big problem, unless somehow it's been declared. It's an absolute mess."

"Well, I have to discuss it with Frost. And where does Hudgell fit in this?"

"He's Rasputin to the Czar probably. Do you have any connections to members of the Pompton board?"

"Unfortunately, no. I am deep with the XelFunds boards but really quite at arm's length with the Pompton board."

"That's a pity because we could certainly do with them on side right now. How does this all play to the conversation we were all going to have at your house?"

"I don't see that it makes a real difference to the core case that we should try to defend the company. Our position will be immeasurably strengthened, though, if what Simon says proves out."

"Oh shit! I was supposed to be meeting with Grace and that maniac Edwards. Seems it's kicked off and Edwards has upped her ask."

"You think she has a case?"

"Come on Fen. She has a huge case. You saw the press this morning."

"No. I mean aside from your professional opinion, do you think she should ask for money for what went on here?"

"All my life, I have cut through the bullshit. Taken no prisoners. You know me, I am the strongest man around here. But I've paid a price. It has been harder than it should have been. I don't wear my heart on my sleeve but I have had to make people treat me like a man instead of a woman and that has distorted me and the world I live in. When I was a kid I learned to harden up. I was treated like a sexual aboriginal in Australia, I couldn't be me. I was not to be admitted. I couldn't be a dyke. I can't even be one now. Even though there are parades for us! I didn't want to be a man, Fen, I wanted to be a dyke. A woman who loves other women. But instead of that, to get on I have had to be a woman who has three loves: the law, money and myself. There Fen, you don't know it, but you've been working with the new holy trinity!" Cynthia laughs and raises both hands, "I should join those evangelicals over at Hillsong!

"So, does Edwards deserve financial compensation? Yes of course she does, because that's the way things go right now in business! But nothing can really compensate for the shit she took. Even though she is a twisted woman, she deserves compensation. How much financially I actually don't know or care. But what happened to her was an assault. A slow assault and then a rape of her soul, Fen. Candidly, what else could he have done to her that would have been worse?"

"He came to see me, you know."

"Yes, I heard that."

"Personally, I don't think he was trying to hurt her when he killed himself. I think he had simply got to the end of himself. Played his game and found nothing. In some way, I think it may have been an act of love on his part."

"My God, you men are total egotists. No wonder the world is so fucked up!"

"But before you dismiss it Cynth, could what I am saying be right? Do you think, deranged as he was, he loved her?"

"You are a bloody romantic, not a realist Fen!"

***

Frost's voice is as jovial as usual. "So how is it going over there, Lucas?"

"The latest on the acquisition front is that the acquisition team has discovered what they think may be an odd capital structure. They are questioning your financial holdings in XelFunds and your ownership interest in the acquirer."

"Who is party to this?"

"Fen, Purvis the CFO, Viser, Cynthia Browne and her side kick Pierre Alverez and a couple of juniors who identified the issue. Fen told everyone to keep quiet and that he plans to bring the matter to you."

"You understand, Lucas, that there is in fact no conflict here?"

"Of course, John."

"All my holdings are disclosed and strictly governed by the board."

"I was expecting you to say that. I am afraid that this is another example of XelFunds being out of control and leadership demonstrating a total lack of loyalty to you and the corporation."

"Leave the matter with me, Lucas. There will be very important work for you, and things to do. Stay in touch."

Lucas is left looking at his phone as a thought runs through his head. *If you play this well you may come out of this in a good place, a very good place indeed.*

CHAPTER TWENTY-ONE

The chosen are standing around in Fen's kitchen. Joe and Rosie are in bed, Alina has left for the day. Cait is in her office on the top floor of the house doing email. Fred the dog is lying on his back, oblivious to those in the room.

People have paired up to chat, as if at a cocktail party. Everyone has arrived on time. To Fen, the scene looks like the dark etching by Riffaut of a prisoner in a crowded room. His eyes sweep across those present: Grace, Cynthia, John, Tom, Steve who has flown in from the Operating Center, Tiffany, Abby and Dean Harris, the head of Fixed Income. He eventually decided to extend the circle and invite everyone whom he felt he could trust. He suddenly feels a deep affection for them all.

Fen places his glass of chardonnay on the concrete island in the middle of the room. "Thanks for being here tonight. I know that you must be wondering, why all the cloak and dagger?" There is a ripple of laughter. "I am new to this job and frankly not sure how to play things." He hears himself speaking but it feels more like scratching his nails on a blackboard than the well-rehearsed rallying cry he has planned. "I am certain that if we are to get through what's before us, I need each one of you to be onboard the bus. Is that the right kind of metaphor?" He looks around the room. They seem open but it's difficult to tell.

"As long as you don't start talking about the ship of state, Fen!" Tom raises his glass in Fen's direction as he speaks.

"You got it, Tom!" Fen returns Tom's smile. "We have come a long way. How far is it from being a band of antagonistic hard-arses to a crew of disgruntled misfits?" There is more laughter this time. "The fact is that we are in a tricky situation. The reporting structure that has been foisted upon us by Frost is ridiculous; it is preventing us working together, and frankly worsening relationships that were already strained."

"Fen, if that is the case, why didn't you invite Lucas, Peiter, and Geoff Peach to this meeting?" Abby asks.

"Because frankly, I do not trust them to be on the bus with us." Several in the room adopt uncomfortable expressions.

"But you do realize that puts us in an impossible position, don't you?"

"Yes, and because of that, if you want to walk away from this conversation I will entirely respect your decision. And that goes for everyone else too." No one moves.

"So, what do you want from us, Fen?" Steve asks.

"I want you to commit to this team and to helping us move forward."

"Understood, but what does that look like?"

"Three things. Honest communication between us. Energy around getting the acquisition resolved. Loyalty to the team and to each other."

"I don't think there is anything there that any of us would disagree with. But is there more to the situation than this reporting anomaly—the problem with Lucas and what that implies about our autonomy?"

"I'll take that one if I may, Fen." Cynthia speaks with her usual authority. "Yes Steve, we do have other concerns. As we have looked at the offer on the table from the acquirer we have become increasingly concerned that the deal is not in XelFunds' interests in terms of the return to shareholders, or general business outcomes, to say nothing of employees who will clearly be eviscerated. In fact, we may be faced with a situation where Frost is doing something which is unethical, if not downright illegal."

"But if we are talking about ethics—new to us by the way—don't we have an ethical requirement to be objective and to act on behalf of the corporation to get this transaction done?" Fen notes that John, who asks this question, has a very red face and wonders if he has drunk a little too much.

"We certainly do John, provided that it is in the shareholders' interests."

"Which shareholders, the people who own XelFunds or the people who own the funds we manage?"

"We must defend both of those things, Steve." Fen looks at him directly as he intervenes. "And that has become more complex as we have dug into the ownership structure of the company."

"Meaning?" Abby asks.

"Meaning, that it looks like Frost and Hudgell have substantial holdings in both XelFunds, for compensation purposes, and in the company seeking to acquire us. They are set to get paid at both ends of the planned transaction. There is some very odd financial engineering going on that does not seem right from a legal or compliance perspective." As she says this Cynthia seems oddly sad. It is as if she has been informed of a death in the family.

Fred's heavy breathing and odd snuffles suddenly become audible as he continues to sleep, legs akimbo, in the middle of the floor.

"Look everyone, there is not a lot more to say at this point." Fen holds his hands out as if weighing something. "I don't want us to get ahead of ourselves. My purpose in having us meet is to recognize that for once we are beginning to act like something resembling a team. That is something to celebrate, given our shared history. It feels a lot better to be one of us now, I think. I want to rally your support, encourage you that we are fighting our way through this and to share with you what we know so far, some of which is great. Some of which is worrying." He does not use the word 'threatening' but it is what they all know he means. "I had also thought of having us sing God Bless America, or even Living in America, but I think we can dispense with that!" Again, there is laughter.

"I just urge us to stick together and keep what we have discussed tonight confidential as we move forward. As my wife would say, 'May the road rise up to meet you and the wind be at your back.'" As he says this, he has a sudden flashback and is filled with the memory of Miles and his funeral.

"Shalom!" Abby replies, not noticing the sudden change in Fen's countenance. The room breaks into animated conversation.

Through all this, Grace has remained conspicuously silent. She has been watching the group's body language. While they sound happy, she senses they are all very nervous, if not uncomfortable, with what they have heard. As she heads to the door, she overhears Tiffany say to Abby, "I like his enthusiasm, it's a breath of fresh air, but can we trust his judgement about this? I never heard Christian talk about any secret compensation arrangements and I am sure he would have been onto it if it wasn't in the company's interests." Grace does not hang around to debrief with Fen. She has an important date downtown.

As people begin to depart, Tom Richter quietly takes Fen aside. "Frankly, you need some help on this one, Fen. Have you considered reaching out to Donaldson? He is the chair of Pompton's Audit Committee."

"Good advice, Tom. In fact, I am scheduled to have a call with him in the morning. I will let you know how it goes."

***

The house is still. The only impression that remains of the meeting is a few trays of uneaten hors d'oeuvres on the kitchen table and the wine glasses that Fen is loading into the dishwasher. Cait drifts into the room, her laptop under her arm.

"So how did it go? You look beat," Cait says.

"I will answer in reverse order. Yes, I am beat. And it went okay, I think," Fen replies.

"You are taking a huge risk," Cait observes.

"I know."

"Are you really sure of your facts?" Cait pushes it.

"It's multi-layered. There are the politics and personalities. Frost is trying to sell us off into a conglomerate and that will almost certainly result in killing our culture and laying off hundreds of people. I don't like that, I think it's a huge strategic error, but accept that if the board decides to do it, it is their prerogative. If it was that alone the situation would be fraught but that's life. Then there is the question of whether Frost and Hudgell are trying to pull off the sale for their personal gain. If that is the case what they are doing is certainly unethical and likely criminal."

"But the last time we talked about this, you said it wasn't clear. That the way compensation is structured there may not in fact be a conflict," Cait says, confused.

"It's not so much compensation as the ownership structure. I don't understand everything. So yes, there is a chance I may have got things wrong," Fen replies.

"Because you are so emotionally engaged with the sale you may have diagnosed the patient incorrectly?"

"Yes doctor, that is a possibility."

"You may be going down a rabbit hole?"

"True."

"If even one of those guys turns you in, you will be toast."

"I know."

"If you do get fired what happens to your compensation?"

"It stops."

"I know it stops. But do you at least get severance?" Cait asks.

"I wouldn't think so," Fen replies.

"What about those millions you have in stock?"

"I'd probably have to sue them to get it but maybe they would have to give it to me since I would argue that I have earned it. You are taking an interest in all this all of a sudden."

"Hardly surprising, is it? The children and I may be out on the street shortly if you play this wrong!"

"Is playing this wrong about the money in your view then?"

"Are you trying to insult me, Fen?"

"Well, why are you making a point of it? In fact, why are you making a point with it?" He has lost all his earlier humor. He feels exhausted. *I have played the Pied Piper and probably the Fool too*, he thinks to himself.

"I'm just trying to figure you out. For years we seem to have spent our lives being shaped by and following your career. AKA the money. And then suddenly money is not an objective. We move to this city because of the money. We move house to here because we have the money. Do you get my drift Fen?"

"Well, maybe I've seen something differently recently." He puts the last glass in the dishwasher and picks at the lights to program the machine, none of which seem to work. Cait walks over, presses the right button and closes the machine. "And that's not the only thing you are good at," he says to Cait puckishly.

"You've got a nerve!"

"That's true."

"But look, Fen, I'm not going to be deflected by a cheap sexual interlude here. Pleasant though that might be every couple of weeks these days. Our future is at risk, right?"

"Yes."

"Is there a 'yes but', because you seem quite relaxed for a man under sentence?"

"Well I am optimistic. In fact, frankly I've been feeling utterly elated over the past few days."

"I wonder sometimes if you are bipolar. Are you sure it's not a psychotic break?"

"Can never be sure of that, Cait. But truly, for the first time in a long time I have taken charge, I am engaged. I think the people here tonight are good people who want to do the right thing. There is a good possibility that Frost will win out but I think we have at least a chance of preventing him from destroying the company and ending the futures of hundreds of people. I am believing that there is a right and a wrong thing here; I am valuing truth over lies."

"It's decidedly odd hearing you talk like this."

"I know, I feel off balance. I am still trying to sort out why I feel so changed."

"This is not unusual—a lot of men go through this. Try to keep your head a bit straight will you, and if not, I have some people you might want to talk to."

"Very funny. This is serious."

"I know. Life seems to be rerouting us somehow doesn't it? I had quite a deep conversation with Alina today."

"That's new."

"It is. She told me a lot about herself. Not so much about her aspirations, more about how she sees the world and how she got to be who she is."

"How did all that come up?"

"Oh, being wolf-whistled in the street, but more, I think, prompted by the piece in the paper today about Miles's suicide."

"Yes, we had thought that it might only be covered by the Times but it was picked up by Huffington and went everywhere."

"It struck me that we definitely are on different planets."

"Me and you?"

"Everyone," Cait says with a smile. "But more, Alina and me. What really drove it home to me was how our conversation kept coming back to her preoccupation with possessions and navigating the social scene rather than anything intellectual or spiritual. The way she frames things in material terms all the time. And I am sitting there having this conversation with her and thinking that I am on some higher plane. My youth spent in doctoring and demonstrating. Thinking about the big questions. Then I realized that in reality I have spent most of my time also thinking about what I should wear, what we should eat, the address we should acquire. The kinds of schools we can get our kids into so they can get a good start, the kinds of friends who will make me feel at home and reinforce the cycle—am I making any sense?"

"I think so."

"Maybe there has been a gap. Maybe, and this is worrying, I am processing some kind of subconscious longing like you. But there again Fen, at least I'm doing it behind the scenes, quietly behind the roar of the money. A call to spirituality of some kind. A different sort of winning as you might say?"

"Odd that we should be circling the same kind of feelings."

"Odd that somehow it's been catalyzed by Miles's suicide. I'm beginning to think that my childhood in Ireland so squeezed any possibility of belief out of me that it's done me permanent damage."

"Maybe Richard III had it right: 'Let's choose executors and talk of wills: And yet not so, for what can we bequeath, save our dispossessed bodies to the ground?'"

"No, Fen, let's choose the opposite. Let's choose life for ourselves and our kids. We need to find a way of grace, as old Sister Elizabeth would say. Until recently all that I could remember of my time at school was being scolded for doing the wrong thing. But recently I remembered. I remembered on the days when I arrived at school broken because of what was happening at home. Sister Elizabeth would take me by the hand. She would mostly say nothing but just sit with me and say from time to time: 'You are safe. God is here. You are safe. God is here.' I think I may want to find safety now." The moment becomes awkward for them both. They feel it slipping away.

"This is such a weird conversation for us to be having. When I think of what I have spent my life doing, I am not sure that I can find any real meaning outside our family. I don't know, I just want something else. But I don't think I want some cookie cutter religiosity. Can you imagine us as those sorts of people? That would finally institutionalize me. But I do keep coming back to what that guy said at Miles's memorial. Despite my misgivings about the superficiality of the tenor of what he said, I keep hearing that verse he quoted,

'I will give you hidden treasure,
riches stored in secret places so that you may know that I am the Lord, the God of Israel who summons you by name.'

Is it reasonable to go beyond ourselves and believe any of that? That there is a God who is interested in us? And what does, 'going beyond ourselves' mean? Is it a quest that we all pursue individually for purposes of self-preservation or somehow can we discover meaning beyond ourselves?"

"I don't know for sure. The last thing I expected tonight was a trip round the universe!" They both laugh at Cait's allusion to The Hitchhiker's Guide to the Galaxy.

"It all sounds totally naive, Cait, but what if it is true? What if winning involves us losing all this?"

It is very late when Fen enters his home office and withdraws a box of white linen writing paper from the lower left drawer of his desk. He writes for a couple of hours, frequently getting only as far as a single page and then ripping up his efforts. Finally satisfied, he completes two pages and places them in an envelope which he is careful to address longhand.

CHAPTER TWENTY-TWO

Ambition is a seduction she does not resist.

Until now she has intentionally formed her identity around a carefully curated image honed to promote her career prospects. She has achieved a remarkable transformation from her roots on Long Island. Has taught herself to manage up, network, know the technical tricks of her trade and become adroit in the dark art of office politics. In the universe she travels, she is not only more capable than her peers, she is more capable than those who manage her. She has also detailed her demeanor and appearance with the rigor of a consumer brand manager, based on an article she read in Forbes at college that stressed the importance of not compromising intelligence and work ethic by dressing unprofessionally. She speaks with a low-pitched voice, often punctured with innuendo. And yet she walks the narrowest line across the thinnest of ice because in her workplace she knows herself to be an exotic, dependent on goodwill of the older mostly white men who determine her fortune. Her work is her life. She has become psychologically and emotionally allied with her captors, her instincts for survival causing her to hold her life in her tightly gripped empty fists, unsure that there is anything else worth embracing.

Nevertheless, she can feel the fabric of her life being rent by recent events. For years, beached emotionally, on the arid Jurassic coast of financial services, she has observed the fossil evidence of love and joy in the lives of others but has herself become stone hard. The only remaining relationship that connects with her soul is that with her mother. As her work has grown to impinge on everything and envelop her time, her visits home have become rare. Her closest relationships outside those she works with are Brian Williams on The 11th Hour and Stephen Colbert on The Late Show, with whom she laughs before falling asleep in the early hours.

She of course maintains the appearance of enjoying the company of girlfriends and will take expensive trips to exotic destinations and lie in a red bikini by the pool until she can steal away to read her office email and texts that reassuringly clog her array of mobile devices.

Since her tryst in Greece with Peter she has been more or less sexually inactive, except for using the vibrator she keeps in the drawer by her bed, and the very rare weekend when she will get blind drunk at a party and decide she likes a man. She invariably regrets the dalliance.

Toying with ideas, philosophy, religion or indeed drugs and alcohol in college left her unscathed and unmoved. She was too serious, too applied, perhaps too insecure to experiment much for fear of dropping the thread of ambition that drives her. Her focus was on the right school, the right GPA, internships, and appearing on the Dean's List. Sometimes, late at night, returning from seeing her mother on the train from Babylon to Penn Station, looking at her reflection in the rain-washed carriage window, she asks herself why she is so driven. Is it because of the stories her mother, Jenna, tells her about her adoption, absent grandfather and experience of rootlessness? Is it because of her experience of being a child of mixed blood in a town and school where she never felt she actually fit?

Or is it because of her father's ambition for her? She saw little of him as a child, yet knew that she was loved. His days as a teacher and guidance counsellor were full, he was passionate about the education of the students entrusted to him. But he was forced to supplement his meager income by tutoring and by flipping furniture and taking any odd job in the summer that he could get hold of. She remembers him working late into the night in the garage of the small ranch house where they lived, refurbishing pieces of old furniture that needed a little love, and the weekends when he would take her in his old pickup around the local thrift stores to see what he might rescue and turn for a profit. Once when walking with him down a nearby street, they came across an old wooden chair with a broken leg. He stopped and picking it up said to her, "See Grace, we can take this chair and make something of it. That's what good people do you know, they take things that are broken and make something of them." Later, when things got tighter, he tried driving for the local taxi company and would come home exhausted in the early hours. When her father died during her senior year on a scholarship to NYU, Grace was devastated, but somehow her resolution to graduate with honors was reinforced by what she knew her father would have expected of her. On Sunday nights, the one day when her father and mother did not work, their house would be full of music and light. The family would gather around the TV and watch Miami Vice, eat pepperoni pizza and laugh at Family Ties on NBC. Grace's grandmother, Fey, would sit on the sofa with her arms crossed and cluck her disapproval. "You have time to watch this," she would say, "but you never have time to come over to the Mission." Grace would laugh as she heard her father reply, "I'm on a mission, Fey, I'm on a mission. It is the mission to feed this family!" On a good night, encouraged by his daughter, her father would bring out his guitar and pick out a song or two. "Maybe I should do a gig or two, instead of driving?" But he never did. On the morning she took her SATs, Scott stayed up after his night shift and cooked his daughter breakfast. Before she left for school that morning he gave her a hug and, holding her, whispered, "You surely are amazing Grace, you can do anything, believe it." He pressed a ten-dollar Liberty Gold Coin minted in 1899 into her left hand. She held it tight in her fist as she walked to school. It is now her most prized possession.

She has chosen to meet Tom at a bar she likes in Tribeca. This is where Grace sits at an outside table, watching the street life traverse the evening air, as she drinks a Moscow Mule served in a copper mug. Fresh from plotting revolt at Fen's house in Brooklyn, she reflects on the price value equation. The price she will pay for abandoning Fen and her colleagues and the value of what she will gain by being promoted to the top HR position in Pompton Financial, recently vacated by Al Jiminez.

She looks at her watch. Tom is late. A young couple speed by with abandon on a very loud Vespa. Neither is wearing a helmet. Grace catches the exultant expression on the pillion rider's face, which precedes her flowing flaxen hair. She remembers Fen's remark, "Why should youth be wasted on the young?" and suddenly feels quite old.

There are contrary arguments running around her head. *Why is Fen so fixated on Frost and Hudgell's unethical behavior, when he has turned a blind eye to Peiter Viser's poor leadership behavior and the alleged trading issues in his group? Viser is a crook but Fen is too soft to deal with him. The leadership team is so dysfunctional. Nobody is really prepared to step up and take decisions which may mean that they are politically disadvantaged. There is no real glue sticking them together. But is that in truth what's driving me to abandon them? Why am I prepared to accept Frost's lack of ethics and not the faults in Fen?* She is not used to this kind of moral dilemma, has no muscle for this kind of introspection or compass that might provide direction. *Truth is, what I'm being offered is a real step up. I can have much more positive influence if I am up at the corporate level.* Her second Moscow Mule arrives. *And how would I turn the offer down without ruining my career prospects? Even asking myself these questions is weird. This is what I get for hanging out with Fen!* She smiles at the memory of them deep in conversation, half-drunk in Boston.

The scooter is back and parked outside the restaurant. Grace watches the driver dismount. There is something about him that gives her the impression that he is from the Islands; as he smiles at Grace and locks his gaze on her eyes, she smiles back. His passenger has dismounted and is walking away down the sidewalk, her short skirt rhyming around her tan thighs. The driver walks over to Grace's table and without breaking eye contact picks up the copper mug containing her drink and knocks it back. "Cheers darling," he backs away still holding her gaze and is gone, running down the sidewalk after his girlfriend. Grace finds herself laughing for the first time in a long time as she orders her third Mule. *Well, if Sister Sarah had two, I may as well have three*, she says to herself.

The street theater over, Grace senses the evening air cooling as she checks her phone for messages. To her surprise she sees one from Frost, "Welcome aboard! Look forward to seeing more of you." She stares at it and is instantly thrown back into thinking about her decision. As she reflects on it, she feels more uncomfortable than ever, as she feels Frost's lasciviousness reaching towards her through his message. *Am I being flat out naive?* she asks herself. *Everything happened so fast.* First the flattering call from Hudgell, saying that Frost positively wanted her for the job and that she would bring a whole new sense of rigor to Pompton's People Function. As she heard him speak, she could feel her skin crawl but the seduction of title and money also weighed heavily. Then Frost called her. He was charming, saying that he was delighted that she would be partnering with him and his team. She asked no questions and it was clear he had little time to talk. But despite her excitement about the new opportunity she cannot avoid feeling that she has abandoned her colleagues and betrayed Fen. *I suppose it's conscience*, she says to herself as she realizes that she hasn't used the word 'conscience' in a long time. She has not spoken to anyone about her dilemma. *And who would I speak to? Not Jenna, this would be totally out of her league. Maybe Fen in another situation, but in this, impossible.* Her feelings of insecurity and isolation paw at her as the fear grows in her of having no one who really knows her. No soulmate. *Maybe the guy on the scooter would volunteer?* she asks herself, as she looks again at her phone, as if it is a lifeline that will deliver her from the evil of loneliness. She wonders if she has ever been close to anyone. She reflects on her mother's experience and what her Grandmother Fey has told her about her life. Despite the hardscrabble road they had traveled they both had an inner core of belief. They had expected less from life but not less from their faith. The compromises they had both made were around sublimation of their ambitions, not sublimation of their beliefs. *But I have never felt the same way. Never encountered the need for the kind of spiritual experience and certainty they have. They lived and continue to live in another time. When I go home it's like entering a different country where the language and currency they use is different. They are happier than me, I think, but not woke to the world.* She has never spoken to Jenna about what it's like for her to work in an essentially hostile world where she feels continuously pushed to anticipate what's required of her to meet the needs of those around her. Provided of course, those needs are aligned with what she sees as necessary for her survival and the agenda she is engaged in for the company.

She has received more messages. They are now sporadic but no less harrowing. It is the same obscure voice. She has come to think of it as being Peiter Viser or someone else in the investment team.

She makes an effort to think about something else, but so often, her thoughts return to her grandmother and the specter of her rape. She begins to enter a dark tunnel of recollection so real that it is as if she is witness to all that happened.

"A penny for them?"

"Better late than never I suppose, Tom."

"Seriously, I had a room full of lawyers. This whole situation is out of control."

"Sit. We've both had enough for one day, I'm sure."

A waiter appears, "Coke please."

"Nothing stronger?"

"Thanks, but I am off the sauce." Tom has a habit of rubbing his neck. "A lot of change for you then, Grace?"

"Yes, I suppose."

"A big move up. How are you up for that?"

The streetlights are washing the sidewalks. "It's odd how this neighborhood can look so derelict during the day but then comes alive at night. It always feels so much more New York here than down in Battery Park where I live." Grace is trying to decide if she will let Tom in past her usual lines of defense. "In a way, I'm glad you are late. It gave me a chance to think."

Tom listens well and lets Grace run. She decides he's the sort of guy that only really comes out at nighttime.

"I have a lot of guilt Tom. I like to think that I am tough. And in truth I have had to learn to be. But sitting here tonight, I feel like I have betrayed my friends. Cheers!"

She signals for another Mule.

"That's strong, Grace. In business, do we betray or simply realign?"

"You sound like some politician justifying abandoning the Christians to the lions."

"It's difficult to rise without some collateral damage. You have to be careful to make sure that people see what you are doing is business. Nothing personal. I keep my business and my personal life separate for that reason."

"So how do you navigate?"

"My master's interests mainly. In general, if I serve that priority I've found I get on. 'Dance with them what brung you.' I got that advice early and it's served me well."

"So no core values or anything?"

"What do you mean?"

"Principles for guiding your life?"

"Hey, I'm Australian," he says ironically. "That stuff is all a bit precious for me."

Grace notes he has the most gorgeous smile.

"No, I'll stick with pleasing my boss, being loyal and promoting his or her interests. I'm undeniably a bit of a Thomas Cromwell. Did you read that book—Wolf Hall?"

"Sorry no. I barely have time for the CNN app on my phone." She has made a decision. "Let's get out of here." She signals to the waiter, hails an Uber and within a few minutes, with Tom in tow, she is opening the door to her apartment. Her one bedroom is a mess, even in the orange light from the streetlamp that saturates the room and paints their faces in dark shadows. She leaves the light off, leads him to her rented couch. "Drink? I can offer you some tonic water? It's that or Poland Spring."

"Poland Spring; always sounds like some uprising against the Russians. I'll go for that," Tom says cheerfully, as he remains standing uncomfortably, trying to get a sense of the room.

Grace walks uncertainly towards the refrigerator, her head still buzzing from the accumulated effect of the three Mules she consumed at the bar. She pulls a half-empty bottle of white wine and two bottles of water out of the seemingly empty refrigerator, which for an instant, washes their surprised eyes with harsh LED light and imprints the room on their memories like some noir movie. Dazed, she shakes her head slightly and brings the drinks with two glasses on a red plastic tray and places them on the coffee table before the couch. They stand facing each other for a moment. It is as if time has stopped. There is the sound of a car door slamming on South End Avenue, the room seems suddenly heavy with Grace's sophisticated perfume. Tom feels her warm breath quickening, and begins to say something as she places her hands gently on his head and draws him down towards her. Time cuts back in, as Tom pulls back from Grace's grasp. Thrown off-balance, they sway for a moment, like some giddy brick tower built by a two-year-old, before falling in an uncomfortable tangle onto the couch, causing Tom's foot to strike the side of the coffee table, sending the drinks flying.

"Ouch! that hurt like hell. Shit!" Tom is sprawled under Grace. In an effort to recover herself Grace pushes her elbow into his shoulder, causing him to emit another yelp.

She begins to convulse with laughter. "I must be more out of practice than I thought." Struggling to her feet she looks down on Tom as she steadies herself against the side of the couch.

"We Australians are tough, but not that tough Grace. You can break us you know!"

Grace pulls herself upright, walks across to the wall light and flips the switch.

They both blink in the stark white rays emitted from the pendant in the center of the room. "Let's try that again. But maybe a coffee first?" Tom is now sitting on the couch leaning forward and rubbing his ankle hard.

Grace has retrieved the contents of the tray from the floor and while the coffee brews they sit next to each other on the couch, each waiting for the other to speak. "I'm sorry, Tom, I got you up here under false pretenses."

"Well, I didn't think that you were going to show me your etchings."

"It's only that tonight I feel so beleaguered, so, I dunno, disconnected, that I don't want to be alone."

For a moment he says nothing and then, "I know that feeling, Grace. I could see it in your face at the bar."

She turns her body and looks with curiosity into his eyes. "I was thinking that there might be something more than business between us. What I had in mind is something more intimate." She has exchanged her usual reserve for a vulnerability he has not previously seen in her.

"Grace, I'm gay. I can go both ways, but truly, I'm gay." Tom says this not so much with pride, but an edge, as if he is revealing some exotic quality. "I like you. I want to be your friend and I would not want to hurt you."

Grace is at first bemused. "So why did you come up here tonight?"

"Because you seemed in such a state when I arrived at the bar. Quite unlike you, Grace. I didn't want to leave you alone."

"I am so fucked up. I can't even get a man."

He says nothing as they both sit with their thoughts.

The coffee machine makes a sighing sound as if despairing at the silence between them. "I'm sorry, Tom. You're being gallant and I've made a fool of myself."

"No worries."

"Is that a statement, or a genuine question, Tom?"

"What would you like it to be?"

"I'd like you to be my friend, if not my lover."

"I can sign up to that."

"Then help me out on this, Tom. I feel sick. I am in love with Fen, or the idea of Fen. I want him but maybe not. He knows I am there, but it's unreciprocated on his part. At least I don't think it is. He's naive, vulnerable and goes around with his head up his ass, but he's good-hearted and even brave. You know, it's more like I'm not convinced I want him to love me but I am convinced that I want him to love the company enough to save it. That's how screwed up I am. But then again I look at the whole thing and see that that is totally impractical."

"I believed at first that Frost should be resisted, that he was trying to destroy us for reasons of power. And maybe my initial instincts were right, but as things have evolved it's become clear to me that there is no way that the XelFunds' team or culture is up to what the markets are throwing at it, that fundamentally the place is broken and doesn't deserve to survive. I tell myself, be pragmatic. In my life I've never had any sense of real fidelity to a particular person or cause. At college other kids would strut around banging the drum for something or another but I was always in the category of: let's do what's practical, what do I like best, what am I going to get out of it? Perhaps I will go this way on an issue or that way. Depends on who's going to be the winning side. I think maybe it comes from my family. I saw what religion did to my grandmother. I saw my mother having to make it on her own in many ways. I really loved my Dad, he was a really good guy, a winner in his own way but not the way for me." Tom sits carelessly on her rented couch, the safe harbor Grace has longed for. She is leaning her head on his shoulder. Their bodies say they are confidants not intimates.

"But that's not all, is it," Tom says softly. It is a statement that requires her answer.

"No, you are right. That's the drama I've cooked up, that's the fantasy I'm in. That's the rationale. Truth is that I am totally confused in terms of my emotions. I'm walking with one foot nailed to the floor. Walking in circles. Before you arrived tonight, I was thinking about my grandmother, how she got raped in Africa." Tom raises his eyebrows. "Long story. But that's how I'm feeling Tom, as if I've been raped, lost any integrity I had and now I'm pregnant with all that's entailed with working for Frost and Pompton. And the father of the child is my ambition. God how overblown all this sounds."

"Do you always talk like this, Grace, or is it those drinks?"

"What's your point?"

"My point is this. You're not for responsible for Fen, the other people you work with, or XelFunds. From what I have seen, you are not going to have Fen. The relationship is in your imagination, and he is in a different universe. XelFunds and the team is going down. Your only choice is to go down with it or do as any smart person would, leverage the opportunities you have to get to a better outcome. After all, if you take this job with Frost who knows what positive influence you may have on him and the corporation?"

It is what she wants to hear. She feels as if she is coming down from a panic attack.

Things begin to distill into perspective. "I am not being a bad person then?"

"No, your grandmother would be proud."

"I think I love you, girlfriend." Tom grins as only Australians can. She says nothing further but leans her head on his shoulder as she slowly slips into a fitful sleep.

Three hours later Tom stands on the pallid sidewalk outside her apartment. Grace can see him from her window talking into his phone. "It went to plan."

"Good job Tom, it's important to have her on board." Hudgell's voice is thin, he's been drinking. "I want Fen to see that he has no allies. No means of retreat. She is going to play a vital part in making sense of our taking Fen out of the XelFunds management team. You think she is up to that?"

"Yes. She is tough. She will deliver. I'll see you in the morning then, Peter."

"You'll be recognized for this, Tom. Goodnight."

The Uber arrives as the call ends. Tom enters the car without looking up at Grace, who wonders who he could have been calling at 3 am.

CHAPTER TWENTY-THREE

Fen is to meet with Frost at 9 am. It is two days since he gathered his compatriots in his kitchen, and nothing much has changed.

'Drifting dissenter
Caught in the center
Of your darling
Mamma's eye'

The words of a song by Outright Alright that he has heard on Pandora rattle around his head until they are replaced by Tennyson's Charge of the Light Brigade.

'Half a league, Half a league,
Half a league onward
All in the valley of Death
Rode the six hundred!'

Somehow everything has come full circle and Fen is uncommonly calm as he sits in his office before his plethora of screens which spout fountains of information. The funds he is managing continue to do well. Indeed, to his surprise, since taking the helm under Peiter Viser the whole department seems to have picked up.

Grace pokes her head around his door, "All good?"

"Yes, I think so. I am going over to see Frost shortly." Fen gives Grace a conspiratorial grin.

"There is something…" Grace's expression is serious. She gets no further, as Fen's iPhone sounds out on his desk.

Fen raises his hand. "Must take this one. Trading issue." Grace waves her hand and leaves. Fen looks after her. He senses her hesitancy, registers a reluctance about her. Something was different in her eyes. He thinks nothing more of it.

Fen can be meticulous if not downright neurotic about his desk. He likes it clear and will consign any odd pieces of paper or pens to the drawers. He finds such a pen and sweeps it towards the drawer he has opened. In doing so, he sees an odd scrap of paper drawn on by Rosie when she visited his office a few years ago. He recalls the way she sat on his lap, fascinated by his computer screens, and feels extraordinary love for her. There is something in the rawness of her suffering that agglutinates yet drives them apart. He takes the paper out and puts it carefully into his jacket pocket.

He walks out of his office, round to the now sepulchral area where Jade used to sit, before making the pilgrimage up Tower Two to floor fifty, where he is to confront Frost. All traces of Jade and the evidence of Miles's suicide have been removed. He pauses for a moment and closes his eyes before straightening his shoulders and walking resolutely to the elevator lobby.

On the way over Fen speculates briefly as to why his meeting with Frost has been moved to a conference room rather than Frost's office. He cannot think of a good reason, but the change heightens his sense of unease.

His nerves rattle, along with the creak of cable as it winds him skyward. He checks his watch. Ten to nine. Time seems to slow. He remembers an unsent love letter to Cait that he came across last Christmas. In his mind's eye he unfolds its yellowing paper. It is an acknowledgement of his frequent absences, physical and emotional, and his inability to express what he felt for her and the children. It contains no poetry, no fig leaf for his true emotions. He felt too vulnerable to send it.

Riding on up, the express elevator makes a couple of stops. He studies the earnest face of a woman who enters and stands opposite, wearing the black weeds and piled hair of a junior corporate officer, her scrubbed face and red lips ready for her mundane routines. There is something of Angela about her. He theorizes as to whether she is happy, sad, or simply indifferent to what awaits her.

He thinks of his days in London; BC, as he often puts it—before Cait, when he was still with Denise. How he had left their flat one morning after yet another session of screaming at each other, knowing that for certain this time it was over. And then going home, all the same, late that night, after a day with the numbers at work, lacking the courage to finish it. He remembers reading When I Have Fears That I May Cease to Be on a wall of King's Cross London Underground station.

'When I have fears that I may cease to be
Before my pen has gleaned my teeming brain,
Before high-piled books, in charactery,
Hold like rich garners the full ripened grain;
When I behold, upon the night's starred face,
Huge cloudy symbols of a high romance,
And think that I may never live to trace,
Their shadows with the magic hand of chance;
And when I feel, fair creature of an hour,
That I shall never look upon thee more,
Never have relish of the faery power
Of unreflecting love—then on the shore
Of the wide world I stand alone, and think
Till love and fame to nothingness do sink'
John Keats, 1821.

As he entered his apartment, he walked into the brutal slam of another evening diatribe. Denise, so lost and unhappy with herself, her life and his imperfections. They fell apart headlong into the dark elevator shaft of ego they had fashioned for themselves as they stood together alone, sharing only the naivety of what they took to be romance. They were, Fen thinks, like wood in water, flotsam and jetsam.

The deceleration stirs him. He steps through the opening elevator doors into the reception area where to his surprise he finds the beautifully preened Angela, Frost's assistant, waiting for him. *She smiles a bit like a crocodile*, Fen thinks.

"They are waiting for you, Mr. Morgan. Conference room one."

"Well thank you, Angela. Looks like I definitely am getting the red carpet treatment this morning." She returns his smirk, a smile he senses that is not to be trusted.

As Fen walks into the conference room, he knows instinctively that something is wrong. That the game he has been playing, however short, is up. Peter Hudgell is seated at the conference table, flanked by Tom Wilson, and to his bewilderment, Grace Rutler. He tries to catch Grace's attention, but she sits with her eyes downcast.

"Do sit, Fen." Hudgell speaks without extending his arm or rising for a handshake. Fen sits, waiting for the first salvo to crack over the table between them.

"Thanks for coming over, Fen."

"You are welcome, but I came over to meet with John, Peter."

"The Chairman is not currently available." The morning light is streaming through the windows as if determined to penetrate the darkness of some fearful lair. Hudgell's palms are flat on the table, his fingers spread wide as if he might suddenly push himself up. *Another croc at feeding time?* Fen asks himself.

"That's okay, I can wait." Fen gazes at the shafts of light falling athwart the table between them. For a moment there is silence, only the ever-present air conditioning whispers its secrets. "And the darkness comprehended it not."

"I'm sorry, I don't understand?"

"The light shining on the table between us, severing the darkness in the room."

The word 'severing' floats in the air; it is as if it materializes before them.

Grace now glances at Fen sitting across the table from her and speaks to him silently with her eyes, *God you are smart, Fen. But I am sorry, they are smarter than both of us.*

"Like a pig about to have its throat slit by a butcher, we all know why we are here. The pig, the butcher, the boys and girls who clean the meat trays." Fen is suddenly filled with a sense of elation, as if he is about to be released from some terrible shackle.

"That is offensive, Fen."

"I apologize, Peter. Truly, no offense is intended. It would appear you have something to tell me?"

"Apology accepted. Let me put your comment aside then." Hudgell shifts uncomfortably in his chair. He has somehow lost the initiative. Regaining something of his composure, he continues. "Fen, you should know that the Chairman and the board are tremendously grateful to you for the way you stepped into the breach following Christian's departure. You have done a fine job in assisting with the transition." As Hudgell speaks, his leviathan throat reddens.

"Thanks for your encouragement, Peter. Are you feeling all right, you seem a little short of breath?"

Hudgell has adjusted to the game and, undeterred, thrashes on. "As you will appreciate, the corporation continuously evaluates the business situation and related leadership requirements. While, as I said, you have done a great job, the board has decided that we need someone who can take XelFunds through what has become a quite arcane acquisition process. We must therefore accept your resignation with immediate effect."

Fen has been expecting them to be on the offensive. But the blow has come early. He feels for a moment as if he has been struck in the face with a baseball bat; his head rocks slightly. "What if I don't want to go?" His voice has lost its command. For a moment, he is a truculent child not wanting the game to be over.

"This isn't a choice, Fen. This is a decision. You are out." Hudgell snaps his teeth, seeking to break the back of his prey.

"As an officer of the company I feel I have an obligation to ..." It is a valiant effort, but Fen knows he is being overwhelmed by the deep.

"Your obligation is to go quietly, Fen."

"I had some discussions with a board member earlier this week, and I think the board may take a different view of this."

"Yes Fen, we understand that you recently contacted Bob Donaldson, the Chairman of the Audit Committee, to express some concerns. He immediately contacted the Chairman and our joint determination is that it is best for all concerned that you resign quietly. You have a great reputation in the firm and on the Street, Fen. Do not put that at risk by making us fire you."

Grace sees him cornered like the remains of a dolphin being savaged by whales and feels nauseous.

"There are certain matters of an ethical nature that..."

Grace wants to plunge in and reach him. Silently she screams, *There is nothing you or I can say or do, Fen. You are a lost cause!*

"You are referring to the executive compensation plan for the Chairman and key executives. This has been properly approved by the board. The board is also aware of certain arrangements with XelFunds' suitor, and has also approved all such arrangements." Hudgell rattles off his bona fides.

"Are those available for review? Would the Securities and Exchange Commission have a view on that?" A last gasp from Fen.

"It is game over, Fen. Listen to the whistle. Hear the closing bell. The session has ended. You are done. Everyone is headed to the parking lot. It will not be necessary for you to return to your office." Hudgell pushes himself up and stands leaning over the conference table towards Fen. "We are being generous here. You tried to conduct a revolt and you lost." Standing triumphantly erect, Hudgell says, "The boys and girls who clean the meat trays will give you the terms of your severance. There will be no negotiations, Fen. No negotiations. My advice is for you to take the money and run."

The door closes behind Hudgell. Fen's voice fills the space that follows. "And then there were three, I suppose. But I am surprised to see you here, Grace. Quite cruel of them to make you come here, really."

"They offered me the job of Head of Corporate HR."

"That's a big job, Grace. How are you feeling about it?"

Grace is silent and refuses eye contact.

"Trust the pay is good." He will regret it later but can't resist it. "Thirty pieces of silver?"

Grace replies, "That was a cheap shot."

"You're right, it was. I'm sorry. It's just that it's not been the best morning."

"Here is an agreement that we would like you to sign following your review with your lawyer. Terms are a year's total compensation together with the value of your vested stock and acceleration of your unvested stock, as provided for in the Equity Holders Agreement. If you do not sign the agreement, which includes a confidentiality clause, you will only receive two weeks' base pay. As you know, you are employed on an at will basis."

"You are very kind, Tom. This cannot be easy for you either. But tell me, what do you actually think? Is there an ethical problem here or not?"

Tom makes no reply.

"And who will be CEO of XelFunds now, Grace?"

"Lucas Aiello."

Fen closes his eyes and after a moment says, "Now that is a surprise."

Grace spends the remainder of her day calming the troops. She has individual conversations with each of her colleagues, reassuring them that although Fen has left for personal reasons he is being well taken care of financially, that there was a huge misunderstanding regarding the financial arrangements around the planned disposal of XelFunds and appraising them of the extremely generous loyalty bonuses, that will make them rich, should the sale go through. She requests that they not reach out to Fen but rather give him the space to separate that he has requested. The only individual to call foul is Cynthia, who screams various epithets at Grace before slamming her office door and booking a one-way flight to Sydney.

Employees are summoned to a town hall meeting which is simulcast across the company by video, at which Frost announces that the rumors that XelFunds is being sold are untrue. The company will remain indispensable to Pompton's global strategy of growth through excellent financial instruments, product and geographic diversification, innovative service solutions and importantly, people. He then introduces Lucas as the new CEO. Lucas chooses the importance of risk management and teamwork as the theme for his address to employees and stresses that no one is owed a job unless they earn it.

The XelFunds management team sit stone faced alongside Lucas like members of a politburo. No mention is made of the dear leader Fen who has recently mysteriously departed.

It is clear that the investment team is singularly unimpressed as they sit together in undisguised contempt and hostility. Barry stands at the back of the meeting room with Frost, who leans towards him and says, "We are going to need your help with this one as well, Barry. We need to win."

It is decided that no announcement will be made concerning Grace's promotion and move to Corporate. She will stay for the time being at XelFunds until things settle. Apparently, word on the negative sentiment towards her surrounding Miles's death has made its way to Corporate. She is tainted merchandise and no longer perceived as an appreciating asset.

CHAPTER TWENTY-FOUR

I walk slowly down the echoing staircase from Rosie's apartment to my Volvo, where I sit steeling myself for the drive across town to our apartment on to the Upper West Side, where Cait and I now live following the sale of our house in the Heights.

The years since I exited XelFunds, or perhaps more accurately, since I was unceremoniously ejected from what was once that hallowed institution, seem to have passed in a moment. For years, I have found it difficult to accept the past is over. I continually wonder if things could have been different. If I had changed direction earlier would Rosie have found herself, by some miracle, been delivered from the hand she has been dealt?

My time and the people at XelFunds are still vivid and alive in my memory. Like characters in some play by Brecht, they inhabit my dreams. Tenacious Cynthia, honest Steve, the warmth of Tom Richter and the weakness of Christian. I find I still have great affection for them all. Several of us from the company made an effort to keep up for a while. But soon we were cast to the four winds. When we did meet over lunch or dinner in some New York neighborhood restaurant, we would talk for a while, but then find that there was little gusto in our conversation. Christian moved to Savannah and passed away a couple of years ago, Cynthia was last heard of breeding horses in Australia, and Steve is very involved with a charity for the disabled.

I also recall the avarice of Frost, serpentine Hudgell and the sad, acquisitive guile of Lucas Aiello. Lucas totally disappeared. I heard a rumor that he got involved with some fly-by-night payday loan outfit in Pennsylvania and lost a lot of money, but who knows if that is true. I find myself in fits of schadenfreude seeking news of them online or in the New York Times obituary section.

But mostly I remember the morning betrayal by Grace.

We came across each other quite by chance in Midtown. It was a cold morning in late November. One of those days when the wind lashes the streets from out of a clear blue sky.

I was leaving the Yale Club in Midtown after a breakfast meeting with one of the trustees of the charitable foundation where I am Chief Investment Officer. Grace and I literally blundered into each other's arms on the sidewalk as she exited a cab and I stepped out of the club reading the front page of the Journal.

"Why, Grace, it's you!" I remember saying in complete astonishment.

She hesitated for a moment as she placed me, "My God, Fen? It can't be!"

"Yes. It is indeed me." I'd often thought of this moment. What I would say if we ever met again.

After Grace and Hudgell ambushed me I was escorted out of the building by a morose, shiny haired young man in a blue polyester blazer. When we reached the lobby level I offered him a tip, which seemed to offend him.

As I walked out of the building, several staff walking in offered me smiles or waved hello. I of course found myself smiling and waving back. It was a sort of out-of-body experience.

I never heard from Grace after that meeting.

I hailed a yellow cab, and was back at our house in the Heights in no time. No one was at home except Fred. We sat on the stoop talking to each other for a long time. It seemed to me that he had had a bad morning too.

"You are looking great, Fen. Decades younger!" Grace said nothing of her obvious surprise at my willowy frame. I've had a couple of minor health issues recently that have thinned me out a bit.

"I'm not so sure how to take that!" I replied. And there it was again, her conspiratorial laugh.

The brilliant early sunlight searched the makeup on her olive skin. Her face had changed perhaps. It seemed to me that her eyes spoke of disappointment. Life had exacted its toll upon her. But she still radiated the same formidable essence. She still dressed as if ready for a shoot for a piece in Forbes magazine. She has haunted the halls of my memory for so long that I found myself searching her face, adjusting my recall. She was still young of course, and had lost nothing of her pugnacious bearing. I wondered how much she had really learned about life.

"And you, Grace, you have not changed a bit! What are you up to these days? Still taking prisoners?" I couldn't resist taking a crack.

"Oh, I am still there," she said defensively. "Still pitching. But not for long now. And you?"

"Yes, still at the foundation." There is a moment of awkward silence that neither of us seems to want to fill. I sense that each of us is eager to express something but is held mute in an aspic of misunderstanding, just beyond one another's reach.

"I think of you when I see them in the news. They do wonderful work."

"Yes, worthwhile cause," I reply and then, "Is there anyone I would know left back on the ranch?" I notice the wind pressing on her collar as it whips around the street, brushing tiny streaks of silver in her otherwise raven hair.

"The old XelFunds distribution and service people have pretty much all gone now. But many of the investment team are still there. You should drop by sometime," Grace says, with the thinnest veneer of sincerity.

"Sure. Perhaps I will. I'm sure I'd get a great reception." I say this glancing away, knowing in my soul now, that there is no possibility of us reconnecting.

"Frost, Hudgell and Aiello are out," she says, as if announcing the result of some baseball game.

I heard that she fought hard to hold on and move up at Pompton Financial. There was a rumor that she and Frost had a thing. But I never believed it. She never did get the top job. Had made too many enemies on the way up. Still the story goes that against the odds she was the last one standing when they finally came for Frost, Hudgell and Aiello—The Gang of Three, as they become known. I remember thinking that the years she spent since we last met must have been lucrative but devoid of passion.

"Yes, that was quite a story. High crimes and misdemeanors, it seems? Front page of the Wall Street Journal. Caught with their fingers in the till. What a surprise." *What's the point of laying this on her?* I asked myself. *She decided to take the last bus out of town. I had the luxury of naivete and walking away. Which of us sinned more?*

"Still got your sense of British irony, then?"

"And you. You are surviving somehow, Grace?" I see the sadness in her, and remember why I miss her.

"Yes Fen, I am surviving. In fact, I'm taking a break soon. I'm going to see if I can find an old friend who is a doctor with the UN in Lebanon."

"Better than Long Island, I suppose." Unforgivable on my part. But I am still angry with her.

"Yes. More terrorists perhaps, but less retail." What she said is funny, and we both recognize it.

"Who's that then?" I'm genuinely interested.

"A guy that I met years ago when I was on vacation in Greece." A passerby brushes past us as Grace speaks. Grace is momentarily off-balance. I catch her arm. Just as I did in Boston.

"How was that. How did you meet, I mean?" I ask as we both regain our footing.

"We just ran into each other and said that we would get together again sometime."

"Romantic. But what are the chances of you finding him after so long?"

"Oh, he is still there, I looked him up through someone I know at the UN. Sent him an email and we reconnected. Easy really."

"Enterprising. I'm pleased for you" And honestly I was. I was happy that the zero that she had carried so long in her core would be healed. "Does this mean the end of kickboxing?"

"Hardly Fen, the streets are still mean."

For a moment more we just stood there on the street, in the intemperate wind, outside the Yale Club.

"There is something different about you, Fen," she said. "You seem, I dunno, composed, centered or something."

A white van with the insignia 'Harry's Bathroom Supplies' clattered by. From out of nowhere, I found myself saying, "I didn't mean to fail you, Grace."

"And I didn't mean to deceive you, Fen." I am not sure either of us was telling the truth. But somehow it was enough.

"Dangerous place."

"The Lebanon?" She asked

"No, life," I said.

"Yes, but I've always liked a bit of adventure. I miss our conversations." I wanted to say more but she is too quick and without missing a beat continues, "Well, I have to get going, I'm afraid. Great to have seen you, Fen."

I remember that we looked deep into each other, for longer than was comfortable. It was the farewell that we should have had years earlier. We embraced more as Americans than Europeans, and she was gone. Swallowed into swirling coats and the breezy morning cacophony. I stood like a lost child looking after her for a long time.

Who was she? Did I ever really know her? We had perhaps been close. And yet not close at all. She was Mata Hari and I was France. I can't think of a suitable quote which will obfuscate my feelings.

She is the phantom who will continue to haunt my dreams.

EPILOGUE

Rosie lives in solitude with herself, amongst others, on the seedier side of Brooklyn. And continues to occupy the center of Fen and Cait's concerns.

Her days, if empty, brim with vacuous thoughts that bombard her brain and assault her consciousness, like the staccato drip from the faucet she hears as a fusillade of water striking the unwashed mugs in the cracked ceramic sink, crammed between the fridge and the closet full of paper plates and plastic utensils.

She regards her studio apartment as a castle built to withstand attack which may only be entered occasionally by family, and rarely by friends. This morning she was consumed by a rowdy inner conversation apropos of whether or not she should consult her doctor about the recurring pain in her hip.

She interrupts her shuffle out of her galley kitchen and leans her gaunt frame against the wall, chewing on a stick of string mozzarella (that she bought on promotion, a word she sometimes likes, an act she has long been denied). Then wanders aimlessly over to the unaccompanied grey leather chair that she has placed before the window and slumps to sit silently in her habitual perseveration. The refrigerator compressor cycles on, a dull chaperone to the stream of her discordant thoughts.

She picks at why passengers are not electrocuted in the steel subway cars that rattle past her building eight floors below her grimy window. And observes the changing weather and light. Restless, she ruminates upon what Siri does when not talking with her as she performs a melancholy karaoke with Sting, whom she has conjured from her new Apple HomePod. She closes her heavy blue eyes, visualizing Sting playing the part of the demanding tenor opposite her, as she plays the exquisite soprano.

She knows herself to be fragile yet brilliant. Her interests are always particular and pursued with a vibrant tunnel vision intensity. A sorter of numbers, sequences, shapes, memories and lists, with capacious recall, she devours books by female authors, especially those who resonate with her life experience on the spectrum. She has somehow felt her way across what she describes as the desert of trippy stereogum funk and the cheap iconography of pop culture, to the symmetry of Bach, the discernible structure of nineteenth century French Realism paintings hung in the New York Met, the writings of Sara Coleridge, Fritz Lang movies, especially The Big Heat and opening chess moves going back to the 1770s. She is also impresario of how to cook black spaghetti, empty the trash, pay bills (that she has laid out in perfect symmetry on the counter of her galley kitchen) write checks, save money and take black-and-white pictures on her 35 millimeter camera. She knows herself to be powerful at summoning images and possibilities. She can live in the future and make it the present—the very best that may happen and the worst that almost certainly will happen.

Her aversion to what is modish keeps her dressed in what to her is comfortable, out-of-step, shabby chic clothing purchased from the dead in the off hours from used clothing emporia on the Lower East Side.

Some nights when she feels utterly isolated, the rat of loneliness gnawing at her soul, she will don makeup and dress to the nines, fantasizing that her life is intact, go uptown to her parents' apartment on the Upper West Side, then on to a bar with her brother. For a few hours her head is clear as she camouflages her emotions. Then, exhausted by small talk it becomes too much, it feels as if panic will bust open her chest and she will flee to her apartment, defeated and crying in the back of an Uber, as her brother, Joe, stands in the street staring sadly after her car.

On such nights she fears herself to be stupid.

She cannot sort people.

She cannot stop the repetition.

She cannot separate from the past.

She does not know if the past is true or if the future is going to be true.

She will not attempt to resolve complexity she has not created or venture to places or people that are foreign to her; such striving blows her emotional circuitry and can render her intellectually helpless.

Most of her evenings end with the same routine. In hope of disconnecting her mind she will pace across the room twenty-four times to shake off her anxiety before switching off the lights.

While always feeling dogged by the stigma of being different, some of the passages she navigates are better than others. As a child, she preferred to play alone, permitting only one or two friends within her wall of non-disclosure. She learned early that other children could be spiteful and hostile, was often bullied and always on the outs. She would form an occasional relationship with another child and create lists of winners of women's soccer games and losers of tennis tournaments, endangered species, Harry Potter characters, planets and solar systems. But the exhaustion and uncertainty of managing any change in routine resulted in frequent meltdowns, destroying the tendrils of many relationships. When childhood meandered into adolescence, she liked herself and others less and the meltdowns became more frequent. Her interests became narrower as she would focus on tasks so intently that the world beyond her bedroom would disappear. Despite efforts to identify therapies, medications and stable routines, Rosie continued to experience the minor frustrations that she encountered as great tsunamis of frustration that would wreak havoc upon the fragile islands of emotional and intellectual development tended by those who loved her.

As she uncoupled from her teens and scraped into college, her tenuous relationship with what she had come to regard as the tyranny of education evolved into curiosity and a love for computer languages. She gradually learned through painful trial and error how to coexist somewhat with the motley crew that were her classmates. Few of her college contemporaries knew and no one understood the depth of her struggles. While socializing exhausted her, she was easily able to grasp mathematics and hack her way through the jungle of bits and bytes in a way that others were not. Upon graduation, despite repeatedly screwing up interviews, she was eventually snatched from the abyss of unemployment by an entry-level job offer at a quirky startup based in Dumbo.

Rosie's family were overjoyed by her success and what appeared to be her increasing stability. This breath of normalcy was, however, short-lived, as Rosie sensed herself slipping back into the lockdown of alienation emanating from her differences. The specter of an uncertain future continued to wander the halls of their lives, seeking to devour any fleeting aspirations they had of true and joyous fulfillment.

And yet Rosie will still recall moments of clarity and warmth from her childhood. Times when she truly deciphered the confusion of emotional and intellectual isolation: running laughing with her brother into the crystal waters of the Caribbean, riding an elephant next to her father on their trip to India, sitting swathed in a tight blanket with her mother looking at fireflies in the Rockies, playing her recorder in her school band, hearing her grandfather read the same story repeatedly, the rhetorical effect of onomatopoeia spoken in his Irish accent soothing her restlessness. And music floating up the stairs on summer evenings when she would lie with Fred the family dog and fall asleep feeling safe. (Rosie would like to own a dog now but her apartment building will not permit it. Instead she has bought a cat with tortoiseshell fur that she has named Peter.)

And on Sundays, when they could all bear it, she would sit in a pew with her family under the tabernacle architecture of Plymouth Church of the Pilgrims. Where she would stand and sit like an automaton and stare at the J & R Lamb Studio stained glass windows glowing behind the galleries, and imbibe fragments of authoritative readings and hymns, which she took in deep as certainties, while her brother and the other children left the sanctuary.

She has two friends who have withstood the ice and fire of her youth. Ruth, who has relocated with her husband to Los Angeles; and Paula, who died of an overdose last year. She still talks to Paula. She fears that now she will be probably be alone forever.

Her medical history remains complex, littered with the occasional hospitalization and a strict regimen of medication, and she prefers not to talk about it. Except on Wednesday mornings with her therapist, and every month with her psychiatrist, and sometimes with her church group, where most of the talk is about what's right and what's wrong, and how all that started and how it will all stop!

By night she wakes at 2 am and habitually imagines walking the dim cloisters of her heart and wonders why her prayers for belonging go unheard and unanswered by a God she has grown to fear and not trust.

On winter days during her lunch break she escapes the assuring claustrophobia of her workstation and tramps down the length of the frigid street to the park. As the brittle ice cracks beneath her insulated boots, she stands gazing at the lake, relieved to be solo. Mesmerized, she watches skeins of hysterical geese descend from the grey enameled clouds, and careen to earth between the half-mast American flags onto the frozen lake.

Returning to her office, she stops by the deli which is a carnival of sharp sounds and colors. A gaunt counterhand in his thirties, wearing a blue and white striped apron, stands on the other side of the plexiglass counter, carving turkey and American cheese onto hard rolls. She notes the name 'Pete' emblazoned on his badge, and joins the gaggle of bawdy construction workers and curt nurses who have formed an impatient line. She yearns desperately to abscond, but shuffles forward and orders the special without eye contact, but studies Pete's movements as he carefully wraps, then slips her sandwich into a brown paper bag. For a microsecond she wonders where Pete learned his craft and acquired his air of utter defeat—perhaps in some desert war where he labored in a tent cooking under the intrusive sun. She can almost feel the visual contrast of Pete's white fingernails and reddened hands against the black surface of the countertop. With horror she sees Pete's thin lips part to reveal his yellow teeth, which unsmilingly wish her 'a nice day' as instructed by Bob his supervisor, who stands watching beneath a blood-red neon Budweiser sign.

Rosie has been making an effort recently and at six she pulls on her black antique leather jacket, shambles back alone down the dank sidewalk, past shuttered stores. Her brain full of the faces, sounds and angst of the day, she stands for a moment trying to decode the graffiti daubed over the concrete wall at the end of Washington, where the heavy blackness of the church door offers access to St Bart's.

Inside the church, the odor of incense lingers on the air, as she sits skittishly in a pew, and stares down the dim silent void that is the nave, towards the empty wooden cross shining in the hard-edged electric light. She sits and self-soothes her emotions, then she is motionless, perhaps for a minute, perhaps for five, before pulling out a familiar maroon covered bible from the rack in front of her. Thumbing through it aimlessly, she reads verses which trigger random thoughts that gyrate and reverberate around her head. Odd fragments stick in her brain.

'Because he loves me, says the Lord
I will rescue him;
I will protect him for he acknowledges my name.'

Sounds good? But assume this 'he' includes a 'she'? She smiles to herself ironically. *From what will I be rescued? Who do I need protection from; beyond the normal million threats, that is? Who have I acknowledged? And what does 'acknowledge' mean?* And yet in her confusion, she feels some comfort, some connection with something. She closes her eyes for a moment and remembers the warm glow of the stained glass at Plymouth. She flips to another page.

'In the beginning was the Word.'

In the beginning, at the start, when things began. Matter from no matter. And no matter what because there is a beginning there must be an end. And what is that end? She finds herself really enjoying the energy of the plotline she has created. Her thoughts are like music. She can feel that something intangible imbedded in the rhythm is almost within her grasp. It lingers just beyond the edge of her comprehension. The clarity, perhaps of a still small voice in the vortex of her medulla. And then the voice of a client from the afternoon looms before her, "You move like molasses, girl!"

And all is recrimination and chaos. She closes her heavy eyes and utters a questioning cry from some primal place deep within her, "If you are here, God, rescue me?" The words ricochet through the empty church then fall lifeless to the stone-cold floor.

She replaces the bible and walks wearily towards the church door. The street is as frigid and hostile as ever.

"I hate this leather jacket," she says to no one in particular.

Sunday mornings around ten, her mother or father will knock on her door. She hears them walking up the stairwell and standing in the hallway before they knock and wonders what they are doing in the silence between them and the door. And she will drink coffee with them as they ask about her week and eventually complain about the state of her apartment. Typically, her mother will start by being interested in her routines, whether she is taking her meds, if she is suffering from headaches. By noon they will have argued furiously about the torn receipts and dollar bills strewn across the floor and the accumulation of abominable takeout food and foul paper plates piled around the trash can and the state of her dress and hair. On her father's visits he will ask her about her job. What she is doing for fun. If she has seen any friends. He will seem impatient, as if waiting for something from her. Then somehow they will drift into how much money she is spending; he will become annoyed that nothing seems to be happening in her life. And he will begin to give her useless advice and be frustrated that she will not take it. She has come to take these outbursts from them both as routine. As one or the other of them becomes increasingly agitated she remains calm and goes through a mental checklist of Wimbledon winners until, their anger spent, they leave, again pausing the other side of her front door.

Rosie sometimes thinks her parents are more unhappy than she is.

Sunday afternoons, Rosie sits on a high stool at the counter in Starbucks, across from the park, with her vicarious gaze, imagining herself to be anyone but her, and questions the meaning of an Everything Bagel. *If it is Everything, why does it have an empty center?* Vulnerable, certain of nothing but her questions, she has long felt herself to be the blameless daughter of an absent father, whatever evidence he attempts to offer to the contrary.

Albert lives an eternity distant, across the hallway from her apartment, and often stands before his doppelganger window, breathing uneasily as he peers at ornamented skies heavy with the gold of a western sunset. Past what he believes to be his sell-by date, he tugs at his greying braided hair and comforts his lone black cat who has just returned from its promiscuous travels. His days are spent without aplomb, in the Midtown fashion district, at a barbarous office suffused with innuendo and invoices for jackets, shirts and ties he will never wear. By night, he hears Rosie across the void of their shared hallway, as she paces incessantly to and fro, above the rattle of subway cars on the metallic tracks that snake beneath their building's windows.

On Sunday afternoons, Albert has also taken to sitting solo in Starbucks across from the park. For defense, he brings a copy of the Times, and reads an article about living as a single black man in the white city. While he scans the newsprint, he ponders the pattern of his life and wonders why of all the places he might have lived, he has ended up living here and working as he does at a business he hates and for people he loathes. He is insensible to the coincidence of listening to the same sonorous Sting tracks on his phone as his neighbor (a departure from Marley), and is unaware of her proximity.

Rosie has also learned that if she takes a book with her to Starbucks, people pay less attention. She surfaces from her reverie of unanswered questions, continues to scan her book for a while, then, as if prompted by something or another, she gathers her uncomfortable frame to leave. The grating of Rosie's stool next to Albert's chair causes him to turn, and as he does so, he recognizes Rosie's face from when he has glimpsed her in the hallway of the apartment block. Rosie's unfamiliar voice apologizes as she squeezes, surprisingly nimbly, by his chair. Fumbling her half-smile, he loses the moment and Rosie is gone, a phantom in the torpor that is Albert's life.

Their questions remain taut and unanswered like the meaning of an Everything Bagel. Or a prayer to her once absent father.

Fen opens their apartment door on the Upper West Side to the sound of Cait's chopping. It's warmer than expected and the aroma of hot fat hangs heavy on the air. He walks down the tight cream-colored hallway and into their kitchen.

"We still eating here then?"

"Yes, Joe and the kids are coming over at three. I didn't know what time you'd be back from seeing Rosie."

For some reason Fen takes the time to look at Cait and says, "'The barge she sat in, like a burnished throne burned on the water. The winds were lovesick with them.' Shakespeare."

"Will you stop that sophomoric habit you have? It is flat-out annoying, you old fool."

"I know."

"How was she?"

"Fine, I think," Fen walks to the fridge and takes out the half-empty bottle of chardonnay he and Cait started last night.

"Anything new?"

"Don't think so. Usual drama between the two of us. But she seems to be doing okay, at least got through another week without a crisis."

"A couple of letters came for you. FedEx." Fen walks to the sideboard and tears open the first cardboard envelope warily. Inside is the job offer Fen has been expecting from a hedge fund, based in San Francisco. He is silent as he reads the cover letter.

"What was it?"

"Nothing" he says. Tearing it up and throwing it in the trash can they keep by the refrigerator.

Cait stops chopping and looks at him. "It was the San Francisco job?"

"Yes, it was that."

"You decided?"

Fen does not answer, but fishes a crumpled yellowing envelope out of his pocket and places it before her next to the chopping board. "By the way, I've been meaning you to have this for some time."

Cait wipes her hands on a red gingham towel, opens the envelope with care, a slight frown on her brow. She stands reading, her right hand holding the letter, her left hand resting on her hip. A tear makes its meandering way slowly down her cheek as she lowers the letter and looks at Fen who is transfixed by her face.

Fen slowly draws in his breath and is about to speak as the dog steams into the room, followed by Sam, their adopted four-year-old, who scrambles around Fen, knocking him aside.

As he runs around Sam shouts, "Hey, Dad."

"Yes Sam?"

"Is it important to win games?"

"Good question, Sam. What sort of games?"

***

Later that night, at around 2 am, when Cait and Sam are asleep, Fen pads towards the refrigerator, planning his habitual nocturnal raid on the ice cream tub. He comes across the second FedEx envelope on the sideboard, brings it to the kitchen table and places it alongside the ice cream.

He looks at the oblong tub and the envelope, and decides to open the tub first.

A couple of spoons in, he opens the FedEx envelope addressed to him longhand, and withdraws a letter with United Nations markings. Curious, he quietly opens the letter which contains two pieces of writing paper upon which is scrawled,

Dear Mr. Morgan,

I write to inform you with great sorrow that Grace Rutler was killed by an IED earlier this month at the border between Lebanon and Syria. Grace died instantly and will have felt no pain. Grace was traveling with me to an outpost to deliver care to a group of newly displaced refugees.

I think the days she spent here with us may have been the happiest of her life. She seemed to be working something out. I know that she felt guilty about the way she treated you and others, and that her life to this point had not been what she had hoped.

I know that she held you in particular in great affection.

Grace and I only had a short time together, though I think we had been searching for each other for a very long time. We loved each other greatly, and she loved the children in the camps.

I would very much like to meet you sometime perhaps, when I am traveling to the UN in the US at some point.

In the meantime, please know a few of us gathered to say a prayer and stood silently to remember Grace.

She will not be forgotten.

Sincerely,

Peter

Peter Foster M.D.

UNRWA

Bir Hassan, Ghoberi

Beirut, Lebanon.

Fen continues to sit very still for a long time. Then begins to write on a yellow pad of paper.

It is a poem of his own making.

Then
Someday,
After the outriders of time
Have passed our door
We shall find
A space of peace

Someday,
After the world slows
Its spun turmoil
Breathing will become the norm
And all this stuff
More tolerable.

ABOUT THE AUTHOR

As Chief Human Resources Officer at a series of global companies, Craig Dinsell mentored numerous international teams and leaders, enabling them to thrive in the face of traumatic cultural, organizational and personal change. He has also been active with not-for-profit organizations, as both a strategy consultant and board member. A course on behavior in small groups at the Grubb Institute in London first sparked his passion for creating diverse and resilient organizations. He studied Theology at the London School of Theology, where he was not a good fit.

Craig has had a lifelong interest in writing both poetry and prose, has made contributions to business books, and plans to publish an anthology of collected poems shortly. He is currently engaged in writing a comic novel.

Craig resides on a farm near New York City with his wife Sheila, occasional flocks of sheep, and Henry, an eccentric golden retriever. *Winning* is Craig's first novel. Henry's novel is still in process.

Made in the USA
Middletown, DE
21 December 2020

29379245R00189